Grey Knights

Walking Grey: Book 2

by
Rachel I

I0461058

Two Cents Publishing

First Two Cents Publishing edition September 2014

ISBN- 978-0989345910
ISBN- 0989345912

For Curt,

Thank you for a lifetime of everything.

For Janie, whose reading is acutely astute, and whose writing is even more poetically so.

And for Connor,

You inspire me.

"There is nothing either good or bad, but thinking makes it so."

Hamlet

Chapter 1

To the police, we're escaped lab rats. Of course, rats don't normally nibble on your brain and claw your heart out, not if you're alive. Does that mean we're worse than rats? At least the rats are survivors. They sneak around in the walls, live off what they steal, and they rarely get caught. In World Religions, I learned about a Hindu temple where the rats are sacred. Apparently, a few people can see through skin and stigma to the intrinsic worth of life.

Curled up safely between Grey and me, her fist clenched around a little splash of red plastic, Amber yawns, rubbing her eyes. The serenity on her face melts the worry lines on mine. Her lids flutter as she realizes she's cuddled up with Greyson. Startled, she searches frantically for me. I guess she's woken up too many nights and found me gone. She used to sneak into bed with me before the Z-Virus turned me into a wolf in her sister's clothing. I pet her hair and she snuggles into my palm.

"Are you tired of watching, Evy?" Sleep crusts the words she mumbles. "I can stay awake to guard you while you take a nap." My lips curl at her ingenuous generosity. She can barely open her eyes, but to reassure me, she opens her fist to expose the red blotch for what it is—a very small pocketknife. "Greyson gave it to me so I would be safe."

Is this the part where I'm allowed to cry? For God's sake! My baby sister sleeps with a knife, not a puppy!

For a six-year-old, life between the battle lines doesn't offer a wide variety of options: shut up, lie down a victim and die; or roar, grab a weapon and survive. It kind of breaks my heart that the little pink princess has been locked away in a tower. But then again, I traded in my tiara and stilettos for a sharp blade and combat boots a long time ago.

Greyson stirs, shifting Amber into his lap. A familiar warm spot kindles in my chest. How can you not love the boy who loves what you love most? That's the way it works, right?

Amber reaches up to rub his shaved head. Her eyes half shut again, she grins. "Greyson got a haircut."

Barely managing a tight-lipped nod, I lean my head back against the seat. The near-miss of a sharp blade exposing his brain, carving him out of my life, catches my breath. I shut my eyes and fade the scene to black. It's over. The ZV-Institute is a pile of ashes behind us.

Greyson passes his palm over his crown. "How do you like that, kid? Pretty smooth, huh? It's the new me."

I roll my eyes lazily, but his bravado drags a smile across my lips. Even bald, the boy sweats charm.

Amber grins, nestles into his chest, and yawns, patting his cheek. "I love you, Greyson."

God! If only Greyson were that easy for me. I really want to slip beneath his arm, lay my head in the soft spot under his shoulder, cuddle up, and breathe him in, eau de zombie and all. But Amber's between us and, probably, those syringes of Greyson's blood I gave to Nicolas.

Funny—well, maybe not funny, maybe excruciatingly dysfunctional—when the guns are firing, the teeth are gnashing, and the grenades are exploding, Greyson and I engage like parts of a well-oiled machine. But after the smoke settles, we can't seem to see each other clearly anymore; the gears between us rumble, rusty and warped.

"Are we there yet, Evy?" Amber doesn't even know where we're going, but she's up for the adventure. I always knew she was a tough little cookie. Even before I got infected, she was so determined to hang with me that she put on her big girl biking shoes and rode next to me down the trails while I worked out. I had to keep a close eye on her because she would die before she would admit she wasn't big enough to go along. And, let's face it, not many six-year-olds can survive a zombie home invasion, jump through stained glass windows, and kick off rabid ZVs from the limbs of a tree without spending the rest of their life collapsed into a silent heap of snot and tears.

I don't know if we're there yet because I don't actually know where we're going. Nicolas doesn't know where we're going and he's driving. I'm pretty sure Greyson doesn't give a damn. He can survive anywhere.

And Smaran, Nicolas's little brother, snores obliviously in the passenger seat. Even when everyone else stirs, he doesn't bother to wake up. Not that I blame him; the virus affected him oddly. He's pretty sick—ground zero for the infection. He must be a year or two older than Greyson and I because he caught it as a college freshman. He and his virus partner were working with his parents in Egypt's Zoser pyramid. He's lucky he's got his brother looking out for him. His partner, an intern from Utah, is already dead.

"I need a lab." Nicolas has had several hours, winding along mountain roads, doubling back, and hiding in dark corners, to figure out a destination. We're trying to get the hell out of the state before it's on total lockdown. It didn't take long for the roadblock on I-80 leading to the Wyoming border to go up. Nicolas detoured south, hoping to outrun the quarantine and catch I-70 into Colorado. "I have a cousin, a doctor, who works at Baylor Medical College. If we can get to Houston, he could get me into their labs."

My eyebrows pop up at the opening of the bright little door marked "Houston". "Amber and I could do Houston. My cousins live on a ranch just outside the city." My aunt Esther and I are close—as close as she and my mother were. Maybe even close enough for her to consider taking me in—grey skin, purple blood, and all.

At the mention of the ranch, Amber slides bolt upright into her seat. "We're going to Aunt Esther's? Can we ride the horses, and swim, and jump on the trampoline, and play video games, and feed the baby cows?"

My cousins live in a gated community, in a rose brick mansion, on a big ranch that no amusement park can rival:

every conceivable toy on the planet, wild cousins roaming free with the chickens, range-fed milk cows, open pantries, round, juicy blackberries fresh off the vine, and fresh veggies basking in the wide Texas sunshine. And did I mention the pond, and the baby ducks, and the dog—a monstrous Great Dane named Primrose? Heaven.

If you have to have your family attacked and eaten by zombies and then narrowly escape the holocaust of your hometown, getting to live on Aunt Esther's ranch is pretty decent compensation. Although, how I can ever compensate for what Amber has lost, I can't begin to imagine. But she's surprisingly resilient and adaptive. I would have expected more...I don't know...whining? catatonic refusals to speak? acute anti-social behavior? The truth is, I think she knows I don't have any more to give, so it's not worth asking.

Amber tilts her head, grins coquettishly, and bats her eyelashes. "Cameron lives at Aunt Esther's house."

Puppy love. Something you don't expect to meet in the apocalypse.

"Hey, I thought I was your main squeeze." Greyson hugs her closer, extracting a healthy bubble of giggles.

Amber squirms around to lay her head in his lap, practically purring. She drapes her feet across my knees. I couldn't be craving Greyson right now anymore if he were warm bread, fresh from the oven. My stomach growls...and something else, something much deeper.

"Sooo...Houston?" Nicolas looks around for general agreement as if we're not a bunch of teenagers, and he's not the one in the driver's seat. How can you not like a guy that treats you like a person?

"Whatever." Greyson hasn't uttered more than five sentences the whole trip and most of them were addressed to Amber. Every twenty minutes or so, he sits up straight, his head bumping the low ceiling, flexes his chest and arms, and stretches his legs out against the cramp of Nicolas's seat in front of him. I have to sympathize with his apathy; the back seat doesn't suit him.

On the outskirts of Price, Smaran shuffles awake in the seat in front of me and ogles the Wendy's flying by the window.

At six in the morning, it's probably not open yet. "Anyone else in here hungry?"

That's a loaded question.

In the confined space of the BMW, the succulent smell of Nicolas and Amber saturates the air. It's like traveling to grandma's house on Sunday with the pot roast and hot apple pie in the back seat. I've finally succeeded in coming to grips with what I am, maybe even appreciating some of the finer qualities of my freakishness, but this car really brings out the wolf in me. Major setback. The virus bangs its fists on the table and my stomach growls.

Amber tugs on my sleeve, frowning. "I'm hungry, too."

"We'll see what we can do, baby." I rub her tummy and squint at the reflection of Smaran's eyes in the visor mirror. "If you don't mind me asking, Smaran, what exactly did you have in mind?"

"Sam." He turns around in his seat and greets me with a gleaming, toothy white smile. "Call me Sam."

I haven't had much chance to get to know him, but he seems to be a younger version of Nicolas—more chill, less responsible. What I really want to know about him, though, is his view on cannibalism. "Okay, Sam, what are you in the mood for?"

Sighing nostalgically, he leans his head back against the seat. "I'd settle for a rare liver and onions, or some tripe, but…" he turns to look me in the eye again "…let's just be honest. Your little sister smells mouth-watering—like my mom's Masala Paneer."

The car veers a little as Nicolas's mouth drops open. "Sam!"

"What?" He meets his brother's shocked rebuke head-on. "It's not like they don't smell it too."

Grey snorts and cracks the window.

"Might as well just say it. Evelyn wants to know if I'm thinking a little Amber, medium rare, would hit the spot. We have animal instincts. She's assessing the threat."

Nicolas frowns in the rearview mirror, but I only shrug. I sort of like Sam. He's not all pathetic and whiney about the virus. He's straight up…and kind of funny. He knew exactly what I was asking and he gave me the only answer that I could trust—the truth.

You have to appreciate a little candor in a grey world. Pretending we're not what we are and living a lie only stigmatizes us and makes it harder to cope with the reality.

Medically, Sam's reaction to the virus isn't exactly like Greyson's and mine. And, to a ZV, there's something more that I'm not sure a non-ZV, not even a doctor, would pick up. We've been crammed together for a while in a small car and Sam definitely smells different than Greyson. The smell activates all my fight or flight instincts like he's a serious predator. His reaction to the virus must be producing some kind of funky pheromone that smells like rotting meat—not just that sexy as hell subtle skin decay I get from Grey.

Sam throws back a chuckle. He obviously gets a kick out of pushing his brother's buttons, which are all pretty accessible.

"It's just not polite." Nicolas shakes his head, mortified.

Sam grins, but then his eyes soften. He likes to play the shock card, but the blood between the two of them runs thick. They're orphans and Sam knows who butters his bread—or, in this case, carves his liver. "Look, Nic, at some point, you're going to have to face up to the fact that the virus is my life now. Let's just live with it instead of pretending that it's not there, or that it's just camped out for the weekend."

"He's got a point, Nicolas. You smell like Sunday dinner to me."

I'm sorry, but it had to be said—and not just to lighten things up a bit. I appreciate that Nicolas can see through the ZV and treat me like I'm still human—because I am. But somewhere it irritates me that he's always pretending the infection is going away, always looking at me like he sees me without the virus, which really isn't me—at least not for now, or anytime in the near future. So, I feel like he can't really see me because he can't look at that part of me.

Sam cracks up and my cheeks feel like they're going to crack because I haven't laughed in so long. Amber joins in just for the fun of it. Not even Grey can resist a quick fist bump. "Classic."

Nicolas's shoulders relax as he gives in to public opinion and cracks a half-smile. "As soon as I see a place that serves vegetarians and carnivores, I'll pull over." Sam nods at me in the visor mirror and the two of us score a win. Nicolas's brother is growing on me—odd smell and all.

"Any requests?" Nicolas asks.

Really?

By the time we pull into the grocery store parking lot in the sprawling metropolis of Price, Utah—where there is a Walmart and two, not one, two, fast food places—the faint glow on the eastern horizon foreshadows the imminent new dawn. Nicolas scouts out a parking space removed from the direct beam of the streetlamps still burning in the uncertain darkness.

When the engine dies, Amber scoots forward to whisper in Nicolas's ear. "Can I have a pizza Lunchable with a juice box and candy?"

"One pizza Lunchable with a juice box and a candy."

"And some Gushers?" She glances back at me to see if I'll object.

I frown, my eyebrows crossing because, basically, Nicolas is funding our road trip.

"And get some Gushers for Greyson, too." The charming little minx is a master manipulator. She whips her little blond head around grinning with generosity at Greyson who is a much easier target for her cajoling.

"My kind of breakfast."

"And a whole box of Gushers, family size." Nicolas flashes Amber one of his prime rib smiles. I get caught in the crossfire and, let's be honest, my saliva glands splutter a little. Amber wrinkles her nose back at him. Life is so much simpler when you're six—and not infected with a 4000-year-old virus that makes you crave human organs.

"The rest of us aren't too picky, but some water bottles would really hit the spot." I could guzzle a lake at this point. Back in Eli—before they burned it to the ground—my Polygamist hideout in the basement of the old Methodist church had a pretty steady supply of water bottles from my brother Cory's underground delivery system. I never really noticed how much water I burned through. After all, I'm a runner. Water has always been my lifeblood.

"That's the virus. It's a thirsty little bugger." Nicolas opens the door and, stretching a little, steps out of the car. "Don't wander off." Who knew the good doctor could be sarcastic?

Through the rearview mirror, I watch the trunk pop open. The zipper from a suitcase grates back. He must have listened to the warning I passed him through Madi's dad. He and Smaran were ready to get out of town when the Snatchers brought Greyson in. Lucky for us, Nicolas is a humanitarian and stuck around. Otherwise, my boy Grey would have been Dr. Christensen's biology dissection project before I got there to unstrap him.

When the trunk snaps shut, Nicolas is no longer sporting his blue scrubs and lab coat. He's camouflaged into looking like any other really hot guy on the street wearing jeans and a brown hoodie that look generic but are probably some expensive name brand, like the BMW he's driving. The sweatshirt is zipped only about halfway and I notice in the light from the streetlamp that Nicolas has a nicely carved set of chocolate bar abs.

Somehow, I really didn't expect that. My eyebrows pop up and the virus does this funky little dance as the thought of chocolate revs up my taste buds. Greyson catches me noticing and I avert my eyes, leaning down to kiss the soft little blond of Amber's head.

Grey's arm hovers above the back of our seat before his hand slides beneath the hair at my neck, massaging the tightness that runs all the way through my shoulders. He hasn't touched me since we bolted away from the burning Institute. The tension between us melts a little and my head falls back, wading in the roaring rush of his skin on mine again. My eyelids flit up to meet his wink. A little competition seems to have thawed some of the chill between us.

As Nicolas strolls away, silence, sudden and uncertain, falls like death on the car. Out my window, the street lamps flicker in the sallow grey between morning and night. Even for this small-town outpost in Carbon County, the empty-ghost-town feel strikes me as eerie. If this were a horror movie, this is the part where I'd expect a zombie to smash its mangled, grey face against the window and bang on the windshield moaning, "Br-ai-n-s!"

What's beaucoup scarier is when the police car rolls up the street, slows at the entrance, and turns into the lot.

Chapter 2

"Shit!" It's nice to know Greyson is still with us. He slides Amber into my arms and pulls out the gun he brought with him from the raid on the Institute.

Again, zombies and guns—two bad tastes that taste worse together. But under the circumstances, I'm afraid the flavor is growing on me, like coffee—the bitterness lingers on your tongue, but it keeps you ticking. I object anyway, on principle. "Hey, let's not jump to shooting people. Maybe he's just here for some donuts."

"Yeah, that would be convenient. Maybe later some nice Marines will show up and give us an escort out of the state." Lovely! The Greyson I know and love is still in there and has made a comeback.

"No, look! He's driving over here!" Sam checks the door of the grocery store. All joking aside, when the chips are on the table, he's got his brother's back.

"It's still mostly dark inside the car. The lamp doesn't reach this far. Maybe he hasn't seen us yet." I slouch down in my seat, below the windows, pulling Amber with me. Her pale hand brushes over the metal of Greyson's gun.

"Don't shoot him yet, Greyson. You can't tell just by looking if they're good or bad. You have to wait and see what they do."

My mouth drops open for a second. Oh, to be as wise as a six-year-old. My hand taps her lips. "Shhh, honey." Greyson's eyes meet mine, and I don't have to say anything. He's just been schooled by a first grader.

"No one's going to shoot anyone. This is just a precaution." Greyson clicks the safety off his gun and then slides down and tucks his head away from the glass.

Our hearing works as well as seeing. The motor hums toward us and then stops behind the BMW. The patrol car headlights flood the interior.

"He saw us," Sam whispers. "Act like you're sleeping, so we don't look suspicious."

"We're the only car parked in the middle of a grocery store lot at the crack of dawn during a zombie lockdown. Trust me. We look suspicious." I pet Amber's hair, wink, and grin to reassure her, but my body is clenched, ready for war.

"Everybody, just calm down." Greyson senses the tension leaking off of me. An adrenaline cocktail is cascading through my veins, churning up my blood. Amber shivers in my arms. For a long time, nothing happens. "He's running the plates." Greyson is coolest under pressure. "Now the only question is, have they got the doctor's face and name popping up in all the databases yet?"

Behind us, the cop's door hitches open. Slow, heavy steps stomp the asphalt. The beam of a flashlight wanders around inside our car, a faint aroma of roast pig trickling in beneath it. Hunger and fear dance like wild natives in my chest, stirring up the fire of the beast inside. My breathing mists up the cold, glass window under my temple. Inhaling deeply, I wipe away the virus impulses and focus on stillness. Wanting this to end with no one getting hurt, knowing it can't, I will the cop to leave, knowing he won't.

My palm slides over Amber's eyes. I'm not about to let her see any more mayhem. She already has enough nightmare material to get her well into her thirties.

Greyson nestles his gun hand against his right thigh. If he fires on a cop, how many more will come after us? We'll totally lose all our anonymity. Our chances of getting out of the state will be pretty much shot—no pun intended. If that happens, my best bet is to jump into the driver's seat and race for the front of the store. If I let Greyson drive, chances are he'll leave Nicolas in the checkout line. I can hear it now. "He's not infected. It'll be easier for him to get out of the state without a carload of zombies." Cold, hard Greyson logic.

Outside the driver's seat, the cop taps on the glass with the butt of his flashlight; inside, Greyson eases back the slide across the barrel. My arms twitch. Amber's heart flutters in my ears. We can't answer; we can't look up and flash our ZV mugs. But, if we don't answer, the charade is over, the cop gets suspicious, and the bullets fly. I brace for the inevitable.

And then, out of the thin night air, Nicolas's voice, like warm caramel, flows muffled through the cold glass. "Hey, officer. Can I help you?"

The flashlight beam disappears. We all exhale. A thin spray of fog covers the windows. The policeman lumbers around the car to the rear passenger side. "Well, sir, there's been an incident up in Salt Lake. Some pretty dangerous individuals are at large. Have any ID on you?"

I reach my hand over to stay Greyson's—the one with the gun in it. "Nicolas can handle this."

"Yeah, and what happens when Doctor Boy's picture shows up on every cop's dashboard and Deputy Dufuss here realizes he let a carload of zombies drive away?"

"Don't worry." Sam doesn't budge from leaning on the window, his face hidden. "Nicky didn't just get where he is because he's crazy smart; he's got charisma." Coming from his little brother, that's probably an understatement.

Outside the car, charming Nicolas has kicked in. What am I saying? Nicolas only has one flavor—charming. "Of course." Plastic bags crinkle against the pavement. "We were visiting relatives when we got the news. Just on our way back to the city. It's been a long trip. Thought we'd grab a snack before we head home to board up the windows." He chuckles.

"Might have to spend the night in a motel. Don't know what the roadblocks look like going into Salt Lake, but the quarantine is on. I know they're not letting anyone out of the state at this point." The policeman's flashlight beam teeter-totters between Nicolas's face and his ID. "Sudhir Nicolas Vadlamani. International Driver's License, huh? French? You don't look French."

"Yes, well, there's some Indian and a little Egyptian mixed in there. I'm a bit of a hybrid."

Amber whimpers and wriggles. My heart stops, drops, and rolls as the beam of light flashes into the car and spotlights her face through my window. She squints, snuggling into my lap. I pet her head and turn away from the pane, letting my hair flop over and camouflage my face, like I'm really half asleep. If the cop only gets a glimpse of Amber's perfectly pink cheeks and clear eyes, it might be enough to let him assume we're all the same. A tender little morsel like her wouldn't stand a chance in a car packed with ravenous zombies. Right?

"What brings you to Utah?" He flashes the light away.

"The CDC sent me here to do medical research at the University."

"A doctor?"

Nicolas looks way too young for the degrees he has—*enfant prodige*. That's his charm; he's ridiculously brilliant, but he never makes anyone feel stupid. If anyone can talk our way out of this, he can. But, Greyson is right. Eventually, Nicolas's face is going to hit the radar.

We're as good as exterminated when this cop connects all the dots. They'll know everything: who we are, the plate number on the car we're driving, and where we were. Right now, they have no idea; for all they know, we could have escaped across the Wyoming border before they ever shut it down. Or we could have died in the explosion.

"Yes. I'm working with Dr. Christensen at the Z-V Institute. My credentials should get me into the quarantine zone."

And now the police will know that little piece of info, too.

I'm doing my best to stay calm, but a virus generated hormone haze is slowly oozing from the bodies of the ZVs in the car. The slightly odd smell from Sam tenses all my muscles, winding them tight, intensifying the instinct to pounce.

"Then I don't need to tell you how dangerous the situation has become—ZV soldiers with guns walked right out of an explosion and hit the streets. The city is crawling with them now. The corpses of the infected adults are rotting in the road, and the kids that go zombie are devouring anything that breathes. The whole epidemic spread like wildfire when some mutants put together a gang and attacked the Institute. You're lucky you were out of town." He pauses for a second and then his voice goes all curious, "I guess you seen a few of 'em up close."

"Yes, sir. Closer than I'm sure you'd care to be."

The beam from the flashlight invades the car again. "Are these relatives?"

"Only my brother in the front. The rest are family friends from out of town."

"Bad time for a vacation. Well, sir, for your own safety, I strongly advise you to check into a motel somewhere near here until the military has the quarantine zone back under control." I hear the rustle of Nicolas's ID closing and the crinkle of grocery bags as the light wanders through the car for one last look. I can't help myself; I hold my breath, only semi-relieved.

"That's good advice. Thanks, Officer." Nicolas walks back around the car with the cop. "We'll look for a place in town." Good move Nicolas. Now the police won't be suspicious when we don't drive off toward Salt Lake.

"We can't let that cop walk away." Greyson's gun hand is tense under my hand.

"Don't start anything. You shoot that gun, and they'll track us down a lot sooner."

"I'm not going to shoot anyone."

The driver's lock pops up and the leather seat exhales as Nicolas settles in. None of us speak, but the key isn't even in the ignition before Greyson throws open his door.

The cop turns around at the front wheel of his patrol car. Before he has a chance to even suspect what's coming, Greyson swoops down on him with the butt of his gun.

"No!" I gasp, more upset that it has to be done than that it's being done.

The police officer is an unconscious lump in less than a second. But Greyson doesn't stop there. He scoops up the guy's chunky arm and takes a bite out of it like he's laying into a turkey leg.

Nicolas jumps out of the car. "What the hell are you doing?"

"Nic!" Sam reaches out to stop him from interfering. He knows as well as the rest of us ZVs it has to happen.

"You're not serious, right?" Greyson drags the limp cop around to the passenger side of the patrol car, away from the view of the street. "You didn't really think we could just let him drive away after he's seen who's in your car, has run your plates, and studied your ID? How long do you think it will take him to figure out he just let the state's Most Wanted slip through his chubby fingers?"

"You didn't have to bite him. That's a death sentence, or worse." And now we know how Nicolas really feels about being infected.

"Well, it's us or them, isn't it?" Greyson glares at Nicolas who doesn't know how to answer. But that's the pertinent question. Is Nicolas US or THEM? Neither side is warm and fuzzy.

The two of them stare each other down until Greyson stuffs the cop's gun into the back of the scrubs Nicolas loaned him.

"Up to now," he explains, because there's always reason behind Greyson's madness, "no one knows which direction we've gone or where we're headed. Let's not leave them any bread crumbs." He shoots a look at the hulking heap. "He's no vegetarian. When they find this guy, he'll be too far gone to tell them anything. That is if they bother to ask before they 'decontaminate' him."

He handcuffs the limp arm to the car door, conveniently ignoring the fact that the old guy has a higher chance of dying outright like most adults rather than slowly degrading while chasing down body parts like the teenagers. "He's not going anywhere. This way, no one else is going to get hurt. They'll assume some rogue ZVs are on the loose down here and waste their time and manpower scouring the town for them."

Nicolas doesn't have a response, but I can see he doesn't like it any more than he liked seeing Greyson and me on the dissection table. I don't envy his position. I don't envy Greyson's. If it were just me, I could let the cop go, take my chances; I'm a big girl. But it's not just me. Amber is everything. She's the hope for a solution that can see grey. She has to be safe.

Kneeling on the back seat, absorbing Greyson's handiwork through the window, she tugs on my sleeve. "Evy, do I need a gun too?"

No words come out when my mouth drops open. God! The worst part is…part of me thinks she might.

Trailing my hands through my hair, I try to find the words that will untangle the knotted threads of this dilemma for her. I get why Greyson bit the cop; I get that someone needed to, but I hate that this is the way our world is now.

I don't want to burn zombies. I don't want to bite cops. I don't want to dress this baby girl in camo and strap a gun to her hip. But they're making it harder not to take sides. The black and white are seeping apart; the grey keeps fading.

Chapter 3

Twenty miles down the highway, the sun shows a sleepy orange face to the grey horizon. The roadblock at the last exit out of Price and the enormous traffic jam take us by surprise. Even down here, miles beyond the infection zone, in the wee hours of the morning, the news has spread like a pack of ravenous zombies. The locals have packed up and are stacked bumper to bumper on the road that leads to I-70 and the Colorado border.

The small convoys of troops passing us on the shoulder and the news reports on the radio explain the mass exodus. We all lean in to hear. Nicolas turns up the volume; he has a clinical interest. For the rest of us, it's the draw of a roadside car wreck—although now, a roadside car wreck has a whole new appeal.

> *The Governor's office of both Texas and California confirmed reports this evening of minor outbreaks of the Zoser Virus, aptly nicknamed the Zombie Virus, in some of their most densely populated areas. The virus was once thought to be contained in the Salt Lake Valley and sexually transmitted over a very narrow population. It now appears to be spreading more virulently as victims are bitten by infected hosts.*
>
> *Following reports of attacks perpetrated by the infected upon the Z-V Institute in Salt Lake City, widespread panic has hampered government response teams in their efforts to isolate and contain the virus.*
>
> *Neighboring states have closed their borders. Travel in and out of Utah, Texas, and California is*

being rigorously restricted. Expect delays, detours, and frequent checkpoints.

Nicolas shuts off the radio. "Well, that explains this roadblock. They're obviously turning people away from I-70." With his finger, he traces route 6 on his GPS. "There are only a few small towns on this road; it pretty much only goes to the interstate."

There's a steady stream of cars heading back into town—disappointed refugees. They can't be any more disappointed than I am; at least no one is hunting them down—not yet. "We're trapped then. There's no getting out."

"Not so fast, Dr. Doom." Greyson leans forward, squinting in the dim morning light washing over the desert. "That's the Huntington exit just off to the right there, isn't it?"

Nicolas nods.

"Then, once again, I can save our asses." He sighs dramatically. "My dad grew up down here. It only takes one weekend at the grandparents' to figure out every street is a dead-end at Bored Central or the desert. Take a right at the fork, before the checkpoint. Head south. There's a bunch of small towns down there."

I lean up to see the GPS. "It won't matter, Greyson. Both routes end at I-70. Even if we go south through all these small towns to avoid this roadblock, the road eventually hits the interstate again before we get to the border."

"Which is why we're not going to use the road." He looks right at me, winds a strand of my hair delicately around his finger, "If you don't trust me yet, at least trust my survival instincts."

How did this get personal? I was just reading the map. My eyes crinkle up and I have to I turn my head and look out the window to keep from escalating into a lover's spat right here in the backseat of Nicolas's BMW. What the hell does he mean, if I don't trust him? As if.

Greyson's finger stays cuddled in my hair. I can't yank it away without doing damage, but I'm not sure I want to anyway.

Nicolas maneuvers to the exit lane. I wonder if he can see the drama playing out in the back seat.

On either side of the exit, there are two big gas-and-groceries facing each other. Cars that have already been turned away from the roadblock are heading back home in a steady flow south. The northbound side of the street crawls along, thick and slow as tree sap, pooling at the highway in Price. A loaded-up Dodge truck, sick of waiting, abandoning hope, jumps out of the stalled northbound line and darts through a tiny hole in the fluid southbound traffic, kicking up a ton of dust on the shoulder to the tune of aggravated horn honking.

"I have to pee." Amber rocks back and forth in her seat when she sees the possibility of a restroom at a gas and grocery. No big wonder, she's downed about a gallon's worth of juice boxes.

"I should get gas." Nicolas glances at the dashboard.

Nobody objects to stopping in the middle of all this mass of people, cops, and soldiers. We've passed tons of National Guard and patrol cars. If the plates on the BMW were hot, we'd have been pulled over by now.

The off-ramp gas station is a zoo. Most of the soldiers are up on the interstate, but a couple of guys in fatigues look like they're on a snack run. Nicolas hops out to pump, leaving the keys in the ignition so the radio can stay on.

Amber is doing the pee-pee shuffle. I have no choice but to get out and walk her into the mini-mart; she doesn't know Nicolas well enough to let him chaperone. Although, the way the good doctor keeps playing fairy godmother to her every wish, he's becoming pretty stiff competition for Greyson.

Sam loans me some glasses and mittens and I pull up the hood from my sweatshirt. It's a little drizzly out, so hopefully, I'll just blend in.

Crowds are our friends. Even in the long line to the stalls, all the women are so ticked off and nervous about the quarantine that no one really notices us. Well, they notice the smell. "These bathrooms reek!" The woman next to me grimaces, fanning the stench away from her face. I nod and duck my head. Amber covers her nose.

After the handwashing ceremony, I divert Amber down the candy aisle out of the mainstream of disgruntled travelers. Big mistake. The giant size Twix on the end shelf attracts her like a megaton magnet. As I'm hauling her away, we pass Nicolas just coming in the store. "I'm going to pay and grab a Mountain Dew." He pulls his wallet out and starts shuffling through the credit cards. "I need something to help me stay awake."

"Can I have a Rolo and gummy worms?" Amber dances on her toes and smiles up at the handsome man with the money.

"Amber!" I flash her a mom look.

Her face falls and Nicolas leans down to catch it with a smile. "Sure! We can't be driving all the way to Texas without any gummy worms."

"And juice!" She is incorrigible.

"Of course!" He rolls his eyes as if any idiot would have known that gummy worms require gallons of juice.

Someone has to be the responsible adult here, so I suggest a banana and some cheese to round out the balanced diet of candy and chocolate.

Nicolas winks at me as I hoist the sugar monster onto my hip and carry her away before she can squeeze anything else out of the doctor.

As I push the door open, I freeze. "Nic!" He turns around, his face on alert.

I nod in the direction of a patrol car that's just driven into the parking lot. The thought of a scene like the last one, playing out in this crowded parking lot, in broad daylight, makes my fists crawl with virus ants. I hug Amber closer and duck my head into the hoodie.

Nicolas steadies me with a nod and a slight hand motion that takes in the milling masses. He's pretty confident we're just another couple of anonymous faces in the crowd. Grabbing a bottle of soda, he hops in the cashier's line as I hustle out to the car.

"What was that all about?" Greyson asks when I dump my blond charge onto the seat next to him.

"I'm getting a Rolo and sour gummy worms." Amber bounds up to him. "You can have some."

The leather seats squish beneath me. "She's warming up to Nicolas's bedside manner."

Greyson fist bumps Amber. "She's not the only one."

"What's that supposed to mean?"

Sam's eyes go wide in the visor mirror. When he catches me watching him react to our semi-private spat, he slides down in his seat and stares out of the car, trying not to be here. He's politer than Nicolas gave him credit for. Amber doesn't even try to pretend she's not listening. She's all ears and she's about to get a higher education.

Greyson squints my direction like he's not buying that I don't know what he means.

"What? It's the blood, right? You're still mad about that?"

He shakes his head like I'm really thick.

It irks me that I feel like I need to justify myself. "Excuse me if I thought risking everything to bust you out of the Institute would count for something. We're alive…in one piece. We're together. What else is there?

That doesn't get a response either, just a deep breath and another skeptical head shaking. What I wouldn't give for a nice, snarky Greyson comeback, anything to break the silent treatment.

He's looking at me like I'm eating him alive, well, you know, figuratively speaking. I don't know what to say, so I strap Amber in.

Finally, he speaks up, but he talks to the window so he doesn't have to see my reaction. "You know, Ev, you really have to figure out who you are before you can embrace it."

My mouth hangs open for a second before Sam interrupts. "I hate to cut the drama short, but that cop is on his way over here."

Apparently, Greyson's little stunt at the grocery store wasn't as effective as we thought.

There's no conference or vote, Greyson bolts out of the car and back into the driver's seat right as Nicolas, juggling his bulging plastic bag of candy, soda, and water bottles in one hand, pushes the door open for some lady with the other. His eyes follow the cop who has drawn his gun. Greyson throws the idling Beamer into drive.

"You can't leave Nicolas!" I yell in chorus with Sam's "Hey! What about Nic?"

The BMW swerves out of the pump lines and squeals away to the exit as the cop fires. The sound of metal ripping metal rocks the car. The parking lot froths into mayhem; people scream and run for cover.

Greyson cuts a sharp right off the driveway and onto the empty shoulder where he hammers down the gas pedal. The car roars forward. Sam grasps the handle above the door; it's that kind of fast. Amber stretches her head up so she can see out and I push it back down in case more bullets fly.

"Wait, Greyson, wait!" She squirms out from underneath my hand to grab his shoulder. "Nicolas has the gummy worms! If you leave him, we won't get any!"

Not exactly my point, but close enough. Better from Amber than from me. It's not the gummy worms I'm worried about. It's the research, and the brains, and, hell yes, the sanity. And we won't get any of that if Greyson ditches Nicolas here.

The Beamer revs past a slow-moving pick-up that looks like it belongs on blocks on someone's front lawn.

On our side of the dotted yellow line, there's a bit of wiggle room for weaving between the dirt shoulder and the lumbering carloads that have already been rejected and sent home. I've got to say, Greyson shines at the wheel of a car like this. But what I said about guns, probably applies to fast cars: don't give them to zombies.

With only Amber in the back seat, there's a lot more slide room. Trying not to squish her every time the car fishtails turns out to be a pretty good work out.

"I'm not really a back-seat kind of guy..." Greyson glances apologetically at Sam, who can't decide if it's better to see the imminent collision ahead or try to spot his brother. Nicolas has totally disappeared in the terrified mob of the parking lot. The cop, sirens blaring, finally squeals onto the highway about half a mile behind us. "No offense to your brother, but all this horsepower is wasted on him."

"What the hell do you think you're doing?" Sam finally adapts to the speed and finds the breath to plead his brother's case. "Nicolas is no thrill-seeker, but he's got us this far. This is his car, for God's sake. You can't just leave him there. He's the only chance we have for a cure."

22

I grab Greyson's shoulder. "Sam's right…"

Veering back onto the road from the shoulder, Greyson cuts an SUV off. The SUV brakes and skids behind us, a minivan slams into him and slides off the asphalt, followed by an old Buick and an Explorer. Dust explodes onto the highway, brakes screech, sirens blare, angry drivers rant. The cop chasing us gets tangled in the mess of Greyson's wake.

"Sam, you have a phone?" Greyson checks the mirror, admiring the quickly receding chaos he's left behind. The cop won't be clearing it any time soon. My ZV boy isn't just surviving; I think he's enjoying this.

Sam nods, mesmerized by the speed, or paralyzed with fear.

"Call your brother and tell him to go over to the station on the other side of the road. We'll circle back and pick him up by the air pump."

Greyson glances at me through the mirror. "What's the matter, baby? You didn't really think I'd ditch Dr. Do Good, did you?"

"I…." Of course, I did. I thought it way back at the grocery store. That's what makes Greyson so complicated and aggravating. He's ruthless, and calculating, and oh, so frighteningly efficient. One minute he's leading his zombie minions in a raid on the innocent villagers, and then the next, out of the blue, in one unsettling act of genuine altruism, he goes against all his instincts and puts his brain on the dissection table to save the ass of the girl that just betrayed him. You never know which direction Greyson is really headed. He is the definition of contradiction.

"I'm not the ungrateful son of a bitch you take me for, but you can't get it out of your head, can you? I'm bad. Doesn't matter what I do. It's camped out in your brain."

"Look, I'm sorry. I know sometimes I expect the worst from you. It's not like you're a saint. But I'm not the treacherous bitch you take me for either. It's just that…"

Greyson wrenches the steering wheel and we U-turn violently across the highway through a small break in the traffic jam. Amber squeals and we slide as far as the seat belts will allow. The car bumps and bangs onto the sidewalk going back the way we came, northbound to the Interstate. I nearly bite my tongue.

"…that you like him and I know it?" Greyson finishes for me.

My eyes flutter to Sam who is talking frantically into his phone and won't hear me. "Of course, I like Nicolas! He's nice. He's helping us. He kept them from dissecting our brains. What's not to like?"

He's also a prince that treats me like a princess. Who wouldn't like that?

But then again, I'm no princess, and the same purple blood that runs in Greyson's veins runs in mine. And in the middle of the chase, every little drop of tainted blood, careening at breakneck speed through my heart, craves Greyson.

He turns to glare at me.

"Watch out!" My arm shoots across the front of Amber as if I could hold her back at this speed in a collision.

Greyson nearly slams into a speed limit sign. Sam grabs the dash and I brace against his seat as we fishtail around it.

"We don't need to do this now." My fingers brush Greyson's neck where the blond curls used to riot. "I love you. You know I love you. Blond, shaved, back seat, front seat, demon, or savior, it doesn't matter. I love you."

No response again.

"Okay?" I nudge his back with the flat of my palm.

No response, but he does take his eyes off the road long enough to flash me that sexy half-smile that's the liver and onions of my life right now.

Chapter 4

A small parade of highway patrol cars, sirens screaming, races toward us down the southbound side of the highway. They spot us across the road, coming back their direction on the sidewalk, but the accident roadblock Grey left on their side slows them down. A cop jumps out of his blocked car and shoots at our BMW across the lines of traffic. Muffled shouting erupts in the stalled cars and all the passengers duck and cover.

We're nearly back to the gas and grocery on the other side of the highway exit before flashing lights force a hole in the traffic jam and barrel across the highway to pick up the chase. The BMW screeches into the parking lot.

"Open the door, Ev!" Greyson pulls up to the air pumps and Nicolas sprints for us.

No one needs to tell me. I'm already leaning over the top of Amber buckled in the center, popping the handle. As I'm falling back into my place, Greyson twists and leans over the console between the seats, grabs my neck and pulls me in. The adrenaline rush of the chase is revving up all his other hormones. My mouth is open when his lips hit mine. He's been trudging through the desert for days and I'm the canteen. But I'm feeling a little parched myself, and Greyson's well runs deep.

Amber is mesmerized; Sam's mouth drops open.

"Thanks for coming back," Nicolas gasps, sliding in and grabbing the seat belt as my back hits leather again. That's the elegance of Nicolas. Does he rant and rave at Greyson for hijacking his car and stranding him at the gas and go? No. He thanks him for coming back.

"Don't mention it." Greyson peels through the parking lot to the back of the market. He accelerates right through a rickety fence into a trailer park. Nicolas winces at the scrape of wood on blue BMW paint. Greyson's eyes, reflected in the rearview mirror, actually appear empathetic. "We're going to have to ditch her, dude."

Nicolas nods. I feel bad for him, sitting in the back seat while someone else trashes his baby. But let's just say it: Nicolas isn't the man you want at the wheel when you're running from the cops; he's much too polite. From the way we're weaving in and out of back streets, it's pretty safe to say Greyson has more experience with this kind of work.

I want to know what kind of plan Greyson has, but I don't dare ask. I'm not sure if I don't want to break his concentration or if I don't want to know that he's improvising.

The car swerves past a wide SUV onto gravel and dirt. We bump and slide to the passenger's side on the shoulder of a decrepit, old side road. "Greyson's a crazy driver!" Amber can't quite decide if this is the roller coaster ride of her life or the prelude to her death. "Is he gonna get a ticket, Evy? Does that mean he's going to have to bite another policeman?"

Nicolas and I exchange glances, pulling ourselves upright by the crash handles above the doors.

A police car finds us as we bump and rattle through the pot-holed street bordering some kind of abandoned factory with the windows broken out and doors boarded up. Sirens flashing, the cop cuts us off at a three-way intersection. Greyson brakes, skids into a 180, and then screams back up the way we came. Shots from behind shatter our back window. Chunks of glass fly into the cab.

I shove Amber's head down as another patrol car squeals around the corner in front of us, boxing us in. We all lurch right when Greyson whips into the wrong lane to play chicken with the oncoming policeman. The cop behind us switches lanes in pursuit.

"Oh, my God!" I drape my body over Amber as the two cars race toward an imminent head-on collision.

"Are you insane?" Sam ducks his head into the pillow on his lap.

Some indiscriminate foreign words shoot out of Nicolas's mouth as he braces against the driver's seat.

At the last minute, Greyson wrenches the steering wheel. The BMW swerves back into its own lane. The desperate squeal of brakes precedes the nasty crunch of metal on metal and the shattering of glass that rattle through the rear window to the disjointed tune of warped sirens. Popping my head back up as we turn down another side street, I see that the cop charging us won the chicken match but totaled his car on the front fender of the cop chasing us.

Thank God Greyson is on our side!

When he's done enough damage to the neighborhood, he races out behind the town into the desert. In a small cloud of dust, we off-road southbound, parallel to the highway for several miles until we spot the flashing lights of some back-up cavalry from Huntington, rushing northbound to Price. Beyond the ridge of a rise that will hide us, Greyson cuts back over to the highway, heading for Huntington.

Go figure. We've banged over curbs, crashed through fences, and rocked the uncharted desert, but it's on the shiny, black pavement that we hit a monstrous nail and blow out a tire. It pops and rumbles like we're giving birth to a helicopter.

"Shit!" Greyson slams his fists on the steering wheel like it's the BMW's fault.

"Now what?" I ask.

"We drive on it. Just not as fast." He brakes, bringing the roaring vibration down to a limping mumble.

Nicolas looks like he wants to protest, but then follows the same logic I do: that it's no use protecting the wheels from damage when this is the last he's ever going to see of his car. It's a cop magnet now; as soon as we get to wherever Greyson is headed, we have to abandon it. I don't even try to see past Nicolas's diplomatic mask to what he's really feeling. I'd rather just go with the façade of serenity; it's comforting to believe one of us might still be sane. To live in this warped world, we have to bend the way we look at it so that it makes sense.

It looks like we're still in the middle of nowhere with no plan and a flat tire when a cop car, racing from Castle Dale to join in the action at Price, passes us. He catches a glimpse of our BMW stumbling down the highway and then whips a U-turn and comes up behind us, lights flashing. Of course, he can't run, so Greyson pulls off the road and stops. The cop pulls in behind us.

"Damn!" Greyson checks his rearview mirror. "At least there's only one."

For the billionth time today, my limbs sip on a nice adrenaline cocktail. I wonder if there's a legal limit on those. My heart thumps and my lungs start heaving as I gather Amber into my chest, doing my best to reassure her with a smile. But she can read all the other body language.

"It's okay, Evy. I have my knife." She nods reassuringly and flashes me the little red case.

My first impulse is to grab the sharp object from the six-year-old. But the old rules have smudged in the new game. "It's just a little knife, Amber. No one will expect that you have it, but don't use it unless you think you can run away." Great big-sister advice. I'd rather be explaining the fashion rules of footwear. "Stay down!" When you're only half size, hiding is a much better survival option than fighting.

The cop, a big burly guy, who looks as if he's used to letting his car do all the police work for him, gets off the radio. "Get out of the car!" He aims the barrel of his authority at us and uses his car door as a shield.

Greyson knows the drill; he gets out with his hands on his head and swaggers to the back bumper of our car, his gun bulging under the back of his shirt. Nicolas looks confused but follows suit, taking up a post next to Grey on the passenger side. Sam coughs, sighs, wraps his blanket tighter around him, and hauls himself around to a position between the two but slightly behind Greyson.

I'm not sure what to do. I don't want to leave Amber alone and I don't want to take her out of the car where the guns are. I decide to leave her hidden and step out of the car behind Nicolas with my hands out in plain sight, but I hang back by the open door where Amber can see me.

Another cop car, which from the looks of it has been chasing our dust, rolls up over the rise behind his colleague, spots the party, and pulls over in front of us, boxing us in.

"You in the blanket," the hefty cop gestures at Sam, "get your hands where I can see them."

"He's quite ill," Nicolas objects politely.

"Shut up and keep them hands up!" The cop prods his gun in Sam's direction. "C'mon! I want to see 'em."

The other cop gets out of his car. He's a scrawny kid, the kind that became a cop to get some respect. The gravel on the shoulder crunches under his shiny boots. He's coming up behind me. My mind is racing because I really don't want them to know that Amber is with me. There's no scenario where it ends well for her if the police haul her away.

Sam drops the blanket and breaks into a coughing fit. The burly cop steps out from behind his door. "I'm going to need some ID."

"Of course." Nicolas reaches for his pocket.

"Hey! Slow it down there."

"It's just my ID." He eases his wallet out of his pocket, holds it over his head, and slips the driver's license out of it.

"Toss it on over here!" The cop waggles his gun and approaches cautiously.

While he looks the ID over, the skinny cop comes up behind me. "Step away from the vehicle, ma'am." He's all serious, with a little hitch of excitement in his voice, like he might actually get to try out his new gun. I glance at Greyson before I turn around. He's watching the chubby guy, but he's got the corner of his eye on me. I don't know what he's planning, but I'm pretty sure he's not just going to stand there. The cop scrutinizing Nicolas's driver's license is keeping a healthy distance.

"We got some live ones here, Lowell," the scrawny guy says when I turn around and look him in the face, keeping my body positioned to block his view of Amber.

Nicolas steps forward to explain why he's traveling with a bunch of ZVs and the cop points the gun right at his head. The doctor's hands shoot up in surrender. "You can see from my ID that I'm with the CDC. I'm transporting these infected patients to a secure facility for research." Nice, Nicolas! Who knew that the doctor could lie on the fly?

"Well, Dr...," the doughy officer slaughters the name on the ID, "Val-dam-na-man-I, looks like you got yourself a little trouble here. Seems to me, this here zombie-boy was driving your car. He done upset some folks back in town there. If it were up to me, I'd shoot the dirty bugger where he stands, but the big shots up Salt Lake want a look at him."

I miss Nicolas's reaction because the scrawny cop is getting nosy about what's in the back seat. I don't want to start anything, so I back off in baby steps as he nudges me away with his gun, but what he doesn't realize is that I'll take a bullet before I let him get a hold of my baby sister. He's not much different than any other guy I've ever met; he took one look at my hair and sized me up—sized me up wrong.

We do this little tango until he pushes me too far and gets a peek at Amber in her seatbelt. "Geez, Lowell, they got a little hostage!" The last word is barely out of his mouth before my brain instinctively launches my foot, crashing it into his gun hand, and sending his weapon spiraling across the street.

Greyson doesn't waste any time. Dropping his shoulder, he charges and body slams Lowell, who goes down firing. Sam yells, struck by the wild bullet and crumples to the ground. Nicolas dives to help him.

Without guns, these policemen are just wimpy, small-town losers. Greyson rolls his guy over, liberating his handcuffs and slapping them on, while I dodge a wild fist from the skinny one and pop up behind him, throwing my arm around his neck.

"Don't eat me! God! Don't eat me!"

My knee stabs at the back of his. He grunts as his flailing stance collapses. With my palm on the back of his head, I force his pointy little nose into the dirt of the shoulder where he blubbers.

"Don't worry, you're much too stringy for my taste." Pulling the handcuffs from his belt, I wrangle his arms around behind his back.

Greyson saunters over to handle the cuffs for me—he has more experience.

"It's pretty much public knowledge who and where we are now." He clicks one metal bracelet around the cop's boney wrist. "No sense in taking a bite out of these guys...not unless you want to play a little Simon Says and send them back to slow up the troops." He grins, clicking the other cuff.

"That's not even funny."

"I wasn't joking."

I shake my head. I'm not going to think about how Greyson can even contemplate making that suggestion. Ten minutes ago, I was thanking the universe for throwing him my way, and just now…I don't know what it was thinking.

"Nicolas," I stand up and brush myself off, "is Sam okay?"

"Does that mean 'no'?"

I only glare at Greyson and turn toward the car. The cocky cop underneath him whimpers. "Please, no! I got a family."

Greyson tugs on the cuffs and jerks his thumb my direction. "So, does she."

And then I remember: Greyson's my family now. He's never let me down—not ever. Whatever else he is, he's mine. I turn around, grab his hand, and draw him away from the temptation.

"How is it, Nicolas?" I kneel down next to Sam. He doesn't really look too bad, not much worse than when Chase took a bullet. Being viral has some benefits.

"The bullet went through his thigh, mostly flesh. How much pain, Smaran?"

His eyes cinch up and he groans. "About a 5." He's obviously spent too much time around doctors.

Nicolas stops probing the wound. "The bone doesn't appear broken, but that doesn't mean the bullet didn't graze it. The wound looks severe but the virus compensates and shuts things down around it, so you should be fine fairly quickly. Can you walk?"

"He won't have to." Greyson strolls to the police car. "Say good-bye to Lady Beamer, Nicky."

Not even flinching or looking back, Nicolas bundles his brother into the front passenger seat of the cop car.

I don't know a soul that wouldn't at least wince at the idea of abandoning his beloved BMW on the side of the road. But with Nicolas, family is everything. Impressed, I grab Amber and hustle her into the back seat behind the cage.

Our destination isn't that far. A couple miles outside of Huntington, Greyson takes a left on a road I'd have missed if I'd blinked. The hill it crosses blocks the view of everything but the desert on the horizon. When I see what's behind the slope, I begin to wonder if Greyson might just, after all, be some kind of superhero.

Chapter 5

"How did you know this was here?" I survey the small airport: no tower, one runway, a little house that looks like it just got built, a couple hangars, and a gas pump. Huntington municipal airport: who'd have guessed?

Greyson shrugs. "Like I said, my dad grew up just down the road in Castle Dale."

"I didn't know that."

"There's a lot you don't know about me, Ev." He passes the little house and heads for the hangars.

"I know enough; not sure I want to know everything. Are there airplanes here?"

"Yeah, my grandpa took up flying after he retired; bought himself a 182 Cessna. This airport was just sitting here falling apart. There was a county budget for it so he offered to run it for them; fixed up the runway, built the new hangars and the house, got some traffic flowing through here—mostly small planes, a few cargo."

"Do you fly?" Nicolas asks the question that's on my lips.

"Nope. Never got around to learning."

I'm wondering what good it is to have a plane and an airport with no pilot. It's not like this is the Matrix and Greyson can just upload a pilot program. Then a tall, thin man, that looks like he might have loaned Greyson some of his features, wanders out of the hangar.

Greyson stops the car and climbs out. "I was hoping you'd be up and kicking around early, old man."

The old guy's face stretches out in shock and then wrinkles into a grin. "Greyson! Your dad's been worried sick! We heard about all them raids and such. They burned the whole town to the ground."

"Yeah, well, they caught me and hauled me off to the Institute before that. Got out before they could get their knives in me, though."

The old guy grabs him and hugs him and I can tell he was deeply concerned. He doesn't even flinch when his cheek hits Greyson's semi-dead skin; he can see grey—and feel it too. Nicolas and I step out of the car.

The old guy nods a hello. "You need a place to hole up?"

"Actually, we need a place to run to." Greyson shoves his hands in the pockets of his scrubs, glancing down at his toe, and scraping indeterminate lines in the dust.

"I see Lowell must've borrowed you his patrol car."

"That's the thing," Greyson peeks up with one eye shut against the morning sun, "I may have a little trouble coming my way, not too far behind." He tilts his head back down the road toward Price.

We wander up behind Greyson. The old guy squints, looking us over, and then he holds out a slightly shaking hand. The trembling is not from the circumstances but from his age; the steel in his blue eyes is as steady as Greyson's amber. He's another guy you want on your team when the stakes are high and the terrain is rough.

Greyson makes the introductions. "Evelyn, Nicolas, this is my grandpa, Warren Childs."

Grandpa shakes my hand and then wraps his other hand around my wrist. "You're a pretty thing, aren't ya? Pretty enough to coax this boy out of hiding."

My eyes go wide as I absorb the brashness and then I grin at Greyson. The apple doesn't fall far from the tree. I've never met Grandpa, but I'm pretty sure I know him.

Greyson shakes his head and rolls his eyes. "So, Grandpa, you up for a little under-the-radar flying this morning?"

"You didn't exactly tell Lowell you was borrowing his car, huh? That the trouble you're expecting?"

"Just some of it." Greyson grins. "Lowell's not the worst of it. Heck, I took Lowell out with one fist. He didn't recognize me, what with the...you know. It's the soldiers and the Feds that have us running."

Grandpa Warren shakes his head, but handles it pretty well, considering. A distant gleam in his eyes even makes me wonder if he's not just a little proud. I guess Greyson's worked his way up to this level of delinquency slowly so it's not quite as much of a shock as it would have been for my grandparents.

Nicolas comes out on Greyson's side. I don't know why I find that odd. I should know Nicolas well enough to realize that he's not going to let some petty rivalry tarnish the way he sees people. "There are some highly unethical, ruthless people hunting your grandson, sir. He's somewhat of an anomaly, and possibly the key to a cure for the virus. I'm afraid things have gotten out of hand and people are using their guns instead of their brains."

"Yep, 'heard about that. The news said them zombies was responsible for that explosion up at the Institute." He squints at Greyson. "You know anything 'bout that?"

Greyson shrugs. "A little. Maybe. Don't tell Grandma."

"I was there, sir. They were about to dissect your grandson…alive." A chill ripples through Grandpa Childs; his face stiffens in shock. Greyson tucks his chin under and rubs his bare head self-consciously. "Evelyn, here, she showed up and rescued him." Nicolas is pouring it on a bit thick. Chase and his minions did most of the work. Grandpa thanks me with a solemn nod. "If it weren't for the two of them, my brother and I would have been caught in the explosion—or the raid. I'm researching the virus. We need to get them somewhere safe where I can continue my work."

"Well, I'm much obliged to you, young lady." He doesn't let on that there might be anything abnormal about the purple-grey tint of my skin, my smell, or the red streaks across my eyes. There's nothing but gratitude on his face. Then again, maybe his eyes and nose aren't what they used to be.

He scratches his chin and looks over at the police car where Sam's and Amber's heads are just visible. "Well, my plane's only a four-seater. Some of you smaller ones might have to double up. The FAA is not going to like that, but who's going to tell 'em?" He grins at Greyson.

"We just need to get over the Utah border. You been to Colorado lately, old man?"

"Let's see now…there's that Blake Field, outsid'a Delta, Colorado, little over an hour from here. Been there a couple times."

"Sweet! You up for it?"

"Yeah, I could get you out there, be back 'fore your grandma even gets up, no one the wiser." Thank goodness Grandpa Warren is an early riser. "Let's see, now. I got 1200 lbs. useable load. We're talking about 30 gallons of fuel. That'll run us about 200 lbs. We got four men at 175 each; that's another 700. Unless the two little gals here weigh over 300 lbs., that'll do her."

Greyson is about to make a wisecrack about my weight, but I glare at him and he swallows it. "Don't want to rush you, Grandpa, but we're in a bit of a hurry. I imagine we'll have some company here soon."

"No trouble. Was heading out this morning anyway. Grandma likes a little alone time. Retirement's been hard on her." He winks at Greyson. "You just pull that car you "borrowed" into the empty hangar over there. I'll tell Lowell it was abandoned here."

"No way. I don't want you mixed up in any of this. Nicolas can follow me in your truck and I'll drive it up to the reservoir and dump it in. We'll let Lowell make up his own story."

The reservoir is only a couple miles up the street. Greyson and Nicolas are gone for about five minutes. By the time Grandpa Warren has the plane fueled and out on the runway, they're back, none too soon. My ZV super-hearing picks up the faint squeal of sirens coming from the north and south. Greyson picks it up too and hustles us all into the cabin.

Out of respect for the pilot's range of sight and for a more or less equal weight distribution, the small lap child, Amber, gets assigned the front passenger lap, and the large lap child, me, gets relegated to the back pilot-side lap.

Sam hops in the back, which leaves Nicolas and Greyson drawing straws over who's going to hold whom. The four of us stand there awkwardly. Greyson is holding Amber. Nicolas, politely I think, concedes the front seat to him.

"You go ahead. You'll want to sit by your grandfather. I'll just climb in the back with my brother." We all know Greyson's not really a back-seat kind of guy.

We also know Charming Greyson is in there; he's just shy. But he apparently knows when the cards are on the table and he's got a great poker face. "No way, dude. You go ahead." He shuffles Amber into Nicolas's arms. "You're the guest. The view's great." He leans his head in where his grandpa is busy flipping switches and checking gauges. "You'll give him the full tour, right, Gramps?"

Grandpa Warren wags him a thumbs up.

And then Greyson just can't help himself. "Besides, Evelyn's not as light as she looks." He grins at me. Jerk. Yeah, I remember. He had to carry me, a sedated lump, out of the Institute when he broke me out. "You know, we zombies have superpowers." He flashes Nicolas a wink and pats him on the back as he climbs in. "No worries. I got her."

I smile, one of those pencil-straight, you're-not-going-to-get-away-with-this smiles and climb in over Sam. As I take my seat on Greyson's lap, I rub my palm across his baby-bald head. "Smooth," I smirk. "Really smooth." He can take that however he likes.

The plane rattles to life—great! Zombie Air—and then we're tearing and bumping down the runway.

In a game of "Would You Rather," I'm not sure whether I'd pick "run from the cops with Greyson driving me in a BMW" or "evade the border police with Grandpa Warren flying me in a very small plane." I'd have to say the takeoff was about as white-knuckling as the near-miss out of the intersection in Price. I can't complain, though. We're leaving the state where they want to hunt us down and chop us up like deer in season.

The flight is about like any other flight I've been on. Greyson's grandpa fills the cabin with an aged, toasted aroma, like coffee and peanuts, that mingles with the fruity-sweet soda and juice smell my little sister has at the moment—probably because of the loads of Gushers and gummy worms she's devoured.

The sixty minutes of flight time glide by, not because we're having fun—or flying, but because it's just so peaceful up here above it all—literally. For the first time in months, nothing is chasing me and I'm not chasing anything. I'm just gliding, leaving the past behind and waiting for the future to become the present. Molded into Greyson's lap, his arms locked around me like seatbelts, my entire body melts into his. I close my eyes to breathe it in and soak it up, a lazy summer day in a lawn chair by the pool.

Out of the window at this height, the mountains seem so much less imposing than when you're in them. I imagine what it would be like to rise so far that the earth fades into a blue ball, and then a point of light, and then disappears into the blur of the universe. I wonder if I'll ever feel like being a ZV is just a grain of sand on an immense landscape.

Overall, Greyson is well behaved. I only have to shove his hand out of the back of my shirt twice. I think Nicolas saw me do it once. Do ZVs blush red or purple? I can't even imagine Nicolas trying something like that. That's not really what bugs me about it, though.

I love the feel of Greyson's fingers on my bare skin, but I don't want Nicolas to see that that's the way things are. Even though that is the way things are. Greyson and I are flames and smoldering coals; we fuel each other. But doesn't fire need a hearth to keep it from burning out of control? Nicolas is definitely brick and mortar—with a very nice mantel. So...I don't know...it just makes me feel weird for him to actually see Greyson and me that way.

Okay, yeah, I did let my lips brush Greyson's temples once or twice when everyone else was admiring the view. I know, I'm a whacked-out hormone mess. Excuse me if it just feels so warm and safe having his arms around me again and some virus that feeds on love hormones is hijacking my brain. Everything seems so much simpler in our tiny, metal bubble hurtling through the open sky—almost everything. Not Nicolas.

The perpetual breath-holding starts again as soon as the plane begins its descent. The psychedelic roller coaster ride down has me clutching my stomach and gasping for air. A couple times, I thought I should throw my hands up and shout, "woo hoo!" as we bounced through the airwaves. The chase, the fear, the responsibility for Amber, it all washes over me like a sonic boom the moment the wheels hit the runway. At least, there's not an armed welcoming party camped out when we land just outside of Delta, Colorado. Someone, push the "EASY" button.

We all climb out and Greyson bear hugs Warren. I think they both know this is the last time they'll see each other. "Thanks, Grandpa."

"Just don't tell your grandma you was in town and I didn't bring you home."

About now I'm wondering how many times Greyson's dad told him, "Just don't tell mom."

"Do you know where you're going?" Warren pats Greyson on the back one last time before he lets him go.

"Yeah, but it's probably better if you don't."

"How you going to get there?"

Greyson shoves his hands in his pockets. "Well…I…uh…you wouldn't want to loan me a credit card? Nic here has been funding us, but he's leaving behind an electronic trail a mile wide."

Grandpa nods and digs into his back pocket. "It'll help that you got my name on your license."

"Greyson Warren Childs. That's me."

The old guy hands him a MasterCard with airline points. "That should do it then. Don't tell your grandma."

Chapter 6

Greyson is only eighteen like me, but his license says he's twenty-five—old enough to rent a car. Why am I not surprised? Or an even better question: why is the car attendant not suspicious? Maybe the scrubs he's wearing under Sam's navy sweatshirt give him a professional look. One way or the other, he waltzes out with the keys to a navy-blue sedan.

Engineering the passenger seating so that Nicolas and I share the back seat, I strap Amber between us. Greyson rented the car so he's driving and Sam is growing on me, but I'm still not comfortable leaving my sister with him in order to ride shotgun with Grey.

I feel a little guilty about my reservations, kind of racist because Sam's really nice to her. He uses the paperwork from the rental car to fold her a couple origami birds to play with. She hasn't had toys in a while—or anyone to play with. The whole trip through the desert goes a lot faster with all the swooping and nesting going on between them. The giggling almost drowns out the news reports. Apparently, my hair in braids makes a terrific castle for queen birds.

We spend the night and grab a shower at a hotel in Albuquerque, New Mexico. I haven't slept in a real bed for ages, well, if you don't count hospital beds. I almost feel human again when I wake up with clean, neatly braided hair and Amber cuddled under my arm. The two of us have the bed near the door and the bathroom. Nicolas and Sam took the other queen bed nearer the window and Greyson had the pullout in front of it, except he's not in it.

I check the time; it's still pretty early to be up and about. Apparently, Greyson and his grandpa have another trait in common. I wonder what kind of story he's going to tell me about what he was doing wandering the city in the early morning hours.

Amber smells like warm honey and cream, making my stomach growl and my mouth water. I should slide my butt out of bed and rustle us up some breakfast because she's bound to be as hungry as I am when she wakes up. But the crisp, white sheets and the downy pillow speak to me right now, and since I don't know when I'll have them again, if ever, I indulge and snuggle up to her.

Bad idea. I should have known better. When I fall back asleep, my early morning dreams are always nightmares. Of course, my nightmares are full of zombies.

We're having a picnic. The skies are blue, the sun is yellow, the grass on my aunt's ranch is green. Amber skips off to pet the baby cows. I'm flirting with Nicolas so Greyson gets angry and I threaten him with a syringe. His eyes cloud over and suddenly they are the sky, frothing black-grey and rolling in thunder. I stand up and shove him away because I was enjoying the sun. He grabs my hand and tries to pull me off the blanket.

From across the field, Amber screams. All three of us turn to see that the baby calf isn't a calf anymore; it's a bloody zombie buffet. There are dozens of ZVs ripping into it. Screaming, I reach for my baby sister, but Greyson won't let me go. Torrents of rain start to fall. Amber is running, running, running toward me. I can't shake Greyson off of me. Amber trips; the zombies dive for her as she crawls away, clawing at the ground. "Nicolas!" I yell, but the hand that reaches for me has claws. The face on the blanket is purple-grey and snarling, the eyes red and blood-shot. Nicolas isn't Nicolas anymore. Greyson grabs me around the waist while the zombie tries to take a bite out of my leg and then a blood-curdling scream rises out of Amber...

No! That wasn't the dream. That was Amber, the real one.

My eyes fly open. It's not Dream Nicolas attacking—it's Sam, flesh and blood! His eyes are crazy as he snarls and wrestles through the blankets to get at Amber. She's huddled down under the sheets, her arms draped around my thighs. With Sam's elbow pinning my chest and Amber, screaming and whimpering, clamped around my legs, I have trouble wriggling free, so I claw and hurl Sam away from my thighs. He falls snarling into the gap between the beds.

"Nicolas! Nicolas, wake up!"

From the other bed, a shadow darts up and sprints past us, heading for the bathroom. Damn! Maybe Greyson was right all along; maybe Nicolas is the cowering type. At least I have a horde of little ZV bodies riding cavalry into my bloodstream, stirring up my defenses.

Freeing up a leg, I punch my knee into Sam's throat when he dives back over the edge of the bed to get to my sister. He gasps and stumbles back as Amber scrambles to the opposite side of the mattress burrowing deep into the tightly tucked sheets.

Sam's so focused on his prey that he still doesn't even see me. I kick him away, trying to unhitch the linens. His grasping claws, sharp and solid like mine—like any other carnivore's— gash my exposed thigh and shred the sheets, ripping through the obstacle to his quarry.

He tears open the stab wound I got at the Institute. The stink of my blood drenches the room and stains the white cotton. My smell distracts him, but it's not nearly as overpowering as the rotting meat stench gushing from a tiny open wound near his temple. Sam is definitely not the same beast as Greyson and me. One glimpse at his eyes and I can see something in his brain has snapped. Nicolas's harmless, mildly entertaining little brother isn't in there anymore; there's no one home but a ruthless predator.

Grunting, I throw my torso at him, constraining his body with my arms as he scrambles after the cowering mound of Amber. I jam my elbow into his kidney and he howls, disoriented. At least now, he's noticed me.

In the split second that he's distracted, I try kicking my legs to dislodge my sister from the sheets. "Get out, Amber! Get out! Find Greyson!" She won't move. I'm not sure if she's petrified or convinced hiding in the torn and bloody linen will protect her.

Catching his breath again, Sam dives for my throat, jaws snapping, a hyena fighting for his kill. Dodging the assault, I lunge forward. Sam misses me by a hair. Feathers fly at my back as, growling and snarling, he shreds the pillowcase instead of my throat.

Scrambling onto all fours, I rip the blankets out from underneath the mattress and shove the little ball that is Amber onto the floor at the foot of the bed. "The bathroom! Find Nicolas! Lock the door!"

All I have to do is restrain Sam—or what used to be Sam— long enough for her to slip away, but he's on my back, snarling, crawling after her before I can turn to face him. A lioness fighting for my cub, I twist and intercept him in a full-body clamp, rolling him to the floor between the bed and the bathroom wall so Amber can escape while he's pinned. He's always seemed a little scrawny to me, so imagine my surprise when we smack the carpet and I'm the one on the bottom, struggling to shield my neck from the snapping, demon jaws. Where did that come from? The Wimp is suddenly The Hulk. "Go, Amber! Go, now!"

She's too tangled up in the sheets to go anywhere and I'm too tangled up with Sam to help. Where is Nicolas?

The hotel door clicks and whines open. "What the hell?" It's Greyson. In less than a second, he's hauled Sam off of me by the neck, dragging him over the top of the Amber lump. Swinging the writhing body around, he hammers its jaw with a cracking blow from his fist that catches the Sam monster by surprise and sends him reeling, crashing into the flat screen against the wall opposite the beds. Now the Big, Bad Wolf is grappling with the Alpha dog.

Sifting through the ball of shredded, putrid, purple-stained sheets, I uncover Amber. Instinctively she claws and kicks at my face like a rabid bunny until she sees it's her sister that's broken into her den. She jumps into my arms, pasting her little body to mine, and we run for the bathroom. Nicolas, who has finally decided to break cover, crashes into us.

"Don't hurt him, Greyson! I can stop this. Just hold him for me!" He's got a syringe in his hand and he's popping a little fluid out the top.

"I have to stay out here to protect you." I peel Amber off of me and slam the bathroom door, commanding her to lock it. Outside, I crouch at my post, panting, the last line of defense.

Greyson's strong; believe me. I've seen him in action and been on the other end of his grip. But it's like Sam is insanely pumped on an overdose of ZV steroids. His teeth are his weapons, and Greyson's throat is his target. Clamped in a death grip, the two of them grapple. Greyson gives ground, inch by inch toward the window, while restraining the deranged mutant's snapping jaws with his right forearm. Sam attacks relentlessly, throwing his body weight, clawing, and writhing. His fangs slice the skin on the side of Greyson's head and the pungent odor of ZV blood bursts fresh into the room again.

Greyson shifts his weight to throw another punch and Sam lunges for his jugular. His predator virus is strong and vicious, but it's not tactical. Greyson ducks, lands a blow to Sam's gut, and then pivots around to chokehold him from behind, betting on whatever Nicolas has in the tube he's wielding.

Sam sees the doctor coming and squirms, snarling and spitting. He butts his head backward colliding with Greyson's temple. Dazed, Greyson staggers, loosening his grip, and Sam breaks away to tackle his brother.

Nicolas is a lamb waiting to be gobbled up. Sucking in a breath, I dart in for back up, but Nicolas must have some experience with Sam's violent aggression because he's expecting the resistance. He dodges gracefully as Greyson recovers and slams into Sam's back, pinning him face down on his own bed. Nicolas jabs the needle into his brother's thigh.

"Hold him down! Just hold him down." Nicolas stands there in his boxers, his bare chest heaving.

We watch Sam slowly deflate. When he's docile, nearly unconscious, Greyson rolls off of him and sits on the edge of the bed. He's got a couple new wounds on his arms and one on the side of his bald scalp. Teeth marks.

"What the hell was that?" He dabs at the ZV blood with the sheet. "Is he ripe?"

"No, no." Nicolas sinks onto the bed, next to the limp body of his brother. Pulling his fingers back through his wild bangs, he breathes deeply, exhaling the tension of the fight. "It's okay." He puts his hand on his brother's head, pets his hair.

Knocking on the door, I manage to convince Amber to open it up. "It's all right, baby. Sam is asleep. I'm here. Open the door so I can hug you, sweetie."

The lock pops, but the door stays shut. When I push it slowly open, I find her huddled beneath the sink cabinet. "Evy, my knife wasn't big enough." She shows me the purple-stained blade. She must have gotten in the stab on Sam's temple before I woke up.

The tension in my heart melts into pity. How the hell is a six-year-old supposed to deal with so much horror and trauma? Maybe I'm fighting a losing battle trying to find a place where Amber and I can escape the insanity and live a normal life. Maybe it's time I realized that a normal life slipped out of our grasp the day ZVs fed on the rest of our family, or even before that, the day the Z-Virus set up housekeeping in my blood.

Gathering her up in my arms, I set her on the sink while I clean the blade, close it, and hand it back. "You were tough, baby. Evy's proud of you." Scooping her up, I carry her cautiously back into the room, shivering and whimpering on my shoulder.

"Dude! I know he's your brother and all, but this is not okay. We've got a little girl here." Greyson nods toward Amber. "Once they get like this, it's over, man, they're gone."

"No!" And I thought Nicolas only came in one flavor. I was wrong. "He's not like them! This is different!" He stands up and paces around. "It must be all the excitement: the police, the car chases, the gunshot wound. It's stirred it up again."

"Again!" Greyson catches hold of the word. "So, this has happened before?"

Nicolas gets more flustered. "Look, everybody, just calm down."

"It's kind of hard to calm down, Nicolas, when your brother just tried to eat my little sister." I'm about one notch short of hysterical. "You should have told us he was like this."

"He's not like this!" He sits on the bed again, with his hands out in front of him, calming the air. "I know it looks bad, but it's not because the disease has taken over. This is not a gradual descent into a total loss of reason. This is more like...an episode."

"An episode? Really? Is that what you call hunting down a small child for breakfast?" I'm still a little worked up on ZV hormones and although I have the claws on my fingers sheathed, the pointy end of my tongue is raw steel. Amber's whole face is hidden in my shoulder. She can't look at Sam on the bed.

"No. No! Like an epileptic episode." Suddenly Nicolas's hands do half of the talking for him, his fingers and palms rounded, attempting to contain the uncontainable. He flips them over, offering us enlightenment. "It's part of his symptoms. He'll be unconscious now for a few hours and then it'll take at least a week for him to get his normal strength back."

"What do you mean 'normal'? The kid was a sickly wimp an hour ago. Suddenly he's tossing me around the room." Greyson has a right to be skeptical. He's surveying the damage to his arms and face. "Which of those do you call normal?"

"This," he motions around the room, "this was the virus. You see, he's fighting it like you are, but there's something about his strain of it that's also invading his immune system. You two aren't like that. Your body is adapting to accept the modifications to your hearing, your eyesight, your motor skills, and your muscles. His is not. He's fighting something more than what has infected your system. That's what I need to isolate. That's what's makes him sick and causes 'episodes' like this."

I don't know who looks more miserable, Amber or Nicolas. Maybe I'm just crazy to think we can all survive together, that somehow there's a solution where we work this out and we're not a threat to each other. What if I wake up one morning and the wolf going after Amber is me? Maybe the only solution is to keep the ZVs away from the uninfected. Maybe black and white is the only safe way to see the world.

"We need to get Amber to my aunt," I say. "Don't you want to see Aunt Esther?" I'm hoping visions of open fields, cows grazing, and cousins playing like puppies will crowd out the nightmare of being attacked by a rabid zombie. Amber shivers mutely but nods in my arms.

Nicolas shakes his head. "I'm so sorry. I've been giving him the injections and they've been working. We haven't seen an episode like this since before we started this treatment. It's the over-stimulation; it has to be." He's crushed, frantic, trying to figure out the solution.

I feel bad for him. I see in Sam the shadow of what waits for Greyson and me. Nicolas can't get discouraged. We need him to believe he can win.

"Don't give up, Nicolas. Whatever you're doing, it will work." I rub Amber's back. "This was just a setback, not defeat."

For the first time since I've known him, I don't need Nicolas; he needs me. Even though Greyson is standing right there and won't appreciate it, I brush my hand against our doctor's cheek. He needs the human touch right now. "Look. Your brother didn't go after you. You were asleep, right next to him, and there was still enough of Sam inside the beast that he came all the way over his own brother to get to my sister instead." It's a chilling piece of evidence, but it's evidence. Nicolas looks up at me, half grateful, half mortified. "That's something." I smile grimly.

His hands cover his face and then push back up through his tangle of untamable bangs as he heaves a heavy sigh. "I'll need to up the dosage, but I'm already running low. We need to get to a lab."

"We'll find you a lab, Nicolas." I pet Amber's hair as she stops whimpering and hugs me. His face hardens in determination, but I can still see the pain of this defeat, a foreshadowing of the pain that will be there if the bug finally gains the upper hand against Greyson and me. Nicolas loves his brother; that's why losing this battle is ripping him apart. It wouldn't be right if he loved me too.

Chapter 7

Now that the fighting is over, if anyone can sympathize with Nicolas, it's Greyson. I don't know how many friends he had to watch descend into brain dead cannibalism. At least Nicolas has his research to turn to. All Greyson could do was lead his friends to the gangs of ZV bashers or the Snatchers to put them out of their misery.

Greyson claps Nicolas on the shoulder and offers him a chance to redeem himself. "Go down and get us some breakfast, Nic. I smell sausage. You might want a to-go bag for Sam. I think he'll be starving when he wakes up." He tosses Nicolas his pants.

That's when I realize I'm standing there in my PINK underwear and a tank top. The purple blood from my thigh trickles down my leg. My chest is still heaving and the boil in my blood hasn't quite returned to normal temperatures, so it's hard to tell if I'm even self-conscious about it. Most of my attention is on Amber who is slowly coming out of hiding beneath my arm.

Nicolas pulls his pants on and nods at my wound. "I have something for that."

Slipping into the bathroom while Grey and I exchange glances and shrugs, he rifles through his medical bag. Bottles and tubes clank against metal instruments until he finally reappears with a tube and gauze. Then he kneels down in front of me and starts applying this pink stuff to the wound on my upper leg.

Picture this: me, in my underwear, the PINK logo scrawled across the front, Nicolas kneeling in front of me, his nose practically grazing the K, as he wraps gauze around my thigh. Every time his fingers brush the skin, a shiver snakes up my leg. I don't think the virus is doing a good enough job of shutting down the sensation in that area. I clench my teeth, to stop myself from feeling anything or, God forbid, from giggling, and stare up at the ceiling—anywhere but at Nicolas, and definitely not at Greyson.

"You have to be careful," the doctor goes on as if it's all just clinical and my boyfriend isn't standing right behind him, frowning. "Most of the infected patients they admitted to the Institute had wounds of some kind or another. I've been working with the guys over in stem cell research. We came up with this. It's not perfect, but it helps. The wounds get infected quite easily because your immune system is already under attack, so secondary infections can turn lethal for ZVs. Of course, with you two," he glances back at Grey, "we don't really know." He smiles up at me. "Better safe than sorry."

I try to smile back at the nice doctor who just patched me up, but, with the emotional soup sloshing around in my blood, Nicolas's hands wrapped around my upper thigh, and his scrumptious smile beaming up at me, I'm not sure what actually surfaces onto my face.

I'm trying to keep this professional, but my quick glance at Greyson's face tells me he's reached the edge of his charm and is about ready to dive off. Nicolas tosses him the tube. I guess house calls aren't covered on Greyson's plan.

The silence churns thickly.

Nicolas slices through it. "What's in that tube is all I have for now. But the research is there on my laptop. Once I get a lab, I'll duplicate my work and improve it."

"Thanks," I say as he stands up. "I'll volunteer for human testing."

"You already have." Snide humor from the charming doctor?

We all stand around, trying to find somewhere safe to look until Greyson tosses me my jeans. These are skinny jeans. They're going to require some wriggling and two hands. I set Amber down and step into one leg.

"I'll just get us some breakfast, then." Nicolas bolts for the door. The doctor always steps out while you put your clothes back on, even after he's already seen you naked.

"I want juice," Amber yells after him. "I need juice, Evy." She's clinging to my leg like a baby monkey that's just been snatched from the jaws of a crocodile. I'm glad she's actually still capable of speech, but it makes it hard to slide my jeans on. Greyson scoops her up.

"Thanks," I say, wriggling into them as the door shuts behind Nicolas, "for…" I motion around the room and my eyes land on the unconscious form of Sam, "…for everything."

Greyson pets Amber's hair. "Hey, why don't you run in there and take a bath? You're as stinky as I am."

Amber grins; she loves a bath, but she's probably just as happy to get out of the room where the Big Bad Wolf that just tried to gobble her up is sleeping on the bed. "Are there bubbles?"

"The bottle is all yours."

She runs off but turns around before she shuts the door. "Evelyn! You stay right here!" She shakes her index finger at me like I'm a naughty two-year-old that just ran away and got lost.

"I'm not going anywhere without you, baby."

The door clicks shut. Before the water goes on, Greyson has his arms around me. He didn't send Nicolas downstairs for sausage because he was hungry for breakfast; he was hungry for me.

At first, he's wringing out of our lips all the mistakes, all the drama, all the fear and anger that have kept us apart for the last few days. And then his hands find the back of my neck and his lips go soft and I can feel he's breathing me in like I'm life to him. I remember now. I remember how Greyson got under my skin. He's the half of me I never knew was missing. His lips move on mine and his fingers slide down my back. My body curves and inhales, filling up with him as his hands glide along my curves. I close my eyes and we're falling. The pillows hug us and I wrap my legs around Greyson's.

"Evelyn! I can't reach the soap!"

My eyes pop open. Greyson leans away and smiles. "You better go get the soap before the bubble monster comes after us."

I'm walking away but he still has my hand and won't let go. He hauls himself up for another kiss. I throw my arms around his neck.

"Evelyn! Did you hear me?"

I giggle. "She sounds like my mom." My hair runs through his fingers as I walk away to do the princess's bidding.

When I finally emerge, slightly soggy, Greyson has gathered up our few belongings. I surprise him in the act of rubbing a thin pink layer of Nicolas's magic potion on his bald head and cheek.

"You were off early this morning." I sift through the mess of blankets for Amber's clothes.

He only nods and reaches for the cord to Nicolas's laptop.

"Where'd you go?" I wonder if he's going to tell me. He's not wearing the scrubs he wore to bed last night. In the early morning hours, while we were all sleeping in, before Sam got hungry, he scored himself a black hoodie and some jeans. I'm not sure how he managed to get into a store, much less buy anything, without setting off a freakshow frenzy—or worse. I'm not even sure he got them from a store. Wishing my mind didn't jump to the worst possible conclusion, I smudge away the picture of a half-mangled body, minus jeans and sweatshirt, lying in the bushes behind the hotel parking lot.

"The car needed gas."

So now it's not "don't tell Grandma" anymore, it's "don't tell Evelyn." I think about letting it slide while I walk back to the bathroom, but I can't do it. I'm not going to let Nicolas's blindness to what I really am irritate me and then turn around and pretend I don't see Greyson for what he is. He's not going to play me the way he's played so many girls. I can't be with someone who evades me with half-truths and lies.

That's what I tell myself in my head while my back is to him, but I'm not really sure. If it came down to it, face to face, I might cave, let him get away with it—whatever it is he's hiding. Greyson and I need each other to survive. Neither one of us will make it alone. And Amber requires two supervising adults.

But then, the thought of letting him lie to me makes me cringe from the inside out. I am NOT that girl. I whirl back around. "So, you're not going to tell me where the new clothes came from?" It comes out a little harsher than I meant it to because I've been chewing on it.

His eyes shift to his clothes and he shrugs—that's all—he just shrugs.

My temperature starts to rise a little. Maybe the virus is still a little worked up from this morning's adventures in Zombieland, but I can't let it go.

When he sees I'm about to bite, he tosses me a bone. "Somebody gave them to me. Calm down."

"Calm down?" Now I'm anything but. "I'm not stupid, Greyson. Last time I checked, no one was organizing charity clothing drives for ZVs. Who just takes off their jeans and sweatshirt and hands them to strangers? You're out there attacking innocent people, or you're leaving a mile-wide pale purple trail right to us and you expect me to just 'calm down'?"

He turns around and glares at me for a second with his mouth open, then his hands go up like he's surrendering. "What do you want from me, Ev?" Somehow the worn-out clichés take on a new meaning when you're a zombie. "Suddenly you can't trust me because Doc Do Good is around and I'm the bad influence? Is that it?"

I can't say anything. My mouth hangs open while I try to figure out how he twisted this back on me. We can't ever stay on the same page. He's reading my words but they don't say the same thing to him that they do to me.

He shakes his head incredulously. "That's it? You really don't trust me?" Now he's mad. "Newsflash, baby! I'm not the one that just tried to eat your little sister. Oh, yeah!" now the sarcasm, "I'm the one that pulled Dr. Do Good's raving monster off of her."

Direct hit. The guilt explodes inside me. I step forward, reaching for him, but he turns away to pick up stuff. "I said 'thank you'." Why does that sound so lame? "I really meant it."

He only snorts. "Thank you?"

"What do you want me to say? You're always saving our asses. We wouldn't be standing here now if it weren't for you. Amber would be infected or dead. Whatever shape they're in, we owe our lives to you. Is that what you're looking for? Because there it is! But give me a break. It's not like I haven't ever put my ass on the line for you."

"That's not what this is about and you know it."

"What then?"

"You want me to say it out loud? It's not enough that it's screaming at us 24/7, in the car, in the plane, in the hotel room. Don't give me that crap, Ev. You know this is about Nicolas. The guy is totally whipped. He's all saying he just wants to help us so he can cure his brother, but he's got it bad. I get it! He loves you; he can't help himself. I feel his pain. But you have to stop jerking me around with him."

"What are you talking about?" I ask, but I know exactly what he's talking about. It can't be hidden. Nicolas is transparent and I'm a lousy liar—especially to myself. "Of course, I appreciate Nicolas. He's a doctor and I have the virus of the century. He cares about people; he's nice; he's trying to help us."

"And what do you think I'm trying to do?"

"I don't know! You won't tell me!"

"So, you just assume Greyson, that jerk-off, is sneaking out to sample the local flavors, rip a few lung burritos out of the unsuspecting villagers?"

That's actually what I was suspecting, but I'm not going there. I don't want to follow Grandma and Grandpa Childs and Greyson's mom and dad in Act Three of the Childs drama. I don't want to fight with Greyson until we can't stand to be around each other anymore. I don't want him to sneak away in the morning. I want him on my team. I want to be soul mates. I want to be that couple.

"I saw your mom and dad, Greyson. The whole town had front row seats to the dysfunction. I heard how your Grandpa— don't get me wrong, he's a great guy and I really appreciate what he did for us—but I heard how he keeps your Grandma in the dark. I don't want us to end up like that."

He's confused because I didn't go where he wanted to take this. He steps back to regroup as the fire fades out of his eyes and the lines along his purple mouth go soft. It's so funny how love has so many faces; no wonder it makes us all a little crazy.

"I'm not my Grandpa or my dad; and they don't have the Z-Virus." He tosses the stuff in his hands on the bed next to Sam and crosses the room. He wraps his arms around my waist and pulls me close. This is what I really want. I want to be close to him; I want to be the only one he tells. He's a head taller than I am, so I have to look up into his face. It's hard to tell if his eyes are a devil's or an angel's; he can go either way. But either way, he's not lying when he says, "Don't you get it? There is nothing, nothing, in this world for me but you. You're my blood, and my brains, and my breath." He leans down and his lips find mine again.

It's true; I feel like we can live off of each other, and not in the zombie flesh-eating way. We're connected with strings that we can't see, which just makes me sadder that he won't tell me where he went. "Then why are you shutting me out?" My fingers caress his neck and shoulders where the blond curls used to be.

He's exasperated, but he doesn't let go. "You want to know where I was?"

I nod and pull him closer, standing on my tip-toes to bring my nose even with his, my lips only a breath away.

The key card shuffles in the lock and the door opens. Greyson and I break away from each other, but the cords between us still hang in the air like the smoke from a candle that's just been snuffed out.

Nicolas can sense it; we all shuffle our feet and avert our eyes as he walks into the room with a couple glasses of juice balanced on heaping platefuls of meat.

"I'm done, Evy!" Amber's muffled voice cracks the stiff air. "I can't reach the towel, and the bubbles are sticking all over me!"

I brush past Nicolas, grateful for the escape.

Chapter 8

We have to cross the Texas border somewhere between Albuquerque and Amarillo. Even after a couple of hours, Sam is still limp on the front passenger seat next to Greyson. He and Amber are definitely not sharing the same side of the car—ever. The border between Colorado and New Mexico was a piece of cake; of course, neither of those states has reported any ZV infections. But, judging by the populace, or lack of it, I really don't think New Mexico cares who wanders over its borders; they're just glad for the company. Besides, when you've already got aliens, what difference do a couple of zombies make? Not that we were advertising.

Just outside of Clovis, New Mexico, Greyson flips on the radio to pick up some news. What we hear is less than encouraging. Chase blew up the Institute only a couple of days ago and things are already looking pretty bad.

> *...Following the discovery of several large pockets of Zoser Virus infection in both Southern and Central California, Governor Sharpton has declared a state of emergency. He is meeting today with White House representatives to seek funding and assistance for both quarantine and decontamination.*
>
> *The state's troubled economy and recent budget cutbacks have left its emergency response teams ill-equipped to deal with the sudden surge of the virus. Of the two known strains, California is reporting a higher percentage of the new "lucid" strain. Carriers of this strain, while experiencing the onset of initial symptoms, seem to resist the virus' lethal effects indefinitely. These*

carriers demonstrate enhanced physical abilities and, in rare cases, a resistance to the appetite for human organs.

The original, largely lethal strain that, in some cases, produces pronounced zombie-type symptoms and rapid degeneration of the host, appears to be more prevalent in Texas, where officials are finding the range of the infected area is now significantly wider than originally projected, with Houston still at its center...

"Of course, Texas has more brain-dead ZVs. They're the beef capital of the world." I think it's a pretty safe bet that California boasts a few more vegetarians than Texas.

Greyson snickers. I try to catch his eye in the rearview mirror, but he's looking past me at the car behind us. He seems very interested, so I turn to see what's caught his attention. There's nothing but a nondescript black sedan.

While the reporter drones on, I explain my vegetarian theory to Nicolas. He nods politely as I list the cases of people I knew were vegetarian reacting differently to the virus than those I knew ate meat. "Of course, my whole theory is based on a total of four test cases, but I have 100% accuracy and it's practically the only thing Greyson and I had in common." Oops. That didn't come out quite right. I glance again at Greyson's reflection in the mirror. He's taking it all wrong. "I mean...before we got to know each other better."

Nicolas nods politely. Greyson refocuses his attention on the newscast. The only way out of the little pit I've dug for myself is to jump. "Madi—you remember her? Her dad called you for me before the Institute invasion—she wasn't even bitten by a mutant. One of Greyson's converts, a total zombie head, got her. But she's resistant and strong like us. Why? She was vegetarian."

Of course, Nicolas is a scientist so he doesn't buy into the idea wholesale, but he at least looks intrigued. Or is he just humoring me? "It's an interesting observation, definitely worth researching. Vegetarianism can change the type and quantity of enzymes present in the digestive system, which could be a factor that leads to the actual resistant element. It's definitely a clue worth pursuing."

"Well, as long as you're at it, you should know that Chase was fine until he got mad and gave in to the cravings. I think that eating people instead of sticking to animal meat is what accelerated his deterioration. He was pretty much just like me and Greyson until he developed a taste for Snatcher guts." The report droning on in the background catches our attention again:

...The governor of Texas called the legislature into an emergency session yesterday. In a heated debate he urged lawmakers to pass legislation sanctioning the use of "reasonable force" to protect persons, property, and welfare. Critics claim that this would essentially clear the way for law enforcement, or any legal gun owner, to fire, at will, on an infected person without fear of prosecution...

"Any legal gun owner?" Greyson scoffs. "That means everyone in the state...and their dogs. Maybe we should seriously rethink our destination."

"We can't. I have to get Amber to my aunt's. It's the only family she has left."

"She has you...and me." Greyson looks over his shoulder, possibly at me, or maybe at the car that's following us.

My hand wanders over Amber's little cupcake cheeks, pushing the blond wisps from her face. "But, for how long?" I meet Greyson's steady gaze in the mirror. If it were up to him, the answer would be "forever." Greyson's convinced we're immortal. But I'm not so sure. And if this is immortality, do I really want it?

My eyes shift toward Sam. Nicolas catches the glance. "She's not safe with us." The wound is still too fresh to pick at it, but the doctor already knows. I feel bad that I have to say it. Maybe I keep saying it because I'm trying to convince myself. Everything about my new life has teeth, claws, and bullets for Amber, but I'm also the only soft pillow where she can lay her head.

There aren't many souls out there that really care what happens to a little blonde in the middle of an apocalypse...my

Aunt Esther is one of the few…and Nicolas. He turns and stares out the window.

"And you need a lab, Nicolas." His research is his coping strategy. It's the rope he clings to so he can pull himself out of the muck that keeps rising up around us—and maybe the rope he'll use to drag us out with him.

Greyson checks his mirror again. He's not glaring at me; he's checking out the black sedan that is still behind us. His eyes are cinched and his brow is furrowed, which makes me nervous because Greyson never worries; he just handles what comes up. Maybe it's the odd sound coming from the car's wheels that bugs him. If it were a bike, I'd think it had a playing card clicking in the spokes. The subtle clack annoys all the ZVs in the car, except Sam. He's still out cold in Frankenstein time-out.

"I wanna go to Estwher's howse," Amber mumbles in my ear around the glob of gummy worms in her mouth and over the rest of the broadcast.

…Lawyers for the Lazarus Knight Church of the Firstborn have issued a statement of sanctuary for ZVs and, based on First Amendment rights, are prepared to file for injunctions against any legislation. In the last week, Ashley Knight, daughter of the late Reverend Ezekiel Lazarus Knight, has issued several calls for the faithful to join her at the Knight compound and no longer fear the coming of, what she terms, "the final transformation." The Knight Church has a sizeable following and substantial private funding.

"Did you catch that?" I tap Greyson's shoulder because he seems distracted. "Sounds like somebody's finally trying to see things from our side of the aisle."

"Doesn't surprise me. Aren't all the church-goers afraid of dying? They're all looking for a miracle, a way to live again after they're dead—immortality?" He waggles his hands and his brows like he's mocking a big show.

"Not like that." I went to church. Sometimes. Enough to know the zombie apocalypse and the resurrection are not the same thing. Nothing is sacred to Greyson.

He goes for backup. "What do you think, Doc? Aren't we some kind of holy miracle, Ev and I?"

Nicolas clears his throat. He's actually going to give Greyson a serious answer. "Well, Egyptians were obsessed with life after death. The virus may possibly be the result of the alchemical experiments associated with that quest. I've already discussed my parents' research on that theory with Evelyn. But since the virus infects the living, not the dead, technically there is no reanimation. I suppose it is possible that, anciently, a deceased host resuscitated, in a manner of speaking, as a result of infection, but…"

I put my hand on his knee to stop the pain. "He's joking, Nicolas. I don't think Greyson believes in life after death."

"I do now." He grins and then checks the mirror again.

"What are you looking at?" I crane my neck around to see the black sedan again.

"No! Don't look back."

"What's going on, Greyson?"

Now Nicolas looks back.

"Nicky distracted me with breakfast and I never did get to tell you where I went this morning." He grins, actually grins, in the rearview mirror. As if! There's no way he was intending to tell me anything about his little field trip this morning. He really thinks he can just smile and make it all go away.

I don't humor him. Narrowing my eyes into little daggers of "you're so full of shit," I cross my arms and look out the window, shaking my head.

"You went out?" The anxious crease of Nicolas's eyebrows vindicates my earlier suspicions.

"Well, you were all dead to the world, and the car needed gas. I gotta tell you, Nicky. That morning, smokehouse flavor dripping off of you is a bit tempting."

Nicolas gasps. Evidently, he's still not used to wry ZV humor.

"Let's just say I needed a little fresh air."

He glances up at the mirror. The black sedan is still snapping away behind us.

Greyson changes lanes. The black sedan slides over, staying a dozen car lengths behind. "I had Sam's hoodie in the front seat so I figured I could slide by at the pump. I nearly did until I was hanging the thing up and, over the fumes, I caught a really intense whiff of open ZV wounds on the air. It's been a while since I actually caught a whiff of myself. You know, you get used to the smell…"

"I can smell you, Greyson." Amber rips into another juice box and I remove it from her hands to replace it with a banana. "You remind me of Flash." With wide, droopy eyes, she solicits my sympathy for her old wound. "You remember Flash before he got hit by the car?" The whole car goes quiet out of respect for the deceased dog.

You'd think with all the carnage she's seen, that particular scene would have melted into commonplace. But she's really still sad. Amber's the youngest so our dog Flash was like her baby brother. It sounds twisted, but I'm actually glad she's still sad; it means she can still feel something. Maybe she's not totally screwed up for the rest of her life and, if we can get her to my Aunt Esther, she has a shot at something normal. "Greyson smells like Flash used to sometimes, like when he got out of the bath and then ran around wild." She checks with me to see if I think the same thing.

"Wet dog smell? Hmmm." My hand cupping my chin, I nod, contemplating the similarities. "Yeah, that's what it is. I think you're right, baby. I just couldn't quite put my finger on it." It's good to be laughing at Greyson again. He takes it well.

"I'm hurt, Ev'. You're nothing but chocolate chip cookies and apple pie to me." Charming Greyson is lethal. To tell the truth, to me, Greyson is all homemade bread, hot out of the oven and smothered in butter.

"So, there was another ZV?" Nicolas prods the conversation back around to the pertinent information.

"This crazy girl jumped into my car and crouched down in the back seat. At first, I thought she could still smell Amber in here, but then she started rambling about a lab, and escaping, and some Mr. Holland hunting for her again. She was scared stiff and her head was shaved like mine." Greyson's hand runs up across his bald scalp.

Nicolas catches the word "lab." "I wasn't aware they had any ZV studies going on in New Mexico."

"Nope. I finally got her to calm down by promising I wouldn't let any lab guys get her."

I don't like the way this is going because the mystery ZV girl isn't here, but some stranger in a black sedan is trailing us. I don't much like the idea of Greyson bumping into mysterious ZV girls either. I know—petty. She was running scared, bald, needed help. But what am I supposed to do? Pretend I don't feel a little territorial so I can be some kind of saint? I don't think so. I haven't spent the last month clawing my way to embracing what I am on the outside just to turn around and go all hypocritical on the inside. I know what I am inside; I'm not going to call it something that it's not.

"Once she calmed down and I passed her a little snack I managed to scrape up," (I don't even want to ask) "she spilled her guts about some pharmaceutical company outside Houston. She thought she was participating in a university study, but it's our Institute of Terror all over again. Said she and her boyfriend made a run for it." He glances back meaningfully at me. "That's where the clothes came from. The boyfriend got caught. She had his stuff in her pack."

Okay, so sue me. It makes me feel better that she has a boyfriend. I wonder if she's going back for him.

"Some Texas Snatchers showed up in an SUV. We played a little street tag."

We already know what that is like. No need to relive it.

"I got them off her scent long enough for her to hit the road—on her way to hook up with relatives in So. Cal. Sure hope they're the kind who care. Whoever takes her in is in for a real shock. She was hacked up—missing an eye, exposed parts of her brain, open wounds over her vitals."

The gruesomeness of it all revolts me; I want to cry for her because I've been strapped to that bed. So why is there this tiny, shallow bubble rising up inside of me that is glad she wasn't beautiful? Fortunately, Greyson's superpowers don't include reading minds or seeing into the deep, dark caverns of the heart.

"Anyway, one of the thugs driving the SUV got a good look at me and was on his phone before he got himself in an accident and flipped his car." He grins. "…not safe to talk on your phone and drive."

"And you think the guy behind us is the one they were talking to?" I nod toward the rear window.

"Can't be sure, but the way she described him, I think the driver is this Holland dude she was so freaked about."

Shivers trace a cold trail down my spine. Why hasn't he called the police or the military? Why is he just following us? "How could they recognize you?"

"There's a database." Nicolas catches Greyson's eye in the rearview mirror. "It was set-up by the CDC. It's classified, but some of the pharmaceuticals might have access, especially if they're working on a vaccine. I'm afraid, Greyson, since you were admitted into the Institute, your information is in there."

"At least what they bothered to collect of it." That was the part that really infuriated and disgusted me. The doctors at the institute were more interested in cutting living, breathing human beings up for the fun of it, than gathering data. Reliving the Dr. Christensen-nightmare turns my stomach. Just thinking about Greyson strapped to that operation table makes me queasy…and so angry that little bubbles of virus juice boil up in my veins.

"They have your picture, your blood work, and a pretty detailed description of your…uh…enhanced abilities." Nicolas can't quite meet Greyson's gaze anymore and takes a peek at the sedan. "He may be hoping for a good look, observing, and cross-checking the data. They didn't care about names. They assigned you a number."

A number? God, that's so dehumanizing! Strapped to one of those tables, you're no better than a lab rat: no more rights, no more dignity, not even the same respect a worm on a hook would get. "At least they didn't tattoo it on our forearms."

Greyson passes his hand over his scalp. "They don't need tattoos. They can just laser the number on your bald head. ZVs don't heal and they don't grow hair."

"Give me some time and a lab." Nicolas drops a consoling hand on Grey's shoulder. "That may change."

"You just keep living in La La Land, Doc. I'm sure the nice man back there just wants to bring us in, feed us, help us find a cure, maybe send us on our way." Shaking his head, he slows down to see if the guy will pass him. He won't. "Not likely. He's waiting for us to cross the state line. You heard the radio: once in Texas, we're fair game. It's legal now. They can shoot us, cut us up and bottle the good parts, or poke and prod at our brains to see what makes us tick. They don't want to learn how to live in harmony with us; they want to figure out how to control or exterminate us."

That's what people do when they're afraid of something. They don't try to understand it, work with it, adapt to it. They destroy it. AP Sociology, AP History, AP Literature: the evidence is there in all of them.

I can only think of one thing that would avert an all-out, frenzied effort to "decontaminate" the planet, burn all of us ZVs off the face of it—total anarchy: no more government, no more roadblocks, no more databases, no more communications, no more military, no more police, no more interagency coordinated manhunts, pure survival of the fittest—and we are the fittest.

Is that all we can hope for now? Anarchy? Can Amber survive in that world? I was hoping there'd be something in between, something civilized and humane. Of course, I look to Nicolas.

His hand covers his eyes. He knows what Greyson is saying is true. He knows he's losing the battle for his brother. Can he still see it, the world that isn't black or white? Or is the grey fading for him too? And when it does, what color will he see me?

Chapter 9

Of course, they're not letting ZVs out of Texas. According to the truckers heading west at the café in Clovis, New Mexico, the roadblock on I-70 is set up just outside of Farwell, Texas.

Nicolas brought back this report and a pile of food from the café. He asked for some raw meat—for his dog. From the New Mexico side, in Texico, they're also not letting the uninfected into Texas. Of course, there aren't many of those lined up on the highway clamoring for a chance to be served up at the zombie fest going on inside the Lone Star state.

The café food is good but not exactly zombie gourmet. Hopefully, if we can get through this last roadblock, my aunt won't slam the door screaming when we knock, and we'll get something more satisfying at the ranch. Right about now, a juicy, red, cow heart would really hit the spot.

Sam wakes up about fifteen minutes after we're back on the road outside of Clovis. The smell of meat must have roused him. I seriously want to find out how much of a risk he might be to my aunt's family, but don't think now is a good time. Too soon.

When he wakes up, he looks around terrified because he has no idea how he got in the car, and chances are, it took a couple brain clicks for him to remember who the ZV driving him around is. Greyson pats him on the knee, "Glad to have you back with us, buddy." He flashes him a grin. "Are you going to play nice, now?"

Sam cranes around to look at the rest of us, and then throws his back against the seat. "I came after her?" He hides his face behind the bars of his fingers. No one answers. "So, I did."

He groans in the silence drowning the car. Mortified, he spins around to face us. Amber jumps back and under my arm because he looks a little intense.

"Look, kid…Amber, I'm so sorry. It wasn't me. You know I'm sick, right?" He looks at me to back him up. I'm not sure I want to. I know it's just a fit, that he has no control over it, but do I really want to teach my little sister to pet the nice doggy that hardly ever bites? "She knows about the virus?"

I lean forward and pat his shoulder. "It's okay, Sam. We understand. That's why we're taking her to my aunt. She's not safe around ANY of us."

Sighing, he shakes his head in his hand. "God damn it!" Nicolas hands him some raw meat. He takes it, scowling. His fist squeezes the bloody lump. "Shit!" He hurls the wad at the windshield.

About a half an hour later, he picks it off the dash and starts gnawing on it petulantly.

As we approach Texico, Nicolas exits the interstate and drives us a couple miles south down a dirt road. Everyone but him piles out and heads east on foot through the farmlands toward the Texas border. Nicolas drives back, gambling on flashing his CDC credentials to drive through the checkpoints. We all breathe a little easier when he pulls up behind us and picks us up in downtown Farwell. But it makes me wonder what happened in the aftermath of the Institute explosion that Nicolas isn't on every agency's wanted list.

Greyson thought for sure the black sedan would show up the minute we crossed the border, but the clicking tire disappeared just outside of Clovis, about the time Sam woke up. Doesn't make any of us feel safe, though. We just wonder when and where he'll pop up again.

It's been a couple summers since I've been to my aunt's. To avoid any other interstate checkpoints, we have to detour from my mom's usual route and go south through Lubbock. Things don't start looking familiar until just west of Katy. That's when Amber starts fluttering and bouncing in her seat. She's only done the trip a couple times, but she can tell by the landscape that we're close. She recognizes the diner on the corner where we used to stop so we wouldn't descend upon my aunt as a ravenous horde. How ironic.

It's been a long haul since the diner in New Mexico and we're all starving. I'm a little worried about how my aunt is going to deal with a carload of zombies arriving unannounced on her doorstep in the middle of the night and decide we'd better not make it a carload of hungry zombies.

Having Nicolas around is handy. He can walk right into a grocery store and buy whatever—no more messy scavenging and hunting, all that dead meat just sitting right out on the counter, neatly cut up into slices—so civilized.

Except things have changed a bit in Katy. Just outside the grocery stores, there are military guys with automatic guns. We lie low in the car until Nicolas climbs back in with his bounty.

Handing Amber a bag of semi-healthy snacks and fruit, he apologizes to the rest of us. "I had to settle for the more basic cuts. It would have been too obvious to go for the organs. There's a soldier standing right at the butcher shop checking temperatures for fevers. Apparently, now that bite victims are more common than couple virus pairs, the…uh…appetite for meat is showing up with the fever. The more obvious skin discoloration and the low temperature that sets in after the initial fever come later. For early detection, they're monitoring temperatures in the quarantine zone. The soldier told me the infected head right for the butcher shop. There have been some raids…and some incidents."

For a brief moment, I wonder why we scurried out of the pot and into the frying pan. But the answer is sitting next to me. Amber needs family; she needs family that won't wake up one day and think her little fingers might taste great with some honey BBQ sauce.

After watching Sam, I don't trust myself anymore…and if I'm honest, I don't really trust Greyson. We eat in morbid silence, actually the ripping of raw meat is kind of loud, but most of us are pretty used to it by now so we don't even hear it.

The grocery stores don't really stock much of the stuff we like: the heart, the lungs, the stomach, the liver, they're second-rate specialty items. The steaks and filets are okay, but it's like eating Chinese food. You're hungry again in about an hour. The virus needs organs.

We're almost there. A massive white Southern-style mansion stands sentinel at the beginning of the county road that leads to my aunt's ranch. As we pass, I grimace at the solitary Christmas decoration on the crescent lawn. An enormous blow-up snowman grins and glows, washing the whole street in an eerie white fog—definitely more of a giant, evil, grinning Stay Puft Marshmallow Man than a merry Frosty.

Amber squeals and dances in her seat when we go under the gate with the Crooked Cross emblem on it. My uncle always said my aunt was the Holy Cross and he was crooked, so he made that their mark. He's not really crooked. He actually grew up a rancher but wanted to be a doctor. Now he's both. I'm glad he has a sense of humor about family.

Family: the wild serenity, the harmonious babble; where everything works even when it doesn't; where they're supposed to take you in when no one else will—even when you're a zombie?

My mom always told me there was no friend like a sister. There were just things you could ask a sister that you'd never dream of asking a friend. I'm close to my aunts. Rebecca is up north in Montana. She's the oldest sister and her two boys moved away a long time ago. I think she loves me because secretly she always wanted a little girl and my mom was willing to share. Rebecca does stuff my mom hates...hated. She shops. My Aunt loves a sale at Nordstrom's as much as I do. I wonder if she'd shop with me now.

I wonder if Esther is going to be happy to see me or if her face will go pale and she won't dare to open the door any wider for fear of letting the infection in.

Esther's house has always been happy land. It's the land of "I love you"s and "I'm so proud of you"s. It's the land of "just ten more minutes," and "okay, but only one more time." She has an open pantry and free-swimming. Bed-making is optional. Chores buy you movies and laser tag; lip smoochies buy you Littlest PetShop toys and Pokemon cards. She reads stories about holding hands and watches movies that end with a kiss. My aunt doesn't just have the glasses that see grey; she sees pink. I know this, but I still wonder, what will she see when she sees me? Should I send Amber to the door alone?

It's close to midnight and we're in a state under zombie lockdown. Christmas lights shower the yard with white light and the winking lights of a Christmas tree in the music room window beckon warmly.

I let Amber ring the doorbell and hang back in the shadow of the shrubs. Things grow around Esther: vegetables, flowers, shrubs—children. For a while, nothing happens. Then, from the back of the house, a light flips on, sending a glow to the front windows. The porch light snaps on. My aunt's face peers through the cloudy glass panels of the front door. The moment her eyes make out who the little creature on the porch is, her face scrunches into confusion and then explodes in elation. The door flies open and Amber is swept up in Esther's happy universe.

"Amber...I was so worried...oh, my little kidlet! Is it really you? Are you okay?" Kissing and hugging, and staring and kissing again, followed by more kissing and hugging.

"It's me! It's me! I made it for Christmas!" Amber rejoices. More hugging.

"I saw the papers and the news...your mother...How did you get here?" She's totally incoherent but now she sees the car and I'm going to have to step out of the shadows.

"With Evelyn and Greyson." Amber turns and points to the car.

"Evelyn is here?" Esther peers into the shadows. I step forward a little. "Evelyn?" It's not like my aunt doesn't know I have the virus. I'm sure she's one of the first people my mom told. I'm sure my mom cried on the phone with her the day I left.

She sees me.

Before I can flinch or blink, she's down the stairs and I'm in her other arm and we're crying together, holding each other the way we've been wanting to hold my mom for all these days that she's been gone. Wrapping my arms around her is like slipping into a pair of fuzzy slippers on a winter's night when I got caught running barefoot in the rain and the tips of my toes are about frozen off. There's nothing like this feeling.

Yes, I have Greyson. He makes me feel whole again like I haven't felt since I moved into the solitude of my polygamist's hide. Yes, Nicolas heals all the parts that are broken in me. But a mother's arms, they leave an empty space that a boy can't quite fill up, and my Aunt almost does, and I can feel that place warm and glowing again. It doesn't matter to Esther that I'm purple-grey, that I smell like old fish, that my fingernails are lethal weapons; it only matters that I was my mom's...and now I'm hers.

"I hope it's okay...that I came."

"Oh, kidlet! Of course, you came! Where else would you go?"

It's late, but she wants to hear the whole story. She beckons my friends out of the car and herds us past the music room stuffed so full of presents that no one can sit on the little loveseat or play the grand piano. I can't imagine what my aunt and uncle could have possibly bought for their kids that they don't already have.

My cousin Craig, the oldest, lumbers sleepily down the stairs. He must have heard my voice; he's always had a cousin crush on me. Cameron stumbles sleep drunk behind. He's ten, four years younger, and a scrawny little ginger who goes wherever Craig goes, does whatever he does, and says whatever he says. He's Amber's hero. She calls him Prince Cameron.

"What are you doin' here, Ev'? I thought you got infected." Craig's never been very tactful or sensitive.

"Craig!" his mom exclaims.

"What? That's what you told me!" He doesn't wait for the fussing, he strides over and bear hugs me. A smile invades my lips. He doesn't care that I'm a little cold and grey. Blood is thick here, even when it has a virus in it. Being blunt just makes it easier for Craig to overlook the grey. "You don't look sick, you just look like you're ready to go Trick or Treating, or something."

"Nice hairdo, loser." I nod at the bedhead rooster tail flapping at me from his forehead. Without skipping a beat, he frowns and reaches up to fix the flaw.

Amber catches sight of Cameron, squeals, and wriggles loose from my Aunt's arms. She nearly knocks the kid over body slam hugging him. He grins and pats her on the back, but after a full minute of unbridled affection, he's not quite sure how to disengage himself.

Fortunately, all the commotion has stirred the sleeping princesses. Paula trips down the stairs rubbing her eyes and squinting in the bright light. Prudence hops along behind.

Catching sight of her best friend and imagination soul mate, Amber relinquishes her death grip on Cameron in favor of a dancing group hug with Paula and Prudence.

My uncle comes out for a while and meets everyone. He and Nicolas hit it off right away—doctor talk.

When Paula and Amber sneak away to the Little Pet Shop heaven upstairs in the girl's room, five-year-old Prudence wanders over to my lap and cuddles in, as if I weren't a lot greyer than the last time she saw me.

Of course, in the end, Aunt Esther is all about finding sleeping arrangements. That's when it gets a little uncomfortable.

"You don't have a shed, do you? Something that locks on the outside?" I have to admire Sam for squarely confronting his disease. He doesn't ever dance around the issue. He keeps a straight-up "good fences make good neighbors" attitude. I can't help wondering, though, if deep down inside it doesn't chip away at his heart, this frank recognition that he's a pariah. Don't we all have some innate need to fit in that festers if left unattended?

This is where my aunt's pink glasses start to turn smoky. "Well, of course, but what would you want the shed for?"

"I'm infected."

Aunt Esther turns serious. "It's not contagious." She turns to me. "Didn't your mother say it's not contagious? You have to get bit."

"We don't know for sure." Nicolas steps into the fog with his clinical clarity. "It's not airborne, more likely the virus is spread by physical exposure, but the incubation requirements are so specific...the risk is..."

"I bite." Sam doesn't do tact; it interferes with frank.

Esther's pink lenses shatter a bit. Her eyes go wide before she recovers semi-gracefully, not sure what the proper etiquette is for hosting rabid zombies.

I try to smooth things over. "He has a rare strain, Aunt Esther. He's not exactly like Greyson and me. He gets these…uh…" I grimace at Nicolas, "seizures?"

Nicolas nods. "I've been working on some treatments. My brother and I would actually be quite comfortable together. We've spent a fair amount of time as tentmates on archeological digs."

"The virus comes from Egypt." I sort of want to detour the conversation. "Nicolas's parents were archeologists."

"Of course, your Uncle Daren can pull the blow-up into the shed, but it really isn't…" Esther follows my lead, making a monster effort to be gracious, but at the same time, I can see the mother bear kicking in. I feel for her.

"No, Mrs. Yeats, it is necessary." Nicolas reaches to shake her hand. "Thanks—for everything."

The awkwardness gets lost in the general shuffle of getting everyone settled down for the night. We just ate, but my aunt is religiously hospitable, and a serious feeding is one of the sacred rites of guests.

Before we can object, the microwave is defrosting a wide variety of assorted raw meat. Sam, Greyson, and I are not really hungry, but it would be sacrilege to refuse the offering and we stuff down what we can and chase it with a couple gallons of ice water. Nicolas politely accepts a makeshift salad while the three little girls raid the snack pantry. I infected Paula and Prudence with vegetarianism the same year I converted Amber. Prudence wasn't all that hard of a sale; she was basically surviving on a strict diet of juice and cheese sandwiches anyway.

The girls dip Oreos in milk while divvying up the stuffed animals into packs and assigning them names and superpowers. Watching them, for the first time in a long time, I feel safe…not for me, for Amber. I did the right thing. She belongs here. Paula has already outfitted her with some animal print pajamas and fuzzy slippers

Amber cuddles in with Paula and Prudence and I take the guest room. I'm gently slipping some running shorts over the bandage on my thigh when I overhear my uncle showing Greyson into Cameron's room next door. Cameron still sleeps with Craig even though he's old enough for his own room now.

"My boys are in the room connected through the bathroom there..."

Silence.

"Evelyn tells me you're responsible for keeping Amber safe and getting the two of them out of town before the...uh..."

"'Decontamination.' That's what they call it." Either Greyson can't hear my uncle's question between the lines, or he's just ignoring it.

Uncle Daren clears his throat. "My wife's much obliged. She and Evelyn's mom were very close. Doris's kids are our kids."

Silence again.

"My boys, they're...uh...just..."

"I'm a heavy sleeper, Dr. Yeats, they won't bother me." Hopefully, my uncle interpreted the ironic grin in Greyson's voice the way it was meant. I'll reassure Uncle Daren before he goes to bed.

The door clicks shut. My uncle hesitates before his muffled footsteps disappear down the hall. Greyson's been driving all day. He's got to be exhausted, but I peek in on him anyway.

"Hey, you." I brush my hand across his forehead. The warm fuzzies at Esther's house melt away all the doubts and demons. The bed creaks as I sit on it. "Thanks. Again."

I expect a sleepy smile, instead, one eye cracks open. He reaches around my waist and pulls me over the top of him. I laugh and he slides his hands up the back of my tank. I wrap my arms underneath him. My fingers slide up his neck and stumble on stubble—on stubble!

"Greyson! Oh my God! You're hair! It's growing." I lean around to confirm with my eyes the evidence from my fingers, and then squinting to see, brush my hand across the fuzz on his crown.

He half grins, an odd mixture of vain satisfaction and jealous appreciation. "A moment of silence for the good doctor's research." He closes his eyes and goes still for about two seconds. His eyes pop open and he slides his hands up the curve of my waist to the hooks on my bra. "And now I'd like to engage in a little medical research of my own."

"You are so going to get me in trouble with my aunt." Giggling, I wriggle up his chest and force his hands down to the curves of my waist.

"She doesn't much like me anyway. A mom's worst nightmare: her daughter brings home a wild, zombie boy. I'm sure the nice doctor is looking pretty good to her right about now."

"I'm sure she really appreciates you saving my ass—and Amber's. She'd probably rather you were a little less purple-grey and had more hair," I rub his crew-do, "but I'm sure she loves you just because you got us here—in one piece."

"Yeah, but I'm going to take you away." His hands stop cold on my hips. He reclines his head deeper into the pillow to look me in the eye. "You know we can't stay here, right? Your uncle has probably already locked the door between the bedrooms and is camped out with his shotgun on the other side, just in case I wake up hungry on the wrong side of the bed."

I take a deep breath, savoring the air of paradise before I return to hell. Rolling off his chest, I lie on my back. Greyson's arm is still anchored beneath me. "You're right. We have to leave. But you can't really blame him."

"I don't blame him. You and I both left home for the same reason your uncle is sitting guard. We can't be sure. We have to leave. Tomorrow we'll have to figure out where to go."

I sigh. In this house, I could almost forget. "I'm just glad I'm not leaving on my own again, Greyson." My cheek seems to fit right into the soft little hollow of his shoulder and I snuggle in. "When I first got infected, I just wanted to be somewhere near my family. I used to watch them play in the fields out the church windows. Now, I don't care where I'm going, as long as you're there. Now that Amber is safe, you are my family."

Greyson's hand strums the back of my hair. The rise and fall of his chest lulls me. Suddenly, running has lost its appeal. I'd rather sleep here in peaceful bliss. I close my eyes and feel what it's like, sleeping next to Greyson. It's quiet and safe and whole.

I want to be closer, so my lips find his. They're soft, full, and sleepy. He cuddles into me, bringing me home. Our bodies attract and it's like we can't get close enough. His fingernails dig shallowly into my skin and I arch my back into the deep rush of feeling. It takes more than it used to for me to register touch and Greyson knows it.

I wrap my arms around him tighter and he rolls over on top of me. The weight of him surrounds me. He wraps me up in his arms and legs and it feels like he's stealing my soul through the keyhole of my lips. But I've unlocked the chest where I store it and it's pouring out as fast as he's pouring himself into the tender void.

When I hear my aunt in the kitchen downstairs, I sigh and tear myself away. "I'm going to go down and talk with my aunt. You need to sleep; you've been driving all day. And I need to go for a run; I've been sitting in that car all day."

He pulls me back. "Run in the morning; I don't need to sleep." Our lips meet again and I know it's not sleep he needs from me right now.

"Dream about me," I say, as my fingers untangle from his. He groans and turns over.

Chapter 10

In the family room downstairs, the TV drones on and on so I camp out on the couch to catch up on what's happening in the world. My mouth drops open as I click through the channels. There's nothing but video after video of gruesome ZV attacks.

The screen crackles and rips with clips from people's cell phones: "Oh, my God! Oh, my God! They're tearing that guy apart!" Sounds of vomiting accompany the scene, the picture lurches, the background shifts to the sidewalk, or the floor of the mall, the street, or the grass, and the footsteps break into a full-out run. "Help me! Oh, God, no!" The image flies through emptiness before clattering to the ground and displaying a lovely view of blue skies and puffy, white clouds, or darkness, or faint pebbles of asphalt as the symphony of snarling and screaming crescendos.

My hand covers my mouth and I forget to breathe as, over and over again, roughly the same story plays out, punctuated by BREAKING NEWS reports with helicopter footage of Los Angeles, San Francisco, Dallas, Salt Lake, Las Vegas smoking and burning. Little maps with rippling red dots moving gradually across the states track reports of new attacks crossing state and city boundaries:

> *...it appears that the largest population of infected survivors are young people between the ages of fourteen and thirty. Older and younger victims appear to die, their organs attacked and destroyed much more quickly by the virus. Reports on the death toll are erratic and unreliable but estimated to be at 1/3 the population of each of the infected cities and states.*

The scales have tipped. The ZVs are winning now. It's spiraling out of control. Somehow, I feel responsible, even though I've never even bitten someone…well, Dr. Christensen, but that was self-defense. I can't say the same for Greyson.

The grey is gone. I'm going to have to choose a side. But one side won't take me, and I can't fully embrace the other because, even though she's with my aunt now, I will always have Amber. Amber, floating above the chaos of the storm with all the innocents like her, she is everything. I wonder if it's too late for Nicolas to calm the waves.

The states are begging for military assistance to protect the surviving populations, but at least half the survivors are infected. Instead of sending troops in, risking contamination, the federal government is responding with quarantines. Only a small chunk of the infected are like Greyson and me. I wonder if they've figured out that the mutants were vegetarians. I wonder if the vegetarians have realized they can't start human organ bingeing or they'll die brain dead monsters like the rest of the carnivores.

I guess that's what the CDC is thinking. The hosts die faster when they DO feed or CAN'T feed. Quarantine is the best option—unless, of course, you're not infected and stuck in one of those states. Then you're pretty much prey.

The screaming stops as the screen shifts to serene white and the intoxicating voice of the Reverend Ashley Knight, daughter and heir of the late founder of the Church of the Firstborn, Reverend Lazarus Knight, in a breaking news story. They run a clip of her most recent sermon that seems to be causing a furor. I listen for a while, mesmerized, not just by the cadence of her speaking, but by how young she is. She can't be much older than I am. And she's not some dowdy pioneer girl with glasses and braids—I'm pretty sure some of her followers weren't just converted by the word. She's so sure of herself; it's hard not to be taken in by her.

> *My brothers and sisters in the faith, fear not! Do not fear the hand of Providence. Do not fear the judgment of the just. "For God hath not given us the spirit of Fear; but of power, and of love, and of a sound mind." Come to*

76

us. Let us bind ourselves together in love and no longer fear. Let us strengthen our power in the unity of love and in the faith of the believers. With sound mind we shall open our eyes to see the fulfilling of the word; with sound mind we shall listen that we hear the word without trembling.

Why should we—the children of promise, the followers of the word—fear the coming of the judgment? Because it consumes the flesh of the wicked? But we are not wicked.

Because it comes to us with tainted skin and the scent of refuse? Open your ears! Hear the words of Isaiah: "He hath no form nor comeliness; and when we shall see him, there is no beauty that we should desire him. He is despised and rejected of men; and we hid as it were our faces from him." But we will hide no more.

Together we will stand in love and power. We will embrace the gift that has come to us out of Egypt...

I'm nearly ready to join up when the camera shoots back to the anchor announcing a ZV attack that evening on the trails along the woods near a golf course. There's actually Go-Pro video footage.

ZVs fall out of the trees. They aren't just a random assortment of citizens gone brain dead. It looks like someone besides Greyson got the idea of recruiting gang members. I can tell that one guy is a mutant, so obviously there must be vegetarians in Texas. The video shows him directing traffic and his mob doesn't actually eat the runner on the spot. They carry him off, screaming and clawing for dear life. Apparently, the golf course now has a take-away menu. The gruesome reality shudders through my organs.

And who stands there and films this stuff? Well, maybe not stands there, the picture keeps shifting perspective; whoever had the camera strapped to his head is running away, glancing back as the horror happens behind him...or her. I guess it's not that different from catching a video of the latest hurricane. It's crashing toward you and there's no changing its path. Only difference is, with a hurricane, they encourage people to pack up and leave.

This is not the first instance of ZV gang violence and officials now fear that many of the infected, evading capture, may have taken shelter in wooded areas, banding together into hunting gangs. Residents in the infected zone are strongly cautioned…

My aunt comes down the stairs in her silk pajama suit. All the cousins are back in their beds. She grimaces at the screen and then pads over to the couch and sits in the same cushion with me, snuggling up.

Her mom warmth bathes me and I bask in it for a couple seconds before it melts my heart and the tears start to fall. It's been so long…so very long and far away since I was a daughter and a mom was out there in the night, worried about whether or not I was safe. Her arms around me, arms that are so like my mom's, crack the shell and all the baby in me oozes out.

As my tears stain her blue pajamas, she rocks back and forth with me, cooing that everything is going to be all right and that I'm safe now.

When Prudence, Amber, and Paula appear on the stairs to demand another drink before sleeping, I scramble to pull my face back together. A quart of juice later, Esther picks both little string bean girls up in her arms and heads back to their room with Paula in tow. As she passes the couch, the little ones both lean in for a hug from me. Esther tips over from the weight shift, Paula jumps into the heap, and we all roll around in a tickle, kissing fest until my aunt herds them up the stairs for the second time.

The news rolls on until I click it off when she comes back and sinks exhausted into the couch again. "It's getting worse, Aunt Esther. You should get out."

"We've applied for an exit pass. Daren is a doctor, so he has a good chance of getting one because we have a sponsoring relative in a non-quarantine state. Your aunt Rebecca told us to come to Montana. We're going to be fine. Some of Daren's colleagues at the University are working on this epidemic. He's had some unofficial news about breakthroughs. They've got some expert here on loan from France. We'll go to Montana, and when they have it all figured out, we'll come back. It'll be a grand vacation." She claps her hands and smiles broadly. Esther is always the optimist.

"You know I can't go with you?"

Her face tells me she didn't know that. That kind of thinking has no place in Esther's World.

"If you're lucky enough to get out, they're not going to let you transport a flaming ZV over the border." Just saying it chills my chest. The virus is a massive stone wall between the warm hearth of my aunt's family and me. It's snowing where I stand outside their window.

"But we could…"

I shake my head.

Her lower lip trembles. She knows. But she can't look the truth in the face because the face is the grey one sitting beside her. It's the face that still looks like her niece, looks just like her older sister, but isn't…can't be. Her eyes fade red around the edges, glistening against her will. "Daren has influential friends…I know he could…"

Plastering up the cracks my aunt opens in my heart, I cut her off. I don't want her to dream. "What do you know about the Knight compound?"

She chuckles, distracted from a subject she doesn't want to look at head-on. "Ashley Knight used to babysit for me—when Craig and Cameron were little. Such a sweet girl." She points out the window. "The Knight ranch—compound, I guess—is only a couple miles west of here."

I nod. For a while, we both stare at the sparkling fruit in the bowl on the table and the shifting pattern of Christmas lights reflecting from the music room onto the entryway marble. I know she wants to talk about my mom. No, she doesn't just want to, she needs to. There won't be any service; there will only be what we say to each other.

My aunt leans over and hugs the guts out of me. "I'm so glad you came here, Evelyn. This is where you belong. It's what your mom always said she would want if…"

The missing words choke us both.

"I know." I have to concentrate to get the words out dry and comprehensible. "Every time she left on a trip she'd get the will out and remind me we were all supposed to come live with you if something happened. I thought it was freaky, but she said nothing would happen if she was prepared." I laugh a little. I can still see her standing in the office summing up all the financials for me. There was no way to be prepared for this.

Aunt Esther stares deep into the blood-streaked green of my eyes. "You miss her."

Okay, she didn't need to say that. I look at the blank TV screen, now just a black reflection of me, and take a deep breath, trying to hold it together enough to answer. As soon as I meet her eyes again, I melt into a pool of tears and snot on her shoulder. I can feel she's crying too. It's what we both need, though—a place to let the tears fall where they won't just dry up and be forgotten.

"It's okay, Evelyn. Amber will be happy and safe with us. Your uncle is a doctor. We'll do everything we can to help you. Can't you reconsider…?"

I pull away and wipe my eyes. "I can't stay here, Esther. It's too risky. That's why I left home."

"Don't be silly, kidlet. I know the news makes it sound like the Wild West out here. But there really are still some sane people—a few at least. And, there's the Knight Church—I'm not sure Ms. Knight is all that sane, but they're right here in the county. The Reverend is fighting heavily in the courts for ZV rights."

Pointing at the TV I get a little agitated. "ZV rights isn't really an issue anymore. It's way beyond that now." The cages are open and the rabid animals are running rampant in the streets. Survival is all that matters. "You have to leave and you'll never get me out of the state. The quarantine is only getting tighter, Esther. We had to be escorted out of Utah on a private, under-the-radar plane! But, that's not what I mean anyway. It's too risky for you and the kids. Don't you realize I'm sitting here trying to decide if you smell more like Coq au Vin or Boeuf Bourguignon?"

For the first time, my aunt looks shocked and leans back reflexively. It's too gross even for her, the idea that I'm really tempted to eat people. I try to cushion the blow, but she needs to know what I am. "I've been able to fight it, probably because

I am…was…a vegetarian. In fact, you all should think about joining Paula and Prudence, just in case…well, you know, because it's more contagious now."

I need to convince my aunt to let me go. I don't want her feeling like she let me down, or like she let my mom down by letting me go. "If you have Amber, then I can take care of myself. It's too hard to keep her safe from both sides. I don't want to leave her…" the tears well up again and start dripping down. Watching out for Amber is my life. Talking about leaving her behind is like imagining dying. If you don't have a purpose anymore, are you still alive? "I have Nicolas; he's brilliant and he's already making some progress. He'll need to find a lab, but I have Greyson, too. As long as I have Greyson, I'll be okay."

"I can tell Dr. Vadlamani really cares about you. Your uncle is very impressed with him. You two seem…"

"We're good friends." I avoid her direct gaze and contemplate the artistry of the pink roses in the painting over the fireplace. "He helped Greyson and me escape the Institute, kept us from getting dissected. He's one of the few who can still see the people behind the symptoms."

When I look her in the eye again, Esther nods like she's humoring my denial, but knows what's really going on.

"He has Sam to watch out for; I have Amber. We have stuff in common." Like that will really explain what seems to be so obvious to everyone. Nicolas needs to get a poker face. "He really wants to find a vaccine or something to help his brother."

"And you."

"Yeah, well, he thinks Greyson and I have antibodies. That's why we're resistant—and important."

"I think that Nicolas is interested in more than your antibodies." She raises an eyebrow my direction. How does she do that? My aunt can sniff out a romance the way I can sniff out a stray dog. I swear, not a single thing has happened since the moment we walked into the house to give the slightest impression that there might be some attraction between Nicolas and me. Is it really that obvious? "It's just the way he looks at you, the way he stands. You can practically feel it floating around in the air."

My mouth hangs open with no words.

"You do have to thank Greyson for me, though. I told him how much we're in his debt for pulling Amber out of that horrible…" She can't finish. She changes gears. "Greyson seems to like you, too. He looks like he's a little more your age. But then, there's not much difference between all of you is there?"

"Not much difference in age; maturity levels, now that's a different story."

"Well, Greyson is very handsome, and obviously very brave, and driven to keep you safe."

That is exactly the power that Greyson has on me. It must be some weird, Darwinian atavism; I can't resist the guy that can protect me, the guy that never lets me down.

"He is ridiculously good-looking, isn't he?" My giggle is intended to lighten things up. "Well, he's a little purple-grey now, and they shaved off his really nice blond hair." Even as I say it, I know that's not the reason I'm not all in. "But he can be s-o-o-o-…." There are too many words to finish that sentence. There's something deeper, a crack between us that's opened up within the last couple of days—and Nicolas has the bridge. I just sigh heavily.

Esther gets the picture. "…s-o-o…teenage boy? Boys mature later than girls, kidlet. He'll catch up. That said, I do have to admit, I have a weakness for good looking doctors."

I can't help but crack a smile. Of course, she does. "Nicolas has a thing for a good-looking ZV. Isn't that weird?"

"Why would it be weird? You're beautiful, even in purple." She grins. "You're smart, you're athletic, you've got gorgeous hair…" she runs a strand of it through her fingers "…and your mother's big, beautiful, green eyes." She puts her hand on my cheek.

I wish I could stay here. "At least, you don't have to worry about me." I'm not sure if I'm convincing her or myself. "You know I have a small army looking out for me. Greyson is a small army all by himself. The only thing I really need is for you to get Amber as far away from the virus as possible so I know she's safe. Go to Montana. Go to Rebecca's."

"We can talk more about it tomorrow."

"No, Aunt Esther, there's nothing to talk about. She's not safe. If they track her back to me, they'll take her. We share genes. My genes are what they're after."

"I want to make sure you have somewhere safe to go before we make any decisions." She puts her hand on my knee and looks me in the eye. I throw my arms around her because it is so nice to be the daughter again. "You should really think about the Knight compound. I think Ashley Knight may be a crazy loon, but she's always been the sweetest little gal and she doesn't seem to be afraid of ZVs."

"Who's that?" My uncle Daren bursts in jangling his keys.

"We were just talking about the Knight compound." Esther stands up to kiss him goodbye.

"Ashley Knight is that little gal that used to babysit for us, right?" He nods at me. "She's crazy now."

"Daren!"

"Took her father's death very hard." My uncle has always been very pragmatic, a straight shooter. "I have to go to the hospital." He points a look at me and makes a quick reference with his eyes to the upstairs sleeping arrangements. I know what he's asking and I nod reassuringly. "Be back in a few hours." He heads out the door.

"He's always on call." My aunt huffs indignantly.

The leather sofa exhales and crunches a little as I lean over and give her a kiss goodnight. "I'm going to go for a run. It'll help me clear my head. I've been sleeping in the car all day and I need the exercise so I can fall asleep."

"Just don't leave the ranch. There's a curfew. In the streets, they shoot first and ask later."

Chapter 11

Running at sea level in Texas is a breeze when you're used to running the mountain altitudes in Utah. You have to love Houston—seventies in winter; you can run outside year-round. It's been a while since I went running just for the fun of it. There's no one behind me, and nothing in front of me—just open fields and little clumps of woods. The Z-Virus hypes up the endorphin rush I get as I push myself. The fresh air clears my head; the world disappears leaving only the rhythm of my feet pounding the dirt path and the beating of my heart. The black sky goes on for miles of nothingness above me. No mountains limit its expanse and the stars shimmer into infinity. A distinct cow and horse flavor wafts through the trees—but I ate before I came.

My mind shuffles through a slideshow of scenarios where I can stay here and life can spin in perpetual summer around me as my lungs and muscles bask in the stretch. I'm not even winded until I'm clear out to the back end of the ranch near the barn where they keep the calves. My uncle would always let us feed them if we woke up early enough. It's the only thing that would induce me to wake up before six a.m. in the middle of the summer.

It's the wrong season for calves, so when my virus enhanced super-hearing picks up uncertain steps in the barn, my first thought goes to fugitive ZV. I'd know for sure if I could pick up the smell, but the door is locked and I've been running so, let's just say in a polite Texas way, "I'm glowing" with essence of ZV.

My insides twist into a whole wad of complicated cross grains as I slow to a walk and approach the door. I know what it's like hiding from the goons with bats, so I want to help whoever is hiding in there. But I don't know what shade of grey he…she is. Could be a putrid-mouthed brain sucker just waiting for one of my cousins to wander away from the house.

Maybe it's some poor girl that was just minding her own business getting on the Honor Roll, applying for Ivy League schools, and earning her letterman's jacket, when some douchebag, rabid ZV hauled off and infected her, and now she has to leave her family, drop out of school, forget her future and hide out in a barn, scrounging around for scraps to survive.

That decides it. What do I have to be afraid of? I'm a ZV, the strong kind. Unless there are more like Sam…

The steps squelch toward the door. This ZV is wearing cross-trainers. It's bizarre though, if I know it's in there, it should definitely have heard me coming. Whoever …or whatever…is in there, doesn't even know I'm here. Could be a bad sign.

Opting for the quick entrance, I smash my foot into the old wooden door. It swings open, revealing a tall shadow, standing at the water trough. I leap and twist, nearly kicking the brains out of the shadow figure before the moonlight catches on his face.

Nicolas.

"What the hell!" I throw myself off balance to miss him and land on my butt in some straw.

"Evelyn! What are you doing here?" He has a syringe in his hand. I caught him finishing up an injection.

"I think that's my line."

Nicolas rushes over to give me a hand up, pocketing the syringe.

Instead of letting him pull me up, I grab his wrist and pull him down on the hay next to me. I need to catch my breath.

He's a little closer than I planned, touching actually, way inside my personal space. Neither of us scoots away.

To fill up the dead air between us, he nods at the huge sinks. "I was looking for water. I didn't want to wake anyone in the house."

Of course, he didn't. "So, you walked all the way out here to the barn? There's a hose in the backyard."

"I didn't walk. I was already out here." He glances at his pocket. We're both thinking of the syringe, but he doesn't say anything and I don't pry. "I needed a run, you know…all the drama. I couldn't sleep."

I'm not sure if I was more surprised to find out Greyson is a vegetarian or that Nicolas is a runner. And then I notice it again, over his trim biceps—the Hollister boy chest. Apparently, it comes in a variety of colors. Nicolas is wearing an unzipped sweatshirt over a pair of shorts and some Nike's. The artistic lines of his calves and thighs are equaled only by his sculpted abs. There's enough moonlight streaming through the windows that little drops of perspiration glitter back at me from the deep lines.

Is this possible? Nicolas is a runner? It dawns on me that I'm staring and I tear my eyes away to look him in the face. "Yeah, I had the same idea."

"You know what they say about great minds." He flashes me one of those spicy smiles he keeps tucked away under his smart-doctor face. "This is a lovely place, even in winter. It reminds me of home. I grew up on a farm in the South of France."

"My dream life! Why'd you leave?"

He shrugs. "Education, work with my parents. But I miss the evening runs and the early morning rides into the countryside."

"You had horses?" I shake my head. Nicolas grew up in my fantasyland. "That's my favorite part about coming here. My aunt started letting me ride when I was about six." I fish a piece of straw off the ground and twist it across my fingers.

"You must be pretty good." He glances over at my bare legs, gets embarrassed that I caught him looking, and then shifts his gaze out the open door.

Nicolas is shy about girls? I probably could have seen that coming; I've heard med school doesn't really lend itself to a rich social life. But he's so freakin' hot, there's no way girls haven't been drooling all over him since he stepped onto the well-trimmed green at Oxford.

It's up to me to smooth over the awkwardness. He looks like he wants to find an escape. His warm, toasty color looks a little off. He's really struggling here.

"I should…uh…" His head tilts toward the exit, but I cut him off. I don't want him to go. I want to talk. Not just about the virus, and the cure, but about life, normal life, the way things used to be for both of us. I really want to know what Nicolas was like pre-ZV.

I mean, he went to Oxford, and he thinks of bringing me a brush when I'm strapped to a dissection table, and he totally spoils Amber, and he's saved my life multiple times, not with brawn, but with brains and charm. Yes, he has trouble just accepting that the virus is part of me. Yes, I feel like I need to be fixed when I'm around him. But, since we've been with Sam, I can understand what drives him and now I see he needs me too. I'm not just the other end of what he wants, I'm a person, a person that has a lot in common with him. Besides, I always wanted to live in one of the little villages in Provence. That's why I took French.

"We moved to Texas for a while." Thinking quickly for something neutral to say, I bring his eyes back to mine. They look a little bloodshot. The pressure of the chase is getting to him. Oxford probably doesn't offer a course in pre-zombie-apocalypse survival. "I actually rode in some rodeos and my Aunt hired me to take care of their horses."

"Rodeos?" He's only surprised for a second. He settles back in the hay and looks me over, nodding his head. "I guess I can see you in a cowboy hat and studded shirt." I have to drag my eyes, stunned and reeling, away from the cheeky grin. He should have to have a license to flash that thing.

"Hey, I'd have made a smokin' hot rodeo queen if we hadn't moved back to Salt Lake." I laugh, trying to lighten things up. It doesn't work. There's too much invisible chemical stuff going on between us. "There's a whole lot of stuff I missed out on by moving back to Salt Lake: friends, the basketball team, horseback riding. I probably wouldn't have gotten the Z-Virus either."

I don't say it, but I realize if I'd never moved back to Utah, never gotten the Z-Virus, I never would have met Greyson—or Nicolas. I can't imagine my life without them now. Life's funny that way: you never really know if you were lucky or not.

Stuff happens and I guess it's not really good or bad, just different.

"Let's go see the horses." Pulling Nicolas up from the hay. I lead him to the stables.

The smell hits me like a freight train when we open the doors. "That's ripe. And I don't even need my ZV hyper-smell."

Nicolas looks a little self-conscious. "I'm sorry. I must smell like roadkill to you, all sweaty after a day in the car and a run."

"Believe me, I wouldn't describe your scent as roadkill. Did you actually just apologize to me for how you smell? I'm a ZV Nicolas. You could bag all pretense at hygiene for a month and I'd just register a musky tang to your spicy aroma."

I've got him there. He's a little disconcerted but recovers in typical Nicolas style. "I wouldn't know. I had a riding accident when I was small. My parents couldn't convince me I needed a saddle: hit my head, messed up my olfactory processes. I don't register smells the same way other people do." He leans over and sniffs me. "Coq au Vin made with a nice Piñot Noir."

"You are so full of it." I shove his shoulder, laughing.

"I'm totally serious."

"Well, if you are, that explains a lot of things. AP Biology: smell is a big part of attraction. I know why I like you, you smell like the slow-cooked roast beef with potatoes, onions, and baby carrots my mom used to make on Sunday before we all turned vegetarian." I indulge in a whiff of it, right off his trim chest. "I can't figure out why the hell you like me." I chuckle. But once the words are out, I shut my mouth abruptly. I must have been drunk on the smell; the words just popped out like a hic-cup—sudden and unstoppable—why you like me.

Looking anywhere but at Nicolas, I tuck my hair behind my ears, mostly so I can turn my head and cover my eyes for a second. The wall covered with bridles and halters develops a riveting appeal. I stride over and grab one. Nicolas is right behind me.

"It's more of a package deal." He's not going to let the slip slide. I opened a door and he's going to walk through it. He comes up behind me, looking over the bridles. "I've always had this thing for smart blondes. But my timing is always wrong. Occupational hazard: too busy working to smell the flowers before they're gone…and then, I can't really smell."

Standing behind me, he's got his fingers in the tips of my hair. I can feel his breath on my neck. My hand starts shaking a little. The hormones are churning and working up the monster inside of me. I should be salivating over the warm aroma of Sunday dinner, but the only thing I can really smell now is a kiss. I can't turn around. I have conflicting urges: throw my arms around Nicolas and taste the candy of those tempting lips, or dig my claws into his chest, rip out his heart and devour it. And then there's Greyson.

Hanging the bridle back on the wall, I take a deep breath and close my eyes, trying to get a grip. I search for something to say, a reason for leaving the barn, getting myself out of this way complicated mix of emotions. "I prefer bareback."

Oh geez! Somehow, I think I just made things worse. I start rambling to cover. "I rode all the time…even after we moved…my family liked to spend Christmas vacations here. It's a nice change from dreary Eli. The weather is always nice." At last! The weather—a safe subject, guaranteed to kill the moment. "I'll take warm and toasty over chilly and grey any day." How is this possible? It's like I have some tragic, Freudian speaking disease. We're only talking about the weather, but somehow it means something more—to both of us. The pause between is just a little too long.

He sounds a little sad. "I would have thought grey would be more comfortable for you now."

"In some ways. I don't have to hide from it." I turn around, mostly to see if he's talking about the same thing I am. "It's who I am now."

I look him in the eyes. He has those long, thick eyelashes girls aren't allowed to have because they'd be lethal weapons. This conversation is going in two directions at once. I can't stop the flow and I wonder if Nicolas sees where it's heading.

I bite my lip and turn to see what's out the window. "But you know, a nice tan, basking in the warm kiss of the sun, it's every girl's daydream." Did I really just say "warm kiss of the sun?" A little AP English kicking in, or maybe more Freud.

Nicolas seems closer than he was before. I'm having trouble breathing and my thoughts are all jumbled. Maybe I overdid the running and I'm getting a migraine. "I wanted to thank you." He drops his hand on my shoulder. The touch takes my breath away.

It's only polite to look back at his eyes, but it's a huge mistake. His eyes are Zoloft—one dose floods your system with serotonin; the world becomes a peaceful, happy place—at least that's what my mom said. "Thank me? For what? You're the one that unstrapped me from the dissection table. Besides that, we'd have been stealing from dumpsters and sleeping in dark alleys for the last week without you. So, what are you thanking me for?"

Nicolas has this shy grin that makes him look like he's only six, instead of six years older than I am. "Warning me to get Smaran out of the Institute."

"Yeah, well, Greyson was behind most of that, I just got him out—with your help." I notice he steps back when I mention Greyson. The kiss has flown. The rush of the run is wearing off. It's not quite as warm in the barn anymore.

"About Greyson…"

Please don't ask about us; please don't ask about us. "I'm not really the expert there."

"He was quite upset about the…uh…incident with Sam at the hotel. Thank you for understanding."

I shrug. "You have Sam. I have Amber. I'd take a bullet to the head fighting for her…even if she was a raving, mad zombie."

"He's not, you know. It's so funny. Sam was always the calm, easy-going one."

Sam is calmer than Nicolas? How is that possible without being dead? "You know more about the virus than anyone. I don't need to tell you the Z-Virus messes with your hormones."

"I know. I just hoped the injections were working better than they are. It probably seems trivial, but it's a huge evidence of progress that he was still lucid enough to not come after me. It gives me hope. Thank you for pointing it out."

"You give me hope, Nicolas." I can't help myself. He still has that little boy look and I want to cuddle him up close. I put my hand on his cheek. Just like that, the kiss swoops back in the air between us again.

He points at the bandage on my thigh. "Is it healing?"

"I don't know. I haven't looked."

"Do you mind?" He kneels down in front of me without waiting for an answer. My leg jitters when his fingers brush the skin. He handles the bandage like I'm some fragile toddler. So, are we going clinical again? I can't watch him. It's too…I don't know how to take this.

The bandage is off. I can feel his fingers caressing the line of the wound. I'm thinking that I'm in over my head and I've got to stop him, but when I look down, he's looking up at me like I'm St. Eve with a revelation. "This is incredible." He rubs his finger along the line, sending ripples clear up my spine. Clearly, the nerve endings weren't damaged. "Have you seen this?"

Even with my ZV night sight, the light isn't strong enough for me to see without leaning over. I grab my mom's phone out of my bra and flip it open. In the little beam of light, a red seam winks back at me. Did you catch that? Red. Not purple. Red.

"Oh, my God!" I stare at Nicolas. "What does this mean?"

Now he's got both hands around my thigh and his face is so close he could practically kiss it. "It means there's something about you, Ev." His eyes meet mine again. "Something more than just being a vegetarian."

The kiss of hope is in his fingers. There are too many emotions sloshing around together between us. Something totally new, totally foreign, starts to breathe between us.

But there's something else too.

In the distance, I can hear the sound of engines coming up the farm road. But that's not what scares me. It's the clicking wheel that flips my adrenaline switch. It's after 1:00 a.m. This can't be good.

"Nicolas, can Sam ride as well as you can?"

He's so confused. "Yes, but he's sleeping in the shed."

"Get him up and get him on a horse. We're leaving and we don't have time for saddles. I'll get Greyson."

"Why? What's…"

"This is Texas, and I'm pretty sure that's a posse."

Chapter 12

A sudden, quick goodbye is better than a long, painful one—like pulling off a Band-Aid. When I storm breathless and panting into her bedroom, my aunt startles awake, reaching instinctively for my uncle who is still on call.

"Aunt Esther! They're here! We have to leave."

"Wait! What?" She's struggling to wake up and sit up at the same time. "Who's here? Where are you going?"

"They're hunting us. The man that followed us across New Mexico just turned up your driveway. We have to go!"

"Who?"

"I don't have time to explain. If these guys haul us away, they'll dissect us alive. You can't tell them Amber is my sister. We have the same gene pool. It won't go well for her." Thoughts of the red stripe across my thigh flash through my mind. I can only hope if Amber ever gets infected, she'll be like me. But then, that's not hope. Hope is that Amber gets away from here, away from the carnage, away from the hunt. "Take Amber up to Aunt Rebecca's in Montana. Please! Get out of here as soon as you can, all of you. I've seen what happens. It's going to get bad—for everyone."

"Let me get some food together for you." She pushes her feet out of the blankets, over the side of the bed.

"There's no time."

Awake now, Esther jumps up and wraps her arms around me. There's too much urgency for tears. "I can't let you go without knowing where you're going."

"We're going to try for the Knight compound. I think it's the safest place for now."

"How will you get past them?"

"We won't. We're taking the horses if that's okay. We can take the back trails. I think we should avoid the roads."

"Absolutely."

"We can send them back, or Uncle Daren can pick them up."

"Don't worry about that!" She kisses both of my cheeks and then the top of my head. "You just be safe. Head west along the creek through the woods. You'll see the Knight brand: the crescent crossed by the leaning t. You know, the moon for night, the 't' for the knight's sword."

"I remember. Thank you, Aunt Esther...for everything." I hug her once more. "I have to get Greyson. Stall them as long as you can. And whatever you do, don't tell them about Amber." I look my aunt in the eye. "She's just another one of your kids now." My heart tightens up to close the gaps left by my shrinking family.

Greyson is already up and dressed when I get to his room at the top of the stairs. He heard the clicking wheel too.

I grab my jeans and sweatshirt from the room next door, risking everything to stop and kiss Amber. The peaches and cream smell of her brings the sting of tears to my eyes—for so many reasons. She doesn't wake up; I'm not sure I want her to—like I said: quick, ripping goodbyes.

Grey and I are dropping out of the window by the time my aunt is opening the front door in her silk pajama suit.

Of course, if it hadn't been so long since we'd watched a good cop show, we'd have known that Mr. Holland would have sent someone to cover the back. We hear the click of a gun as Greyson's feet hit the patio.

Greyson has no gun. I made him leave it in the car when we got to my aunt's house. What was I thinking? This is Texas. Even my aunt has a gun. But, with my little cousins sleeping behind the window to the left, it'll be much safer if we take this guy out quietly.

The problem is he seems to be well aware that we're not the average deadhead zombies. "Mr. Holland don't want anyone to get hurt. We know all about y'all. Y'all're wanted, and the gov'ment boys will shoot you dead where you stand."

What's scarier than jumping out a window and coming face to face with the barrel of a trained soldier's gun? Jumping out the window and coming face to face with an amateur whose gun hand is shaking. Hunting refugee zombies is obviously not this guy's day job.

"You just come along with me, nice and easy, now. We got people can deal with the Feds. We're from a research facil'ty. We want y'all alive."

Greyson and I exchange looks. Is that supposed to make us feel better? We know exactly why they want us alive and we'd rather be dead than let them take us. "Y'all come with us nice and easy, and no one gets hurt."

I don't move because who knows where this guy is aiming and because I know Greyson is all over this.

"That sure is nice o' y'all. What's yer name?" Greyson mocks his accent with a bad imitation.

"Raymond. Raymond Godfrey."

"Well, Raymond, Raymond Godfrey, I met one of the ZVs from your 'research facility' and she told me she thought the service there wasn't at all what the brochures promised." Greyson inches toward Raymond.

The gunman's eyes dart all around, the gun following drunkenly their crooked path. He tries to croak out a call for help, but only comes up with a wheeze.

I'm starting to get anxious. How long can my aunt stall Holland at the door? My ZV survival instincts are kicking in and Raymond smells like a nice, warm dish of yellow liver and onions.

"Now that wouldn't be very smart, Raymond." Greyson is reading the panic on his face and interpreting the nervous twitch of his fingers squeezing the butt of the pistol. "You know all about me, don't you?"

Raymond nods.

"Then you know I'm fast, and I'm strong. You should also know, that unless you hit me right through the brain with that thing," he inches forward again, nodding at the gun, "I ain't goin' down."

The wild-eyed man points the gun in the general direction of Greyson's head.

"By the looks of it, you ain't had the proper trainin' for that ther' gun, so I'm gonna come an' take it from ya', just to make sure no one gets hurt." Greyson is moving closer all the time and it looks like Raymond is having a little trouble with his motor skills. He's trying to speak but nothing is coming out. Apparently, we're that scary.

Greyson pushes his advantage. "Now, if you were to try to call out, or shoot me, afore I got my hands on that gun, I'd still come fer it—only faster and harder. And, y'all know what? I might jest have to bite ya in the process."

Even in the vague light of the back patio, I can see the guy blanch.

"You know what happens then?"

Raymond nods.

"I bet you do." Greyson is back to his own, chillingly serious accent. I'm totally glad he's on my team. "In less than a week, that purple sludge we call blood will putrefy your veins and shit up your brain. Is that what you want, Raymond?" He holds out his hand, inviting the agent to turn over his gun.

Above the sloping patio roof, my cousin's window cranks open and Craig, rubbing his eyes, croaks out, "What are you doing out there, Ev?" Cameron's carrot top and eyes appear in the corner under Craig's arm.

Craig's voice startles Raymond who jerks back, his trigger finger twitching violently. The crack of a shot thunders through the still air of the quiet neighborhood. My cousin grunts and then groans, flopping forward over the windowsill.

A string of raw swear words spewing out of his lips, Greyson leaps at Raymond's gun hand. The stooge twists and rolls, but he's no match for a mutant ZV. Raymond's arm jerks around his back with a nasty crunch as Greyson yanks the gun from his fist.

"You don't shoot kids, you bastard!" he hisses. I forgot that the flames that burned up his best friend's niece still lick at Greyson's gut, maybe more than at mine. The virus is raging all over his face.

I smell the baby backs-on-the-barby aroma of Craig's blood before I see the red stain spreading across his shoulder. Cameron bellows for his mom.

"Oh, God! Craig!" I yell, reaching toward the window too far above my head. "They shot him!" They shot an innocent fourteen-year-old boy! They shot my Aunt Esther's boy right in front of his little brother. She takes us in without a flinch and they show up and shoot her little boy!

Suddenly I'm not on my aunt's back patio anymore. I'm right back in the bushes in front of the Eli jail watching fear-crazed fascists tear holes in a sweet little six-year-old with their shaking guns. I wish they'd shot me instead. Why can't these barbarians keep their madness to themselves? Why do the innocent kids have to be in the middle of it?

"Mom! Mom! Dad!" Cameron's face disappears and his screams punctuate Craig's groaning and howling.

The sound of men yelling and running erupts from the front yard.

Raymond writhes, screaming and groaning. I'm pretty sure Greyson has lost all his control and he's gonna shoot the guy, or worse, claw his heart right out of his chest. But Greyson only whacks him on the head with the butt of the gun. Raymond crumples limp to the ground, his head banging and bouncing against the concrete patio. Grabbing my hand, Greyson whips me around, away from the window.

"No!" Tears sting my eyes and well up. "They keep shooting kids!" I try pulling away from him because I want to do something, anything, but he won't let me go.

"His dad is a doctor. Let's get the hell out of here."

He's right. He's always right—coolly, chillingly right.

Across the ranch, there are fences, childproof locks, trees, dogs, and more fences. There's no way Holland and his men can keep up. But at this point, the goons shouting in the distance behind me mean nothing. All I can see, as my running shoes stomp along the dirt paths to the stables, is my cousin's crumpled face above the bloodstain oozing across his t-shirt.

And then, I've left Amber. It's the right thing to do. Right? She'll be safer with my aunt and uncle. She'll be happy with her cousins. Oh, God! I may never see her again.

If the running doesn't steal the breath from my ZV charged lungs, that thought does. My chest double-pumps to compensate for the gasping. The hundreds of microscopic electrical filaments attached to the need inside of my baby sister rip from their sockets in my brain and my heart. Sparks at the raw ends shower my veins with the sting of their unleashed power. Greyson reaches for my hand as we pass the barn and the cold, solid, grey of his skin grounds me.

We make it to the stables with a huge lead. Nicolas and Smaran are already mounted up outside.

"Head for the woods! The creek runs west. Follow it!" My hand reaches for the latch on one of the stables. Either my ZV smell or the general panic makes the occupant prance and snort anxiously. But these horses know me. They're confused by the contradiction of scents.

Nic and Sam gallop off into the trees while Greyson unlatches the door next to mine. Of course, he can ride. Greyson grew up on a farm in Castle Dale.

"You are the smart one, Evy."

Really? He's going to bring that up now?

"Horses." He grins like I couldn't possibly have imagined he was talking about anything else. "They can't bring their cars into the woods."

We grab bridles off the wall and don't bother with saddles. We just ride Prudence's chestnut stallion Romeo and Paula's black mare Shadow, following the distant thud of Nicolas and Sam galloping through the woods, ducking low lying tree limbs hanging over the meandering dirt horse trails. We're pushing a pretty good pace, closing the gap, when Greyson pulls up short. Romeo's sleek, red coat glints and flickers in the moonlight as he dances impatiently, flicking his head up and back.

"What is it?" I rein in Shadow.

"Don't you smell it?"

I haven't been paying much attention to anything but the road and catching up with Nicolas…and Sam. I feel like some kind of bloodhound following Nic's scent; the woods practically reek with it. But now that I actually put my nose in the air, I can smell something else too: ZVs—lots of them.

Chapter 13

Greyson curses under his breath. "It's not enough we have to run from zombie butchers, now we also have to keep Dr. McDreamy off the zombie *hors-d'oeuvre* menu. We really need to pick a side and stick with it."

Peering through the trees, I try to instill in Greyson some sense of the gravity of this situation. "The news said ZV gangs in the woods were picking people off and hauling them away." I'm terrified for Nicolas because if that's what's going on here, he might as well be wrapped in tin foil. Do I see my horror mirrored in Greyson's face? No, I don't.

"Food Storage. Good plan." In the moonlight that filters through the trees, he looks like he's actually wondering why he never thought of that. "You never know when the food supply will run dry...or...just run." He thinks that's hilarious.

"That is not funny, Greyson. Nicolas is a sitting duck out here."

"You think?" He sniffs at the air again. "He smells more like halibut to me." I cannot fathom how he can take this so lightly. But I don't say anything because he's jumped off his horse and seems to be tracking something—no surprise there, since his hunting trips with his dad were the inspiration for his mom's animal rights lectures and vegetarianism. Finally, he gets serious. "You catch up with Nicky and Rage Boy, give them the heads up. There's a mob of ZVs over the other side of the creek. I'll check it out and catch up."

I spur Paula's black mare on. "C'mon, Shadow, we've got to sniff Nicolas out before they do." Nicolas and Sam shouldn't be too hard to spot. They took Craig's and Cameron's horses: one is pure white and the other is a pale grey; they'll both show up in the moonlight.

Ten minutes down the creek I catch the glimmer of a horse's flanks between the leaves. I don't want to call out, just in case, although, what's hunting Nicolas won't need to hear him to know where he is. The horses aren't moving fast, probably because Nicolas doesn't know where he's going. I've ridden these trails past the Knight ranch a few times over the years, and even though the dark skews the landscape, I'm starting to get glimpses of familiarity. I'm also starting to get heavy whiffs of ZV.

Once I catch up to Nicolas and Sam, we can move a little faster. That will get us out of the woods at least, which will be safer for Nicolas, but riskier for the rest of us. I hate having to fight both sides from the middle. I just want to find some neutral ground and I'm gambling on that being the Knight Ranch. I'm not worried about Greyson falling behind. I couldn't lose him, not if I wanted to.

I'm finally close enough to make out human silhouettes astride the horses. "Nicolas, it's me! Wait up!"

Sam keeps plodding along but Nicolas reins in and turns. He looks relieved to see me, but not for long.

My hand hasn't even finished waving when a black form with a yellow bandana around its head, and pale grey arms protruding from a black muscle shirt, drops out of the tree and pulls him off his white horse.

Jabbing my heels into Shadow I race through tangles of leaves and branches that rip at my clothes. Oddly enough, my only thought is to pray, Please let this be the kind that drag off their victims and don't eat them right away. Please don't bite him; please don't bite him. Yes, it would probably simplify things if Nicolas were a ZV like the rest of us, but I don't want that—I really don't want that.

Shadow hasn't even slid to a complete stop on the damp ground before I'm off her back. Another figure has swooped down on Sam, but he's confused because Sam is a ZV and they're locked in a standoff.

The ZV with the bright yellow bandana wrestles to get a rope around Nicolas, but the doctor has had his share of sparing with rabid ZVs and he's no easy target. I'm not going to give his new friend a chance to decide it would be easier to eat his meal on the run than to try to carry it out. Swooping in off my horse, I throttle the ZV's neck in the crook of my elbow and pull him off. "Go! Go, Nicolas!"

"What the hell!" The ZV can't figure out why a fellow ZV would pull a perfectly good piece of fresh meat out from underneath him and then let it get away.

Nicolas hesitates. I can see he doesn't want to leave me alone to fight off the terrorists but has no idea what to do. "Get the hell out of the woods, Nicolas, and we'll all be safer! There are more!" He knows I'm right, but can't bring himself to retreat. "I'm a ZV, Nicolas. I can handle this. Go!"

If the ZV that jumped Sam were a mutant like the one that's heaving, and squirming in my arm, I'd be worried for him, too. Outside of the little episode at the hotel, he doesn't stand to raise the odds in any ring for his weight class. But his attacker is in pretty shabby shape even though he was still coordinated enough to climb a tree, or maybe he had help. It's more of a sumo-like, shoving match between the two of them.

The infected predator I've collared is swearing up a storm and nearly pulls me over his back off the ground. Maybe it doesn't look to Nicolas like I can handle it but he doesn't quite know how to jump in.

Sam finally doubles his ZV over with a quick jab to his nose, grabs Nicolas, and shoves him toward his horse. The ZV stands there confused like this wasn't in the script. The smell of ZV blood leaks through the fingers he has clasped to his face.

I can't hold the leader ZV anymore and he writhes out of my grip, mad as a swatted hornet. At first, he's a little surprised, hard to tell if it's the chauvinist how-could-a-girl-take-me-on thing or the hair. The looks I get are usually about the same for both. His face warps to anger pretty quickly when I round kick him in the chest. I don't really want to do a lot of damage because, you know, "do unto others," and I, personally, would definitely prefer as little damage as possible. The ZV hits the ground, gasping for air, as Nicolas kicks his horse into a gallop.

"Shit! You stinking Zeta bitch." All his *I*s sound like *E*s. "You don't come on Miguel's turf and steal his carnitas." Catching sight of his buddy gawking like an idle robot unleashes the viral fury that ignites with embarrassment at one of his minions watching a girl take him down. "Chico, don't just stand there! Go get our meat!"

"He's infected, Miguel…like us. And he stinks…like death." His flunky's eyes shift between Miguel and the trail that swallowed Sam and Nic. "He's strong."

"Mine was still fresh! Get your brown ass down there and bring him back." The goon nods and disappears into the dark of the trees. Sam will just have to cover his brother while I handle Miguel here.

"I'm doing you a favor, Miguel." I brace for another attack as he hauls himself up. It would be nice if we could just talk this out. Didn't any of the other mothers preach "use your words" like mine did?

"I don't need your charity, chica." He launches himself at me, fists swinging. He's done some fighting and although I manage to block his first couple of hits, when he goes ballistic, my feet fly out from underneath me, and my head thuds back into the dirt. I'm on my back underneath him before I know what hit me.

"Damn!" He leers down at me. "I didn't know the Zetas came in your flavor, baby. I might just have to have me some of this." He reaches for my shirt, but I'm no sorority drunk and he can't handle me with one hand. I'm glad I threw on my jeans and sweatshirt before I left.

My fists pummel his face until he collars my wrists and slaps me. The offensiveness of it stings more than the contact. The beast inside me goes wild. The cocktail the anger stirs up unleashes a furor he's not ready for and I give the punk a dose of my knee.

He learns pretty quickly that the arms do less damage than the legs. Groaning, he falls back, while I take advantage of his distraction to writhe onto my side. But ZV's don't feel stuff quite as intensely as I wish he did. Before I can break free of his straddle, he flips me so that I'm on my stomach with his hand on the back of my head shoving my face in the damp soil. Ramming his other fist between the pounded dirt and my ribs, he snakes his arm up my hoodie.

This is not going to happen! Livid and snarling, I thrash like a bull with its balls tied up, tossing him off my back into a bush. By the time I've rolled over and heaved my body up, he's already leaping back at me. We crash into the tree behind me, branches break, I lose my balance and we roll to the ground. He's got me head-locked, with one arm pinned behind my back under his knee.

Is it at all strange that the moment I'm wondering where the hell Greyson is, he shows up? Well, I don't actually see him show up. I hear the hooves, and then the growling, smell the scent, and suddenly the weight of Miguel flies off my back.

I already know Greyson can handle himself. I've watched him take on certified zombie soldiers before. But that's a different kind of fighting, more civilized. This is a street fight and Miguel pulls a knife. Do ZVs really need knives? At least Greyson has a gun now, the one he pulled off of Raymond.

"You know you're just going to damage me with that, right?" He nods at Miguel's blade. "You'd have to get me through the brain."

"I might get lucky."

"I'd say today is definitely not your lucky day." Grey pulls the gun out and points it at Miguel's head.

Yes, I'm freakin' furious that Miguel slapped me. Yes, I hate him because he tried to rape me. No, I don't want him shot through the head. I don't have to object because Greyson's voice is as cool as it is deep.

"Let's you and I talk, zombie to zombie. You see, I saw your little posse across the creek. Mostly white guys."

"Hey, gringo, you don't judge me. They deported my dad for defending himself at a bar. My mom's illegal, so all she can do is clean house for a bunch of white women that can't wipe their own asses."

"Frankly, I don't give a rat's balls about your politics, dude. That's not your world anymore. You're a ZV; nobody cares. Your only politics is surviving. Now I'm going to do you a favor." He swaggers into Miguel's fight circle. "Instead of giving you a bullet in the brain, I'm going to give you an education. You were vegetarian before you got infected, weren't you?"

Miguel looks shocked. He glances back at me because the leaves rustle as I start to stand up. He pivots, retreating and waving his knife a little between Greyson and me. "That's right. I got a medical condition. How'd you know that?"

"Because Evelyn, to whom you owe a very polite apology, and I have been around for a while. Now you listen up. You lay off the human hamburger."

"Why should I? They've been living off our sweat for years. It's about time we evened up the score."

"See? There you go again. You're not brown; you're not black; you're not white or yellow or red. You're grey—a ZV. That's all. Game over." Greyson wipes the air with his free hand to illustrate. "Bottom line—you keep eating people's guts, doesn't matter what color they are, that virus goes after your grey matter. You end up like your little white stooges, brain dead, decrepit, and hungry."

"How do you know that?"

"Does it matter? You must be feeling lucky if that's a gamble you want to take. 'Cause I'm afraid we'd all be better off if I just blew your brains out now. You're giving the rest of us a bad name. Those slobs decaying in the woods, that's one thing—they have no choice and they're as good as gone anyway—now or later, doesn't matter much. But you and me, we're the future. We can own this place. You get it?"

Miguel squints at Greyson. I know how he feels. Anybody has to wonder if Greyson is for real. To him, being a ZV is a gift. But I guess if it gets this guy to stop hunting down people like rabbits, I'll go along. The knife relaxes in Miguel's hand and his stance loosens. "Why are you telling me this?" His beady eyes dart my direction.

At least he knows he's a dirtbag and doesn't deserve any help. Or maybe I'm wrong. Maybe we're all dirtbags some time or another and what we need is some help. Either way, my blood is still boiling and I'm a little pissed that Greyson hasn't taught this dickhead a thing or two at the end of his fists.

"Because you're a survivor. So, survive." Greyson stuffs the gun in his jeans again and walks over to Romeo who is sampling the green buffet under the trees. "Let the rest of them fight it out."

Fuming, I follow his lead. I have nothing to say to this rapist, so I whistle to Shadow. She knows me pretty well and she's an easy but perky ride. I can't stop myself from shoving Miguel as I hustle by though. "Prick!" Greyson stares him down while I spur Shadow into the woods.

A couple minutes later, he catches up and matches Romeo's pace to Shadow's, even though the trail is really only wide enough for one and he has to maneuver around underbrush. "Are you hurt?"

That's the thing about Greyson. I'm not at all down with his ZV supremacist, survival of the fittest philosophies, but he's got that "I would die for you" core that keeps leaking to the surface and clouding the clear waters.

"Just my pride." I'm struggling not to vent. Payback isn't normally my MO, but that son of a bitch just tried to rape me. And Greyson let him walk away. If Miguel had had me strapped to an operating table and been coming after me with a scalpel, Grey would have ripped his throat out. I don't see the difference? Either way, I'm being violated by an asshole.

"Sorry." He reaches over and tugs back on Shadow's reins. She comes almost to a stop, but can't quite control her jitters.

"For what?"

"For not beating the shit out of him."

Looking him in the face right now would be disastrous. Miguel doesn't deserve the death penalty, but Greyson should have done something. I'm still mad as hell. "I've seen you do a lot worse for less."

"Only because some people need to get a taste of how the grey half-lives. This kid wasn't going to cut you up."

"No. Just rape me." Does he really see a difference? If he keeps going down this path, he's going to find the dragon at the end.

"Yeah, good luck with that. You can take care of yourself."

I roll my eyes, even though it's true. Frankly, I'm glad he sees me that way. I like that, to him, I'm strong, even if he has to keep saving my ass. I've saved his a few times. It's that kind of world now. Out here, nobody survives long without friends. His frank vote of confidence soothes the rage a bit. "Your chivalry overwhelms me, Sir Galahad."

Greyson grabs my reins and pulls Shadow close enough that he can touch me. Moonlight filters through the thinning trees and shadowy branches frame our silhouettes in the dusky light. "If he'd actually got through your defenses, really hurt you, I'd have shoved my gun in his mouth and splattered his infected brains all over these trees, ripped his heart out with my fingers and crushed it in the dirt." Sometimes Greyson scares me—in this really intense, eerily attractive way. "I told you. No one—nothing—can come between us. You and me, we are the future."

I only wish I was as sure of the future as Greyson is. But I think my eyes are too blinded by the smoke of the past to see the future clearly.

"But since he didn't hurt you," Greyson lets my reins loose and clicks Romeo ahead, "I let him go—because he's one of us."

One of us. Us and Them. That's what the future looks like, at least to Greyson. But I can't bring myself to call Miguel "us" just because he's the same shade of grey. I don't pick my people by the color of their skin; I pick them by the choices they make.

Chapter 14

We catch up with Nicolas and Sam on the farm road across from the fence that marks the Knight property. Huge floodlights illuminate the road up to the woods. Hopping off my horse and grabbing the bridle, I run smack into a big, old hug from Nicolas.

"Evelyn, you have to stop risking your own safety to save me. That ZV that jumped me was lucid. He could have hurt you."

Oh, God! Isn't this awkward? My face flushes. I can actually feel the heat. I was kind of hoping the drama of a zombie attack would just conveniently erase the little episode in the barn.

I fight off the instinct to look back at Grey. I have no idea what's written on my face right now, but I'm sure it's a story I don't want to tell.

"Nicolas, you still don't get it." Almost imperceptibly, my feet retreat until I've disentangled myself from his arms. "You're the one with the little bottle of pink miracle cream. We lose you, we lose hope of a cure." That was clinical enough, right?

Apparently not for Greyson. "Not that we're looking for a cure."

I turn on him. "Really Greyson?" In a flat second, I've unzipped my fly and shoved my jeans past my bikinis to my thigh, whipping my phone out of my bra to highlight the scar healing there. When I pulled off my running shorts, I didn't have time to admire, but I noticed that the gash was fading to rose. Now, the whole area has turned living-skin beige.

Greyson jumps off Romeo to have a closer look. He comes nose to nose with Nicolas who can't resist another assessment of his clinical trial. "I for one wouldn't mind having my own personal stash of this stuff." I'm still too irritated to feel self-conscious about a couple of guys checking out my thigh. Besides, I'm making a point here.

"I'm still running tests, but this looks very promising." Nicolas traces a finger along the faint pink scar.

Greyson swats his hand away from my thigh. Good thing, too, because it kind of makes me shiver. The skin all around the old cut has regrown nerve endings. I haul my pants back up and brush the top of Greyson's head. "If we can get Nicolas a lab, you stand a pretty good chance of growing back those curly blond locks of yours, boy."

Greyson doesn't say anything, but I think Nicolas's stock just went up.

We have to ride along the fence until we come to a metal gate marked with the crescent moon and the leaning 't'.

Greyson clicks Romeo around to face the rest of us. "So, what do we do? Knock?"

"Or not." Eight feet of chain link, that wasn't here a couple years ago when I last rode out this way, towers above our heads.

"There are security cameras all along here." Nicolas points up at the top of the gate and down the fence.

"I don't remember those from the last time I rode by here." Our safe-haven is starting to feel a little less secure.

"Things have changed. There are predator ZVs in the woods." Greyson turns and focuses down the road. "And it sounds like Holland has tracked us here."

The clicking car rattles up the farm road. Behind us, in the woods, the static of walkie-talkies closes in. "Who is this guy?"

Nicolas answers. "Pharmaceuticals are big money. Holland, if that's who he is, is not going to just walk away from you two."

"Then, between the mad scientist and the crazy preacher girl, I think I'll take my chances on the other side of that fence." Greyson hops off his horse to unlock the gate. By unlock, I mean he shoots a hole through the lock.

Alarms squeal and floodlights flash, illuminating the entire east side of the compound. The headlights from the clicking car now bounce into view.

Greyson's right. I'd rather take my chances inside. We're not out of range by the time the cars on the road reach the fence, but I'm pretty sure they're not interested in shooting us—as if that would do much more than put a hole in us anyway. There's not much comfort in knowing they want us alive.

Once inside, we gallop toward an enormous white building with a giant cross on the roof and a very large, round window. Everything's bigger in Texas, including the churches and the bugs. I think I just swallowed one. I guess that's not all that traumatic for someone who craves cow guts.

A cloud of dust rolls toward us from the compound beyond the church and about three Jeeps roar out of it. This couldn't be worse than what's waiting on the outside of the fence. Right?

One Jeep screams to a stop behind us, cutting us off from jumping out of the frying pan and back into the fire. Greyson pulls Romeo back and positions himself in front of me. Nicolas does the same with Sam. A guy in camouflage with an automatic gun jumps out of each Jeep surrounding us.

Nicolas doesn't give them time to get the wrong idea. He jumps off his horse. The guys all train their guns on him, but no one starts shooting. I'm not surprised. Nicolas doesn't exactly look threatening.

"I'm Nicolas, CDC, former head of research at the Z-V Institute in Salt Lake City." He waves and holds out his hand. Does he really think one of them is going to shake it? He's spent too much time around diplomats. The only diplomacy these guys know is "don't shoot until they're on your property."

But I guess he read his audience pretty quickly. These aren't guys that you want to introduce yourself to using some suspicious, foreign name like Sudhir. They might shoot you just because they don't like the sound of it.

It's just barely noticeable, but after his introduction, the grit in the air softens just a tad. The smoothness of Nicolas's voice has that effect on people; it has that effect on me. "We're sorry to have activated your alarm system, but my three friends here are infected with the Zoser Virus and I'm looking for a safe place to lodge them while I continue my research. We heard that the Knight Foundation might be sympathetic. Is there someone I could possibly speak with who would have the authority to give us sanctuary?"

"'The Lord hear thee in the day of trouble and send thee help from the sanctuary': Psalms 20." A tall brunette with dark eyes steps out of the back seat of the first Jeep. "But since He is not here yet, I will have to do. I am Ms. Ashley Knight, Minister of the Lazarus Knight Church of the Firstborn. I will indeed grant you sanctuary here Dr. Nicolas riding the white horse."

She turns to her guards, "Brothers, point your guns at the strangers at the gates." The soldiers pivot and aim in the direction of the black sedan. I recognize the portly silhouette of the guy we think is the infamous Holland.

Imagine my surprise when Ms. Ashley paints on a welcome smile and walks toward the fence followed by her camouflaged groupies. She walks like there are clouds under her feet instead of solid earth. When she waves her lily-white hand, it flutters in the lights like a delicate petal tousled in the wind. "Why Brother Scott Holland! It's been too long since we've seen you." Now I know where the girl gets her preaching talent. She's a born actress.

"With all respect, Ms. Knight, those two ZVs are armed and dangerous."

I can't help myself and yell back. "I'm not armed and you're dangerous one. Your goons shot my cousin—an innocent fourteen-year-old boy."

"My, oh my! Is that true, Brother Holland?"

Holland looks uncomfortable under the glare of the spotlights and Reverend Knight's inquisition. "That was an unfortunate accident provoked by the male ZV as we tried to apprehend him. The boy suffered a minor wound. He'll be fine. We have a mandate from the Governor's office to apprehend all vagrant ZVs and remand them to treatment centers for their own safety and the safety of the public."

"I'm very glad to hear it. But I'm afraid that these are not vagrants. They are fellows in the Brotherhood of the Firstborn. You see I, too, have a mandate, from a much higher authority, to be the instrument whereby His word shall be fulfilled. Now if you had studied the word with more diligence, and if you would open your eyes and see, you would recognize that right here, right now, you are witnessing the fulfillment of the holy word of the Apocalypse. Out of the east the word has come to us."

She turns to us, smiles, and then announces her good news to the gun-toting priests. "Brethren, like a thief in the night, the messengers of the Lamb have arrived. Open your eyes and see the gift that has been sent to us. Count the horses. Are there not four? Are they not the four horses of the Revelation?" She points to each, a satisfied, pearly white smile gracing her face. "One white, one red, one black, and one pale."

She's totally right. That is so freaky.

"Hear the words of the Revelator: 'Come and see. And I saw, and behold a white horse: and he that sat on him went forth conquering, and to conquer.' Now I ask you, brothers, is it only coincidence and not the work of divinity that Doctor Nicolas rides the white horse? And is the Greek meaning of "Nicolas" not 'conqueror'? Let us not be blind and deny this great manifestation of the divine will, but let us rejoice at the good news: the hour and the day are upon us, and here before us is the sign of that day."

Wow! She's good. I kind of feel like raising my hands and shouting "Hallelujah!" She talks like the Bible, which makes her sound like the ultimate authority. Maybe I was wrong. I told the doctor he should go by Sudhir, the name his parents gave him, because it means "great scholar" and that's who he is, but maybe Sudhir was meant to be Nicolas after all.

Holland isn't convinced. "Excuse me, ma'am. I don't think you understand the danger here. One bite from the young man on that red horse and you're all infected, as good as dead, or wishing you were."

Somehow, instead of being terrified, Ashley finds that amazingly funny. "Why, Mr. Holland," she giggles playfully, "you have opened my eyes. 'Whoever has ears to hear, let him hear' for the Revelator also saw the red horse. 'And there went out another horse that was red: and power was given to him that sat thereon to take peace from the earth, and that they should kill one another: and there was given unto him a great sword."

Well, there, she's missing something, because Greyson has a gun in the back of his shirt, but I'm pretty sure he's not packing a sword.

She's not finished, though. "Have you not read the words of the prophet? 'He hath made my mouth like a sharp sword'?"

Oh, she is good. I squint to see if she's got some notes, or a Bible, or something. But this is all off the cuff. And I thought I spent too much time studying Shakespeare.

Holland is getting frustrated. The guns of his men tip downward with each of Ms. Knight's arguments. "We don't want any trouble here, Ms. Knight, but I'm going to have to insist that you turn over custody of those infected young people to me. You're welcome to do as you please with the young doctor there, but those three fall under my authority."

"Well, Mr. Holland," Ms. Ashley doesn't skip a sweet, little beat, "as the Good Book says, 'agree with thine adversary quickly.' You can talk to my lawyers first thing in the morning and settle this question of 'authority'." Her handful of soldiers steps menacingly closer.

The light is bright enough to see Holland go red in the face. His half-bald head and paunchy gut scream, "I'm the kid that got teased in school and is now exacting vengeance on any poor soul that happens to fall into my petty, pudgy hands." He's a loser.

Apparently, he's been on this turf before, because at the mention of lawyers, he backs his men off, but he's not happy about it. He slaps one upside the head for not getting out of his way fast enough. I don't ever want that man to touch me. Crazy loon or holy saint, I'll take Ms. Ashley Knight over Scott Holland any day.

Chapter 15

The Knight compound is a group of long buildings that form the sides of a rectangle capped with an immense church on one end and a sprawling mansion on the other. The empty center makes a nice courtyard if you don't mind feeling like a monkey in the zoo, watched on all sides through the windows. An old, white, ranch house and barn sit a way back on the far west side of the compound but still within the fencing of the acres of property recently bequeathed to Ashley Knight and her younger brother Daniel by their late father.

"Welcome, weary travelers! You have found rest. May you find peace in the Lord and his righteous judgments!" The immorally good-looking Ashley flashes us a toothpaste commercial smile through wine-red lips while patting Shadow's neck. It has to be some kind of sin for a preacher to be that beautiful. Her long black tresses match the coat of the mare, and her pale white skin practically glows in the glare of the floodlights. She surveys our mounts. "I recognize these fine horses. How is it you came to be riding the four horses belonging to the children of my neighbors Dr. and Mrs. Yeats?"

"Esther is my aunt. I'm sure she'll send my uncle Daren over to pick them up in the morning."

"Nonsense. I wouldn't dream of troubling him. Do you think when the Apostle borrowed an ass to fulfill the scripture and bring the Lord triumphant to Jerusalem, that he asked the kind owner who supplied the providential animal to come and fetch it back?" She giggles at the absurdity. Her camouflaged "disciples" follow suit. "Of course not! Brother Simon will take these blessed animals to the barn and see that they are well tended and then returned."

A small, thin soldier, whose camouflage looks a little big for him, nods. "Yes, ma'am!" He and another of the men lead the horses away through the prairie grass, past the church, and toward the barn, which must still be in use. Crop fields surround the entire compound.

Ms. Knight beckons us away from the gate toward the back of the church. As we get closer, I see that there is another, smaller chapel building facing the back of the church. The two structures are separated by a narrow, cement sidewalk and about ten feet of grass. A porch light illuminates the smaller structure adorned with a sculpted depiction of Christ separating the lambs from the goats. On his right, angels tip a holy grail to the mouths of the waiting lambs. On his left, a ravenous wolf devours the unworthy goats.

Between the enormous white siding chapel, adorned with a spired steeple and clock tower, and one of the two matching white dormitory buildings, a little stone path leads to the courtyard at the center of the compound.

Even in late December, the flowers, illuminated by street lamps positioned at the corners of the garden, are beautiful: blue, yellow, pink, purple—all the colors of heaven. On one end of the park, a full-sized stable, complete with life-sized wise men, shepherds, sheep, donkeys, the holy family, and an enormous star hanging above, celebrates the season. At the center of the park, a carved marble cross, a radiant gold sun rising from the horizontal beam, hovers above a bubbling fountain pool. A grassy picnic area with gazebos, white wrought iron benches, patio swings, and a wishing well lead to the mansion at the end of the park. What Houston calls Winter, we Northerners call Spring. Fireflies spark in the cool night air among the shade trees. The whole fairytale setting is a demented contradiction to the handful of camouflaged, automatic rifle-toting "disciples" escorting us through the park.

One guy always takes the lead and appears to be Ms. Knight's personal bodyguard. He's really tall, with dark, close-cropped hair, a very square jaw, and a monster long stride. He is obviously ex-military. Of course, the first thought through my head is, "what made a convert of this guy?" And then I watch the lines on his face loosen just a tiny bit when Ashley touches the sleeve of his coat and says, "Brother Travis, would you be kind enough to go to the kitchen and ask Juanita if she would be willing to find a little late supper fit for these messengers of the Lord?"

The answer is simple—he's converted to the lovely Ms. Ashley Knight. He nods and double times to the steps of the very southern mansion presiding over the far end of the courtyard opposite the church.

Just slightly less impressive than the church, the mansion boasts upstairs balconies and columns surrounding a huge wrap around porch. Ushering us past the stone lion sentinels, up the front steps, Ashley welcomes us inside with a serene smile. "Let's get y'all situated for the night and then we can sort things out in the morning."

It's only for a brief second, if my ZV senses weren't still revving in overdrive from the chase through the woods, I might have missed it, but our charming hostess gives me the once over, sizing me up. That, I'm used to. It's the nearly imperceptible, competitive eye scrunch at the end that sends a tiny shiver up my back and across my shoulders. What are we competing for?

And then she totally gives the game away by falling into step with Greyson and taking his arm as she glides through the massive, black double doors. Is it possible that Nicolas isn't the only one on the planet with more than a clinical interest in checking out a viral resistant zombie?

Don't get me wrong, here. I'm aware that not more than a couple hours ago, I was rethinking my stance on Nicolas, balancing on the edge of a kiss, wavering between brilliant, charming, good guy, and cool, grey hero. Who could blame me, though?

Yes, I know Greyson would go…no, has gone…to hell for me…and Amber. But let's face it. He's ruthless and sometimes his trigger finger fires a lot faster than his brain. He is totally an "end justifies the means" kind of guy. I'm not like that. I plan stuff out, think about doing the right thing, the way Nicolas does. And, in the last couple of days, Nicolas has clocked a pretty tight record of non-violent ass saving. He donated the getaway car, funded our escape, bought our groceries, talked our way out of a close call with a cop. Hell, he's the guy with the little tube of cream that's returning the pink glow to the skin on my thigh and a little fuzz of stubble to the bald spot on my scalp.

I know; I know. Greyson's convinced we're soul mates—at least he was until the blood sample thing got between us. But what exactly makes me his sacred other half?

People change, but deep down inside, I can't shake the memory of who Greyson has always been—the kid that dumped my best friend Julie when she needed him most. So, I have to wonder, if there were another option for Greyson, someone who bought into his "superhuman, evolutionarily dominant species, man of the future" worldview, would he still be so devoted to me?

In the marble entry, in front of the double staircase that winds up both sides to an enormous balcony lined by closed mahogany doors, the Reverend Ashley Knight's next words tell me I'm about to find out. "Welcome to my home." Totally harmless, right? Not! She's not talking to all of us. She's smiling directly at Greyson.

A younger, Latino girl with long black hair wanders in balancing a tray of hot tea. The only thing the virus craves as much as organs is water. I guess nothing really lives without it. I help myself to a glass and swallow greedily. Sam and Greyson have the same monster thirst I do, but Nicolas just takes a polite sip.

Her gaze drowning in the gold of Greyson's eyes, Ashley motions to one of the two armed disciples left, "Brother Jacob, would you be kind enough to escort Ms….?" She waits for me to fill in the blank. When I don't say anything, she's forced to turn her head and look me in the eye.

"…Evelyn. Evelyn Cross."

"Ah…Ms. Cross. Jacob, would you escort our guest to one of the dorm rooms in the sisters' wing?" Brother Jacob is a tall ginger with freckles, who wears his cap low like he'd rather not be noticed. She gestures to her left, "And brother Paul, please show Nicolas and…?"

"This is my brother, Sam. But…I'm afraid we may require…"

"What my brother is trying to put delicately," Sam steps in front of Nicolas, "is that I bite. I have an aberrant form of the

116

virus that, like Greyson's and Evelyn's refrains from slowly consuming my organs and my brain, but unlike theirs, has not evolved enough to grant me predator superpowers." At this point, Ashley gives Greyson the once over, and let's just say I'm not thrilled about the look of smoldering hunger on her face. "Instead my brand of Z-Virus saps my energy and leads to violent, mindless, organ bingeing zombie episodes."

Nicolas looks mortified. But it's not so much that Sam gave them away; what really bothers Nicolas is that his brother sees himself as such a monster. "He has…seizures." The doctor tries to delicately soften the impact of Sam's bluntness.

I remember the look on my Aunt Esther's face when she heard the disturbing truth about Sam. Of course, I expect the same politely hidden shock to flash across Ashley's face. Instead, Ms. Preacher Girl smiles graciously, the way a spider would upon making the acquaintance of a fly. "Y'all mustn't fret about that." She waves the news away with a flick of her dainty, white wrist.

Brother Travis emerges from a hallway and whispers in Ashley's ear. She smiles and nods. "It just so happens, Sam, you are not the first of your kind to seek asylum here among the Church of the Firstborn. I knew when you arrived astride the pale horse that you brought Death in your wake. But here, among the faithful, we know that only the sinful shall die. Those who are among the righteous will be changed in the twinkling of an eye to dwell forever on the New Earth."

Is she serious? Psycho girl actually thinks the Z-Virus is some gift from heaven! I chance a glance at Greyson. He's totally amused. I can see where his head is running right now.

"For you, Sam," Ashley graces him with a game show hostess smile, "…and of course for your brother…we have particular accommodations. Travis, would you be so kind as to arrange a room for Sam and his brother in the Hall of the Judges?"

When she says that, Travis takes a quick look at Sam before he dutifully replies, "Yes, Ma'am." So now I know even if Her Worship's holy water is laced with LSD or something, Brother Travis is still walking around in our dimension. The look he gave Sam was tinged with just enough healthy revulsion. His whole body tightened up in a gut instinct survival stance. I could smell the hormone spike. Nice piece of info to file away. But even more intriguing is the news that there are more ZVs like Sam.

My guess is they're taking Sam and Nicolas to the smaller building behind the church, mostly because it's separate from the other dorms, but also because it's got that façade of the judgment between the goats and the lambs. Being separated prickles my suspicions. You know what they say, "divide and conquer."

The teenage girl stacks our empty cups on her tray as Brother Travis starts to usher the Vadlamani's toward the front door into the courtyard.

"I really don't want to appear ungrateful, Ms. Knight..." Nicolas clanks his mostly full cup onto the girl's tray as she passes on her way to the kitchen.

"Please, call me Ashley. You are, after all 'The Conqueror' of the Revelation."

"Well, what I'm really seeking is a way to conquer the virus." Our hostess's lovely white brow furrows beneath her jet-black bangs.

Nicolas hasn't quite tuned in to the insanity going on here. Fortunately, the crazy preacher girl isn't the only one who went to Sunday School and can BS her way through a text analysis. Bridger, my ex, was the grandson of a Methodist minister, and I didn't ace AP Comparative Lit for nothing. "What he means is," I step in front of him, "that he is looking for a way to purify the virus, target its defects, not with a sword, but with the bow of his intellect. The bow's not really a weapon, it's just the ingenuity that lets the weapons have a broader range." That was pretty good, at least a "B+" worth.

Ashley nods. "The white horse! Of course! The symbol has always been such a mystery. Why would the color of purity carry the conqueror? And now, the message is so simply clear."

"And that's not all." I'm going for the "A." Ashley clearly has money, influence, and lawyers. If we can get her to shelter us ZVs and finance Nicolas, he stands a decent chance of coming up with a cure. But it's plain she's not interested in a cure, so I'm just spinning things to get her on board. "He not only is going forth to conquer, but he already has. Look!" Unzipping my jeans again, I flash them a look at the pretty pink skin surrounding the scar on my thigh. "Nicolas has already vanquished some of the virus's degenerative effects. This was a stab wound. And look at the skin around it. It's like that part was reborn."

Ashley and her guardsmen ogle my thigh and then Nicolas.

"Nicolas can conquer every flaw of the virus. When he's finished with it, the virus will bring about a pure transformation." I beam at the doctor but my eyes tell him to get in character.

"Well…" Nicolas starts to object.

Greyson picks up on cue, cutting him off. He leans his head toward Ashley. "They shaved my head before we escaped. Nicky's little potion did this." I'm not too thrilled about the light brush of the hand that Her Reverence bestows across Greyson's crown.

"Oh my!" She gasps and shivers a little as she caresses the fuzz. Was that just surprise…or something else?

Staring pointedly at our way too ethical doctor, I drag her attention away from Greyson. "All you need is a lab, right Nicolas?"

He's confused but he plays along. "Well, yes. We'd been studying this virus for a while before it began to spread. My parents were the first to discover it."

"Yes!" Ashley nods enthusiastically. "In Egypt. The virus was brought forth out of Egypt and that was you and your parents, Dr…?"

"Vadlamani." Nicolas stretches out a hand.

"And Sam." Greyson jerks his thumb in Sam's direction. My ZV boy is getting bored with the conversation, but I can see he's not wasting his time. He's casing the place, forever resourceful.

"Yeah, that's me." Sam raises a hand. "Z-Virus ground zero."

"So, you were the first infected?"

I have to wonder why Ms. Ashley is so intrigued by the origins of the virus. What exactly is her agenda?

"Sam was the first, but there was a girl." Nicolas is a walking encyclopedia. He can't help himself; he just spews info. "The virus is over 4000 years old. We believe the Egyptian alchemists stumbled across it, or possibly created it, in their search for eternal life. That's why the mummification processes are so heavily linked to the urges brought on by the virus."

Ashley drinks it all in like a devout disciple at the feet of the master. "4000 years! It can only be divine providence that this virus of immortality has come forth in these, the last days. And what, may I ask, revived this dead virus?"

I know the answer to this question. "Love."

"Excuse me?" Ashley either doesn't follow or she thinks I'm making a joke that isn't very funny.

"Love!" Read my lips!

"Well," Nicolas interjects apologetically, "technically, it is the mix of chemicals present in the first stages of falling in love that formed an ideal incubating environment for the regeneration of the dormant virus."

"Love is a bitch." Sam's murmur doesn't quite escape Ms. Knight's attention.

Nicolas looks tortured. "Unfortunately, we weren't aware of its existence and took no precautions. The virus isn't airborne, most likely it was inadvertently passed from an infected surface into the human membrane as we studied the infected artifacts." Nicolas slides closer to his brother but Sam leans away. "Sam and the undergraduate research assistant he fell in love with were heavily exposed. She succumbed to some of the uglier symptoms of the virus."

Sam tries to pull off a poker face, but the grief and anger leak through, and his stone visage warps into a botched sculpture, badly carved.

"In truth, Sam," Ashley touches his shoulder, genuinely moved by his pain, "I quite sympathize with your sentiments. I am sorry for your loss. I recently lost my own father…" she trails off, gets lost in the haze behind her eyes, and then blinks, breathing deeply the present. "But here, we know that God is Love. Love called this virus of immortality forth from Egypt. So, once again, God has brought salvation out of Egypt."

Turning to her soldier disciples she declares, "Brothers, Watch! For the season of the harvest is nigh. The final judgment of mankind is upon us. It will bring about the change of the righteous in the twinkling of an eye. Are we not among the blessed to be standing here watching as scripture unfolds in our midst?" She showers Nicolas with the sanctity of her smile. "You, Nicolas, crowned with the laurels of victory in knowledge, will go forth conquering until you have purified this gift of the Almighty."

"Actually, I…uh…" Nicolas stutters, unsure how to just let her live with her delusions. "I'm trying to isolate what makes Greyson and Evelyn strong, but attacks my brother. I guess you could say," he glances uneasily at me, "I'm looking to purify the virus."

Well played, Nic! Before he stumbles, I step in. "And don't forget the ointment that restores the skin's ability to heal." I'm still standing there with my fly open and one thigh exposed, glad I opted for bikinis instead of a thong when I went running. I illustrate the cream with the proof on my skin and then hike up my jeans.

Ashley is all ears and eyes. I can't say I'm not glad to distract those bewitching brown eyes from Greyson, but the hard intensity in them tells me she's no wilting lily. This girl is a Steel Magnolia if I ever saw one. What is her real agenda? "And Nicolas, could this ointment of yours possibly be used to stimulate the reknitting of broken bones in those touched by the gift, martyrs wounded by the unbelieving?"

"I'm working on that. Actually, if I could just contact my cousin at the Baylor School of Medicine in Houston, I believe he could supply me with everything I need to continue my research. Although we haven't isolated the various mutations of the virus, we've made some excellent progress toward alleviating some of the negative symptoms."

"This is most wonderful news. Brother Travis, will you assist Nicolas in contacting his cousin right away?" She stifles a yawn. "Oh, my, excuse me! It has been a long and trying day. Nicolas, perhaps you would rather stay, get a restful night's sleep and then be about your business in the morning?"

"Actually, as long as Sam and the others are safe, I wouldn't mind getting in touch with my cousin Richard as soon as possible. I know it's late, but I'm sure he'll put me up for the night, and then we can get started first thing in the morning. The situation is becoming more urgent."

"May the Lord reward your dedication to the cause! I will wish you all a good night. Sleep in the peaceful rest of sweet Jesus."

Brothers Travis and Jacob shuffle Sam, Nicolas and me out of the foyer, but Ashley slips her arm through Greyson's and leads him away whispering, "May I take the liberty of speaking with you in the privacy of my study for just a few minutes, Greyson, rider of the Red Horse?"

The only consolation I have as I'm being hustled out the front door to the sisters' wing of the compound is that at least he looks back over his shoulder and winks like he knows what game we're playing here. But I'm not sure he DOES know.

Chapter 16

Brother Travis leads Nicolas and Sam back down the path to the chapel. Jacob steers me toward the sisters' wing on the west end of the courtyard. Nicolas breaks away, running across the lawn. "Evelyn!" His face is urgent and his mouth opens with some hugely important parting message he wants to leave, but then no words come out like he can't remember what he was going to say, or maybe he can, but the words are sticking. "You'll be okay here, right?" I can see he's as edgy about the charade going on here as I am. But he really needs to get back to his element. And the naked truth is, what's best for Nicolas, is best for all of us. "As soon as I've gotten settled with Richard, I'll come back and make sure..."

"Don't worry about us, Nicolas." I shrug. "It's a little odd here, but Sam, Greyson and I aren't exactly the in-crowd. We can do odd. To tell you the truth, I feel a little like a wolf that has sneaked into the flock."

He grins and then his eyes find the sidewalk. "I...uh...I still haven't thanked you properly for..."

"Don't Nicolas. You've had my back as often as I've had yours. We all need each other. It's more than just need, though..." I can't stop myself, I lean over and kiss his cheek, in a friend zone kind of way—but not. My lips linger against the smooth, warm, olive of his skin... "you're my family, Nicolas."

His whole face breaks out in this beaming smile like I just let the sun out of a jar. "I'll be there for you, Evelyn. Always."

I nod, turning away before any more feelings seep through my skin. I'll be fine. Obviously. I can take care of myself.

Only thing is...as I watch Nicolas disappear across the courtyard...I'm alone in the middle of strangers—no Amber, no Greyson, no Nicolas, not even Sam. A couple hours ago, I was wavering between cool, grey, teenage mutant and tall, dark, dreamy doctor. How did I end up with mute, camouflaged, cult soldier?

The large clock on the church steeple chimes eleven. "So," I attempt to break the foot of ice between my escort and me, "are all the 'sisters' in this building and the 'brothers' in the other dorm across the garden?"

No answer. Just the heavy clomping of boots down the tile hallway. At least, if they come for me, I'll be able to hear them several doors down. Making a mental note of the emergency staircase at the end of the hall, I take another shot at extracting a bit of info.

"I guess my friends and I are the only ripe ZVs you have in here, right? The rest of the girls are all members of the church?" I already know the answer, but I'm hoping to melt the ice a little. The muted scent of the infected hangs about the courtyard, too faint for any but the most discerning nose. If there were any infected members inside this building, mutant or otherwise, I'd have sniffed them out.

At least this time he glances back at me with a look like I'm a total blonde, which I am, sort of, in a honey-colored kind of way, but not like he's thinking. Guess that means somewhere, maybe not in this building, they've got a few organ junkies.

Brother Jacob opens the door to the small room at the end of the corridor on the second floor. I'm a little freaked that the door has two locks—a chain on the inside for privacy and a key on the outside. I guess in a cult that worships zombies, you sort of have to take precautions to make sure the gods don't devour the disciples. That's probably a good sign. They haven't had occasion yet to learn that mutant ZVs, like Greyson and I, don't pay any attention to locks. We just kick the door in.

The room looks a lot like the Hampton Inn my family always stayed in on the drive to Texas. There's a nice, clean, white tile bath, a single bed with white sheets and blankets, and white gauze curtains over a wide window that looks out over the courtyard on the church end.

"I don't have any bags," I joke lamely, 'cause the guy is just standing there like I'm supposed to tip him or something.

Finally, Brother Mute speaks up. "I gave you a room with a great view of the sidewall on the Hall of the Judges."

"Thanks?" I glance at the window and wonder what's so great about the sidewall that Brother Jacob would break his vow of silence to tell me about it.

"I recognize you…from the TV."

"They have TV here?" Looking around the room again for the TV I missed on the first glance, I'm disappointed to see only a simple frame wooden desk and a matching nightstand decorated with an alarm clock and a Bible. They keep it right out in plain sight, not in the drawer. No phone.

"In the main hall. You're one of the mutants." Now that he's talking, Brother Jacob is missing something. He doesn't have the deep woods Texas twang. He definitely should have said, "one of them mutants." So where did he come from?

I hold out my hand. "Evelyn Cross, mutant ZV from Eli, Utah. And you?"

He doesn't take my hand or the bait to catch a little info. He just nods and clomps out of the room. Yes, it's disturbing when the door shuts and the bolt on the outside grinds into the lock. Visions of my "all expenses paid" stay at the Z-V Institute charge into my head. A rush of adrenaline scrambles my heart and I can't breathe. My muscles all contract and I need to run even though I realize these doors are paper thin and there are no armed guards on the other side—at least not yet.

My animal instincts kick in and I check the other exit in the room. At least there aren't bars on the windows, but they're blocked so they don't slide more than four inches. Cracking it open, I inhale the fresh night breeze and try to think logically through the fringe of fuzz coating the edge of my brain. I should have grabbed some sleep at my aunt's when I had the chance.

The window doesn't actually look out over the courtyard because it's situated at the end of the building, not on the side. Small trees, that haven't been around quite as long as some of the shade trees in the garden, reach up toward my window on the second floor. Thick bushes camouflage the foundation below me. It does have a nice view of the Hall of Judges, but there's really nothing to see there on the side wall. Shaking my head, I survey my new home.

This is a nice place, especially if you're into white, which I'm not really, but I can adapt. I try to breathe in the sense of security, think of the positives. Amber is in the safest place I can think of. Holland and his Snatchers can't get to us. The congregation here is more likely to pray to Greyson and me— well, Greyson for sure—than bash our heads in. So why am I so freaked out?

I pace the room a bit, knowing I should just take advantage of the nice, comfy bed and get some sleep so I can start thinking like a rational ZV, but something is bugging me, keeping me on edge. Maybe it's Greyson. He's with HER.

Okay, yes. I'm jealous. Rationally, I've always known he was a player, but apparently, he's convinced some part of my brain—maybe it's my heart, a soft, weak part that wanted to believe—that he is inevitably, irrevocably mine. And now that I think about it, I'm kind of mad. He told me it was all about me, that I was the only one that ever mattered; all the other girls were just keeping the seat warm. Was he just playing me? Or did it all disappear over one little dispute about a syringe full of blood, maybe a little insecurity about my other friends? Must not have been all that deep if one little cut can sever us.

Our last kiss, the one that drew me in and swallowed me up before I left him sleeping in my cousin's bed, haunts my lips. God! I was so taken in. I slump down onto the bed. The mattress is surprisingly cushy and the blanket is teddy bear soft so I fall back and wallow for a minute. I guess since I don't have to take care of Amber...my body physically cringes at the separation...I don't need Greyson. I can take care of myself.

I really thought, though, that he...you know...actually...okay, I'm just going to say it...I thought he loved me. No, it's not that. I thought he loved me enough that he was done being a player. And now the first beautiful groupie spouting, "O Mighty Greyson!" comes along and he waltzes off with her. It's hard to tell if I'm furious or just crushed.

No! I am not crushed. I am not that girl.

Pushing myself off the bed, I stalk over to the window and slam my palm against it. I need to go for a run.

Whirling around, I glare at the locked door. I'm breathing too hard. I know what's going on here and it's not just Greyson.

It's not even that funky, vaguely familiar, but hard to place smell floating in on the breeze from outside. What's really under my skin—besides the virus—is that for the first time in a long time, I've lost my raison d'être—my reason for being.

Amber's safe with my aunt. We're safe, relatively, in this compound. Greyson's buddied up with the "camp director" securing our place here. Nicolas has a lab so he can keep working on saving the world. Sam—well Sam is busy just trying to stay human. And apparently, he's now risen to the calling of judge. So, what about me? I fold my arms across my chest. For the first time in a long time, I don't know what the hell I'm doing.

My ears twitch; very quiet footsteps, like slippers, pad up the hallway. They stop in front of my door. Is this an ambush? The knock is just a formality because I can't really open the door from this side. Stepping quietly behind it, I wait for the jingling of the key.

The door cracks open. The warm, spicy smell of bloody organs wafts into the room. "Sister Cross?" A girl with a very small voice taps lightly on the open door. My stomach growls and I start salivating.

The girl's nose appears in the gap, but she can only see into the bathroom. I'm all revved up for the hunt so I have to take it down a notch. Obviously, I don't want to hurt this girl, but one way or another, I've got to figure out what that odd smell is, what it is that's going on in this place that has my animal instincts bristling.

The crack inches a bit wider.

The second her toe and lightly browned hand appear, I pounce. Grabbing her wrist, I haul her through the doorway, blocking it with my body. Her plateful of cow guts splatters and shatters against the bathroom door, shards skidding across the tile. A clear, plastic water bottle, full of Kool-Aid, rolls across the floor. The girl gasps and starts to scream so I spin her around and smother her mouth with my other hand. She's shaking like she's having a seizure.

"I'm not going to hurt you! Don't scream!"

She doesn't respond. Can't say I blame her. A full-blown ZV just grabbed her. That would scare the shit out of anybody.

"I'm going to let you go, but if you try to scream, I'll have to stop you. Understand? I just want to talk to you, okay?"

She manages to nod and I slide my hand away from her mouth while maneuvering her into the room. The key is still in the lock and, just out of principle, with a quick whack of my palm, I snap the head off, leaving the rod stuck in the open position. Already, the air flows a little more easily from my nose to my lungs.

Quietly closing the door, I slide the chain into place and turn to my visitor. The room is saturated with the heavy odor of liver. For a second I close my eyes and savor it, breathing it in like a pint of Ben and Jerry's Coffee, Coffee, Buzz, Buzz, Buzz.

Imagine my surprise when I open my eyes and the girl is kneeling down at my feet mumbling, her thick, straight jet-black hair tumbling over her shoulders. It takes me a few seconds to recognize the words:

"...is my shepherd, I shall not want. He maketh me to lie down in green pastures: he leadeth me beside the still waters. He restoreth my soul: he leadeth me in the paths of righteousness for his name's sake. Yea, though I walk through the valley of the shadow of death, I will fear no evil..."

"Sweetie, you don't need to pray. Seriously, I'm not going to snack on your heart. Although, you do have a nice cinnamon smell, like my mom's sticky buns." I thought I'd lighten things up with something amusing, but her deep brown eyes get really wide and her shoulders tense up. I should have figured if she's a disciple here, she's probably pretty gullible and can't really spot sarcasm. I backpedal, stepping away from her knees with my hands up so she can see I'm not a threat. "It was just a joke; a bad one."

"This...this...isn't the...judg...the judgment?"

"Uhh...No!"

She starts to breathe again, panting. "Reverend Knight told us we should always watch and be faithful because it could come anytime, like a thief in the night...and you were..." Her eyes wander back to the door.

"Well, it's not today." Before I lean over and start picking up pieces of the plate and tossing them into the trash, I pick up the bottle, unscrew it and guzzle half of it. Apparently, this makes me much less intimidating and the girl slowly gets up and starts helping me, but keeps a wary eye out.

The tasty little morsels of cow, I run under the sink and set on the sparkling soap dish. She watches me entranced like I'm the zookeeper getting ready to feed the tiger. "I'm actually not hungry 'cause I stuffed myself with relatives earlier, but I'll hang onto this until morning."

Looking horrified, she nods.

"No! No! Not like that. I didn't eat my cousins."

Her face relaxes, but her eyes are still wide open and I think she's holding her breath.

"My aunt fed me some cow."

As she breathes again, I hurry to reassure her.

"I don't need to eat all that often."

She nods obediently, still watching me like I'm a coiled, rattling snake. I seriously need to find some way to chill the tension in here and get a little info.

"Soo…you must help out in the kitchen."

She nods.

"And does everyone have a job here?"

She nods again. This conversation isn't going anywhere fast. She's still got her tiny, brown hands folded in front of her white frock like she's praying. The only way to get her to unclench them is to offer her one of mine.

"I'm Evelyn. Evelyn Cross."

Her eyes dart back and forth from my face to my hand. She's got her lips cinched between her teeth. Finally, she stretches out her hand and shakes my fingertips. "Christina. Christina Trujillo."

"Come on." Walking past her, I pull the chair away from the desk and offer its services before sinking down on the edge of the bed.

Gazing longingly at the door, she sidesteps tentatively toward the chair and sits on the very edge. To be less intimidating, I slouch back on my elbows and swallow the saliva swirling around my tongue. I wasn't lying when I said she smelled like my mom's homemade cinnamon rolls, the ones dripping with thick glaze.

"Do you normally deliver food to the ZVs?" Might as well bring the elephant out of the closet.

"Well, not really." She stops and looks around, like maybe the walls have ears, and then whispers. "That's why I thought it was so strange when I saw what was on the plate, that a...uh...one of the judges...was here in the sisters' wing."

I'm the only ZV in here. That's interesting. They must keep the rest of them in the Hall of the Judges. "What about the brothers' wing? Did they take a special plate to a new "Judge" over there?"

"No. I don't think so. Brother Travis escorted a new Judge to the Hall, but there wasn't anything for him. Only Brother Travis is worthy to take food to the Judges."

Damn! That means they haven't given Greyson a room in one of the dorms. He's still chatting with Ms. Ashley...or worse. The scowl inside my head must be worse on my face.

Christina shoves the tip of her thumb in her mouth and tears at her fingernail, glancing furtively at the door. She's only about thirteen or so. I wonder if someone is waiting for her. Even though this place kind of makes me want to look over my shoulder, at least it's safe from Bashers and Snatchers—for the moment. I don't want to raise any alarms that would get us kicked out before Nicolas gets himself set up with his cousin.

"Christina, are they expecting you somewhere? Is your family here with you?"

Wrong question. Tears gloss over her eyes. The cinnamon smell gives way to a slight aroma of salt and vinegar. "My mother..." she gulps, blinking to keep the tears back, and then wrings her hands, "...my mother was...judged. She wasn't worthy."

"Oh, God! I'm sorry. Was your mother bitten by a ZV? In here?"

"No! Not in here. On the trail...we were running...and the trees...from the trees..." The words fail her; she chokes and sobs, illustrating with her trembling hands the horror of ZVs falling on her mother from the trees. The present slips away from her eyes; fear glazes them over. Her chest flutters, trying to keep up with the air she's gasping. She's gonna pass out.

Springing off the bed, I slide onto the corner of the chair next to her and wrap my arm around her shoulders, petting her black hair the way I do Amber's. At first, she stiffens, but then she turns her head into my shoulder and relives the nightmare through her sobs as I rock her back and forth.

"I'm so, so sorry," I whisper when the moaning subsides into whimpering. "We're a lot alike, you and I, Christina. My mother and I were close too. She was…killed…in a ZV raid on my house."

Sniffing, she shakes her head. "My mother wasn't killed; they took her!" Gazing at the floor as if the scene is playing there in all its terrifying wonder, she stammers, "I screamed…and she yelled, 'RUN,' and I wanted to help, but there was another one…they were chasing us… 'Mom! Mom!' I screamed… 'RUN!' she kept yelling…and they were snarling." A shiver rocks the girl's body as she shakes her head, still not quite ready to believe what she saw and heard. "He carried her away!" Her baby eyes search mine for an explanation, a reassurance she knows isn't there but desperately needs to find. "A big yellow bandana…and a black muscle shirt…he took her."

Miguel, the rapist! The colors: yellow bandana, black muscle shirt. It can't be a coincidence.

"Took her" is so much more horrific than "killed her." The image of being abducted and held for food storage turns my stomach more than the thought of being ripped apart by wolves. I'd rather be dead than hopelessly, mercilessly at someone else's disposal. I've been there, helpless, hopeless, strapped to a table, staring up at blue-gloved hands with scalpels. I'm never going back. The memory makes me forget to comfort Christina for a while.

Her shoulders shiver under my arm. Christina gasps and chokes. I do my best to pull her back into the present. "So, you came here?"

Biting her lip, she grabs onto the emotional life raft I've just tossed her. "No." Wiping her nose, she pushes away the tears. "I'd watched Reverend Knight on TV, but I never really believed any of this was actually happening…until…until…"

I have to squeeze her shoulders to keep her from slipping back into the mire of the memory.

"I didn't go out, I didn't call the police, I didn't answer the phone. I locked the doors, closed all the shutters, and hid in my room. When the doorbell rang, I was too scared to come out. But, somehow Ms. Ashley knew I was in there."

Somehow? Somehow my ass! I'm not buying the Kool-Aid that sweet Reverend Ashley is trying to sell us. This place has something insidious going on. I can smell it.

"She yelled up to my window that the Lord told her what happened to me and sent her to save me from my fear. She's so sweet, and when she talks...I feel so calm, so peaceful." Just talking about the Reverend releases all the worry lines in her face. "Listening to her, I wasn't afraid, so I let her in. And she saved me. She taught me the Word and I'm not afraid anymore. When the Judgment comes, I'll be saved."

Now the kneeling and praying when she was attacked by a ZV starts to make sense.

"So, let me get this straight. When you see a rabid ZV, teeth chomping and blood dripping from its claws, you plan to kneel down and let it bite you?"

Her eyes round out when I put it like that, but she stiffens her shoulders. She folds her arms and looks up at the white plaster on the ceiling. "Yes! I'll be saved because I believe the Word of the Lord's mouthpiece, Ms. Ashley Knight, and I obey. I'll be changed in the twinkling of an eye to a new life where I won't have to be afraid because no one will ever hurt me again."

Poor gullible child! "Sometimes fear is your friend, Christina. Take my advice. You see a ZV, you run."

She doesn't want to believe that. "...though I walk through the shadow of the valley of death, I will fear no evil..." she recites, closing her eyes.

I try to hide my exasperation but a little sigh leaks out. I really want to help this girl. She has no one. Her mother was abducted by ZVs and now she's got herself all tangled up in the web of this crazy cult. She didn't just stumble in here. They went out and got her; Ashley hunted her down. Why?

I can't just leave her to the spiders, but at the same time, do I really want to pop the life raft that's keeping her afloat? What if it's headed towards the rocks?

I'm afraid I'm going to have weave myself into the web if I want her to hear me. "Listen, Christina. I'm a Judge, right?"

She nods doubtfully.

"I'm even one of the four messengers of the Apocalypse sent to Reverend Knight." Her eyes grow wide as my credentials sink in. "Well, this is my message: If you're not going to run, at least be a vegetarian."

Now she looks at me like I'm the crazy one. Maybe I am. I don't have any scientific proof, but so far, I have a 100% accurate theory that the herbivore population resists the virus. Who knows how long you have to have been a vegetarian for it to matter? But, if Christina is hell-bent on letting herself get bit, there's only one thing I can say to help her.

Grabbing her by the shoulders, I twist her around in the chair we're sharing to look me in the eye. She's scared witless. Good! "I don't want you to ever touch a piece of meat again. From now on, all God's creatures are sacred, and you don't eat them. Do you hear me?"

She nods quickly, holding her breath.

Just to be sure—and maybe for a little drama—I tack on, "If you even think about nibbling on a piece of animal flesh, when the Judgment comes, I promise you, you will be eaten alive." I'm pretty sure I can guarantee that if a rabid ZV doesn't fulfill my prophecy, the virus will.

And then things get really awkward when she slides off the chair, kneels at my feet again and says, "I promise. Save me, Lord."

Maybe I've been a pariah for too long, but this falling down and worshiping thing is worse than screaming and running. Jumping out of my seat, I reach down and haul her up to her own two feet. "Christina, stop doing that! You're all alone, now. You have to take care of yourself. No one can save you but you. Learn how to fight! Learn how to run! Stop following."

Her mouth drops open. I must sound totally insane to her. Throwing my hands up, I pace the room until my brain figures out what to tell her.

"Look! Stop letting other people tell you they can save you! They can't. Listen to what they say and make your own plans. Trust yourself."

Sitting on the bed in front of her, I grab her hands and look up into her eyes. "I'm not dying from the virus, neither is my friend Greyson. We don't know for sure, but we think that the only thing we had in common was that we were both vegetarian. I've seen a couple more cases like me and they were all vegetarians. We resist devouring people's organs and stick with animals. My friend Chase was like us until he got angry and started snacking on human livers. After that, he went downhill fast. Dr. Vadlamani is researching the reasons why, but for now, that's the best advice I can offer you."

"So, I have to stop eating meat so I'll be ready for the Judgment?"

Exasperation seeps out my nose. She really just wants someone else to tell her what to do. "No! Look inside. Do you really believe deep down that God sent this virus to separate the evil from the good? Personally, I think that's ridiculous because I just met the ZV that took your mom, and he's just like me and Greyson, but he definitely wasn't good. If it helps you not be afraid, and that's all you care about, then believe it. But if you can learn to live with the chaos, you can make your own choices about what you believe, and maybe you'll decide..."

My rant gets cut off mid-sentence when my ZV hearing picks up a very muffled screaming trickling in from the 4 inches of open window. Peering into the darkness I ask, "Did you hear that?"

She glances anxiously at the door, self-conscious like she's not supposed to be here. "I better go..."

She backs apologetically away, her hands slipping out of mine. "I promise I won't eat any meat..." As I shake my head, she pushes on the broken knob and slips out the door. She just doesn't get it. Oh well, if the virus acts the same with someone who has just become vegetarian as it does with someone who has always been vegetarian, at least when she lets Ashley talk her into letting a ZV "judge" her, maybe she'll turn out like me. That's better, isn't it?

The faint screaming, followed by almost imperceptible whimpering, draws me shivering to the window. I've heard screaming like that before, as I watched the slow, painful, ripping of organs out of the still living. The worst part of the sound is not the revulsion that wrenches my guts; it's the attraction to the kill that slithers up inside of me.

Looking out, I recall again that when Brother Jacob locked me up in here, he broke his silence long enough to tell me how privileged I was to get a room with a "great view of the sidewall on the Hall of the Judges."

Of course, that's where my eye travels first, not just because that's what Jacob said, but also because there's a bulky, black silhouette of a man loitering at that corner. A little flame sparks to life in his hand, lighting up the red end of a cigarette. With my ZV night vision and the help of the burning butt, I can see the shadow is Brother Jacob. He must be standing guard. For what?

The red embers flicker through the shadows of the trees between here and there as he takes a drag. When he drops the cigarette, he holds it at an odd angle behind him. I survey the area, connecting the dots between the screams I heard and the hints he was obviously dropping, but don't see anything. When I refocus on his face, the whites of his eyes bore through the crack in the curtains into mine. He knows I'm watching. I think he was counting on it.

Raising his hand, like he's going to take another drag, he stops, focuses on my window again, and then flicks the cigarette to the ground. Is he trying to say something or is he just worried because I caught him smoking?

He strides over to where the butt landed. My eyes follow. I can see the red glow in the dirt. But that's not what I'm interested in anymore. Behind Brother Jacob's foot, at the level of the foundation, is a grated window about two feet long and maybe eight inches wide. His toe finds the smoldering flame and smashes it out as he peers back up at my window.

Silent boy just spoke. There's something about that grate and he wants me to know what.

I jerk away from the window and gasp when I hear the faint brush of wood on wood as the door opens behind me. Standing in the open doorway, her thick black hair and red lips a distinct contrast to the stark white plastered all over the room, the Reverend Ashley Knight frowns at me.

Chapter 17

The frown disappears under Ms. Knight's serene hostess mask, so I throw on my grateful guest face to counter.

"Did I startle you?"

That was the point, wasn't it? "I was just getting some fresh air. The courtyard is lovely."

"It brings moments of," she drawls, strolling past me to the window, "solace and comfort to those that have lost loved ones to the First Judgment." Peering through the pane, she rotates her head from side to side, checking out my view and breathing deeply the smoky crisp scent of winter coming.

"Like Christina?" My slight mocking of her innocent, church girl voice may not have been as subtle as I intended.

Turning, she stares me down, and then her lips curl up like petals blooming on a grey day. "Poor child. Her mother never came back so we can only assume the worst—she was unworthy. Such a shame." She bows her head.

"How can you…?" Indignation that she could manipulate a poor, innocent little girl like Christina by telling her that her mother was a sinner because a depraved ZV abducted her boils over inside me.

She cuts me off. "I understand there's a problem with your door?"

I have to remember to play nice; my claws are starting to show. "Oh, that. Don't worry about it."

"We feel a sacred obligation to ensure the peace and safety of each member of the flock." It sounds like she's concerned for my safety but I know she's wondering if the beast behind my purple eyes can be tamed.

"Believe me, I can take care of myself, and I won't be feasting on your flock. I stick to animal organs." Nodding toward the kidneys on the soap dish I thank her for her hospitality.

"You're quite welcome. I understand that you delivered your holy message to Christina. I must admit, at first, I was quite astonished since the Lord has always chosen to speak His word to me, but then I remembered the scripture, 'from the mouths of babes'."

"Excuse me? My holy message?" My eyes and forehead crinkle up in confusion.

"Yes. You are the rider of the black horse."

My mind searches frantically through all my Sunday School files for what the apocalyptic black horse meant.

Pleased that I'm at a loss, Ashley supplies the scripture verbatim, "'I looked, and there before me was a black horse! Its rider was holding a pair of scales in its hand. Then I heard what sounded like a voice among the four living creatures, saying, 'A quart of wheat for a day's wages, and three quarts of barley for a day's wages, and do not damage the oil and the wine!'"

Oh God! Now I see it. I just told Christina not to eat meat. The revelation says only wheat and barley, and oil and wine.

"The authorities have always interpreted the black horse as bringing famine," she continues, gloating, "but you have brought us clarity, the judgment of the balances will be determined by those who hearken and do not hearken to the message of the black horseman."

Exasperated, I sigh, my head tilting back so I can contemplate the blank slate of the ceiling that has no answer for this madness. "It's only a theory. Nicolas hasn't confirmed anything yet."

More subtle screaming and moaning seeps out of the Hall of the Judges, crescendos, and dies. Ashley doesn't flinch. Most likely, I'm the only one that can hear it.

"We don't need numbers and theories from science when we have the Holy Word of prophecy."

"But I'm no prophet."

She humors my denial with a silent smile. "Rest well in the peace of the Lord."

She flips off the lights, still smiling serenely, and slips out the door. The girl is totally out in space.

Falling back on the cushy white mattress, frustrated—and most probably bored—I close my eyes, just for a second, wondering what the hell is going on here in the Institute for the Religiously Insane. Somewhere along the winding trail of my thoughts, I slip into a deep cavern of sleep.

The red glare of 4:01 a.m. accosts my eyes when they pop open. Where the hell am I? The white curtains, the white walls, the white sheets and blankets all float slowly back into existence. And trailing on their fine, clean threads is the smell, Sam's smell, only much stronger and tinged with a hint of ZV Supreme which means that unless they're hiding a mutant ZV collection here, Greyson's not too far away. Come to think of it, I've never really noticed much of a ZV Regular smell here. The gates of heaven don't seem to be welcoming the organ munching, brain dead brothers and sisters into the flock.

Since I never bothered to undress, I roll off the bed and wind my hair into a nice tight knot as I peer out the window. I didn't expect to see him, but Brother Jacob isn't hanging about the Hall of Judges anymore. An orchard of trees between my window and the Church casts a thick mob of shadows in the faded light of the courtyard lamps. I can't really see anything, but I can smell that Greyson's down there.

I really want him to be down there. I want him to have sneaked away from Ms. Ashley to find me. I need him on my team. A slight breeze shifts and morphs all the black shapes below. Even with my ZV night vision, I can't spot him. Why doesn't he just toss a pebble up or whistle or something? He probably doesn't know which room they assigned me or maybe there's a guard just out of view of my window. A place like this doesn't let the sheep wander off. I'll have to go down there.

As I turn, the corner of my eye catches a flash of color. Spinning back to the window, I scan the spot but find nothing but trees and shadows of trees. I know I saw it, over by the edge of the orchard closest to the Hall of the Judges. It was yellow, bright enough to see even if I weren't a predator. Although in this darkness, it might have been green shimmering yellow in the lamplight. But it's gone now.

The plate of bovine innards calls to me from the bathroom. Astonished at how hungry I am after just a couple hours of sleep, I tear off a little morsel of heart and pop it in my mouth before slowly turning the knob on the door. Heart definitely is not my favorite—kind of tough. It seems a little dried out and crunchy around the edges for just sitting out for less than a night. I'd expect that in Salt Lake where it's so dry, but here in Houston, my aunt can leave cupcakes uncovered on the kitchen table and they're still moist in the morning.

Chewing quietly, I poke my nose out. The hallway is empty. Surprising. I thought for sure Ashley would post a guard outside my door until they could fix the lock. The exit stairway is the door next to my room. No windows.

At the bottom of the stairs, the exit door has no window. An armed disciple could easily be standing guard on the steps.

Turning the knob, I wait for some response and then pull the door open a tad. The breeze snakes through the small crack and tells me there's no game out there, only predators. "Greyson," I hiss, peering into the thick hedge of bushes that lines the dorm. No answer. In case I'm upwind from a guard just around the other side, and Greyson's freaking that I made noise, I slip out, edge toward the corner, and lean around. Behind the dorm, there's a nice sidewalk bordered by a ten-foot stretch of grass. Beyond the lawn, I can make out the shadows of a slide and swing set with some kind of treehouse climbing wall. No sign of an armed guard. Very bizarre. When I start thinking about it though, I figure it's not all that strange. If I knew there were rabid ZVs on the premises, I think I'd probably be inclined to stay in my room at night. Fear guards the flock here.

The bushes rustle behind me and I breathe a sigh of relief, as the *parfum de Greyson* wafts up. Smiling, I begin to turn around, when a muscle-bound arm wraps itself around my neck and drags me backward off the steps.

"Nice to see you again, Zeta Bitch," the voice behind my ear growls.

It's Miguel. That explains the flash of yellow and the smell of mutant ZV. Sucks for him because he never had after school Karate 101. If he had, he'd have known the first move they taught us was how to escape a chokehold.

Grabbing his arm with both hands, I tuck my head into the crook of his elbow while shrugging my shoulders. Leaning forward, I wrap my right leg around his, trapping his calf, then spin 180° and pull him across my body. He's totally not ready for my defense. Slow learner, this one. He should have figured out what I can do when we fought in the woods. After jamming my left elbow into his windpipe, I swing my leg around, catch his ankles with my foot and knock him flat on his back. His skull thuds against the cement steps, and he groans. I back off.

"Didn't you and I already have this conversation earlier tonight?" I'm sucking air and forcing myself to refrain from stomping on his face. "What the hell are you doing here?"

Spitting blood, he wipes his mouth and snarls, "Miguel doesn't answer to white zeta bitches like you."

Okay, I've taken about all the virus can stand from this tool. Shifting my weight left, I pull my right leg back to speak to him in the only language he can understand—a foot in his mouth.

Behind me, around the corner, twigs snap and boots squelch in the moist dirt of the flowerbeds that surround the building. Finally, Her Reverence's soldier boys are getting around to doing their job.

I've spent so much time roughing up big dumb Snatchers and military chauvinists that underestimate me upfront once they get a look at the hair, that I forget that Miguel is one of us ZVs. The encroaching guard distracts me for a second and Miguel seizes the opportunity to flip himself up and leap away. Miguel is a bigger threat than the unsuspecting holy warrior coming after us around the bend, so I lunge after my ZV nemesis, but faceplant empty-handed in the dirt when combat boy tackles me from behind.

Normally tossing him off would be no problem, especially if the crowd of scrawny boys in camouflage that escorted us in here were a good sample of the Church of the Firstborn's finest. One sniff tells me I'm not dealing with an ordinary machine gun disciple. I've got another mutant ZV on my back; he smells just like Greyson and Miguel. That must be what Ashley is up to; she's not just recruiting her own little army like Chase, she's recruiting officers to command it.

As I scramble to roll over to my stomach so I can kick this guy off of me, Miguel crashes away through the bushes growling, "I know where you live, bitch." He needs some new vocabulary.

The guy on my back grabs my wrist as I roll between his legs so I slam my elbow right in his groin. "Shit!" he backs away, doubled over, as I flip my hair out of my face.

"Greyson!" All the adrenalin escapes in a rush with a sigh.

"Ev! What the hell are you doing out here in the middle of the night?"

Squinting in the shadows I lean back on my elbows. "What am I doing here? Well, let me tell you. Somebody had to get busy figuring out what these crazies are up to because you're too busy getting busy with Ms. Ashley."

The acid shooting off my tongue doesn't burn the target the way I hoped it would. "Jealous there, Ev?"

"Should I be?"

He just shakes his head and grunts, pulling himself upright. "I never really figured you for the insecure type."

I'm not the insecure type. "You seem to be getting pretty cozy with Her Worship. Have you joined up already? Nice camo." The familiar clomp of boots came from the nice little uniform Greyson's been issued.

"What's up with you?" He frowns at the toxic aftertaste of my sarcasm.

"Oh, nothing. I'm just being attacked by a ZV rapist while you're making a play for Ms. Ashley."

"ZV Rapist? That was Miguel?"

"I told you. You should have put him out of commission when you had the chance. But, don't worry about it." Of course, just saying that tells him he should worry about it. "Like you said, I can handle myself. Didn't want to interrupt your little date."

Greyson squints at the remark, but he's more pissed about Miguel. Looking out through the bushes, hoping to maybe still catch a glimpse of yellow, he swears. "I'm going to have to do that kid some damage."

Shaking his head, he turns back and reaches out a hand to haul me up. "And there was no 'date.' How many times do you want me to tell you this? Everything I do is about you. I'm in there kissing up to the crazy girl to make sure Nicky gets what he needs and Holland's Snatchers don't get their hands on your tight little ass in the meantime. Besides, I've spent the last twenty-four hours or so sleeping off that spiked tea our holy hostess fed us."

I take his hand to pull myself up, but he can tell by the way my brow is all scrunched up that I'm not convinced. "Twenty-four hours? We've been asleep that long?"

"Yeah! It's Christmas Eve. Merry Christmas, baby!" He yanks on our linked hands, crashing me into his chest. "Shit, Ev! Every thought I have finds its way back to you somehow. You eat at my brain all day and all night. Hell, you're the reason I'm out here right now. My ZV superpowers picked up screaming so I broke out of my stateroom in the Ashley mansion to make sure they weren't keeping me sedated while they outfitted you for another stay at the Institute."

Honestly, it's totally impossible to look into the golden-brown of Greyson's eyes and not be swallowed up by the intensity there. He's got his fork buried deep in the middle of me, the last filet mignon, rare and juicy, on a grill surrounded by a horde of ravenous Boy Scouts hot off the hike. All the irritation melts away in his arms. My fingers find his neck, brushing the lawn of spindly shoots sprouting where the soft curls used to bounce. The camo cap he's wearing made me forget it was ever gone.

And then his lips find the tenderness in mine, and it doesn't matter anymore, none of it. Miss Ashley and her entire Church of the First-Born melt away. My pulse races; my breath comes too fast for my lungs. Every cell ignites at Greyson's touch. The animal instincts rumble between us. Maybe he's right. Maybe in the world that's coming, in this race to adapt to the rules of the virus, Greyson and I are the future.

"You're a terminal illness, Greyson." Catching my breath, I break away, dropping my head onto his chest.

"But I'm also the cure." He tangles his fingers in my hair and kisses the top of my head, breathing me in. "When will you start believing me when I tell you I love you? Only you.

Always. Even when you don't think I do. I've got your back, baby."

With Greyson, it's not my back I'm worried about; it's my heart. I turn away, embarrassed? scared? overwhelmed by his honesty? You tell me. "You heard the screaming too?" I don't want to—I'm not really able to—dissect the emotion. Too many hormones and foreign bodies rule my bloodstream and send mixed messages to my brain.

"Yeah. Reverend Ashley was preaching the word to me. She wants me to share a little of my ZV love with her congregation. The girl is obsessed with the virus. She thinks if I bite them, it'll separate the good from the evil, bring immortality to the good, and the hell of a zombie existence to the bad. Seriously, to her, I'm the hand of God."

Convincing Greyson he's God's gift to mankind is definitely not a hard sale. I'm starting to understand his attraction to Ashley. "You're not actually going to do it, right?"

"I can see why she'd want to take her chances." He shrugs, considering the possibility. "Face it. The war is coming. You and I, we're the winning team. Why wouldn't they want to join up?"

Unbelievable! My foot recoils into the crunching leaves below us as I shove his chest away. "Greyson, people could die!"

His hands go up, his palms flying open. "I thought you just told them all to be vegetarian." He totally can't figure out why I'd be upset that he plans to infect a couple hundred of Reverend Ashley's lambs.

"I did. But we don't know for sure that's how it works. How did you know that, anyway?"

"Travis, Ashley's main soldier boy, came in and whispered in her ear. Then she starts spouting a bunch of crap about you delivering your divine message through the mouths of babes."

"The mouths of hidden mic's, more likely. They must have this whole place under surveillance. Which makes me wonder why they didn't catch a glimpse of Miguel. I mean, if they knew there was a mutant ZV wandering around here, you'd think they'd send some disciples with guns, even if they were planning to invite him to stay."

"Unless they already have."

"I thought about that too. Do you think Ashley is assembling her own personal Zion's ZV Army?"

"It's possible; with my help, she could make her own soldiers."

"I can't believe you're seriously buying into her BS."

"I didn't say I was."

"You didn't say you weren't either." The only response I get out of him is a quick little bounce of his eyebrows. "I know reading isn't your thing, but have you ever heard of 'The Man Who Would Be King'?"

"Nope."

"It doesn't end well for the guy who wants to play god."

"Who's playing?"

Sighing, I shake my head. Greyson is never going to get this. I can see it in his face. I'm never going to convince Superboy that what he is, is not what everyone else wants to be. And in the end, that's what draws me to him—the casual self-confidence that shrugs off the horde of frown-faced conformists that I still feel the need to stare down.

Because of Greyson, I don't see myself as a monster anymore, but I'm no ZV goddess either. "Forget it. Let's just figure out why Miguel was slithering around in the dark. We ought to know what we're signing up for before we get sucked into the hive. It can't be a coincidence that he was lurking in the bushes about the same time we heard the screaming."

"It was pretty faint, almost like it was underground, but I figured it was coming from the Hall of the Judges."

"It was louder for me; my room is just up there." I point out the second-floor window above the trees.

Greyson takes my hand and we rustle to the edge of the bushes. The glow of the courtyard night lamps reaches the corner where my escort Brother Jacob was standing earlier. "See that tiny window? About the time I heard the screaming, the soldier that brought me here was standing right there." Kneeling down to stay in the cover of the leaves, I point across the orchard. "He lit a cigarette and tossed it right at that little window without even smoking it. I couldn't squeeze a word out of him the whole way up to my room, but then, when he was ready to leave, he made a point of telling me that he knew I was one of the mutant ZVs and that my window had a nice view of the Hall of the Judges. He was either really socially awkward, or he was definitely trying to tell me something that he didn't want the mics to pick up."

Greyson crouches next to me. The gritty brim of his camo cap brushes my temple. "Isn't that where they took Sam?"

"Yeah. You don't think…?"

We're both wondering if all the excitement from the chase in the woods brought on one of Sam's little "episodes"—thus the screaming.

"Who knows?" Greyson slides slightly ahead of me, pokes his head into the open, and scans the courtyard. "The way he went after Amber, I wouldn't put it past him to skip dinner and go straight for a little disciple dessert." He takes a whiff of the air. "The smell of these people reminds me of my grandma's homemade wheat bread, dripping with butter."

"That's another thing I've noticed." I venture out next to him to get a better whiff. "The smell. Really suck it in."

Greyson raises an eyebrow and then sticks his nose up, nature's new bloodhound hunting. At the Hall of the Judges, he picks up the scent and sniffs again. "Old blood. Gone bad. Someone left their ZV out on the counter a little too long."

"Do you recognize it? You've smelled it before."

"If you're trying to get me to say out loud that it smells like you, I'm not going there. Besides, it smells more like Sam than you."

"Exactly. Glad you noticed."

Grinning, he nuzzles the top of my head. "You smell the best after you've been running. Reminds me of horseback riding in the canyon by the river."

"So, what are you saying? I smell like a sweaty horse?"

"Delicious."

"You're sick."

"So are you."

Rolling my eyes, I get the train back on the tracks. "The odor hangs on the air. Sam's only been here for a few hours. It took that long for it to fill the car."

Greyson bends his head to look in my eyes. "They've got another one like him here?"

"Don't you remember? Ashley didn't even blink when we told her about Sam's 'condition'. She said he wasn't the first of his kind to seek asylum with the Church of the Firstborn. They've got another one of them in here."

Greyson sniffs again, "At least one. How is that possible? I assumed he was different because he caught the virus from the source before it had a chance to mutate in the rest of us."

"I don't know. But Nicolas needs to know about this, and we need to get a peek into that room."

Shifting on his knees, Grey glances back to the porch showered in yellow light. "We don't want to get caught snooping around. Ashley's crazy, and her boys have guns. Let's play her little game. I know my way around girls like her."

"I bet you do."

He grins shamelessly.

"Watch out, baby." I stand up. "I'd lay pretty good odds she knows her way around guys like you." Bending over, I let my lips brush his forehead before I disappear through the shrubs to the back exit of my dorm.

Chapter 18

The church bells wake me up, but the timid tapping at the door drags me out of bed. Squinting at the red digits 8 0 0 on the alarm clock, I figure I slept another 3 hours. Oh, God, these are crack of dawn Christians.

"Ms. Evelyn," tap, tap, "it's Christina. Would you like to come down to the dining hall for breakfast? We're having a special Christmas Eve service afterward."

The decorations are everywhere, but I just haven't really caught the Christmas Spirit yet. I can smell Christina's sticky bun aroma wafting through the crack beneath the door. The cow guts are still sitting on the counter in the bathroom. I shove one in my mouth, just to be safe. Pulling back the chain, I open the door.

Christina gasps a little and then sinks to one knee with her hands folded and her head bowed.

"Stop doing that," I growl at her, which probably doesn't help. "Whatever the Reverend told you, she's wrong."

She struggles to her feet. "You mean the Lord wants me to eat meat now?"

"No!" This is exasperating. "I thought we went through this last night. There's a chance the virus reacts to vegetarians differently than it does to meat-eaters. If you're really going to follow these people off the cliff, you'd better have a parachute. But, I'm telling you, Christina, walk away. Get out of this place."

"I want to obey." Her big brown eyes cloud up and plead with me. "But I can't go out there. It's…it's…they took her…"

I'm a jerk. It's 8:00 o'clock in the morning—give me a break. "It's okay, sweetie." Throwing my arm around her, I pat her shoulder and give in to the game. "Just don't eat the bacon."

She nods and hands me a little wad of neatly folded white clothes. It's some underwear, a white tunic style dress, and a little white sweater. I'm not really into the post-apocalypse neo-polygamist style, but since I've been wearing these jeans for a while now, I imagine they're pretty ripe.

Holding the drab dress up to my chin, I ask, "Does it come in green?"

Of course, Christina thinks I'm serious. "We only…I could ask…"

"White is great!" Slipping into the bathroom, I wriggle out of my jeans and slide the clean stuff on, noting with a huge grin that the stab wound on my leg is now a tiny pink trickle through a round human-colored oasis on my zombie tinted leg. Unfortunately, my white dress seems to make the grey and purple in my skin pop.

Slipping into the little white flats, that look more like ballet slippers than shoes, I breathe a sigh of relief that I have long legs and can pull this ensemble off. I fill the tub with some water and a little of the shampoo, dunking my clothes and swishing them around in the suds. The smell of spring flowers invades the bathroom. Even if they have a laundry service here, I'm not letting my jeans fall into the wrong hands. I'd never see them again.

There's a little drawer in the bath with a toothbrush, toothpaste, and—a brush! I don't have to wash my hair all that much, because the virus doesn't bother producing oils for it. Once I've parted it to cover my small shaved spot, that is now displaying a lovely, carpet of hair sprouts, I brush it to a nice shine. It's pretty safe to say my body is getting plenty of protein. Before leaving the bathroom, I toss my street clothes, still dripping, over the shower curtain rod. Their dark, rigid stiffness gashes the flowing, white serenity of the room.

My makeover manages to wring a minuscule smile out of Christina. "You have really pretty hair." She can't quite keep herself from petting it.

We stroll out toward the big church. In the daylight, the Hall of the Judges wall with the small grill window winks harmlessly at us. We follow the sidewalk past the grove of trees and double back on the other side toward the courtyard.

Inside the church, the enormous chapel lies through the double doors straight ahead, but off to the right, behind a smaller set of double doors, a large assembly room beckons us with Christmas Eve breakfast all laid out on long tables decorated with white tablecloths and little holly garland centerpieces. The merry pine boughs, wreaths, bells, and stars spreading their Christmas cheer across the room totally erase the encroaching grey tide of the Apocalypse outside. No wonder people are flocking here.

I thought this only happened in movies, but when I walk in the door ahead of Christina, the whole place falls silent. All the eyes hit the doorway, or more specifically, me, and my lovely, greyish purple complexion.

Not that I haven't had my share of people watching me and applauding. I lettered in track as a sophomore. But when the stands were full of cheering spectators, I was focused; the adrenaline fueled the race. I could funnel the nervous pressure of the chanting faces into speed. Here, there's nowhere to run.

I'm looking for somewhere to hide when a tide of women, in all shapes and sizes of white, engulfs me. They all drop to their knees; those in front start kissing my shoes, the hem of my dress, and tips of my fingers. "Thank you! Thank you for bringing your message of salvation!" A few tears drip onto my foot. Running from ZV bashers and their bats is one kind of creepy, but this is a whole new level. I'd have to say being adored makes my skin crawl just as much as being abhorred—two sides of the same coin.

Finally, Greyson, seated at the front of the room, on a raised dais, before a gigantic white screen, catches my eye. He's chilling in an all-white suit, grinning next to Ashley, whose dress, by the way, is a whole lot classier than anyone else's—some lacey, partly sheer, clingy number with a very low-cut neck. I can even see the white tips of some stiletto pumps peeking at me from under the tablecloth up there. It's been a while since I wore heels.

The love and adoration make me teeter like I'm on the top of a narrow little pedestal and the ground beneath won't stop shaking, but Greyson thinks the whole ZV worship gig is hilarious. Just under the thin mask of mocking, though, there's a glint of power hunger in his eyes. I think it's the way his eyebrows are slanting, or maybe I'm still getting used to the Greyson sans hair. But seriously, he looks a little puffed up in his chair at the top of this whacked-out world.

The Reverend Ashley stands up and puts an end to the worship session. "Brothers and Sisters, we wish to welcome among us the Rider of the Black Horse of the Apocalypse, a true messenger of the Lord. Sisters, please take your seats."

While the crowd wanders obediently back to their tables, Christina ushers me to a chair on the stage, on Ashley's left hand, away from Greyson. That doesn't stop him from leaning over and winking at me. I really don't think he has a clue about how seriously demented these people are.

Gazing out at the sea of upturned faces, I notice a disturbing pattern. There are no older people in the crowd. Most of the men and women range from about early twenties to maybe thirty. The room buzzes a little with the constant motion of kids. Half the diners at the tables are Christina's age or younger. Judging by the size of the room and the number of tables, a rough guestimate puts the strength of Ashley's congregation at about 500 or more souls.

The voice of the Reverend sings out, "The Word of the Lord has come! Just as the Jews celebrated the Passover before the final hour of sacrifice, we, the children of the Church of the Firstborn, will heed the words of the messenger riding the Black Horse and refrain from all meat until the Day of Judgment. That day is coming and will soon be upon us. Let us be prepared to stand before the judgment bar. If we do not fear, then, as in the words of Isaiah the prophet, chapter 49 verse 19, his name will be 'written...on the palms of [our] hands. Always in [our] mind...'

"By the 'sword of his mouth'..." She flutters her lily-white hand toward Greyson. The lights dim on cue, and behind us, a larger than life projection of him in his white suit towers over the stage. "...this messenger will print in blood upon our hands the mark of salvation. The righteous and obedient sheep will be made strong and incorruptible to inherit the earth after it is laid waste. The wicked goats will rot in their excess, consumed by the fire within."

"Lord save us!" The congregation clasps their hands and shouts in unison.

In a clip from the news, a small herd of brain-dead ZVs shambles down a forgotten highway strewn with burned-out vehicles and blocked by collisions. In the distance, the wreck of a small plane spews smoke over the road.

The adults who don't have the right hormone soup to accommodate the virus die fast, faster than they can get to a hospital with all their organs still whole, but apparently not faster than they can get their teeth into a couple good human steaks. Every mouth in the gang is smeared with the juicy remains of their last human kabob.

The dangling shin of the leader finally rips and sloughs off as he drags it across the asphalt. A couple of ZVs in the middle crash forward, jerking to a wrenching, gut-churning death as their peers trample mindlessly over them. The whole group, their faces gashed, semi-severed limbs barely clinging to bloody tendons, their clothes tattered and blood-soaked, could easily make the cover of Cosmo: Horror Edition.

"The world beyond the gates of our holy city is falling to flames and demons. The wicked are burning…"

"Lord have mercy!" rises up from the auditorium.

Another newscast begins to play. Craning my neck, too close to the screen behind me, I can barely decipher the footage of bodies being decontaminated with flamethrowers. The anger of injustice, the fear of burning, and the despair of loss flood my chest. For a second, I bury my eyes in my hand, but that only shifts the scenery to shadowed pictures of Krystal, Chase's niece, her little body engulfed in flames. I want to get up and run out, hide from the nightmare that will never fade, but there's nowhere to go.

The report shifts to aerial shots of Dallas, Los Angeles, Salt Lake City—entire neighborhoods choked in smoke.

"We will not burn! The Children of the Firstborn will rise up triumphant, reborn. We will partake of the balm sent to us by the messenger of the White Horse. No longer will the chosen righteous fear the wounds of the sword or the decay of this world. The people of the church will be victorious and vanquish all death and decay."

"Hallelujah!"

To my utter amazement, the screen shifts to a picture of what can only be the pink scar on my thigh. Even though I know this compound has more surveillance than Big Brother in the Brave New World, seeing my bare skin flaunted on the big screen, in an auditorium packed with people, violates me on so many different levels.

Horror, anger, anxiety—there's too much emotion sloshing around in my blood. The head of the virus rises up in my cells and growls. I have to physically grasp the edge of the starched, white tablecloth to keep myself from diving at Ashley, ripping out her throat and clawing the screen to shreds. Overreaction? I know. I'm a ZV. That's what we do.

But I'm a mutant ZV; I can control the urges. I don't have to give in. We have to give Nicolas time. We have to wait until we have a viable plan B before we torch plan A. So, reigning in my breathing, I grit my teeth and glare at the screen, avoiding, at all costs, eye contact with Greyson.

The torture goes on. "Brothers and Sister! We have been warned. As the word came to the prophet Ezekiel:

The word of the LORD came to me, saying, 'Son of man, I have made you a watchman for the house of Israel; therefore hear a word from My mouth, and give them warning from Me: 18 When I say to the wicked, "You shall surely die," and you give him no warning, nor speak to warn the wicked from his wicked way, to save his life, that same wicked man shall die in his iniquity; but his blood I will require at your hand. 19 Yet, if you warn the wicked, and he does not turn from his wickedness, nor from his wicked way, he shall die in his iniquity; but you have delivered your soul…

'21…if you warn the righteous man that the righteous should not sin, and he does not sin, he shall surely live because he took warning; also, you will have delivered your soul.'

Pausing strategically to survey her minions, Ashley allows the implications of the scripture to sink in. "We shall indeed warn our neighbors." She nods, smiling benevolently, and then turns to shake her finger accusingly at the screen behind her. "Look upon this evil that threatens them. Destruction stalks them like a thief in the night."

153

A news report with a broad red stripe, "Breaking News: Warning! The images in this report may be disturbing," crackles across the screen. At first, I can't tell what's going on and then the announcer tells us a private security system recorded a ZV home attack this morning in broad daylight. The reporter seems a little breathless, standing in front of an abandoned neighborhood. "Early this morning, 911 calls flooded dispatch. ZV gangs mobbed neighborhoods scattered across the county. The County Commissioner called out all available law enforcement and requested assistance from the Governor, but the raids continue unchecked as the Federal Government refuses to send troops beyond the quarantine lines."

The screen shifts to the Police Commissioner. "We just don't have the manpower to cover an emergency like this. The National Guard is already strapped along the borders, but the virus has infiltrated the state. There's nothing we can do. Our men go in and they don't come out."

The scene shifts to the narration of the anchor. The warning wasn't lying. The home security footage is gruesome, but I only cringe for a few seconds because one of the ZVs, in a yellow bandana, chases down a kid that looks about ten years old. The terrified boy bolts right out the front door, but he's not anywhere near fast enough. The ZV doesn't chow down on him when he catches up. Instead, he throws a bag over the head of his prey and tosses him over his shoulder.

The only thing more terrifying than watching a boy snatched right out of his house in the middle of the morning, when he should have been camped out in an armchair, in front his game console, shooting up zombies with his buddies on Blue Tooth, hoping to find the newest version of the game in his stocking tomorrow morning, the only thing more terrifying than that is catching a glimpse of the giant snowman with the creepy Ghostbusters marshmallow, monster grin on the kid's front lawn, between the white Southern mansion columns.

I gasp, sitting bolt upright as synapses in my brain fire, and messages collide. Suddenly my heart is racing and there's not enough air in this crowded meeting hall. My nails dig into the tablecloth.

I know where you live, bitch. That was the last thing Miguel said to me. I thought he meant here, but he didn't. Somehow, he knew where my aunt's neighborhood was. Oh, my God! This is revenge! Oh, my God. I have to warn them. Amber!

My chair clatters to the floor as I shove it back and bolt from the stage. Greyson jumps to his feet. Ashley just keeps going on, a runaway engine speeding down the tracks toward the divine ravine. "For one holy week, this week in which we celebrate the coming of our First Salvation, we will broadcast, proselyte, preach the word and the Gospel of the messengers, gathering in the harvest of the pure, and then, on New Year's Day…"

The double doors slam shut behind me as I race out of the chapel.

Chapter 19

The compound fence looms nine feet above me, only five strides away, when Greyson finally runs me down, grabbing my arm. "Where the hell are you going? I told you! We have to play this game."

Jerking my arm away, I shove a toe in one of the chain-link holes. "Didn't you recognize it? That was THEIR neighborhood!"

"Whose?"

"My Aunt's! I have to warn them." Grabbing hold of the fence, I shove my other foot between the links. "Miguel said, 'I know where you live,' before you tackled me and let him get away last night." Why did I throw in that little piece of info? Because I don't want this to be my fault? Amber, my cousins, my aunt and uncle, it can't be my fault if something happens to what's left of my family, to the people I love. Not again. I can't even think about what "something" is.

I shouldn't have come to Texas. I shouldn't have brought to their doorstep this nightmare that stalks me. But I had to find somewhere safe for Amber. I thought I was doing the right thing. But the right thing and the wrong thing, they're all mixed up now and I can't sort them out.

My family has to be safe. Please let them be safe! I have to get back and warn them. My hands and feet propel me up the gate.

"What makes you think Miguel's going after your aunt's family?" Greyson jumps onto the fence about a foot below me and climbs up beside me.

"The Snowman."

He reaches his arm over. "Seriously, Ev. Are you alright?" He looks like maybe he's worried the virus has gone to my brain. Of course, that would be as tragic for him as it would be for me…I mean, if I'm losing my mind, we're the same, and he will too—eventually.

But I'm not losing my mind. In fact, right about now, the tiny ZV bodies floating in my brain are waking up to a nice adrenaline and hormone shower. "I recognized the house from the Snowman on the news video. It's on the corner at the front of the road in my aunt's neighborhood." I don't bother climbing down; I've jumped farther out of windows. Launching my body away from the metal, I free-fall the last couple of yards. Dirt puffs around my feet as they thump onto the ground, my knees bending to absorb the impact.

The thud beside me is Greyson. "Are you sure? It's Christmas. There are probably hundreds of those on lawns across the state."

"I'm sure." I don't have time to argue. The scenery outside the compound looks a little different than it did at night. The sun is rising over the top of the trees to the east, throwing a golden mist across the woods. I spot the entrance to the trail at about the same time I see dust from a Jeep racing from the compound to the fence.

Greyson follows as I sprint for the break in the trees where the path starts. "You don't have to come with me. You can go back and run your little con. Like you said, 'I can handle myself'."

Trees flash by as I push myself to run faster. My little white commune dress and ballet shoes aren't exactly trackwear, so I hike up the skirt to stretch to a full stride. Amber is at the end of this trail. The only thing standing between her and Miguel's cannibals is me.

Greyson keeps stride with my pace. He's as immune to the venom on my tongue as he is to the virus—they just make him stronger. "I'm only playing that game to keep you somewhere safe. If you're out here, there's really no point in me being in there, is there?"

The virus inside of me is raging, pounding through my tainted blood, screaming in my head. Nothing boils it up more than anger. So, excuse me if I can't stop and get all warm and fuzzy about Greyson.

Pictures of my parents, lying ripped apart on my kitchen floor, images of my brother Cory, shot through the head, a piece of human liver still dripping from his fist onto the Institute floor, they all stab at my brain as I run. As the visions haunt my imagination, I see Amber on the kitchen floor too, where she doesn't belong, mixed in with the blood and the dying. I can't let this happen.

How could I have left her? I could see on the TV that things were so much worse than I thought. I saw the ZV gangs and the quarantines. It looked like the same old war I've been fighting. I just didn't imagine that, even if the tides were turning and the ZVs were winning, the war would reach my aunt's door.

When the trees break into an open field, I can see my uncle's red barn in the distance, but the house is hidden. The pasture glistens tranquilly in the morning sun. That's not a good thing. The horses we borrowed should be out grazing. Maybe they haven't been returned yet. I don't stop running to look in the barn as we round the bend in the path and the pink brick of the house surrounded by its black iron fence appears. My ZV hearing picks up a faint churning squeal, sirens or alarms, coming from inside.

Speeding up a little, like the last 100m of a 400m, the rhythm of my footfalls beat out the thoughts that I can't erase, that keep ringing through my brain. They have to be okay; they have to be okay. This can't be my fault, not again, not again, not again.

If they're not okay—my cousins jumping on the tramp in the cool of the morning, sneaking wild blackberries from the bushes, as my aunt scrambles up a dozen eggs and a side of bacon, Amber playing chase with the Great Dane that's bigger than she is and checking the coop for eggs—I don't know if I can survive.

Please be okay, please be okay. I'm sorry I ever came here, I'm sorry I brought this to your house. I'm sorry. I'm sorry. I'm sorry. Please be okay. By the time we reach the back gate, my chest is constricted around my heart, and tears streak my cheeks.

My hand is on the latch. Greyson grabs it to stop me from yanking it open and puts his finger up to his lips. Oh, God, no!

I can smell the mutant ZV hanging in the air. But that's not all; there's smoke, lots of it. The fire alarm blares.

He nudges me aside. In the backyard, next to the fence, there's a small orchard of fruit trees. The yellowing leaves hang ragged but stubbornly persistent, refusing to fall until the first serious frost of the winter. Peering through the jagged lines of their bony limbs, I can make out a body on the grass between the trees and the swimming pool. My fingers clench, my breath stops, my hand stifles the scream on my lips that can't find enough air to live.

Greyson stretches out the white sleeve of his suit to block me from shoving past him, but I have to know. Ducking under his arm, I sprint into the yard, fading from tree to tree. My nose can't help me. Between the smoke and the heavy scent of ZV, I can't sniff out any trouble before it comes my way. I start wondering if Holland came back here, or if the ZVs are still here, and if they are, whether they're lucid, or ravenously decaying.

Honestly, I don't know if my aunt and uncle are holed up inside with their guns cocked, waiting to shoot anything grey that shambles out of the trees. After all, they're Texans. My Aunt Esther shot a nine-foot snake out of a tree with a .38 Special Revolver with laser pointer. It took her 5 shots and only two actually hit it because she'd never shot a gun before and didn't know about the kick.

If I end up with my aunt's little red laser dot on my forehead, I'll be useless to Amber…but then again, I wouldn't be a danger to the rest of them anymore.

Crouching at the edge of the grove, I'm close enough to see that the body is the remains of a ZV, one that wasn't in very good shape to start with. A hole in its head and a matching bullet gash across his throat ooze purple goo.

My shoulders relax with a sudden surge of hope. "Aunt Esther, Uncle Daren!" I start to run for the house as Greyson slides in behind me and grabs the sleeve of my sweater. Our Church of the Firstborn whites aren't quite splattered enough with dirt to be camouflage. We're pretty visible.

Even though the body sprawled out in front of us is a ZV, we still don't know what we'll find in the house and, whatever it is, it knows we're here. That could be good if it's my aunt wielding her .38 Special with laser pointer from behind the kitchen counter, or not so good if it's Miguel because there's obviously been a ZV invasion here. Between Holland and Miguel, for the sake of my family, I'd choose Holland. He's an asshole, but he won't eat them—at least not literally.

The back door is wide open, which is pretty normal for my aunt's house, but bacon-laced smoke spewing out and a trail of blood smeared across the patio aren't. The blood's not purple blood either. I can't really think about what that means, and making up my own story isn't an option because there aren't any possible endings that don't leave my heart collapsing in on itself.

The dog isn't barking her head off either. She goes wild when the doorbell rings. There's a dead body on the lawn and she's not on her leash; she should be barking the house down. I need to know what's going on here. I really want everyone to be safe, but I can't see that happening.

Greyson guesses at the dramas playing in my head. He braces my shoulders with his arm. "C'mon. Let me go first."

Nodding, because I'm afraid saying something will break the lump in my throat that's damming up all the fear and pain in my chest, I fall in behind him. Half crouched, we cross the lawn, hold up for a minute at the grilled fence around the pool, and then double-time to the patio. On the driveway courtyard, visible through the front gate, my uncle's Mercedes blings pleasantly, informing us that someone has left the door open with the keys in the ignition. Whatever shit happened here, my uncle was on his way out when it erupted. The bloodstain stops at the gate, but there's another body, or at least what's left of one, drying in the sun by the open door of the car.

I almost don't want to look.

"It's not your uncle." Greyson knows what I need to know before I ask. "He's wearing a suit."

"Do you think Holland came back here?" I grasp at any hope that floats by. "He knew I didn't have Amber with me anymore when we showed up at the compound." That could have happened. Holland could have come back here to find

Amber. Maybe the ZVs had it out with the suits. The thought makes me feel sick and better all at the same time.

Greyson shakes his head. He doesn't know any more than I do. He looks like he wished he did. "We've got to go inside. Amber would hide, if…" He doesn't want to go there. "She was hiding when I found her—the first time."

My eyes close, cringing against the reality that my little sister has now been exposed to two gruesome nights of zombie invasions. I can't stop the picture from playing itself out in my head—the screaming, the teeth, the claws, the blood, the running. Even if we figure out a way to jerk this insane world back into something that resembles normalcy, she's never going to recover. A crash inside the house sends a tongue of flame out a shattered window.

"C'mon!" Greyson grabs my hand resolutely because we all know you're not supposed to run into a burning building. "The place is on fire. We have to make sure they're not still in there." We slide along the back wall of the house until he can see through the window in the French doors. Glass crunches beneath our feet, the smoke hovers suspended around the house, a ghostly shroud.

The palm plant inside the door lies sideways, the guts of the pot smattered across the floor. To the right, in the family room, the couch is flaming. Between the charred pot stand and the burning sofa, another body burns. The smell is definitely torched ZV, unmistakable. I've smelled it before, many times. It's pretty obvious what happened here. The ZV went for the bacon, caught fire, and didn't notice until it was too late—one of the drawbacks of deadish skin sensation. He must have got distracted by better menu options in the family room, got shot, and hit the ground by the sofa, lighting the place on fire. The question is, who shot him?

Just above us is the window to Craig's room. Glancing up, I stumble on another possibility. "Maybe the whole family was still at the hospital. My aunt would have packed all the kids into the car to take Craig to the ER."

Greyson nods ambiguously, his lips tight, not wanting to fan the kindling of my optimism—the bigger the flame, the colder the chill when reality douses the hope.

His back plastered against the wall of the house, he leans his nose over into the gaping doorway, a cop scoping out a gruesome crime scene. Crouching low beneath the choking smoke, because ZVs still need air to breathe, Greyson scuttles through the French doors into the kitchen dining room, motioning for me to crouch down behind him.

The chairs are tipped, shoved away, sprawled out chaotically across the floor. I can't stop myself from thinking that one of my baby cousins, or Amber, tried hiding under here. I inch closer. Greyson holds me back with the flat of his palm pressed against the air behind him.

A heavy cloud hangs over the kitchen—most likely eggs and bacon burned to a black pulp. The burner is probably still on, which really doesn't matter now that the family room is a walk-in oven. The alarm beeps and squeals obnoxiously.

Snatchers or no, we have to make sure Amber and my aunt's family aren't anywhere near this place. "Esther! Amber! It's me, Evelyn…I'm with Greyson!" I only hope they can hear me over the crackling of the fire and the blaring of the alarm. The thing is, though, whoever else is lurking in the house knows who and where we are now.

By the way he straps his arm across my chest, pushing me away from the scene in the kitchen, I think Greyson isn't as worried about stumbling into a nest of tranquilizer toting thugs or militant ZVs as he is that I'll get a look at what's really in there.

His head creeps around the corner of the table to see what's behind the counter separating the dining area from the cooking. The pressure of his forearm on my chest forces me back. An overwhelming aroma of charred bacon and sausage suffocates the room. But my ZV senses aren't tingling over bacon. The mouthwatering, "come and get it" smell isn't pork; it's much stronger. Nothing gets me drooling like ripe human organs. I shiver and try to convince myself it's probably another suit. They always come in packs. Greyson has a full-on view of the kitchen now; he's exposed up to his shoulders. No gunfire. No wiz of darts.

"Whatever happened here," he inches closer, "I think it's over. We need to sweep the upstairs for Amber."

"And my..." the smoke gets to me and I cough out, "cousins." My ZV super hearing probes for some minute response to our intrusion—the creak of a board on the steps, a muffled footstep on the carpet, the cock of a gun—but only the quiet ticking of the grandfather clock my aunt inherited from Grandma pecks muffled at the heavy shell of the fire and alarm. Under the circumstances, you'd think it would stop, hold its breath, and wait to see whether or not life should keep going. But it doesn't. It just keeps ticking away, one second, just the same as another.

Even though he's creeping ahead, coughing, Greyson's still trying to hold me back, away from his view of what's behind the counter. What he's forgotten is that I already know what's there because I can smell it as well as he can. The room reeks, a crowed bar of ZVs and mutant ZVs wrapped in a churning, smoky film of human guts.

Crowding Greyson, I press against his hand until the edges of a bloody puddle seeping across the tile assaults my eyes. It's definitely not a ZV and the options of who it could be are shrinking. Elbowing Greyson aside, I lean in for a closer look, my heart pounding out a sinking anthem. This is my fault. This is my fault. I brought this here. I'm no saint—hell follows me wherever I go, ripping apart and devouring everything I love.

A glimpse of the hem of blue scrubs, stained red, chokes me.

Chapter 20

"Uncle Daren!" I gasp, not caring who or what else is in the burning house. Springing across the dining floor to the other side of the counter, I kneel beside his mangled body, struggling to breathe through the sobs.

My uncle took my mutant friends and me in, and what did he reap from his generosity? He's a ZV meal, interrupted and abandoned, propped limply against his kitchen counter, a .45 dangling from the arm that's still there, his guts exposed.

My eyes burn, well up and spill over, stinging my cheeks. "Oh, God, Uncle Daren, I'm so sorry. I'm so sorry." My hands are up; my eyes dart from one bloody mess to the next, not knowing where to start.

My uncle can barely move, there's blood everywhere; he stares glassily at the island counter in front of him. Gasping for air, he rolls his eyeballs toward my voice. "Help them!" It almost kills him to crank those words out, the "m" gurgles and rolls in his throat.

He's dying. Right here, right now. I can't do anything about it. Oh God! I should just die with him. I should have gone to the Institute months ago when they came for me. I should have let them chop me up and study my brain. Then all the people I love would still be alive.

The whole room is murky behind my tears and the smoke, but the wheezing and syncopated gasping from my uncle tells me he's trying to say something else. Swiping at the puddles blocking my vision, I lean forward so he can whisper. His mouth opens, but nothing comes out. His eyes roll up. My breath sticks and throbs in my chest because I love him and he's dying. Greyson figures out what's going on faster than I can and sprints for the stairs before my uncle can exhale, "up…"

His head falls forward, dangling from his neck onto his crimson soaked chest.

Grief smothers my senses until realization rips a hole through the fog of guilt that's blinding me. Greyson has taken off because more of the family must be upstairs in trouble.

I'm only two steps behind Grey, but as my foot hammers onto the upstairs landing, the door to the right down the hall slams shut and the crack of a gunshot splinters the dead stillness. In front of the door, Greyson leaps for a shadowy figure in a yellow Bandana. Their bodies collide, grunting and slamming against the walls. A vase crashes to the wood floor, scattering green glass at my feet on the edge of the stairs.

The two ZV mutants crash against the wall, snarling, a blur of yellow bandana, saggy jeans, and stark white, crew cut. It's definitely Miguel. Growling and grunting, he and Greyson grapple, slamming each other against the walls, pulverizing the drywall and jolting the pictures off their hooks. More glass shatters as the frames hit the floor.

My first impulse is to join in the brawl. Churned up by the anger and grief that have nowhere to go but into my blood, the virus has released the predator, raging and famished into my veins. The fury propels me into the fray, roaring, but Greyson fends me off. "Your Aunt, she's in there…"

Taking advantage of the distraction, Miguel lands his fist squarely on Greyson's jaw. His head jerks back as Miguel breaks free. A new bullet gash swelters across Miguel's right cheek. My aunt must have been clocking some hours at target practice, so he hasn't managed to carry her off already.

I don't need prodding. Greyson can take care of himself against a punk like Miguel. As soon as I get my aunt out of here, away to someplace safe…someplace safe; where is that?

The gunshot I heard must have blown the gaping jagged hole in the first door past the landing—Craig's room.

I spring for the handle, yelling, "Esther, it's me, Evelyn. Don't shoot!" Throwing the door open, and ducking inside, I smash into Craig. Esther is sitting on the floor, directly in front of the window, her .38 Special with laser pointer targeting the door.

"Get him out! Get him out!" She flips her gun wrist frantically in the general direction of her son. Tears, sweat, and dirt stain her face, scrunched up in pain. Blood gushes around a ragged bone shard protruding from a gaping rip in her left shin. Her blood laces the smoke saturated room with a bitter iced tea tang.

Thank God! Esther's leg is broken but she hasn't been bitten!

Greyson's never let me down, but I'm not willing to stake my aunt's life on him handling Miguel. Rushing to her side, I slide my arm around her back.

"No! No! Leave me, Evelyn. I'll manage on my own. All that matters now is getting Craig out. Take him to the hospital."

"I'm not leaving you here. The house is on fire. You won't make it out like this!"

The tangled mess of Miguel and Greyson crosses the open doorway. My aunt's hand shivers as she raises the gun to her knee and fires. The air cracks and shudders as the bookcase behind the ZVs explodes in a storm of shattering glass and ceramic. "Listen to me, Evelyn," she gasps. "Just get Craig to the hospital." Her eyes cinch and her face convulses, sweat drips from her forehead, soaking her bangs. Speaking is painful...or maybe this is what it looks like when a mother faces losing her child. "Holland has Amber."

"What?" It wasn't supposed to be this way. I left to protect my little sister, to keep my aunt and her family safe. This is all wrong.

"They came to the hospital while Craig was in for the bullet wound. Holland said he would get us out, up to Montana with Aunt Rebecca, if you were willing to help him. He was holding the girls there while we came back to pack a few things." She takes a deep breath, swallowing some of the pain, and licking her parched lips. "He said he was going to keep Amber if you refuse."

The first thought through my head is that they want me to hand Greyson over to them. I can't—I can't choose between Greyson and Amber. But what about my aunt's kids? They have no father now because of Greyson and me.

God! Greyson should have stopped Miguel when he had the chance. Now he's going to have to kill him anyway. If he'd just shot the asshole mutant in the first place my uncle and aunt would still be alive and well and living in paradise.

Outside in the corridor, Greyson flies past the doorway, grunting. Miguel stomps past in pursuit. Rolling and landing on all fours, Greyson vaults forward, smashing his head into Miguel's chest, driving both bodies back down the hall.

"We can't worry about that now, Esther. I'm getting you both out of here!" Craig is clinging to my arm. Usually, he likes to play the tough, cool cowboy, but that was before he was shot in the middle of the night, and then stalked by ravenous, flesh-eating ghouls. About now he just wants to latch onto someone bigger and stronger and get the hell out of Dodge.

The walls shudder in the next room. "Shit!" Greyson moans.

Miguel answers with, "God damn ZV gringo!" The wall between us shakes again to the tune of muffled growling. On our side of it, Craig's poster of Tiger Woods crashes to the floor, the black frame splintering.

I anchor my free arm underneath Esther's knees.

"You can't carry me, Ev. I'm out of your weight range. Please, just take Craig! He's all that matters now."

"Don't listen to her. She can't even walk." Craig's eyes bore into mine. "I'll help. Here," he leans down reaching with his good arm, the one without the bandage. "I'll help you lift her up. She can hop between us. We'll be faster like that."

"No, it's okay Craig, I got this. Majority rules, Esther. You forgot I have ZV predator strength now. I'm more of a leg girl than an arm girl, but I can fake it in a pinch." My aunt wraps her arms around my neck. She grimaces and groans, tears pooling in her eyes, as I hoist her up. The .38 Special clatters to the floor in front of the dresser. "Stay right behind me, Craig. I'm counting on you to keep up." As if I needed to prod him.

In the next room, books hammer heavily onto the floor, maybe a chair snaps—I guess it could be bones—I can only hope they're Miguel's. At the end of a long stream of grunting and huffing, with a deep, resonating crash, glass—that can only be the window—shatters. It doesn't take ZV hearing to recognize the thud on the patio below. One of the mutant ZVs has tossed the other out the window. The question is, which one?

The doors to the two rooms are right next to each other. Smoke hovers between them, slithering in through the open archways. Racing out into the alarm drenched hall—well, not really racing, I'm carrying my aunt in my arms and my cousin is clinging to the skirt of my dress—I crane my neck just enough to see the gaping hole in the window next door and all the little puzzle shaped chunks of shatterproof glass scattered across the floor.

Apparently, both Greyson and Miguel fell through. The room is empty, but through the smoke that seems so much thicker now, I can make out a greyish arm clinging by the fingernails to the wooden sill—not pasty white greyish, toasty brown greyish.

Before I have time to take another step down the hallway, the arm flexes and heaves. A crescent of yellow creeps above the sill as I stride toward the stairs. If I can get Craig and Esther outside, Greyson and I can take on Miguel together—that is if Greyson didn't break anything critical in the fall. The stairway is only a few steps away, around the corner.

"Oh, shit!" I only think it at the top of the landing. Craig is the one who actually says it, coughing and gasping before he drops to all fours—really threes because his right arm is in a sling.

I'm not sure if the stairs to the kitchen are on fire or not, because they do a switchback halfway down, but the blast of heat coming from the enclosed stairway, heat strong enough for even my half-dead ZV skin to register, has turned the shaft into a virtual chimney. The roar of the fire almost drowns out the squeal of the alarm.

"The window in your bedroom, Craig! It's the only way out. Greyson's down there. He'll help us. C'mon! We have to lock your door before Miguel gets back in."

Esther starts choking and mumbling. I think she's delirious.

Crawling beneath the thick layer of smoke, Craig scurries into his room. To my oversized senses, the vapors are noxious.

I hunch, hacking away, and scamper after him only to practically bury my head into Miguel's gut. The force of the collision knocks me on my butt and Esther tumbles from my arms.

The smell of her blood triggers Miguel's unruly, ungoverned craving. He dives on her like a starving wolf on an injured baby lamb.

"Hell, no, you son of a bitch!" Instinctively I lash out with the body part nearest his putrid mouth. My foot cracks his cheek and his head lurches back.

But my reflexes weren't fast enough. My love isn't deep enough. My ZV strength isn't strong enough to keep the infection from invading the only other woman in this world that I love enough to call "mom." Miguel's teeth rip away a mouthful of skin, blood, and sinew from my aunt's neck as she shrieks with terror.

Oh, God, No! No! No! Not this too. Not Esther!

The implications pounce through my mind like a rabid cheetah. Esther's an adult. She's either going to die from the virus right away or go cannibal, sucking brains while it devours her organs slowly and torturously. And then the horror strikes me. Miguel is a mutant. He'll control her.

Vaulting myself to my aunt, I gather her up and toss her into Craig's room. She rolls, moaning, through the doorway.

Furious, Miguel goes for my hair, yanking my head away from the bedroom door.

At least I make for a great distraction; Miguel can't resist the opportunity to take me on, even if it means losing his prey. As he launches my shoulders against the already cracked bookshelf, one-armed Craig drags his mom's broken body into the room and slams the door against the rising smoke and raging ZV.

My head pounds against the wooden shelf, cracking it, and then I dodge just in time for Miguel to bang his fist into the solid wood behind me. The missed punch tilts him into the empty shelf and gives me a second to slip from underneath him.

My hands land on an enormous, leather-bound family album. Hauling it up off the floor as I straighten up, my head slightly reeling, I swing my body and arms in unison. The book slams Miguel's face, cracking his lip and interrupting his counter attack.

"Zeta Bitch!" he yells out, blood streaming from his mouth. The putrid stink of fresh mutant ZV squirts through the haze of smoke.

I have to get back in Craig's room and get my aunt and cousin out the window. It might just be the blow from the bookcase ringing in my ears, but I'm pretty sure I can hear Greyson calling from the patio. I only wish I could believe firemen will show up soon. But I know good and well, from the newscast this morning, there's not enough of them out there. My aunt and uncle's ranch is on the outskirts of the city. We're on our own.

Gripping the book with both hands, I fling it at Miguel's head. While he ducks and covers, I pivot for the doorknob.

Miguel swats at the book. It thumps against the floor, scattering smiling, family photos across the hall.

The door flying open surprises Craig in the middle of the room, dragging his mom, delirious, to the window. Esther chokes and rambles, "Barbecue, cough, cough…left on, cough, hack…burning ribs. Can you smell the ribs, Ev?...cough, cough, hack…"

No! God damn it! No! This can't be happening. The only reason Esther would be hallucinating about ribs on the BBQ right now is that she's starting to smell Craig. He always has that meaty, sweet and tender smell of ribs to me too. It's especially strong because of the open wound in his shoulder.

Miguel jumps me from behind. My right hand stretches for the ground as we tumble through the gap in a billow of smoke. Landing on my side, I pummel him with my elbow to get him off my back. He tries to throttle me, wedging his arm around my neck and yanking on a handful of my hair.

A lucky thrust backward lands my elbow in his windpipe. Gasping, he rolls to his back, dropping my hair and clutching his throat.

"Go, Craig, go! Out the window!" The window in this room sits above the roof of the patio and slopes gently toward the ground floor. Even with his bandaged shoulder, my cousin should be able to handle the short drop.

Twisting away from Miguel, I crawl toward my aunt. Her gun is still on the floor by the dresser. All I have to do is grab it and Miguel's reign of terror could end.

"What about my mom?" Craig stands his ground over her.

"Go!" Esther whimpers, hardly audible above the roar of the fire. "I'm bitten, Craig. Just get out! Evy, get him out for me!"

"Don't listen to her." My cousin's eyes bore into mine. "She's gonna be fine. You got infected and you're fine."

I don't have time to explain to him that being infected by exposure to the couples' virus isn't the same as being infected by a bite, or that his mom wasn't vegetarian.

He probably has no idea that most adults die from the fever before the virus works its cannibalistic mayhem. And I'm pretty sure he doesn't care that there are three types of ZV: the rare ones like Sam, the mutants like me, and the slowly self-destructing organ junkies like most of the infected young adults out there. To Craig, the only thing that matters right now is getting him and his mom the hell out of here.

"I got her! Just go!" I snarl, reaching for the butt of the .38 Special.

Craig hesitates, looking between the window and his mom, and then finally strides over and slides the pane open. He peers out.

My fingers nearly have the gun, but Miguel sees where I'm going, dives for my leg, and hauls me away from it. I'm not fooling myself. Miguel is stronger than I am. He's been on a hunting spree all morning and the virus is supercharging his animal instincts. The best I can hope for is to not let my aunt down and give Craig the cover he needs to get out before Miguel takes me down.

Flipping my body over, I kick my leg in a wide arch to wrench me free from his grasp. The jolt knocks him off balance giving me barely enough time to spring back on my feet before he regains his footing and takes a swing at me. Miguel has a nasty left hook. My whole brain vibrates when his knuckles crash my jaw. Shit! I could get seriously broken here. But what does it matter? My insides are already shattered. It's all I can do to keep standing as my nemesis follows the left with a right to my stomach.

The sensations in my skin may be reduced, but my organs are all up and running normally. As I double over, gasping for air, Miguel's knee meets my face halfway down. The impact jars my neck and my nose absorbs the blow with a crack that echoes around inside my skull. My eyes sting and well up. Pain radiates up into my head, the smoke clogs my lungs, and the realization that I'm not going to win stabs my conscience.

There's a good chance my aunt is already dead or on her way to becoming a full-blown, decaying ZV. Only one thing really matters now. Craig has to get out. Greyson's got to be down there. He'll keep my cousin safe and he'll go find Amber. He'll do it for me.

"Get out of here, Craig," I can't see him, but my breaths rasp and heave, willing him to safety—at least for the moment. "Go! Go find Greyson!"

"You see, rich bitch…" Miguel can't resist gloating, but the smoke clogs the flow of his words, choking off his moralizing, "cough, cough…in the end, it's…cough, hack…"

A jolting crack of the gun leaves his sorry mouth hanging open. ZVs can absorb the bleeding from a bullet wound, but their bones break as easily as anyone else's. Miguel's leg buckles beneath him and he falls to the floor at my feet.

Even before it registers that I have only a few seconds to get my cousin out of this burning nightmare before Miguel recovers, I wonder where the shot came from. The hope that Greyson has managed to climb up through the window flashes up from deep down inside me. Through burning, blurry eyes, I squint and then stop gasping when I focus in on Craig, standing in front of the dresser, his mom's .38 Special clamped in his hands.

Wiping the trickle of purple blood from my lip, I muscle through the throbbing in my nose and my gut and hobble to the stunned boy to unstrap his fingers from the trigger.

Miguel groans and curses behind us, maneuvering around his broken leg, trying to stand. Glancing back at him, I figure I've got about ten seconds. I run to the open window to check for Greyson. The grey smudged white suit he's wearing stands out in stark contrast to the stone of the patio. He's there below the window, just starting to haul himself up. The fall must have knocked him out for a while. Once I lower Craig down, Greyson will figure out what's going on.

The virus is already cutting off my pain receptors and stopping up the flow of blood from my nose. Shoving the gun in the back of my jeans, I hustle over to Craig, still standing dazed over his mother. Wrapping one arm around his bandaged shoulder, I sweep the other down behind his knees and lift, already turning toward the window. Something catches and tugs us both back.

My aunt snarls, clutching the boy's ankle.

Oh, God! It's happening, and not just to some stranger on a news video. My aunt, the little sister that my mom loved as much as she loved her own daughter, the only other person on earth that can fill the void my mom left in my empty soul, has shit for brains and is clawing at her son's leg, desperate to devour her baby.

Why? Why does it have to happen like this? Why? I know why and the knowing clogs my brain, choking me. It's because I brought this here. I unleashed evil on their home the minute my foot hit their doorstep.

Miguel stops struggling, looks up, and laughs, but then chokes on the smoke that has invaded the room through the open door.

"Esther!" I yell in the voice I save for Amber when she's heading for the street and not looking for the oncoming car that's going fast enough to obliterate her existence if she doesn't stop and look at what she's doing. "That's your son. That's Craig!"

Her eyes darting and her chest heaving like a caged hyena, she turns her head to the sound of the familiar name. Her son thrashes his leg wildly. She stares at his face, two animal instincts fighting for territory in her brain. The mother instinct wins. The putrid bug invading her veins hasn't overpowered it yet.

Maybe it would be easier for her if it had. I recognize the storm of horror churning behind her eyes, the ominous black clouds of a dawning realization that life has struck you with a bolt of fate more horrifying than death.

It's not the pattering of the virus eating at your grey matter that worries you, or the almost perceptible dripping decay of your organs inside. It's the nightmarish vortex that spins, gathering dust and jagged debris, looming large and viciously violent on your horizon, the twister that sweeps away choice and leaves behind it the vision of a grey and battered morning of waking to find you've ripped apart and devoured all that you love. That is what terrifies and disgusts you.

Even through the burning haze, I can see the tears welling up in her eyes.

Racing to the window, I shoo Greyson off the ledge so I can dump Craig out into his waiting arms. "Go! Get him in the Mercedes! Now!"

"Where's your aunt? Get the hell out of there!" The house heaves and crackles.

"What do you think I'm trying to do? Just get Craig in the car. Amber's at the hospital. You have to get there…whether I get out of here or not."

"What? What the hell are you talking about?" He sets Craig down on the patio. "Toss her out and get your ass down here!"

Behind me, the house shudders, the alarm shuts off abruptly and then the floor on the landing crashes into an inferno of flames below. Heat blasts up from the raging hole. But even more frightening than the floor falling out, is the shadow of Miguel upright, shambling, one leg broken on its hinge, toward my aunt. I can't leave her here with him. Maybe someone can help her…maybe Nicolas…

Turning back, I scream, "For God's sake, Greyson! For once in your life, just do what you're told! If we're not out of here in 5 minutes, you take Craig to the hospital and GET AMBER! Do you hear me? Get Amber!"

Stinging tears invade my eyes and the exasperation on my face softens to a pleading desperation that Greyson can't resist. Shaking his head, he locks eyes with me. His iron stare wills me to come out of this inferno. Grabbing Craig's sleeve, he sprints away to the car without looking back.

I pivot from the window and hurl myself at the smoky silhouette of Miguel. "Go, Esther, Go! Greyson's in the car with Craig…"

The impact of bodies cuts off my words as Miguel and I stumble, a wrestling mass, toward the raging pit of fire and brimstone behind us. Esther lumbers up and hobbles obediently to the window. Miguel twists violently out of my grasp and then wrenches my arm up and behind my back as he shoves me to the floor.

Boards crack and moan beneath me as I struggle to my feet. Miguel, hunched over, his face contorted and cramped with anger, limps tenaciously after my aunt, hacking out the ashy smoke and dragging his broken leg.

"Where do you think you're going, cow! Get your white ass back in here."

She stops at the window, hesitating.

Lurching my body forward, I snag Miguel's ankle with both hands and snap my arms back. With one of his knees shot out, he has no leg to catch his balance. The room resonates with the thud as his elbows, and then his face, collide with the wooden floor.

Rolling, I drag his foot toward my head with one hand while reaching for the gun at my waist with the other. A shot at close range could forever rid the world of this scum.

With Miguel down, the trance of indecision releases my aunt. She starts climbing out again, but Miguel is still fast as a cat. He twists, hissing, and lurches forward, swinging. The right barely misses my face as I heave the gun around, but the left connects with my armed fist. The .38 Special flies out of my hand, skittering across the floor.

Miguel and I lunge for the weapon. My fingers kiss the hard metal first, but the damn asshole is taller and his arms are longer. He whisks the gun out from underneath my nails. Crouching low, he targets my brain with one hand and uses the other as a crutch to heave himself up, leering smugly at my body crouched in front of him. About a foot off the ground, the cloud of smoke floods his lungs and he breaks into a coughing fit.

That my story would end with me going down in a burning building has always seemed inevitable. I knew that when I watched a Snatcher in a black uniform torch an innocent six-year-old with a bandaged wound. I just never imagined another mutant, someone like Greyson and me, would be the one to take me out. Maybe Greyson is right. I can't stand in the middle anymore. There's no reconciling the two sides. Coexistence is not an option.

At least, I'm going down giving Esther a chance to survive. Maybe saving the people you love is worth risking everything for, even survival. Maybe saving your mother's little sister is good karma and someone will save mine.

Maybe those are the very reasons why my aunt throws her leg back over the windowsill and, before I even have time to gasp, throws herself on Miguel's back. Instinctively, I know why she's doing it. To her, I'm her dead sister's daughter. To her, I'm the one that can save her children. She's a threat to them now. Of course, given a choice, she's going to pick me to survive.

But it doesn't have to end like that. The distraction is all I need to give me time to get off my butt and launch myself at the wad of flesh that is Miguel wrestling Esther. My aunt is a true mother beast—gnashing teeth and swiping claws. Wobbling on his injured leg, Miguel stumbles as he wrenches around to rip her off his back. The two of them tumble into me, the crack of a bullet unleashed shatters the monotonous raging of the fire, and for an instant, silence explodes in a bubble of stillness.

Chapter 21

Is this how it always ends? Me driving away with Greyson, the people we love nothing but ashes in the flames we're fleeing? Staring out the window at the Pines and Popcorn trees filing past, my head accepts the naked truth that if the human race is going to survive this plague, then it will always have to turn out this way because Greyson and I are infected. So, we can't win, or else the infection wins.

The highway is deserted. After this morning's broadcast about the raids, anyone with half a brain left is on the freeway headed east to the Louisiana state line, fleeing the grey tide rushing in from the west. The few cars on the street are wrecked on the shoulder, the drivers slumped over the seats. The only reason for going this way would be to rush to the hospital, but the virus is pretty quick once it decides to kill its adult victim. It can't be pleasant, a swarm of tiny, piranha microbes frenzy feeding at your organs, stripping them away before you can make the fifteen-minute drive to the ER. Maybe it's better that Esther went quickly with a bullet.

Greyson navigates around an SUV stranded across the dotted yellow lines of the two-lane highway. In the front seat, two rabid teens, sisters in matching plaid pajama pants, squabble over the juicy innards of their mother, her blood streaked through their long, blond hair. Greyson sees it too, but there's nothing we can do now. When he looks away though, focusing on the asphalt ahead, I catch a flash of regret on his face, the look of a guy who just passed a Five Guys but is in the car with his vegetarian girlfriend.

Am I like him? Yeah, I caught the whiff of the feast as we went by. The Chinese Buffet aroma seeped in through the vents and mingled with Craig's bloody rare, hot off the grill, steak odor. My stomach growled; the virus fidgeted in my blood. But the revulsion smothered the hunger.

It doesn't make me feel any better that I didn't actually tear into my family with my own predator thick, sharp nails and rip the flesh off their bones with my teeth because my parents, and now my aunt and uncle, are just as dead. I loved them and now they're nothing but rotting carcasses because I'm infected and the virus spins around me, a twister devouring everything in its path.

Craig sniffles in the back seat. It's a good thing I sent him with Greyson. One of Miguel's ZV goons was hanging out in the garage, waiting for someone to jump in the car my uncle left running. My uncle. The images—the blood, the guts, the shuddering last breath—crash my brain. My chest isn't big enough to hold all the pain anymore; it's ripping at the seams— or maybe the tightness is my heart shrinking. I want to close my eyes and squeeze the nightmare out, but it's always there in the darkness waiting for me.

My elbow on the armrest, I turn to the window so Craig can't see me in the mirror. Dropping my face into my palm, I sob, scrunching my eyes and my mouth tight shut.

"Evelyn, where are we going?" I almost don't recognize the tiny voice from the back seat. Being shot, hunted by zombies, and then snatched off the shelf like a tasty little morsel of Oreo by your own mother, robs a kid of his self-confidence.

"We're going to the hospital." I try not to break down in tears, try to sound like a grown-up who knows what the hell is going on. "Your brother and sisters are there."

The back seat is silent until Craig murmurs so softly that I only hear because I have mutant ears, "They took him."

Maybe I didn't hear him right. Twisting around, I lean over the seat to look my cousin in the eye. "What did you say?"

His anger amps up the volume. "One of the damn ZVs took Cameron before my dad could grab his gun!"

"Oh, dear God!" All this time I assumed Cameron was at the hospital with the girls. Poor Esther! How do you live through your little boy being dragged off by grey soldiers? How do you live through the sudden silencing of your husband's gun and knowing the reason for it? How do you live through being bitten and transformed from a loving mother to a ravening predator? I guess, in the end, you don't.

My poor cousin swipes at his eyes, rubs his hands across his pale face, and starts reliving the terror in disjointed murmurs. Everything in the car disappears for him, everything but the nightmare. "My dad was in the kitchen making us some eggs and sausage while my mom and I were packing." He gulps back a sob in his throat. "The feds at the hospital kept the girls 'cause mom didn't want to leave Amber alone."

His mouth cracks into a frown, his eyes welling up. At least he didn't see her die. In his head, his last image of her is alive…trying to take a bite out of his shin. But she was fighting! He can cling to that—she was fighting the virus.

"Two agents followed us home. The other agent, he must have taken off when his partner got…" Craig doesn't even know how to word what happened to Holland's man, splattered all over the concrete. The hamburger remains were still smeared across the driveway when he was escaping to his dad's car. He searches his empty palms for the words and then just skips over the scene.

"Dad yelled at mom to get her gun. But then, when we got to the bottom of the stairs, he told her to get me out of the house. They were already inside."

His eyes get crazy, darting back and forth trying to see everything that happened at once. "Dad was shooting. But the idiot ZVs didn't even care if they got shot. They just kept coming. One of them grabbed Cameron."

His fingers kneading his hair, he tries to wipe the memory from his head. "Cam was bleeding. This ZV in a yellow bandana grabbed him from the other one and dragged him away onto the patio." The images get the best of Craig. His eyes pucker and his head falls to his knees. "Do you think he got bit, Ev? Is he going to die? Why did they carry him off like that?"

Coping with not knowing is worse than the gruesome reality. For all I know, they've carted my little cousin off for food storage. But why is Miguel only taking kids? In the newscast, it was a kid he dumped over his shoulder and ran off with. "I don't know, Craig. There's a chance he's still okay. The blood we saw on the patio was red. It wasn't purple like mine. Some of the ZV gangs are dragging kids off without infecting them."

It's the only hope I can offer. Craig's eyes go round and his mouth drops open. He's not breathing. I can't leave the story like this, make him swallow the pill without the sugar. I have to lie to him. "No, that's good. The police are looking for them. Greyson and I, we know who the ZV in the yellow bandana is. We'll be able to help them look for Cameron."

Greyson shoots me a look, a reality check to make sure I know that what I'm feeding my cousin is a load of crap. My eyes plead silently with him to back me up.

He glances back through his mirror, throws his arm over the seat, and ruffles the kid's hair. "Bro', you're gonna be okay. We're going to the hospital." He turns back to the road. Craig doesn't respond so he looks back again to check the road. "We'll pick up your sisters and get you to your aunt's house in Montana. There's no one up there. The lab guys will have time to figure out a way to stop the tide of the infection before it gets to you."

Craig's eyes narrow and he slaps Greyson's arm away, a hot, angry tear slipping down his cheek. "They killed my dad and dragged my little brother off! The guy in the yellow bandana was grey, like you!" He glares at Greyson for a while and then stares out the window.

He's in the anger stage now. I know the pattern. I know what it's like to lose your parents and your little brother. His anger needs to go somewhere, but it should come to me. I'm the one that brought this to his family. It was my idea to come here. I'm the one that ticked off Miguel. I'm the one Holland was looking for.

We zoom past an overturned mini-van. The dead driver dangles upside down, locked in his seatbelt. A ZV claws and gnashes at him from the back seat, without quite reaching because his leg is trapped under the car. The zombie and the driver have matching buzz cuts. A black kid in a school uniform, jaws snapping, shambles over to the wreck from the brush by the side of the road. They're in the rearview mirror before the inevitable squabble over the carcass breaks out.

"This isn't Greyson's fault, Craig. I brought them to your door. I'm so sorry...about everything." All the tears that I haven't had time to cry explode in my brain and hammer at the back of my eyes. I have to scrunch the lids to hold them back.

Craig's brow crinkles up. He hasn't put everything together the way I have. At least he's stopped crying.

If I lay the truth on the table, he'll maybe transfer his fury to me where it belongs. It'll give him some closure. "Those agents, they were looking for me. They want to know why I'm different from the other ZVs. And Miguel, he wanted to hurt me, so he came here and hurt all the people I love. I'm so sorry, Craig. I shouldn't have come here." My teeth clamp down on a little chunk of my lip, trying to overwhelm the guilt with immediate pain.

Craig won't answer. He only stares out the window so all I can see is the clench in his jaw. It all settles heavily on me, everything that has happened in the couple of days since I showed up on their doorstep. I feel like I have to explain. "I shouldn't have come here. But Amber...she's so little Craig. I wanted her to be with you. She's lost everyone."

His head snaps back, meeting my gaze. "She hasn't lost you." Through the narrow slit in his eyes, he's looking for a fight.

"No, she hasn't..." I know what he's getting at. This is bait, and he really needs someone to bite, but what he needs, even more, is to realize what's facing him now. "And Paula and Prudence still have you."

From underneath crossed brows, he lifts his eyes to mine. Now he knows what I'm getting at. Resting my forearm on the ivory console, I lean through the gap between the seats. He has to get this. It won't just save him; it'll save his sisters.

"It's on you now, Craig. Your whole life has just shrunken into one small game: get Paula and Prudence to Aunt Rebecca's in Montana. After that, you decide. But until then, that's what you do. You channel all the anger, all the pain, and all the grief churning around inside of you. You channel it into that one play. Every choice you make, every word you say, every thought you think, and every action you take: they all lead to that one point. You will get your sisters safely to Montana."

He nods, eyes sober, letting the responsibility sink in. "I'll try. Mom and Dad..." he chokes up a little on the names, "...that's what they would want me to do. I'll do my best." He's still not manning up. His shoulders hunch, his fingers fidget, and his words cower.

"No, Craig." Reaching back, I grab his good arm, forcing him to look me in the bloodshot eye. "You won't 'do your best.' You WILL get those girls to Aunt Rebecca. You'll do whatever it takes. Just like I'll do whatever it takes to get Amber out of Holland's claws and away from this war zone."

Those words burn like poison on my tongue. I can't help but glance over at Greyson. His eyes meet mine and there's a question behind his dented brows. Are mine answering it? Does he know that Holland is holding Amber in exchange for my help? Does he think, no...not think...does he believe I'd betray him to save her? The real question is what do I believe I would do?

"And you're going to start right now." I ignore the questions that aren't here and now.

"What do you mean?"

"I mean I don't want you to even think about eating another piece of meat: no pork, no chicken, no beef. From now on, you're vegetarian, just like Paula."

We're closer to town now. The local chicken chain flashes by. It was a weekly habit for my aunt's family. Craig's eyes follow it hungrily. But it looks deserted: no cars, no lights. I kind of doubt anyone's showing up for work today. From his story, I gather he hasn't eaten this morning. He'll have to wait until we get to the hospital.

The carnage on the road in the town isn't as gruesome as I imagined. ZVs attacked mostly in the neighborhoods at night. When we pass the Target and the BestBuy, a few looters are running through the parking lot, their arms full of electronics. In front of the grocery store, a hooded middle-aged guy toting a rifle is pushing a cart full of groceries down the street. He must have decided to bunker up rather than evacuate.

"What? You want me to eat salad? What does that have to do with anything?" Craig looks at me through the rearview mirror like maybe the virus has made my brain go soft.

Everyone in my aunt's family lives on a thick and steady diet of animal flesh, except for Paula who turned vegetarian when Amber and I did, and Prudence.

"Everything! Listen carefully, Craig. The mutants, the ZVs who don't go brain-dead and start scarfing their family members, they're all vegetarians. If you get bit…" terror invades his face. I know the feeling. It's hard to decide which is worse, being hunted by the beast, or being the beast. "…you need to be one of them because that's the only way you can still keep your sisters safe. I don't know if the amount of time you've been a vegetarian makes a difference, but let's pray it doesn't. You're starting now, because no matter what happens—no matter what happens—you will get your baby sisters to Montana."

"But…but…aren't you coming with us?"

"No, I'm not."

His eyes widen into panic.

Chapter 22

From the mall parking lot, distant gunshot cracks punctuate my response. I can't go with Craig. I want them out now. I don't want them sitting around in the middle of the holocaust waiting for me to do what Holland wants. I want them out of the state before I agree to do anything.

My arm falls away from the console as I slump back into the bucket of the seat, staring out at the mayhem growing as we move toward the residential areas.

Here, it's not just teens rising up open-jawed against their elders. In the driveway of a little blue siding house with pink and white curtains, a mother, her face smeared with bloody clumps of flesh, stands crying over the carcass of a kid in pajamas. As we pass, I'm not sure if it's the virus eating her from the inside, or the horror of what it just drove her to do that doubles her over, clutching her gut.

Where are the police? There should be police. Have they abandoned the city to the ZVs? If they have, the fires will be coming soon. I cement my resolve, inhaling deeply through clenched teeth.

"Look! They're not going to let me leave with Amber until I..." My eyes dart Greyson's direction. He catches the hesitation and glances over. "...until Greyson and I help them. But I think I can bargain with them, get them to make a deal to get you and your sisters out...in exchange for...whatever they want. I owe that much to your mom and dad..."

My head drops; my eyes stare at my grey hands—the purple fingernails, the ghost images of bloodstains I can't quite wash away. "...they lost everything because of me..."

On the last word, I nearly bite my tongue when Greyson's foot stomps the brakes. The tires squeal, the car swerves and lurches to a stop in the middle of the highway.

My head shoots up as the virus activates all my fight or flight hormones. My first thought is to grab Craig and run, because there has to be either a herd of newly minted ravenous, mindless zombies racing down the highway or, at the very least, a squadron of blowtorch-toting National Guards. "Look, would you just stop?" Greyson scowls, turning to shake his head at me and slamming his palms against the steering wheel.

The shock of seeing nothing but random papers tumbling among the looters on the accident-dotted road disorients me until the words bore through the chemical fuzz and I realize he's flat out ticked at me. That's even more astonishing. Greyson pretty much chills every situation. He swallows all the darts my tongue shoots at him and spits out the points. I've gotten the silent treatment, the ironic jab, the cheeky grin, even the hurt puppy dog, but never the injured wolf. Apparently, his immunity to feeling isn't impervious. I'm not even exactly sure what's bugging him—other than a 4000-year-old virus that's hijacking his bio-chem.

Or maybe I do know. The rules have changed. The grey has washed away in the bloody tide and the war has begun. The middle is gone and I have to choose sides. Greyson knows I can't choose his side. I'm just not a supremacist—and I have Amber.

"Take a look at the highway, honey!" That wasn't a term of endearment.

Turning my head away, I fume—What right does he have to go all self-righteous jackass on me right now? I just lost half of the dwindling family I had left, and I'm on my way to the hive to stick my honey colored-head in among the killer bees to sniff out my little sister.

I'm too angry to say anything so I contemplate the scenery. About every hundred yards or so, all the way up to the bend in the road, there's some kind of accident, or abandoned car facing the wrong direction. Angry grey smoke snakes dot the horizon. I guess my aunt's house isn't the only one that's gone up in flames.

We've already passed a couple ragged-looking teens with bloody hands and ripped pajamas. They wander dazed along the broken yellow meridian, or sit along the tree-lined sidewalks at the side of the road, staring blankly at their blood-stained fingers, trying to wrap their viral heads around what they've become. Unfathomable self-disgust drowns them in the receding wake of the viral feeding frenzy. I know. I remember the first time I hunted down and devoured the warm, pulsing organs of a living creature—but the creature wasn't my own race; it wasn't my own blood; it wasn't my own family.

The devastation in their eyes collides with my own in a deafening thunder of silence. Greyson's ranting rattles and bangs inscrutably in my head, a broken shutter flapping in the howling hurricane. The smattering of smeared red on my soot-soiled white dress glares up at me accusingly. The rusted crimson on the hem is my uncle's blood, the sticky purple-tinged red blotch, splattered across my chest and buried in my nail beds, is my aunt's.

Deliberately I turn my head back to face Greyson, desolation weighing down the corners of my eyes and mouth, a hot tear running through the stiffly caked ash on my face. His white shirt and pants are a shredded mess of mottled grey, black, and red—like mine. Somewhere, he ditched his jacket. What a joke! What a sick, twisted, pathetic joke—dressing us up in white! My laugh has no mirth in it.

"You're laughing?" Greyson's mouth hangs open, stunned, hurt—mystified.

He can't see it? Apparently, I have to enlighten him. "They dress us up in white like this," I motion viciously at my blood-stained, ash-smeared, white dress, "trying to turn us into angels. But the grey bleeds through, doesn't it? and the blood? and the fire? We're not angels, Greyson. We're demons. We bring destruction. All this, it's my fault. I shouldn't have come here. I…"

His eyes forbid me to go on as he shakes his head. "That's what I'm talking about. How does everything end up being about you? You had nothing to do with this!"

"I had everything to do with this! Miguel told me he knew where I lived."

"He knew you lived at the compound. How could he possibly have known where your aunt lived? We met him in the woods. You could have come from any of the ranches around here."

My eyes screw up at his completely thick inability to assess the situation. "And I suppose it's just some big coincidence that the next morning, my aunt and uncle's house becomes the zombie Alamo!"

"No! It's not a coincidence. The entire neighborhood got hit. Hell, look around! The whole city is crawling with ZVs. The only coincidence is that your aunt and uncle live here. Reality check, baby! The acid rain is falling on the whole state; this isn't your own personal pity storm!"

"God, you are an insensitive prick!" The viral juices carbonate the anger in my veins. I can almost feel it fizzing in the tips of my fingers, bubbling up to my heart and my brain. Most of the time, charm and chivalry float around Greyson, an intoxicating cannabis haze, numbing the senses. But the rage clears my head and steals my breath. I grab a lungful more as Greyson glares, open-mouthed, wondering, who the hell is the bitch in the seat next to me?

But, I'm not the one wearing the mask, making innocent victims believe I'm something I'm not. I'm totally willing to let the beast in me hang out. "The first time I met you, I was disgusted. I knew right then you were a user, a vicious pack-hunting, alpha wolf. I ran away from you then, and I should never have stopped running!"

Whatever my tongue was stabbing at, I punctured it. Greyson isn't a lie-down-and-take-it kind of guy. The viral tension in the car leaps up a couple notches.

Craig takes cover, slumping down in his seat, out of sight of the mirrors.

"Ev, you can run from me all you want, but wherever you end up, I'll always be there, because, you and I, we're two sides of the same coin. You just refuse to turn around and see me."

His accusations stick hot to my skin, searing through the pores. Recoiling from the burn, I spit back at him, my index finger all up in his face, "You are so incredibly arrogant. I am not like you! We may be infected with the same strain of the virus, but the deadliest bug in your head is your own ego, ripping through and devouring anything with a heartbeat to feed its insatiable voracity!" I can't stop myself. I shove him and all his superhuman delusions away from me.

The corners of his face wrinkle up in disbelief. "Seriously?" He rubs his hand across the naked dome of his head. "I risk my ass, not to mention a few of my ZV friends, to pull you off the Institute dissection table, I run decoy for you and Amber and end up shaved and strapped to a table of my own, book you and your friends an all-expenses-paid charter flight out of a burning state, get tossed out a window running cavalry for you and your cousins, and you're thinking that makes me an arrogant son of a bitch?"

I roll my eyes the way my mom used to when my arguments were totally PMS, out of touch with reality, and clueless. The virus, still rampaging through our veins, feeds on the anger juices and spikes into a toxic venom of rage. "Motivation is everything, Greyson. You know you only did that for yourself. Your overinflated bubble of ego wants to rule the world and some sick mating instinct of the virus has cowed you into thinking you need me to do that. I am your trophy. You want me, Greyson. That's why you do what you do. Evil or Just, you don't give a damn, as long as you get what you want."

"Of course, I want you." He growls, the virus in him responding instinctively to the outburst of mine. "I want you the way I want water and air. Does that make me a selfish tool?"

We're both distracted when a couple newbie teenage ZVs run by, glancing over their shoulders. But we have our own shadows haunting us. We can't stop to gawk at theirs.

"Don't kid yourself, Evelyn. Everyone wants something. Altruism is just a straw shoved into an ice-cold glass of self-righteous Kool-Aid."

"That's the most jaded, absurd load of crap I've ever heard. You're so twisted you can't see anyone else straight. Look around you. Sometimes people just do what's best for someone they love; what's in it for them never even crosses their mind."

"I'm not the one with the warped lenses, honey. Believe me. I've seen a whole lot more of what's out there than you have. You're the one who's down here in the sludge looking for some moral high ground, perched somewhere in the middle of what we are and what they are." He nods at my tattered and stained clothes. "But your little white dress is just as dirty as mine, babe."

The thing I hate most about Greyson is that he instinctively targets the most acutely vulnerable weakness of his prey. No insensitive skin covers the stains and scars the virus has left on my soul; they're out there, exposed—and he just keeps ripping at the scabs. "Tell me, did you run because it was best for your family, or for you? Because they're dead now. Wouldn't it have been better for them if you'd just gone off quietly to the Institute? And why did you come here? For Amber? Last time I checked, that decision landed her firmly in the hands of the enemy. Wake up, Ev! You're a survivor. Your hands are just as bloody as mine."

And that stings. No, it doesn't just sting. It rips into my heart and explodes, spraying guilt shrapnel across my chest and into my head. He's right. Shit! He's right! Burning tears fume at the back of my eyes. I can't sit in the car with the truth anymore. I can't look at myself in his face, bald and covered in the ashes and blood of the world that's dying. I don't want him to be the reflection of me.

My chest ignited and throbbing, I jerk the lever of the door and shove it open. "You know what, Greyson? You're right! This is not my fault." That gets his attention. "It's yours!"

Not what he was expecting.

"You could have killed Miguel right there in the woods on the first night we met him. We both knew what he was. He was going to rape me right there in the middle of nowhere. And you let him go. You let him go again when I had him under my heel outside the compound. Why did you do that? You're fast. You could have hunted him down. My uncle, my aunt, my cousins, they'd all be home scarfing eggs and bacon this morning if you'd just taken care of business. But, no! In your sick little world, Miguel deserves to live because he's 'one of us,' 'a player on the ZV supremacy team'. He gets to go on leading his gang of zombie minions, wreaking his havoc, tearing families apart, and spreading his disease because he IS you. You can't condemn him without condemning yourself. You both live by the same Holy ZV Bible. I don't know who's crazier, you or

Ms. Knight back on the looney farm. Maybe you should take another look there. She's drooling all over herself to get you to take a bite out of her so she can be your own personal ZV whore."

As I slam the door shut behind me, Craig's head pops up from below the seats where he took cover from the firestorm. He's not about to be left alone in the car with angry Greyson.

Our hands unlatch his door simultaneously. Reaching in, I grab his arm and haul him out. "C'mon Craig! We're walking!" As he scrambles out, I lean into the void of the empty back seat, "We're going to make a deal with the demons holding our sisters, not because we might be able to get them safely out of hell and up to Aunt Rebecca in Montana, but because having my organs probed with sharp scalpels and no anesthesia will make me feel better about myself, give me a sense of moral superiority." The slam of the door echoes up and down the deserted street.

Greyson doesn't even turn his head to look at me. He stares out his window, his eyes fixed on the clump of trees lining the opposite side of the street, and his knuckles wrapped white around the steering wheel.

We're twenty paces down the sidewalk when my uncle's Mercedes roars to life behind us and screeches a U-turn back toward my aunt's neighborhood...and the Knight compound.

Grabbing Craig's hand, I squeeze it tight.

Another twenty paces down the sidewalk and my mind screams, Greyson's gone!

How is that possible? The rowdy bugs in my blood settle into a dormant slouch. The cloud of anger disperses leaving behind a grey sky on a stripped landscape. Suddenly I'm a tiny boat, my anchor snapped and sinking to the bottom of the vast ocean. I'm sturdy, sound, and waterproof, but alone, drifting and bobbing on the churning sea. Turning my eyes away from the vast, blue expanse of profound mystery behind me, I set my course for the dot of land that is Amber.

When the fine-tuned hum of my uncle's car has dispersed into oblivion, an ominous clicking fades into the void of its wake. And then I catch a vague whiff of...what? burning pig?

The two sensory inputs collide and I realize the black sedan is coming my way, leading a trail of flames.

"C'mon Craig!" I break into a run. "We have to get out of here. Now!" That's what happens in my head, out of instinct. But, you can't run from your destination; so, what I really do is just keep walking hand in hand with stark reality. Greyson is gone!

Chapter 23

The clicking chasing us crescendos. The black sedan pulls up alongside Craig and me, slowing to a crawl to match our pace. The passenger window grinds down.

"You know there are two ways we can do this, Ms. Cross," Holland announces.

"And you know I don't need to be a ZV to smell the little BBQ you're hosting behind us. You also know you have my little sister so there's really only one way this is going to happen. What do you want from me? Greyson? He's long gone…we had a…difference of opinion." My voice chokes up; I swallow to hide it, meeting his eye, making sure he gets what I'm saying. I won't be talking Greyson into cooperating or luring him into their rat lab.

"Your mutant boyfriend is no longer the prime threat. His kind are a dime a dozen out there. The virus reacts the same way in any bitten adolescent with a vegetarian diet." That catches my attention and I glance down at Craig to make sure he got that piece of info.

He's all eyes on Holland, fidgeting, dying to ask about his sisters. But he's not sure if we're all on the same team here and he doesn't want to give away the game. With a slight shake of my head, I encourage him to let me do the talking. From the looks of it, Holland has all the cards, but I must have a wild card I don't know anything about or he'd have just left me here to burn.

A couple infected kids, blood and guts smeared on their hands and faces, run up to the driver's side of the sedan from the opposite side of the street, yelling and begging for help. The girl, a hoop in her nose and an asymmetrical blond butch topped with a red and white-striped baggy beanie, bangs on Holland's window. Her boyfriend stumbles up, holding his gut, his face scrunched in pain. They must be newly infected; their clothes are still crisp and untattered.

Now that they've fed the need, the virus has receded enough for their humanity to resurface with their survival instincts. The odds are good she's a vegetarian and he's not. The blood on their hands probably belongs to someone they knew and loved. My heart breaks for them. They still think they're human, that other humans will feel some compassion and want to help them.

"Please! Help us!" She jerks her head back over her shoulder, her thickly lined eyes wide with terror. "We're sick! We got attacked. Kyle needs help. We...we..." Her hand shivers on the top of the car. She bursts into breathless sobs unable to speak what they've just done. "They...the Snatchers... (I'm a little surprised to hear that term out here. Maybe the scope of the infection was bigger than I ever imagined.) ...they shoot us in the head and then the Guard, they sweep up behind...burning all the bodies. We need to get to the hospital. They'll help us. Please!" She flashes an uncertain smile back at Kyle, reaching one hand to help him while knocking at the window with the other.

Holland listens, nodding, his lower lip pushed forward like he's considering helping them. His window starts to whir down as he leans slightly to the passenger side.

The tightened muscles across the ZVs face relax, a glimmer of hope brightens her eyes and she waves her trembling, blood-crusted hand out to encourage Kyle. "We won't hurt you!" she assures Holland. "It's gone. The hunger is gone. I think we're gonna be fine."

"No, honey, you're not going to be fine." Holland peers through the widening gap, swinging his right arm toward the window.

Snatching Craig into my chest, I shelter his eyes. Holland's gun practically touches the mutant's forehead before she realizes what's happening, before she realizes what the world has become, before her future hits her between the eyes, before the deafening crack splatters her grey matter across Kyle's cheek. The second gunshot drops Kyle as he reaches to catch her fall.

The looters at the Gas and Go across the street chuck their goods and run for their truck. The guy filling up doesn't bother to unhook the nozzle before jumping in the driver's seat and squealing away.

I totally want to freak, scream, cry, melt down into a viral frenzy, maybe dive in the car and rip Holland's guts out. But I've seen callous sadism like this before. I'm not going to feed his hunger for submissive fear. Instead, I channel the beast inside, channel it into the cold, calculating strategy of a hunter. All the shock, I reroute into calming my cousin. It's good camouflage.

Tossing his gun on the seat and leaning back to continue our conversation, as if he hasn't just murdered two teenagers, Holland levels a pedantic stare at me. "Now, I'm no scientist, but from what they tell me, we carnivores have an abundance of some enzymes that break down proteins. When you don't have enough of those in your own organs because you're a vegetarian, the virus takes another path for survival. It turns you into a predator to encourage the absorption of the enzyme from other meat-eaters' organs."

Holland must really need my help or I'd already be lying in a puddle of my own putrid, purple blood. "So why are you still stalking me?"

"You? We're not interested in you any more than your delinquent boyfriend. It's the kid we want."

My heart freezes. "Amber? What do you want with my sister?"

"You teenagers, you're all alike. You can't wake up and realize the world does not revolve around your pathetic little existence. We don't care what happens to you or your little brat sister. She can burn along with you. Living in your world, she's nothing but ZV bait. She'll end up with the bug biting at her brain the way it does yours. No, we're only hanging on to her for one reason. We need her to get what we want from you."

Placing my hand on the crevasse that lets the window disappear when you don't want to look through the tinted glass anymore, I lean down. My hair falls forward so I have to tuck it back. Licking my lips, I glare into the eyes of the sadist holding my sister. "And what is that?"

"It's classified. And you don't have clearance."

Chapter 24

Five hundred yards before the hospital, a Humvee and a camouflage Jeep block all but one lane. We're idling in a line of at least 20 cars. I'm in the back seat with Craig, behind Holland, leaning against my window so he can't read my face.

Honestly, I don't know what the hell I'm going to do. I can't run, because I have to get Craig to the hospital, get him and his sisters to my aunt in Montana, and get Amber back. For the moment, Holland and I are going the same way. He's holding all the cards, but one, and for me to get anything on the table, I'm going to have to play his game. I guess the first thing I need to do is figure out the rules. All this time, I've been thinking Holland was after Greyson and me. I rack my brain trying to figure out what kid they're talking about and why they need me.

Craig drools and snores, slumped over my shoulder, exhausted. It's been a long, crazy night for him.

Holland huffs. "Shit! I don't have time for this!" He turns the wheel sharply, crossing over the dotted yellow line into the other lane. Abruptly, he stops, straddled over the median, so a passing forest green Bronco has room to squeeze by on the shoulder.

The middle-aged driver in a tattered Cowboys ball cap navigates the passage while craning his neck back to the barricades. Following his gaze, I watch a couple Guards duct tape the wrists of a teenage kid in jeans and a graphic t-shirt too smeared with blood to read. The dad's eyes meet mine. Is the twitch guilt? Fear? A warning? Maybe it soothes his conscience to see he's not the only parent dropping off an infected kid.

As armed soldiers lead the kid off to a big old army transport, a couple other cars ahead of us ease their noses around to make U-turns. Maybe they have someplace better to be. Or maybe some parents just can't quite bring themselves to walk away. I hope the infected kid in their back seat can find the guts to cut the cord for them.

"I thought we were going to the hospital." The edge in my voice slices through the strained silence that hangs in the car about as heavily as Holland's stale buffet odor. Even if I did eat people organs, I'm not sure his would tempt me.

"We're not." He hits the gas and accelerates through the stop sign, turning right without slowing. My instincts scream for me to lean over the seat and rip a hole in his jugular with my teeth, but my head whispers patience. If the predator strikes too soon, the prey bolts.

"Look, we had a deal." My nails dig into the worn leather of his bucket seat. I slide my head right so that I can see the crossbar of his eyes in the rearview mirror. My back feels cold. I don't have Greyson there anymore, covering it. "The only reason I'm sitting quietly back here is..."

"We don't have a deal." He sneers at the word, glancing up to meet my stare. "You're not already a toasted corpse littering up the road because you might be useful to me. If you're not useful to me, you'll be back out on the street waiting for the mop-up crew." He turns right again.

Does he realize I can literally rip his head off before he has time to grab the gun gleaming on his passenger seat? Of course, he does. But he has Amber. And he's the only chance my cousins have of escaping the infection zone. I have to play nice. "Where are we going then?"

"Baylor has an off-campus lab building near the hospital. A couple of their professors were working on the Z-Virus long before the bubble popped. We've appropriated a floor of the office space in the building for our operations. That's where we're holding the girls."

A relatively modern glass and steel block rises out of the trees from the middle of a nice park with diagonal sidewalks and a fountain spilling water into a bed of river rocks. A security gate blocking the entrance to the parking lot, a patrol of about twenty armed Guardsmen, and what looks like a temporary command tent in front of the fountain announces that we've reached zombie central. Barricades, crawling with guys in green combat uniforms, surround the whole park. Civilian bodies litter the perimeters. The security around the building means business.

"How come the military is camped out here when the city is practically under attack?"

"This is National Guard." Holland gestures with a thumb toward the tent. "The Army and Air Force are only authorized to maintain the quarantine perimeter around the states already infected. They're standing border control while the Guard handles the mayhem inside." He snickers and shakes his head as the parking guard waves him through the gate. "What a joke! After last night's attacks, the virus has exploded in exponential proportions. We have five days to evacuate before they torch what's left."

"But why? Why are they doing that? The virus kills most people, and the kids that don't die, eventually get eaten up from the inside. Why don't they just let the virus run its course and then take back the city?"

"Because we're not talking brain-dead organ snatchers, here, missy. The lucid, stalking predators like you," he casts me a slit-eyed glare through the rear-view mirror as he slides in between a couple parallel lines drawn on the asphalt, "lead the others around in coordinated pack hunts, feeding on the rest of the population. We've already had a couple patrols get ambushed and turned. So now the mutants have armed zombie soldiers taking on the other troops at the borders. In five days, there won't be an uninfected yellow dog left to howl in the streets and the pack will migrate toward better hunting grounds." He shoves the door open and hauls himself out.

The war isn't coming anymore; it's here, in full force. The grey has washed away, defining the stark line between black and white.

Grabbing Craig's hand, I follow Holland across the nearly empty lot to the front doors. He doesn't even bother turning around to make sure I don't make a run for it. Where would I go? I'd just end up back here looking for my little sister and my cousins. At least this way, I don't have to break into the building. What's really driving me, though, is what the hell Holland wants. A wrinkle of hope twitters in my head. Baylor.

That's where Nicolas's cousin was working. Dear God, please let Nicolas be here!

Holland escorts the two of us through the front door metal detector, past a gauntlet of security guards, and the reception desk. I must not be the only mutant they've had in here, because Craig, with his bandaged shoulder, gets more frowns than I do. This establishment isn't child friendly.

Once the stainless-steel elevator doors ping and slide open, Holland ushers us in and hits the -3 button below the parking level.

"No corner office with a view of the city?" I quip, hanging by the tips of my nails to the cracks in my confidence.

"We're not going to my office. The labs are below ground." My heart drops with the elevator. It's easier to escape from above ground than below. The motion of the descent jostles my equilibrium. I straddle the sway, an escaped rat in a swinging cage, delivered neatly back to the lab.

The metal box hits the ground floor and the doors gape open. We emerge into a long hallway. Is it comforting or creepy that the white walls, steel trimmed observation windows, and shiny blue tile sparkle, more antiseptic, more clinical than the make-shift, sloppy science of the Salt Lake Z-V Institute? At the converted burn ward, still under construction, the whole crew exuded "amateur." I'm dealing with professionals here, or at least that's what this building screams.

Of course, Holland doesn't stop to reassure us. He plows a path down the hallway, expecting us to follow. Craig clings to my arm, smearing the blood and ashes on our skin. We turn left down a new corridor blocked a few yards down by double metal doors.

"I want to see my sister and my cousins."

"You're not in charge here, Ms. Cross, and nobody gives a damn what you want. We're talking apocalyptic contagion; you're just another casualty." He shoves open the door to a huge open lab surrounded by small, observation rooms. The windows to the small rooms are tinted, one-way mirrors. About six exam tables with blue restraining straps sit in rows surrounded by medical machines and trays of operating utensils it would take a medical degree to identify.

A shiver scrolls up my spine to my shoulders. Surprisingly, Holland strides to an observation room, opens the door, and ushers me in. He wedges his arm between Craig and me as I step over the threshold into what looks more like a typical doctor's office exam room. Craig's eyes snap wide and his mouth gapes open as his hand slips from mine.

"It's okay, buddy." My eyes bore into Holland's, seeking out a shred of decency. I don't find any. "You want to see your sisters, right?" I can't make any promises. I've already broken too many.

He nods, scanning Holland's pudgy face with uncertain eyes.

"You're alive and uninfected, kid. Count your blessings. He shoves him back out into the lab as I reach to hug him good-bye. The door clicks shut, locking automatically. There are no windows—I'm buried.

Chapter 25

There are no Dr. Seuss books on the counter next to the sink. In fact, when I open the cupboards, they're empty. Maybe at one time, they saw patients here, but those days are gone. There's a door that leads to a small, attached bathroom. They must be planning to leave me here for a while.

A rolling doctor's stool stands next to the exam table. I don't want to sit on either of those seats. The best option is an antiseptic corner behind the door where I'm not visible through the observation window camouflaged as a mirror.

I pull my knees up and try to wash out the trailer clips of my fight scene with Greyson. The tide of my thoughts keeps rolling them onto the sandy canvas of my mind.

Find Amber. That's what I have to focus on. But I know, deep down, through and through, I can't keep Amber safe without Greyson. Alone, I don't need anybody. But right now, I don't even know how I'm going to get her out of here. I'm an idiot. How did I let Grey get under my skin? How could I let him crawl out again? Without Greyson, Amber's future is a dusty pile of ashes swirling around in the *terre rasée* of my memories. God, I hate that I need him! I hate that, to survive, I need the part of me that is his other half.

Jumping to my feet in disgust, I pace the room, a caged cat, rubbing my arms as if I could actually be cold. The room is only a shadow of something that once was, outlines of cupboards and a sink, but nothing inside, nothing that gives it life and purpose. How long are they going to keep me in here?

My back slides down the wall in a corner of the room. When my butt hits the cold tile floor, I hug my shins and drop my head into my knees. The vent hums tenaciously, not a tune, just a monotonous whirr forcing air in where it doesn't belong. Sometimes, it lulls me to a restless sleep.

Every time I startle awake again and realize where I am, I need to cry; I want to cry, but the tears won't come. I damned up that spring a long time ago. The Knight compound, my aunt's house, everything seems so unreal in this tiny, isolated room underground.

A couple of times, someone slides food in through a slot at the bottom of the door. They know I only need to eat once a day. Does that mean I've been here for a couple days?

Sitting on the floor, my eyes focus on the crack between the tile and the wall. A tiny grey spider scurries about in the dust, spinning a small web with all the intensity of its survival instinct because that's what spiders do. Doesn't she realize there's no food here? The web won't change anything. She's just spinning sticky threads of hope. Hope is a chocolate-covered razorblade. I'm down to the sharp, tongue-slicing edge now.

I must have fallen asleep staring at the spider. When my eyes open again, she's gone. The motion sensor lights have shut off. Only a small blue emergency lamp glows in the backsplash of the metal sink. The room has no windows, so the sun can't hint at what time it is or how long I've been sitting here. My mind clicks back on and rifles through the stacks of unfinished business: Amber, my cousins…Greyson.

The soft padding of footsteps in the hall outside the lab, that my mutant ears picked up before I was even conscious, must have woken me. The shoes don't squelch with Holland's heavy plodding. They shuffle, a lightly padded swagger—someone young and male, in sterile booties. Should I get behind the door? Plan an ambush? I can't. I have to find out what Holland wants from me. He's my best hope for getting my cousins and Amber out of the war zone.

This must be hell then. A demon is my best hope.

Before the key rattles in the handle, the hot, juicy tang of beef seeps in under the door. Feeding time. The keepers are bringing the meat to the caged cat. I don't bother to look up when the door clicks open. The web next to my right thigh has swallowed my attention. There's a minuscule brown bug suspended in the strands. My arms crossed over my bent knees, my head drooped onto them, I watch it struggle, dying so that the hope woven into the strands that bind it can live.

The door clicks shut again.

"Meez Cross, are you okay?" A subtle French accent seasoned with a hint of humanity and genuine concern startles my senses and lets me breathe.

"Evelyn." Without looking up, I mutter into my folded arms. "No one calls me Ms. Cross—unless they want to cut me up or use me—oh, right, that would be you."

"I'm sorry you've been here so long...Evelyn. Dr. Pêsqué had a number of situations that required his immediate attention. He would have come himself but he's finding it difficult to resolve some of them."

Apologies? To me? Oh, that's rich. I'm the worm in the apple and he's excusing himself for removing me into a safe little cup. I'm lucky I didn't end up as sidewalk road-kill under a combat boot or sliced open on a biology lab table. "Of course, he is. He's a doctor and there's a zombie epidemic running rampant in the streets. Who gives a damn about one infected teen trying to protect her six-year-old sister that she hasn't seen for...days?"

Why do I always do that? Someone shows a little kindness and I bite his head off, no not like that—figuratively. Fear. It has to be fear. One drop of sympathy can seep into the tough leather that is my soul, soften it up, open all the pores that have withered shut. The weathered skin is the only armor I have.

As much as I don't want to look kindness in the eye, my brain demands a face to go with the caramel and coffee voice. Slowly, resentfully, I lift my eyes, past the elastic rimmed booties, up the baby green scrubs hanging carelessly on slim hips, along the tattoo rippled across a lean and trim right bicep, and then across the rough stubble of a dark goatee flanked by a diamond stud earring and accessorized with a splash of deep, brunette bed head.

I must have been in here a lot longer than I thought because I'm pretty sure I'm hallucinating. What kind of doctor looks like this? Seriously, the organs he's offering make the virus tingle with excitement in my stomach, but all I really want is to take a bite out of him—and I'm not so sure I mean in the ZV zombie kind of way. It's getting harder and harder to separate the viral urges from my own.

I'm totally expecting the guy to flash me some "Blue Steel"—no, this kid is definitely "Magnum." Instead, I get a smile—the kind of semi-melted, dark chocolate truffle smile I haven't seen since I walked the hallways of a public high school.

"He's not that kind of doctor. He's more involved in research. But we've had some breakthroughs that demanded our full attention and needed to be pursued. Dr. Vadlamani, the head researcher from Salt Lake City where the breakout began, has arrived recently with some critical findings and data."

"Wait! You know Nicolas?" A new layer of chocolate coats my razor blade of hope. "Who the hell are you?"

Inside I'm feeling a little like purple Jell-O gone rancid, so I forget that, given the hostile ZV takeover going on outside these walls, I look a little more intimidating than I feel.

The kid steps back slightly, but grins. "They told me you were spunky."

He massacres all the vowels in the words, dressing them up crisply, rolling them neatly on his tongue. "Did you just learn that today? Do you even know what," I imitate his accent on the word, "spunky means?"

He shifts his weight. He's self-conscious about his English. Nothing compared to what I would be if I were speaking French here, but enough to give me a foot up between us. "Sort of. I mean my mother is American so my English is pretty good, but I've spoken French most of my life. That's why Dr. Pêsqué asked for me." He steps forward, dragging his free fingers, through the mess of brunette on his head, like he forgot his manners, and then offers me his hand. "Ryan Samson. Nice to meet you."

Is he serious? Does this place look like a single's bar? Rolling my eyes, I grab the hand and use it to haul myself up instead. My knees creak; I must have been asleep for a while.

Ryan was just offering a handshake, not a hand up, so he loses his balance and teeters a bit. Our shoulders bump as I rise up and he leans forward. We both reach out to steady the other. The tray of gooey giblets tilts and squelches to the ground as he grabs for my shoulder. Our eyes meet briefly in the wake of the clatter. This up close and personal, I can see he's not much older than Greyson and I. My shoulders twitch and I grimace a little at the thought of the mess I've made with Grey. But Ryan doesn't know that and takes it personally.

"I'm really sorry, I didn't mean to grab you like that…I lost my balance." He backs abruptly off my shoulder and waves at the blood-tinged mess on the white tile floor. "Oh, Mon Dieu, I've ruined your dinner."

"Not to worry. I've eaten worse. Trust me." To illustrate, I bend down, knees popping, flop the plastic plate over, scoop up the steamy slop of rare liver and onions—sans onions—and plop it back onto the plate.

"No! Really! I can get you some fresh…" He holds his hand out to stop me—you know, grab the dirty pacifier from the baby.

Smirking, I clutch a fistful and rip off the corner. The meat melts in my mouth, sweet, tangy, and just a little smoky. My eyes shut for a second as I breathe in the taste of it and the virus narcotic trickles into my veins. The buzz shivers from one of my resident junky microbes to the next. I open my eyes, tilting my head at the mortification—or is it fascination—on Ryan's face. "You're not seriously worried I'll pick up some nasty germs, right? Because it's a little too late for that." What is it I'm enjoying here? I never really pegged myself for the kind to pierce my nose with safety pins, spike my hair, and wear black lipstick just to get a rise out of people.

"That's what I heard. Your immune system is hyper-resistant, no?" Not the response I expected. There's no shock here. I'm not a mutant viral to him; I'm the neighbor girl with a new Kawasaki Ninja 300 and he'd like to take it for a test drive. "Nicolas says you're a kick-ass fighter and you resist the cravings for human flesh as well."

This is new. I'm not sure how to respond. The savior/saint worship was just plain awkward. But this is different. The blatant naïveté of him catches me off guard. My footing slips, sliding into his objective appreciation for the silver lining on my cloudy grey.

I claw at the brakes. "And you believe him? You shouldn't be so gullible. The city is crawling with mutants like me. Who do you think is causing all the trouble out there?" I step menacingly forward. "We're smarter too—in a cunning predator sort of way."

He nods appreciatively.

"The grey guys in the middle have taken sides, Ryan. And it's not your side." My right toe slides forward, nearly touching his left, a challenge between us. "I'd suggest being a little more cautious."

The last thing I expect to hear is the click of a safety on a Glock that he slides casually out of the back of his scrubs and swings around between our noses. "Oh, I am." He waggles his caution at me with a grin. "My dad is military. That's another reason Dr. Pêsqué asked for me."

I step back. Now it's my turn to appreciate his toys. Much as I'm morally opposed to guns in general, given the current circumstances, I'm finding many practical uses for a boy that knows how to use one. My dad always told me, "Expediency trumps virtue." I guess he was right. At this point, I'm having a hard time believing there's such a thing as an absolute. The whole game board has been upended and all the cards shuffled into a hopeless mess.

I back down, a crooked smile cracking the thin line of my lips. "You and I, we're going to get along." This boy is a whole new breed for me. What would I call it...friend?

"That's what we're hoping." He shoves the gun back behind his shirt.

"So..." I hop up on the counter next to the sink, "what's the deal, Frenchie?"

"A trade." Snagging the rolling stool with his foot, he takes a seat across from me.

"A trade?" I point my toe at his chest. "You seem like a nice kid, Ryan. Let's just do a reality check here. Holland has my cousins and my little sister Amber. He knows I'll do whatever it takes to get them out of the quarantine zone. Now take a look at me. I'm missing one shoe, my dress is smeared, smudged, tattered and burned, I have no pockets, and nothing to go in them if I did. What the hell are you hoping to get from me?"

"The plague—and its cure."

I shake my head like I'm dealing with an amateur. "Look, I don't know what you're thinking, but Nicolas already has all the blood work from me and Greyson. He's got some nice little creams he's developed to handle the symptoms, but the cure isn't there."

"We don't want your blood. It's a dead end."

"I could have told you that. Vegetarian thing, right?"

"Well, that's a big part of it. Some effects from the neural net responses to the self-deprivation come into play as well, but that area is definitely not the most urgent focus of our research."

"Then why am I here? Why are you holding Amber hostage?" I lean in closer to get him to focus on the critical issue. "What do you want?"

"Sam. Nicolas Vadlamani's brother."

Chapter 26

"Sam? What does he have to do with anything?" My first thought is that Nicolas has made some progress on figuring out what makes Sam different from the rest of us, what makes him sick even though he was vegetarian like me.

"It's complicated."

"Try me."

He glances at his watch, "Well, it would require some history."

Cocking an eyebrow, I invite him with hands wide open to note my pitiful lack of pressing appointments.

"Ah, oui, c'est ça." Oh, that's right. My French is still alive and kicking. He checks his watch again, which makes me wonder what's pressing outside this little room, and then shrugs in his little Frenchie way. "Have you heard the name 'Tanner'?"

"Everyone in Utah has heard the name 'Tanner.' Which one? Congressman, Businessman, or News Anchor?"

"None of them. This is a boy who caught the virus. His girlfriend died, but he didn't."

"Oh, Gavin Tanner. Of course, I've heard of him. He's the reason the ZV Institute couldn't go door to door collecting all the infected kids. His family financed a big lawsuit and he won. Didn't hear much about him after that—of course, I was a little under the radar, hiding out in a hole under a church."

Ryan's face scrunches as he scoots his rolling stool back to the examination table and leans against it, folding his arms. His short scrub sleeves crumple up and a rose nestled between the words, *"sagesse,"* and *"courage,"* bulges across his bare bicep. Okay, so it's a wisdom and courage type of tattoo. The tips of letters peek out from the neck of his tunic—a very strategically placed tattoo, easily camouflaged with a white-collar shirt and tie. His prominent dark brows wrinkle up. "In a hole under a church? This is too much, Evelyn." Geez, he's sensitive too? The word phrasing, like the vowels, is just a little off, but a perfect match to what the French would be. "You have no family?"

"Not all American families are rich enough to own armies of lawyers. Forget about it. Ancient history. No one cares." Pity is poison. It melts your heart right out of your chest and makes you think someone should do something about all the shit that's flying your way. "Amber is my family. Let's just focus on the present and getting her the hell out of here."

"But..."

"Look, if you're concerned about me, you can scrounge up some jeans or scrubs. I'm not picky." We both look at my tattered disaster of a dress. "And shoes would be nice."

"No problem...but…"

"Let's just cut to the chase here. What does Gavin Tanner have to do with anything?"

The flickers around his eyes and mouth tell me he's struggling to overcome a natural chivalric tendency, but he finally gives in and gives me what I want. "Gavin's father didn't trust the political climate, so he packed his son up and sent him here on a private jet to stay with relatives. His relatives have ties to Baylor, and the Tanner's have been funding research toward a cure using Gavin's samples."

"That's great and all. I wish them success. I'll donate. But what does any of this have to do with Sam, or you and me, for that matter?"

"Everything. When Nicolas showed up, his research significantly advanced the study. Dr. Pêsqué is a colleague of Nicolas's parents. They were both studying different aspects of the virus in Paris when the Vadlamani's died. Richard, Nicolas's cousin, was working here at Baylor when Gavin first arrived. He recognized the virus immediately and called Dr. Pêsqué to consult. Since Dr. Pêsqué worked in la Marine"—the French words for the Navy slip naturally off his tongue— "for a large part of his career, naturally he called my father for support. I've been working as Dr. Pêsqué's intern. He was intrigued by the opportunity to study the infection in a living, human host, but did not want to depend on the government of the infected country for the security of our team."

As Ryan rambles through his meandering explanation, sometimes my attention wanders, distracted by the French inflection. I force my head to focus on the pertinent information. "My father was willing to provide Naval support as part of a National Security procedure. But, we've been very discouraged. Even with the data from Gavin, we found no breakthroughs. And then Nicolas arrived with his data from Sam. Gavin and Sam have the same reaction to the virus."

Now I see where the long trail is leading. "The comparison of the two showed you the common thread."

"Précisément!" He grins. Shall we just call that smile "French Silk Cheesecake?" He's quite pleased that I caught on. A little too pleased, though, like he wasn't expecting me to.

I'm a little offended, so I venture to break out a little rusty French to demonstrate that I'm not a stupid, monolingual American. *"Enfin, il n'y a pas que la beauté chez moi,"*—a rough equivalent of "I'm more than just a pretty face." I smirk.

He raises an eyebrow and does that Frenchie move with his face, raising his eyebrows, turning down the corners of his lips and nodding his understated approval. *"Alors, là, tu as raison."* My favorite words in the language, "You're right."

"So, what's the common thread?"

"Gluten. Both Sam and Gavin were gluten intolerant. We think that's how a 4000-year-old virus managed to revive itself."

I know about gluten-free. My twin brothers were intolerant. Cooking at my house was an adventure. Amber and I were vegetarian, the twins were gluten-free; there was hardly anything left to eat besides fruits, veggies, and salad.

"Which kind?" I ask. "Celiac? Does it interact with the ZV virus? That would make sense because that involves overstimulation of some antibodies, right?" His eyebrows flick up. He's impressed I know there are roughly a couple types. "My little brothers were intolerant..." I don't finish my explanation because I still can't talk about the family I've lost. Maybe that's why I drive all my focus to preserve what's left of it, instead of mourning over the ashes. I clench my jaw, and harden the corners of my eyes, sandbagging against the hot pricking that threatens rain.

Ryan looks down at the ground for a while and then cocks one eye up at me. "Nicolas told me what happened to your family. I'm sorry…"

"So am I." I pinch off the trickle of sympathy. "So, is that it? Celiac disease causes the mutation?"

"Actually, we're not certain. And that's the problem. There's a newer field of study of non-celiac patients who demonstrate an innate immune response to gluten rather than a specific antigen response. About 1% of the population will suffer from Celiac disease, which essentially attacks gluten with antibodies that destroy the lining of the intestines allowing toxin seepage. But there is another 6% of those that don't have celiac disease but are still gluten sensitive and respond positively to the gluten free diet. The research isn't conclusive yet as to what causes their symptoms."

"So, Sam and Gavin were both this minority type of gluten intolerant?"

"Exactly. Their bodies were essentially attacking the virus like gluten, but not with antigens, with an innate immune response that activates K-Cells—killer cells…"

"…and causes the 'zombie episodes'?"

"Well, yes. We think."

"So, what's the holdup? Get your samples; do your tests; find the cure."

"That would be so much easier if we still had access to the samples."

"Don't you? Oh, my God! Did something happen to Sam?" I lean forward, my elbows on my knees, my hands flying wide in astonishment. "He was fine when we left the compound. I thought he was getting medication from Nicolas." I can't even imagine how torn up Nicolas will be if he's lost Sam—then again, maybe I can. Glimpsing how I would feel if it were Amber shakes me to my core.

"No, no. Sam is fine—at least as far as we know. It's just that, he's in the Knight compound, and getting samples is out of the question. I'm not sure you heard, but Ms. Knight has made some type of religious proclamation and restricted all access to the compound."

"So? Look around, buddy! This place is crawling with military. Why don't they send some over and pull him out? We need that cure!"

Ryan shakes his head, gazes at the tile, and sighs, scooting the stool a little closer, which makes me have to bend my neck a little more to make eye contact. "I'm afraid our conversation has misled you...*euh*... Evelyn." He glances up to make sure I'm still okay with the first name basis. "The cure isn't exactly our first priority at the moment. And...the Knight compound is way too far into the infection zone. All the military they've left us are burning and pulling back. They're not sending any troops in. I'm afraid your variety of the virus...not you, of course...the others...create too much of a predator. It's like trying to fight a city infested with highly trained terrorist cells. And the worst of it is, one bite turns our guys into an armed enemy."

Now it's my turn to lean back and cross my arms. My head rests against the spackled grey cabinets behind me. "I understand what they're up against. But they don't really think they can contain this with the military, right? And, seriously, what could possibly be more important than the cure? That's the only way they're going to actually contain the infection."

Ryan takes a deep breath and then glances at the door like he wants to pass me info I don't have the clearance level for. "*Écoute,*" he glances at the door again. "I'm supposed to wait for Holland and Dr. Pêsqué to present the..."

"The deal?"

"Their plan." He rubs his forehead, trying to figure out how to break some bad news to me. "You need to know what happened to Gavin."

I put my hand over my mouth. Whatever happened to Gavin, is most likely Sam's fate—and, judging by the look on Ryan's face, it's not hopeful. Poor kid! The virus dealt him a tough hand. Poor Nicolas! I suck in some air and harden the little lines around my eyes. "Just tell me." My fingertips grip the edge of the blue Formica counters.

His mouth pressed in a line and pulled to one side, he glances back at the door, weighing his decision.

"Tell me."

This is a boy that always does the right thing. He's been raised military—honor and orders—but somewhere in there, he had a mom that gave him a heart. His eyebrows furrow just a tad over his brown eyes. It must be the eyes—or maybe it's the reluctance to break faith. For some reason I can't quite put my finger on, the strings of his empathy spiral delicately across the space between us, winding themselves around the cracked, burned, and shattered stone that is my heart. The bottom line is: I trust this guy—the same way I can't bring myself to trust Greyson, not implicitly, because I can't trust someone in the crunch if I don't trust the curve of their instincts on life issues.

The threads wafting out to connect me to Ryan can't be pheromones, because my smell is far too strong for any of those to possibly tunnel through to him. Maybe Ryan just likes my outdoor BBQ char smell, or maybe he's been cooped up too long in a basement lab and is craving some fresh air, at break-neck speeds, around treacherously winding mountain roads, and I look like a way sick bike.

Either way, a bond is spinning between us. This must be what happens when you meet the person you'll one day call your best friend. From the first second, all the science converged between us and I feel like we're a pair, like we've been connected in a previous life and know each other on the inside even if we're strangers on the outside.

Or maybe, let's be real, it's just his job to tame and train the beast.

With one last glance at the door and his watch, and a resigned shake of his head, he opts to spill his guts. "We think the virus has bonded, converted, mutated—we won't know exactly until we get some samples—with the K-Cells."

That doesn't sound promising to me. A virus with zombie symptoms hooking up with the body's own killer cells. "So...what happened to Gavin?" I don't really want to know the answer. The screams from the building behind the chapel where they were keeping Sam on the Knight compound still haunt me. A shiver slides up my spine as Ryan's eyes tell me more than his words.

"The information is still very sketchy. We have intel reports. Holland has an informer on the inside of the Knight compound."

"The Knight compound? Wait. I thought you had Gavin here." Words and smells tap at my memory. Sam's odor had been lingering around the compound a lot longer than he had. Ashley said Sam wasn't the first of his kind they'd "welcomed" there. The wolfish hunger in her eyes when she heard about Sam's "condition" bugged me when we first met. Now it scares me, and it's hard to scare me these days.

"Gavin and Ashley Knight are cousins. His father wouldn't allow him to be housed in the research facility."

"Can't say I blame him. My dad didn't have the funds to put me up in an armed hotel."

"Everything was going smoothly, until Dr. Vadlamani's cousin, Richard, started noticing some progressive mutations in the virus samples we were receiving. Not long afterward, the Reverend Lazarus Knight, Ashley's father, died suddenly. There was no autopsy. The funeral took place on the compound—very private affair. And then all the cooperation stopped. The samples stopped coming."

Amber's little episode with Sam in the New Mexico hotel replays itself in my head. My breathing kicks up a gear or two. "Did Gavin have…episodes? Zombie episodes?"

"If he did, the compound kept them secret. But when Dr. Vadlamani shared his research and samples from Sam with us, he exposed the commonality between them and we were able to trace a similar pattern in the samples from Gavin. But Dr. Vadlamani was administering an agent that was slowing the mutation in Sam's cells. From what we gathered from his cousin's research, we think that the Knights were doing just the opposite with Gavin. They were actually accelerating the mutation."

I jump off the table. The predator in me needs to pace. I have a really nasty intuition about this. Sam was completely out of his mind, possessed with the virus when he went after Amber. If that happened to Gavin, who had no Nicolas around to control him, there's no way he could have resisted the cannibal urges.

214

Rubbing my arms and pacing back and forth between the door and the back wall, I try to organize my thoughts, find the point of action, so I can process the information calmly and objectively. "So, is Nicolas working with his cousin Richard, now? Have they come up with what might be going on inside the compound?"

Ryan hangs his head and then looks up at me, biting the inside of his lip. "We lost Richard. Dr. Deshpande died last night in one of the early raids." He stands up like he needs a route of action as well. Maybe it's not just the virus that has me pacing. "We think it was a planned attack. Our man on the inside has some pretty good evidence that Ms. Knight has enlisted some of the mutant ZV gang leaders. The kidnapped victims, the children, we suspect they're ending up in the compound. Where..." the narrative stops.

I stop. In the calming blue paint on the walls, Ryan can't seem to come up with the words to finish. He doesn't need any. I can guess. It only takes a couple brain waves for me to connect the sparks in my mind.

Oh, God! They took Cameron, my little ginger cousin. They dragged him off in front of my uncle!

Closing my eyes to shut out the worst of the possibilities, I push my palms against my temples, willing the images to go black.

Ryan's hand touches my back. He's close. The faint odor of Herbs de Provence breaks through the darkness. "They took my cousin...in the raid on my aunt's house. What are they doing with them...the kids? Do you think...?" I glance up at his eyes, looking for the answer. "I heard screaming from the building where they took Sam."

"We don't know." He shakes his head, unable or unwilling to respond.

They don't know? They need to know what they're dealing with here. Ashley Knight is psycho. "The Reverend, Ashley, she's planning a Day of Judgment. She has wild ideas about the virus being some sort of demented resurrection."

"We know. We monitored the broadcast. That's the least of our worries."

How is that possible? There's something worse than a whole compound of religious fanatics willingly allowing a ZV to infect them? My mind runs unbridled to all the possible dark scenarios, painting pictures and mashing up images from the past. Suddenly the human part of me needs to sit down. My knees are weak and the ground under my feet is rattling. I reach blindly for the stool on wheels. It slides back against the exam table as I sit. Ryan steadies me with a hand on my shoulder.

"Our man on the inside…"

"Jacob." I fill in the missing info reflexively, tonelessly. "His name was Brother Jacob…at least on the compound."

Ryan looks a bit perplexed.

"He didn't say much, but he showed me to my room. He was doing his best to pass me some info…but, I got…sidetracked." Miguel must be one of Ashley's hired ZV food suppliers. That's what he was doing on the compound the night I heard the screaming.

"Well, the information he gathered has led us to believe that a third type of viral has surfaced."

"What? More like Sam?

"Not exactly. Sam's virus isn't technically much different than yours. It's just the way his body reacts to it. But under the right conditions, specifically the introduction of human organs into the diet…"

A surge of bile rises up my chest. It's not so much that Sam eating human organs disgusts me. I've seen enough of that. It's the screaming I heard from the Judgment Hall. Think about it. Which would you rather? Be chased down, tackled, and devoured by the beast in the jungle OR be kidnapped, locked up in a box, and then dropped deliberately into the cage with nowhere to run, nowhere to hide, all hope of a fight gone?

What really makes me shiver in revulsion, though, is the cold, calculating insanity of the keeper who delivers the living, squirming victim to the cage.

Ryan doesn't notice my reaction because I keep my features frozen—stone-hard—in the face of his clinical explanation, oh, so far removed from the tearing, ripping, and shrieking. "…it will mutate again, triggering some psychotic reactions in the carrier…"

And now my heart breaks for Sam because I've seen those "psychotic reactions" in the flesh. I've seen them kick in and hunt down a six-year-old while she slept. What Ryan means is that the virus has won. The Sam we used to know is gone.

"…and a lethal reaction in his bite victims. But once they've died, the virus reactivates certain functions of the brain and then…"

My ZV ears pick up the sound of squishing soles stomping toward the observation lab before Ryan's do. My head turns instinctively toward the door. Ryan stops abruptly as a key jiggles in the lock again, longer this time, unlocking it. The knob turns and Holland's crumpled suit follows his scuffed and faded Oxfords into the room. The place is overrun with the uncut and uncensored aroma of over-cooked ham left too long on the counter. My feet recoil the rolling chair from the door, instinctively, just a few inches, before I plant them firmly in the tile square below.

"…and then, full-blown, ravenous, mindless, organ-sucking zombies—the living dead." Holland glares at Ryan.

Chapter 27

No wonder Holland hauled me in here. What's the saying? Fight fire with fire. "And that's where I come in. You want me to go in there and take out this new monster."

Holland nods toward the mirror and a camera in the corner of the ceiling. "This is a monitored observation room." He turns to Ryan. "That information is above your clearance level, Mr. Samson."

Instead of cringing, Ryan bristles and straightens up, looking down his nose at Holland, a French cooked *Steak au Poivre* squaring off with an *American Salisbury*. He's clearly been around Holland long enough to have nurtured a healthy contempt. "Dr. Pêsqué is not concerned with your 'levels.' We are here with the French *Marine*, and as his official interpreter and assistant, I have equal access to any and all information that he has."

Before Holland can respond, the door behind opens up again, ushering in an arm piled with neatly folded jeans, a black sweatshirt, and a small, clear plastic hygiene kit, complete with a travel brush. Before the face even breaks through the crack, the heavenly Sunday dinner smell gives it away. One whiff and I'm off my chair and practically skipping toward the door. "Nicolas!" The clothes scrunch up between us and the plastic sack tumbles to the floor as I throw my arms around the familiar smell and the logical, reasoning sanity behind his eyes.

"How are you?" He leans back to delve through my bloodshot, purple-rimmed irises to the wounds hidden behind them. The cut on my nose attracts his attention.

The rushing flow of Nicolas's empathy always seems to flood everything around him and makes the ground soggy between us. Letting go, I deflect, glancing over at Ryan. I want to stay on solid ground. "Where's Amber, Nicolas? Is she safe?"

"She's fine. She's with your cousins." He won't give up. "I heard about what happened at your aunt's…" Digging in his pocket, he produces a little tube of his miracle cream, opens it, and dabs some on my nose and cheek. I've been avoiding my reflection in the observation mirror. Miguel left me pretty banged up.

"Yeah, it was bad." I cut him off so I don't have to wallow in my mourning. "Thanks for the clothes." I take them, stepping back until I bump against the solid rock that is Ryan. "You have my cousins, right? Is there a way to get them to my Aunt Rebecca's in Montana?"

Holland sneers. "We don't have resources for babysitting orphans."

I glare at him, my mouth open, ready to shoot darts of venomous vowels.

Ryan steps in. "I have resources."

Holland bristles and squares his shoulders. "You people don't get it, do you? It's not about 'save the children' anymore. We're looking at total destruction." He pokes a finger at Nicolas. "If the compound has turned your brother, they have a vicious, calculating, zombie-spawning predator over there. The ZVs are sheep in comparison to these living dead wolves."

"So…" it hurts me to say it, but I think it hurts Nicolas more. I watch his face as I put the horror into words, "…they've 'turned' Sam into this new mutant whose bite creates actual zombies—not just ZVs? His victims are the dead walking? We're not talking about very sick, living human beings anymore?" I need to sit down. My head drops and my arms flex to haul me up on the counter while I gain a little time to deal with the reality of the bona fide zombie apocalypse—started by Nicolas's little brother.

"Exactly." Nicolas's face hardens into a clinical mask. "You know Sam reacts differently to the virus?"

I nod at Ryan. "He's already told me about Gavin and your research."

Nicolas glances back. Ryan looks just a tad defensive but adjusts his stance to stand his ground.

"Good, then." He's not actually happy about it. "We believe that once the gluten intolerant begin ingesting human organs, the virus uses the new chemical environment to mutate, combining with the killer cells activated by the gluten. The effect of a bite from a carrier is…"

"Disaster." Holland just can't shut up.

"Lethal." Nicolas stares him down. Authority—another flavor of the doctor I have yet to sample. "In this mutation, the bite results in death, and then a sort of virus-driven pseudo resuscitation."

"So…what? You think Ms. Ashley is turning Sam into a zombie factory?"

"We don't think." Holland jeers at us amateurs. "We have intel. And that's not what Ms. Ashley is doing. She's masterminding a religious revolution by spawning an army of zombie converts."

"Not everyone is interested in an army, Holland. Ms. Ashley is operating under the delusion that this is the resurrection." I'm wasting words because his skull is too thick for any new ideas to penetrate the fog.

Nicolas shakes his head. It's not so much that Holland is jumping to conclusions as that he's not following a logical train of thought. Nicolas is methodical. "Once the virus mutates in the gluten intolerant host, the reaction in new bite victims is self-destructive. The virus initiates a massive manufacturing and conversion of the body's own k-cells, effectively killing the host. We can't be sure because we have no observation cases, but extrapolating from the rate of reproduction in healthy blood samples, we're hypothesizing death in under ten minutes."

Ryan jumps in at that point, the med-student side of his brain kicking in. "But while the k-cell modified virus is killing the body, it's also heading straight for the brain. Once the host is dead, the virus hotwires the engine and the body is back up and running."

Nicolas isn't totally down with Ryan's description. Ryan flashes him that forgive-all grin he has—at least, I'd totally forgive him—and Nicolas shakes his head and rolls his eyes. "That is just theory. As I indicated before," he focuses pointedly on Ryan, "we have no observable data on that point."

Ryan is overly enthusiastic. "That's not totally true."

Holland's not about to be beaten to the punch of his own intel report. "Our man on the inside…"

"Brother Jacob," I interject again. We're finally getting the conversation back around to him.

"That's his cover name." Holland narrows his eyes at me. "He was attempting to establish communication with you when you went AWOL."

"He did establish communications with me and I did NOT go AWOL. I watched my family's neighborhood being attacked by a ZV herd and ran to help them." Pinning my stare on Holland, I nail him to the wall. "Oh yeah, you don't believe in helping people. You just shoot them down in cold blood and leave them bleeding in the street."

He ignores me, convinced my priorities are all screwed up. But, seriously, what's the sense of saving the world from the monsters if the saviors are just monsters of another breed? "We have confirmed visuals."

"Of what?"

"Of Reverend Lazarus Knight. 'Brother Jacob' has observed the dead man walking. We have zombies, Ms. Cross, certified living dead. Your friend Ashley Knight is manufacturing them. The ZV raids and kidnappings are most likely food stores she's stockpiling."

"She's not my friend." The implication, the worst of my fears, raises its gory head and distracts me. Oh, God! Miguel and his goons dragged my cousin Cameron off.

The possibilities collide in my mind, one more gut-wrenching than the last. He's either zombie dine-in or the mad reverend is planning to convert a bunch of kids, create some kind of zombie cult where the leaders are mutants and the minions are full-fledged, ravenous, living dead. They could drop bombs on them and they'd still shamble, mutilated, bloody and burned, jaws clacking, out of the smoke and ashes. Or worse. They could swarm out of the dust. What if they're like me?

The virus has enhanced all my predator instincts. Hell, my fingernails grow pointed now. Is this seriously happening? I thought it was bad enough when kids were getting the insatiable craving for human flesh and then dying from the virus that was consuming their guts. At least once they died they stayed dead. Now they're just dying right off and morphing into mindless human meat grinders.

Holland claps. "Good. If she's not your friend, it will be easier for you to eliminate her."

"I'm not 'eliminating' anyone. I've lived life as nature's perfect predator and managed to never kill a living soul. I'm not going to start now." I shift uncomfortably on the counter...I did bite Dr. Christensen in the lab—no telling how that finished. In the end, I guess the monster is inside of all of us. It's just more visible in me. Sometimes the teeth and the claws have to come out or we won't survive. I shiver.

My head slumps, thinking about my family, my aunt and uncle, that they'd still be alive if I'd never brought the Z-Virus to their doors. Maybe I am a killer. Just because I didn't do the actual biting, doesn't mean I didn't kill them. I'm a virus myself; exposure to me is lethal.

"Why don't you just get 'Jacob' to bring Sam out? There's not really any point in keeping your man on the inside anymore now that the state is being evacuated."

Holland squints at me like I'm the totally thick one in the room. "Because our communication channel has been cut. The Reverend Ashley announced she had plans for the New Year. But on Christmas Eve, after it swallowed up your boyfriend again, the whole compound shut down. We have no idea what's going on inside. Our man hasn't checked in. Surveillance has detected zero incoming and outgoing traffic since. The place is a black hole."

"Do you think...?"

"We'd torch the compound, just to make sure none of the new breed escapes." Holland stares belligerently in my direction, knowing that he just told me Greyson is in there. "But Dr. Vadlamani here insists we need samples of the mutated virus."

Nicolas steps between Holland and me. "We have an extraction plan to get Sam out of the compound. We need the virus in his blood, or this new strain will wipe us out before we have any hope of containing it. You and I are the only ones that can get in without provoking a war we don't have the manpower to win."

I'm not sure what makes Nicolas think we can get in. If Ashley has already started her little resurrection rituals, the place could be crawling with the new breed.

"Wait a minute. Before we go all commando here, I want to get a few things straight." I shrug off the self-pity and uncertainty raging in my head and breathe in the one driving force that disperses all the clouds of self-doubt, anger, fear, and…whatever. Amber will survive. She'll survive because I will do whatever it takes to make that happen. And now my cousins are melted into that metal bar that stiffens my resolve.

Jumping off the counter, I plant my feet in front of Holland, my arms crossed. I'm not going to beg from behind Nicolas. "I'm not doing anything until I personally see my sister and my cousins on a flight out of here."

"Non-negotiable! I'm not wasting limited resources on non-essential targets."

"Non-essential to you!"

Nicolas reigns in the argument. "Agent Holland," Agent? What agency is he working for? "I think you would agree that the prime initiative, at this point, before we completely evacuate, is to extract the one source that could yield vital data essential to my research. We have to know what we're fighting before we can fight it. Dr. Pêsqué is adamant that samples from Sam are a critical key to unlocking my parents' work on the virus. I can't go back to Paris without them."

Holland's not impressed; he's kind of angry. "I don't have the resources." He steps toward me, his chest breaking into my space, intimidating me. "We do have bullets to spare."

My left eyebrow inches up.

"We could just off one of the little brats every couple of hours until this mutant bitch gets her priorities straight."

My heart stops. I've seen this fiend in action. This isn't an empty threat. The virus…no, maybe it's just flat out indignation…floods my veins with rage. Holland's pig meat odor swirls saliva around my tongue. My fists shake with the strain of restraint, but I can't unleash the beast in front of

Nicolas and Ryan. Diplomacy has to run its course before the claws and teeth come out.

Nicolas looks appalled. His mouth opens but nothing comes out.

Ryan drops an arm between Holland and me. He's not astonished. His dad's a general; he's familiar with these tactics. "I have resources. I can have them on a helicopter in half an hour."

Holland turns a disdainful stare on him. "Those children are in the custody of the American government. You can fly your little helicopters wherever you please, but our detainees won't be on them. Not until SHE…" he pokes an accusative finger at my chest. The touch of his flesh on my body triggers a chemical chain reaction that nearly gets his neck torn out. Did I just growl? I back off, breathing hard, not because I'm scared of him; I'm scared of me.

Nicolas knows the signs. He places himself strategically between Holland and me on the pretext of getting in his face. "We're wasting resources arguing this point. The extraction plan is time-sensitive. The timeliest resolution is for us to dispatch the children in order to secure Ms. Cross's cooperation and unwavering focus."

Nicolas is a tower of impregnable chill. You can't help but want to nibble on a guy like that.

"Non-negotiable. We will retain control of the children until Ms. Cross," I hate the way Holland says my name, "has completed the objective."

From behind Nicolas, I interject. "Non-negotiable. I'm not going anywhere until I know my sister and cousins are safe."

Ryan breaks into French in frustration. "*Nom de Dieu! Écoutez!* We find a compromise. I arrange transport for Evelyn's cousins. Dr. Pêsqué and I will assume responsibility for Evelyn's young sister and guarantee her safety until the mission is accomplished."

Staring at Ryan, I size him up. Do I trust him that much? I just met him. I don't even know this Dr. Pêsqué. He could be another Dr. Christensen for all I know. But Ryan's head is cocked, his eyes boring into mine, tugging on those invisible threads of this new race called friendship that he drilled into the stone casing around my heart. I do trust him.

Call it instinct—I am a beast and I sense an ally here. If he promises to fly my cousins to Montana, he'll get it done. If he says he'll guarantee Amber's safety, he will. And I know his government has an intimate interest in guaranteeing his. If Ryan's military sense of duty isn't enough to get the job done, the compassion that bleeds right through to his tattoo will finish it.

"To my aunt's house in Montana."

Holland doesn't say anything while he glares at the three of us—a bunch of bleeding-heart liberals that don't have a clue what it takes to save a country. He stalks out of the room, shaking his head. "The extraction operation starts at 0800 in the morning. Total evac of this facility begins at 1000 hours. By nightfall, this place will be a hole in the ground. Get your shit together." The door slams behind him.

Chapter 28

Sometime before 8:00 a.m. the next morning, wind whips across the landing pad on top of the university research building. The helicopter blades spin ruthlessly and impatiently, scattering my hair in flashes across my face. The panorama from the roof paints a picture of how desperate the crisis has become. Pillars of smoke dot the landscape, spiraling into the big Texas sky. From the smell of them, not all the fires are buildings, products of the ZV raid that burned my aunt's house. The "decontamination" process is in full swing.

A pile of smoke streams up from the east toward the airport. On the highways and the surface streets, the flow of traffic has stopped. The odd angles of the cars smashed into little packs speaks volumes about the cause. The damage is worse than I thought.

I can't help but wonder how many secret covens of ZVs a populated center like this has been hiding. We know the virus wasn't airborne, but with its highly selective incubating environment, people could have been exposed, picked it up, and propagated it across the country without even knowing they were carriers. Holland and his goons in black are evidence that Salt Lake was not the only populated center with a ZV Institute. How widespread is this? Three pairs of arms engulf me as I digest the scenery.

"Evelyn! Where's mommy?" Prudence whines, clinging to my knees until I swing her onto my hip. She brushes tenaciously at the little strawberry blond hairs, incessantly raiding her face. All three of my cousins are still in their pajamas.

I don't have time to feel or think about what I'm seeing, even if I want to. The focus here is on getting them somewhere safe, somewhere so sparsely populated that no matter how the virus explodes, they'll be isolated from the infection, at least for a while…long enough for Nicolas to do his work.

Smiling broadly, I kiss her freckled cheek. "You're going to Aunt Rebecca's ranch in Montana for New Year's!"

Her brow creases, but before she can pick at the wound her parent's deaths have left festering in my mind, Craig jumps in. "Are you coming with us?"

He already knows I'm not. This is his way of begging without begging. "Remember what I told you." Crouching down, I set Prudence on her feet and wrap the two little girls up in my arms for one last hug-fest.

Paula is old enough to guess at what's going on; her face crumples and then her eyes muddy up with tears. I can't be sure if she's swatting the tears from her cheeks or the blond curls that keep whipping into her eyes. Prudence's little brain can't even imagine the gruesome reality of what's happened to her parents. "These girls are your responsibility. This is what you do. You make sure they survive."

Craig nods, swallowing hard. His eyes crinkle and spasm as he fights the tears squeezed out by the weight of his new responsibility.

Ryan steps up behind me, placing an urgent hand on my arm as I straighten up and squeeze Craig's shoulders tight.

"We have a pretty tight flight schedule…" he ushers the three of them toward the spinning blades.

Craig whips back around to where I'm standing flanked by Holland's goonies. "What about Cameron?"

What about Cameron? That is the question. I'm going into the hive and chances are he's hidden away inside. My aunt's face is there in Craig's, pleading. There's so little time left. To secure Amber's safety, I have to get Sam out, and I don't know what the situation will be. I don't even know if Cameron is still alive. But I can't look at my aunt's face and tell her I won't go after her boy. I can't tell her he's lost, because she gave up everything to take Amber and me in. I owe this to her. "I'll find him. He'll be with me!"

Ryan hustles the children into the copter and then ducks, running back as it veers away to the north.

The wind is still rioting as he reaches our little group by the door. "They should be in Montana in about 3 hours." He grins at me. This is a boy that's always had the world at his fingertips, but he's been shopping for approval his whole life.

Lucky for him, approval is on sale today. I'm so relieved I throw my arms around him before I even realize what I'm doing. It's like the walls have crumbled and water starts rushing out. The damp stream on my cheek brings me back to reality and the sensation of his palms on my back. This hug goes both ways.

Stepping back awkwardly, I swipe the trickle of tears from my face and run my fingers back through my hair before I get my composure back and face him again. We're not finished. "I need to see Amber."

He hesitates. "*Euh…*" No doubt there's some pretty heavy pressure from Holland.

"Look, I took you at your word. I'm trusting you with the only thing that matters to me in this god-awful mess. Now you trust me."

His eyes and mouth tighten. It goes against the foundations of his military culture. He's more of a 'trust no one' kind of guy. But those strings he screwed tight inside me, they pull both ways.

"I swear I won't try anything. Nicolas and I go way back. I won't leave him hanging. I know what it's like to have the only family you have taken hostage."

Ryan's eyes soften up but the line on his mouth is still stiff.

Leaving this building without seeing Amber again is simply not an option. She has to know I came back for her. Ryan has to let me see her. "I get it. Back in that exam room, it seemed like I don't care about anything but getting my way. But the truth is I know Holland. People are nothing to him. I don't think he realizes that without the people, there's nothing worth saving. I had to play hardball to make sure my cousins were safe."

I'm not going to win unless I put everything out there on the table between us. "One of Reverend Ashley's little minions murdered my aunt and uncle…" Here they come again, the jagged splinters of guilt swirling around in the tsunami wave of pain. I can't finish my sentence.

He doesn't make me. His face melts. "C'mon." He makes a gesture to Holland's men signaling that he'll take over from here.

They shake their heads. "We've been detailed to escort Ms. Cross to Dr. Vadlamani's car. We don't leave her side until she's belted in."

A protest opens Ryan's mouth. Rolling my eyes and shaking my head, I stop it with a hand on his arm.

Our little playgroup catches the elevator to the ground level. At least they don't have Amber chained up in the dungeon. There must have been a company daycare here because the room we walk into has tiny tables and chairs all in a row and shelves of toys. The sun shines brightly in through the windows, the landscape and mayhem outside hidden by a cheery green hedge of bushes.

I don't get a very good look, because a squealing missile of blond hits me waist high and nearly knocks me off balance. "Evelyn!"

Amber vaults into my arms and I hug her like this might be the last time. Her little arms anchor around my neck and steady me in this sea of chaos. Suddenly, I feel stable, focused, and secure. This is my raison d'être. These little pink hands will always find love when they reach for it. I live to ensure that solid fact.

She raises her head from off my shoulder, her brows creased dramatically. "You left me!"

"I know, baby. I'm sorry." And I really am. I defend myself to myself as much as to her. "I thought you would be safer if I wasn't there. I thought they'd let you go with Aunt Esther to Aunt Rebecca's in Montana where you'd be far away from the sick people."

"Well, they didn't! And then they took Aunt Esther away! And then they," she glares, pointing at the nasty men in black standing watch at the door, "took Paula and Prudence away and wouldn't let me come too!"

"But now I'm here. You're going to be just fine." I cuddle and tickle her until she grins again.

"Where's Greyson?" Her head bobs on both sides of mine, searching for the boy that's always got my back.

Is that a knife in my rib cage? My teeth and lungs clench against the stab of her utter confidence that he should be here with me. I glance back at Ryan who is checking his very sophisticated watch. His eyes pop up for a moment at Greyson's name. I wonder what he knows about him. Why wonder? He's been collaborating with Nicolas and Holland. I'm sure he knows everything.

"Remember when Greyson helped us get away from the bad guys at the church and then I left you in the car while I went to get him out of the Institute?"

Amber's nose wrinkles while she thinks. It probably seems a lifetime ago to her. "When the building blew up?" Her little face brightens, pleased she found the answer.

I nod. "He helped me again. We had to get Craig away from his house. So now I have to go get Greyson again."

"He shouldn't let the bad guys catch him every time. Next time, tell him he should just stay with us and we can get away together." She smiles brightly, having just solved one of life's irritating problems, and frames my cheeks in her two pink hands.

I don't have the heart to tell her that, this time, Greyson chose to go with the bad guys. I'm not sure she'd understand. I'm not sure I understand.

Okay, yes! I'll admit I was a bit hormonal; I was crazy angry that some punk ripped apart the people that I loved—the people that loved me—because there aren't very many of them left. But Greyson aggravates the fury and feeds the viral urges. He's like an obsession with hot salsa. It burns, but the taste is irresistible.

"Okay." She sighs dramatically. "Let's go get him. They don't have any gummy bears or juice boxes here anyway and there's no one to play with."

Shifting my weight uneasily and hefting her a little higher on my hip, I break the news to her. "You can't go with me, sweetie."

Her eyes narrow and then her shoulders sink in around her neck. "Are the bad grey people there?" In her eyes, I can see ghosts of memories plastered to the back of her imagination, ghosts that will haunt her every time she closes her eyes. At least she still makes a distinction between good grey people and bad ones.

"You know they can't hurt me, right?"

"Yes." She's silent for a second. Ryan checks his watch again. He's under pressure but too compassionate to push me. He knows as well as I do that the outcome of our little plan isn't guaranteed. "Evy?" She caresses my grey cheeks and her wide eyes beg for the truth. "Wouldn't it be better if I was like you so they couldn't hurt me either?"

"No!" It's my gut response. But it's also the reason I'm not with Greyson anymore. That would definitely not be better. We are not angels, immune to death and destruction; we are demons that spawn it wherever we go. It's a constant fight to keep the monster inside chained up, and there's no guarantee that we'll always win. "No. It wouldn't be better."

"But then I could go with you."

I look to Ryan for backup. He buries his anxious scowl under a sunny smile. "*Euh*, you don't want to go with Evelyn. She's not going to have any fun. You and I, we're going on a helicopter ride and a big boat. Evelyn has to go to work with Nicolas."

I lean over, a half-grateful smile on my face, to pass off my precious bundle to Ryan, wondering about the boat ride. It wasn't really on the schedule of activities.

She slides over, wrapping her arms around his broad shoulders and shamelessly planting a little pink kiss on both his cheeks.

"Ryan is from France." Her face structures itself into her best imitation of a kindergarten teacher. "That's how they kiss there."

"I see you know each other already."

She puffs out her chest, and for the first time, I notice she's sporting a brand-new set of Christmas jammies. There's a Disney princess on them I don't recognize. It's been a while since I was at the movies. "He brings presents, too."

"Yes, I know he does." He just conjured up a helicopter to grant me half of the only Christmas wish I had. I wonder if he can come through with the other half. I guess that depends on how naughty or nice I am. Given the situation, I think I'm going to need to be on the first list to get what I want. I kiss Amber's sweet, rosy cheeks and breathe in her cupcake aroma. She's probably not had a decent bath for a couple of days now.

Her blond brows take a dive toward her nose. "You missed Christmas!"

I have to check with Ryan. The dates are all fuzzy now. He grimaces apologetically, so I know I missed a couple while I was in solitary. "We'll have a big party when I get back. You'll be having so much fun with Ryan, you won't even know I'm gone."

"That reminds me." Ryan rummages inside the pockets of his camouflage jacket. When it emerges, his hand dangles a long leather case trailing straps. "I thought it would make a nice accessory to your ensemble." He grins.

I hold up the knife, wondering what I'm supposed to do with it.

"Sometimes, a gun isn't quite as convenient." He leans down, tilting Amber my direction, and touches my thigh. "Strap it on there, by your right hand." I've never really pictured myself as a knife girl, but I'm all for broadening my horizons and follow his loose instructions. "Looks good." Ryan steps back to appreciate the effect of my new accessory.

Amber tilts her head and then leans into his ear whispering too loudly, "Can I have a knife for my jammies?" she asks, patting her thigh. Ryan's eyebrows go up as mine drop in the center. "A pink one."

Ryan sighs and nods ambiguously. For a pregnant moment, we stare at each other, each of us thinking we should probably have the other's job. Impulsively, he leans in and kisses me on both cheeks. "Au revoir. Bonne chance."

It's a totally standard French good-bye, but I'm an American and it feels like so much more. Opening the door, he heads down the hall with my sister, as my guards steer me in the opposite direction. Amber throws her arms around his neck and waves at me. Should I be worried that it's become second nature to my little sister to be handed off into the arms of whatever boy happens to be handy at the moment? A girl has to do what a girl has to do, right? Maybe I should just be grateful she doesn't cry on Santa's lap. "Give Nicolas a kiss for me!" She kisses her palm and flings it regally in my direction.

"I will!" Looking back as I walk forward, I wonder if this will be the last time I see her. My animal instincts trust Ryan, but no one cares about Amber as much as I do. I promise myself she'll see me again.

Whatever it takes…

My guards escort me to the elevator and out the main entrance. The sun on the eastern horizon, oblivious to the plague ravaging its empire, shines jubilantly over its crisp, pristine blue estate. Birds twitter in the slightly ragged trees, snuggling in for the winter.

Nicolas is waiting out front in the driver's seat of an idling white Honda sedan. Holland stands implacable outside the passenger door, a large black duffle bag at his feet. He dips my head under the frame as I climb in like I'm some sort of juvenile delinquent he's arrested. Instead of reading me my rights, he details the parameters of our mission, as he opens the back door and tosses the bag onto the seat. Metal clangs inside and I know what's in it.

Chase tossed us a bag like that the night he visited us in the church. I wonder where the combat boots are. Apparently, my civilian cross-trainers will have to do.

"Secure samples of the new strain." That's all Sam is to Holland. I watch Nicolas flinch, but say nothing. "Evacuation of this facility begins at 1000 hours." He leans into my window to speak directly to Nicolas. "We will extract and transport you from this building to the French aircraft carrier, Dr. Vadlamani, at 1100 hours. If you have not secured the new strain, you leave without it." He looks directly at me. "All other personnel are expendable."

Thank God, or maybe just Ryan, that Amber is no longer Holland's personnel. "They're purging this place. The bombs drop at 1200 hours."

Chapter 29

Three hours. Three hours to snatch Sam out of the compound and find Cameron so I can take him with me—if he's still alive. Please God, let him still be alive. And three hours to warn Greyson before the firestorm hits. If we're late, we have one hour of wiggle room, and then we're human BBQ with all the flesh eaters.

Nicolas pulls away from the curb and drives toward the edge of town for about fifteen minutes. The motion of the car resurrects my last conversation with Greyson. I play it on continual rewind, sighing and tensing at the appropriate cues. The wires of my indignation and frustration poke out of my head, stiffening the air between Nicolas and me.

"Nice knife," he teases.

I play along, attempting to drown out the drama cycling in my head. "You like that?" I pat it firmly. "It's the new fashion out of Paris."

We exchange awkward, professional smiles. Both of us have a job to do here. We're back to colleagues, miles away from the quiet intimacy of my aunt and uncle's barn.

"I'm sorry." He takes his eyes off the road for a second to check my response.

"For what? Flying my cousins out of the infection zone? Prying Amber out of Holland's jaws?"

"That was actually Ryan's doing. I'm afraid I can't take any credit for that."

Again, thank God…no, Ryan. I'm starting to see a pattern here. It's not that I'm atheist or anything; it's just that when the salesmen are as nuts as the Reverend Ashley Knight, it's hard to take the product seriously.

"Holland's agency is heading up the research right now, more from a security point of view than a scientific one. He's all we have to work with, and he can be a bit of an ass."

"A bit? I would say he's the definition—full of shit. Pardon my French. I have a demon virus in my head."

He allows himself a chuckle. The ripples of it gently vibrate some lighter air to my side of the car. "Really, I'm sorry for forcing you into this. I didn't think I could get Sam out without you." His eyes veer from the road to mine for a second, until he reads on my face that there's nothing to apologize for. If he'd paused to look a little longer, he'd have seen doubt there, maybe a little pity. Sam…there's not a lot of hope on that horizon.

"Nicolas, you've saved our asses multiple times." I allow a little velvet to slide over my tongue. Nicolas is like that; he needs kid-glove handling. "You're like the last hope we have for a cure. Of course, I'm not going to leave you hanging. Of course, I'm going after your brother with you. I was only negotiating tough about 'the extraction plan' to make sure Amber and my cousins were safe from that murderous bastard Holland. Pardon my French."

A half-smile flashes across the severe lines of Nicolas's face. "We were hoping we'd find Greyson with you." He tilts his head a little. "He's quite good at…"

"Mayhem and chaos? Yeah, he is." I don't trust myself to say too much more. Greyson stirs up a bunch of hormones and emotions that shoot injections of the virus into my brain and cloud my logic. "Did you track him?"

"Back to the compound. Our communications went down shortly after that. Holland wouldn't authorize any attempt to retrieve him."

I knew he was headed back to the compound. I knew it, but I was hoping he wasn't. Who am I kidding? He can't help himself. He was born to be worshipped. The need for adoration drives him the way the craving for organs drives a ZV.

Deep down inside, I've always known that the chain that bound him to me was his hunger. I don't want him to worship me; I don't want to worship him. That makes me the never-ending quest, the challenge that won't die. And what if, in the end, I'm not the elusive prey he thinks I am? What if one day he took me down? The thrill of the chase would die then, wouldn't it? And then, what's between us would be nothing more than an empty, gutted carcass.

I know what kind of a state he was in when he went back to Ashley because I put him in it. Those chemicals that were marching around in his blood, looking for a throne to usurp, could only be highly explosive when combined with Ashley Knight.

Nicolas doesn't know what happened between the two of us. He thinks we're still one big, happy family and that I'm pissed he couldn't convince Holland to go after Greyson as well as Sam. "In Paris, things will be different." He offers me an olive branch. "My parents and Dr. Pêsqué were very close. Ryan's father has tremendous influence."

"We're going to Paris?"

His eyes dart my direction. "You didn't know?"

I shake my head. I've dreamed of going to Paris since 7th grade when I took my first French class. Of course, in my dreams I wasn't grey and putrid with a nasty appetite for rare, gourmet, human organs smothered in red sauce.

"Apparently, Dr. Pêsqué was working with my father to manipulate the virus. The body function enhancing symptoms it exhibits in certain hosts…"

"Like me?"

He nods and smiles like I just scratched off a game card and won a free order of fries. "Yes! Hosts like you. They thought that strain of the virus could be mutated to actually work toward curing the body of other diseases." He checks my reaction. Nicolas. He's always the doctor. For him, it's not so much about the zombie apocalypse as it is about the new field of research. I nod encouragingly.

"Oh! That reminds me." He reaches into the back seat and shuffles around in the bags. His hand can't quite feel out what he's looking for, so he turns around in his seat. Normally, I would freak and grab the wheel to keep us steady, but there's not much traffic on the wreath-lined streets.

The place is practically a ghost town. The ZVs have gone underground for the UV light hours. Only odd, coat clad, recently bitten adults stagger along the sidewalk in the direction of the medical building. Chances are they won't get there before the virus has eaten holes through their organs…even if they do, there's no help there but the open end of a machine gun. "Here it is."

Nicolas produces a small cubed box wrapped in metal foil. Only Nicolas would bother to find wrapping paper and a bow in the middle of the zombie apocalypse. But I have to admit, with the silver and gold bells dangling from the street lamps, holly and pine boughs strung along the storefronts, the shiny silver wrapping under my nose, Nicolas's smell of rare prime rib filling the car, I almost catch the Christmas spirit for a nanosecond. "You missed Christmas." He offers me the box.

"I haven't been much in the holiday mood. I missed Thanksgiving, too."

He nudges the gift my way as he maneuvers the car around the small tangle of a motorcycle, a sedan, and an SUV. Only part of the motorcycle driver is still trapped under the bike.

I take the box, feigning embarrassment. "I didn't really get you anything."

Of course, Nicolas looks mortified that he's created awkwardness and starts to apologize, stumbling around the words.

Chuckling and shaking my head, I cut him off. "Nic, I'm joking." Under the wrapping, there's a small box and inside is a whole pot of the cream he used to heal the cut on my thigh and regrow Greyson's hair, not to mention the patch of mine that's now long enough to stand out straight and wave from the side of my head. I have this insane urge to lather up in the cream, see if it will turn me pink again, but I know it's more of a first-aid kind of thing. Who knows how many chunks of hair and skin I'll lose before Nicolas manages to find a cure for my strain of the virus. "Thank you, Nicolas," I manage with a great imitation of a smile. It's been an overall shitty holiday, but between Nicolas and Ryan, the grey in the putrid clouds seems to have a touch of shimmering silver to it.

"I'm sorry that's all I could come up with for you. I developed some for Dr. Pêsqué. We plan to incorporate the cream's active ingredients into our research with the new strain of the virus. One of the reasons we were able to convince Holland to…uh…recruit you…"

"You mean instead of shooting me in the head?"

Before he can conceal it, one of the disapproving looks he usually saves for Sam's inappropriately blunt remarks leaks out across his face. No wonder my aunt liked Nicolas right out of the gate. They both have a taste for rose-colored glasses. "…to assist in the research, was that you're a proven non-threat…"

"An asset?"

He ignores me. "…and your strain of the virus which enhances the body's survival functions…"

"My predator skills?" A smirk leaks across my face. I don't know why I can't resist getting under Nicolas's skin. Maybe because his skin is so inviting—let's just say mouthwatering.

This time he cuts me off with a look. I've seen that one on my aunt's face too. "We think that a hybrid could turn this new K-cell virus on itself, or at least give the body what it needs to neutralize it. I won't be able to focus on actually curing the strain you have until we get Sam out, assess this much more virulent mutation, and find a way to neutralize it."

"What if we…you…can't, Nicolas?"

He looks at me like I'm speaking one of the few languages he doesn't—pessimism. I don't think Nicolas has allowed himself to consider the possibility that Sam might not be just the way he left him. His little brother has been in the compound for several days. All I can think of is how quickly Chase deteriorated once he started giving in to the cravings. Ashley wants Sam the monster. I saw it all over her face the first night she laid eyes on him.

Nicolas concentrates on the dirt road that leads through the woods to the Knight compound. It's been dry the past few days. Little puffs of dust billow around the edges of the car as we bump along in silence. Finally, he turns to me, his eyes deep, focused somewhere in the past. "We have to get Sam out of the compound. We need the new strain from the source, as well as samples from you, to stand a fighting chance at creating a vaccine or a cure."

"No, Nicolas. We need you."

Closing his eyes and breathing deeply, he reaches reluctantly into his pockets. What he draws out, I've seen before—sterilized packages of blood sample kits.

He drops them in my lap to free his hands up so that he can make a U-turn, pulling up along the fence in about the same spot Holland was parked the night we took refuge here, but facing the opposite direction—for a quick getaway, I imagine. "I need Sam," he whispers, as we pull up to the gate.

I nod. I don't need to tell him that I understand. I don't mind jumping into his fantasy for a while. He's been happy to play in mine and Amber's. Besides, the chances of Cameron still being alive are about as good as the chances of Sam still being human.

A vague breeze ruffles my hair as I step out of the car. The tenderly chilling ping of metal on metal draws our attention to the gate latch, playfully kissing the post of the chain-link fence. The lock has been shot through. Apparently, not fast enough though. A clawing, pasty hand clings tenaciously to the intertwined steel of the gate, supporting a camouflaged sleeve, shredded, crimson drenched, and ripped at the shoulder. Blood still drips over the darkened puddle of mud below the gaping open end.

Here and there, inside the gate, partial bodies dressed in white, but now smeared with their own purple ooze, litter the yard.

"Half are decapitated, mutilated." Nicolas looks a little pale for a guy with a naturally dark complexion. "The others look like they've been shot through the head."

"What kinds of guns do we have?" I open the passenger side door to rifle through Holland's black duffle bag.

Chapter 30

Smeared footprints lead through the gate and off into the woods as well as back to the compound. Most of the steps fleeing into the trees are smaller than the sole of my shoe. Okay, I have big feet. I'm a runner. I'm tall. I need bigger feet for balance.

What I mean is, most of the footprints leading out of the gate belong to fairly small people—children. The smell of ZV blood hangs light and spritzy on the air. In the pines across the road, a smear of sullied white flutters against the dark earth.

It's a girl about twelve, a blonde...used to be...now she's more of a wine stain blonde. I bite my lip. Her skin is grey like mine, now fading. All her pieces are still there, except her head dangles over her shoulder, exposing a gaping purple rip in her neck. She was a mutant and yet she was attacked. Whatever it was that stalked her, it went for the jugular, like an animal.

The ticking of my watch reminds me I have limited time to rescue Sam, find Cameron, and get back to Amber, assuming all those things are still actual possibilities. The quiet abandon here isn't hopeful.

The soldiers seem to have had mechanical difficulties. One of the Jeeps that came to greet us the night we checked into Hotel Ashley is belly up in the field just inside the gate. Can't tell if it was chasing or being chased.

The smell of freshly spilled uninfected blood tells me the guys inside weren't ZVs yet. A crimson mud skid stretches away from beneath the Jeep toward the corner where the buildings intersect. When I glance up at the surveillance cameras mounted on the fence, I notice they're off.

I slide my arm through the black strap of one of the few guns that Greyson showed me how to use and toss a handgun to Nicolas, but I'm not sure he'll know what to do with it. He's more of a diplomacy guy. I used to be a diplomacy girl, and now I have a semi-automatic rifle thing slung over my shoulder and a handgun stuffed into the back pocket of my jeans. Of course, I used to be a vegetarian too. Things change. You run in front of the tide, or you drown in it.

The compound is eerily still: no Christmas music wafting softly over the roofs from the loudspeakers mounted on the corners of the buildings, no zombies wandering aimlessly around the perimeters. I almost wish there were. At least then, we'd have some chance to observe what we're up against. At the moment, we're operating on theories.

"So, what do we do now?" Nicolas asks.

I guess that makes me the team leader. The thing is, I'm not just responsible for the mission; I'm also responsible for making sure nothing happens to Nicolas. Holland probably refused to give us any of his people because he considers Sam a "non-essential asset." Odds are the only reason we're here is because Nicolas insisted and Holland has Dr. Pêsqué in his back pocket to cover for Nicolas if…something happens. It's my job to make sure nothing happens.

Strategic assault isn't exactly a subject they offered at my high school. I'm only drawing from what I picked up hunting strays back in Eli, well, that and a couple of one-man infiltration jobs into the Institute.

Glancing behind us at the car, and then back in front at the open field between the back of the Hall of Judges and the fence, I sketch out a plan. "Nicolas, what if you just wait for me in the car? If we go in here together, I have to defend both ends. No problem for me because I'm already a ZV, but if Ashley has infected the whole congregation, you, on the other hand, are a walking dinner bell."

Nicolas looks offended. "I'm not going to send you in there alone. All we have are hypotheses drawn from insufficient data and samples." That frightens him more than rabid ZVs. He pulls the gun out of his pocket. "Believe me, I can use this if I have to." The way it dangles awkwardly from his fingers, I'd have to say I don't believe him.

Shrugging, I turn back to the church and sigh. "Well, let's do this then."

The gate squeaks a little as I open it. Pausing, I wait to see what kind of bedlam I've just summoned. I'm not too worried. I'm better at guns now than I was the night Greyson and I had to fight off Chase's mutinous soldiers. I noticed then that the adults aren't all that agile when the virus is consuming them. Of course, Ashley had a bunch of younger people camped out in here. That must be the method to her madness. They have a better chance of surviving the onset of the symptoms. And then, I made the brilliant move about letting them in on the vegetarian thing. That's better for them, I guess, at least they have a decent chance of remaining lucid if they can stick to the strict diet. Odds are they haven't been depriving themselves long enough for it to become an instinct.

For the moment, the biggest concern I have is that if any of the new converts are interested in getting their teeth into Nicolas, and they're mutants, they're a pretty good match for me.

The gravel crunches beneath our feet. Nicolas's hardy steak and eggs aroma wafts by on a gentle tailwind, making its way into the courtyard and up the nostrils of whatever grey goons are rummaging through the compound's empty pantry for breakfast. As we approach the overturned Jeep, threads of an idea begin to weave themselves into a plan.

I tug on Nicolas's sweatshirt. He jumps and then swings the gun in his hand around aimlessly, checking for targets.

"Sorry! Didn't mean to startle you. I have a plan. Let's use your morning coffee smell as bait."

His eyes widen as his eyebrows raise.

I nod at the Jeep. "I'll cover you from here. You just stand out in the open…and…smell yummy. If there are any ravenous ZVs about, I'll be able to pick them off before they get anywhere near you."

"Are you any good with that?" He nods at the semi-automatic rifle gripped in my hands.

"Good enough for ZVs."

"That's reassuring."

"Better than walking into a nest of them inside a building with nowhere to run."

He has to give me that point and wanders reluctantly about 20 yards away from the Jeep. I cover the ten steps to it and crouch down, leveling the rifle in his general direction, my sites fixed suspiciously on the lovely little hedge that Ms. Knight planted around the back of the church/Judgment Hall complex, most likely to secure the privacy of her elite religious revivals going on inside.

I don't want to walk blindly through the narrow passage between the church and the boys' dorm right into a smoldering hive of full-fledged zombies, hobbling mindlessly about, waiting for a sniff of something as tasty as Nicolas. I need to see them coming.

Now that I'm squatting here, the twitter of the birds catches my attention, or I should say the lack of it. Everywhere else in the county, they're swarming in to ride out the winter. What could possibly shut up a migrating flock on a compound so close to the forest? There's a little pond out by the farmhouse. This is bird heaven.

My nose answers the question—the predator scent. Sam had that odd smell, the odor that made the virus inside me tingle, firing up all my fight or flight impulses. Just below the stronger ZV blood perfume, lurks the vague stench of the predator. A faint scraping, cloth on gravel, trickles around the corner of the Jeep. At first, I think someone might still be alive in there, maybe just now regaining consciousness.

"Hey!" Dipping down, I look in the dark crack beneath the frame, my gun poised, my finger on the trigger, just in case what's alive in there isn't supposed to be.

"Behind you!" I hear Nicolas yell too late. A snarling animal, claws slashing, broadsides me. We roll sideways, exposing my stomach. I'm lying on my back, nose to nose with what used to be Brother Jacob. Everything about him is human, but the eyes. The eyes are dead, trancelike, deep purple. There's no one home inside anymore.

The side of my gun, still grasped in my fists, presses up against his throat, barring the shrinking distance between his snapping teeth and my head. His fingernails scrape at my neck, the skin peeling thinly behind them. My muscles start to quiver with the tension of holding him off. This thing is strong, like me, and what it's doing, it's doing out of instinct.

Lurching forward, he grasps and gnashes at my head, not my gut, the organ payload. I crane my neck, dodging away from the teeth. It's not interested in devouring me; it wants me dead.

Grunting with effort, my back scraping against the sharp stones ground into the dry dirt, I inch my knees up and flatten out my feet. Breathing in deeply to gather momentum, I holler, extending my knees, driving my soles into its gut and catapulting the goon off of me. "Run, Nicolas!" The body thumps and grinds against the gravel.

Rolling to kneel, I glance in Nicolas's direction before swinging back to confront the ZV locomotive rebounding back down the tracks. My jaw drops. Nicolas fumbles with the gun he's just fished out of his pocket while the bushes around the Hall of the Judges vomit more ZVs—and they're fast.

"Oh, Shit!" He back-pedals, desperately trying to remember how to undo the safety and load the chamber. Now isn't exactly the time to figure out how to do that. One of them has already crossed half the distance between the building and us. Once in the wind, I can smell them. They're more of the same, predators like the one behind me that drops its head and charges. Works out well for me. The carrot top makes a pretty good close-range target that not even I can miss.

Recovering from the jolt of the rifle's kick, I spin to start picking off the rest of the herd that the smell of Nicolas has lured into the open before they descend on him and pick his bones clean. I swing the gun around, just in time to stare into the dead eyes of a zombie in a white shirt and tie racing out in front. The whole herd sprints down on me in V formation, a coordinated attack pattern, totally ignoring the perfectly delicious aroma of Nicolas pâté.

"Nicolas! Just run!" With barely enough time to bring the nose of the gun around, I take down the leader.

One of the two behind the shirt and tie, a zombie in military fatigues, leaps over the fallen corpse. A boy in a ripped and stained white shirt trips on it and catches at my ankle. The military zombie tackles me, his head slamming into my gut below the gun. As I fly backward, my finger twitches on the trigger. The bullet zings, nicking the last of them, a teenage girl in a white dress, trailing behind, already injured. It only slows her down; she keeps coming, trailing a leg as I fall, distracted because I recognize the girl with the long dark hair. It's Christina.

The gun strap flies away from my shoulder and the rifle clatters to the ground. My head bounces off the dirt. The weight of the soldier zombie snapping at my jugular keeps me from sliding into the rabid jaws of the boy clutching my ankle. Keeping the soldier's putrid teeth at bay, I squeeze off his windpipe with my fingers, wondering briefly if the thing needs oxygen to function. Neither one of the zombies bothers to take a bite out of me; they're going for the kill, not the meal.

Just the smell of them has the virus raging through my veins, pumping up my muscles, hyping up my adrenaline. This isn't a hunt; it's a fight to the death for territory. The soldier's eyes reflect vapidly through the purple orbs.

"Get off of me!" Twisting violently, I throw my weight to flip us on our sides and rip the Glock from my pocket. The white-suited boy growling at my foot squirms, but can't quite extract himself from the heap of the body he landed on. All his writhing and yanking on my ankle can't stop me from stabbing the pistol into the temple of the soldier grappling with me and blowing out its infected brains.

Shoving away the corpse, I jerk myself forward to sit up before Christina can shamble her way into the mix. Arcing my arm up from the ground, I put a hole in the head of the demented choirboy snapping at my heel.

A straggler, a little chunky in her pleated white skirt, lumbers up, landing a high-heeled foot in one of the corpses between us and launches herself at my head as I'm pulling myself to my feet.

My gun arm flies forward. Christina lunges for the nearest part of me as I fall and traps the pistol. The flopping, cushy breasts of the zombie matron catch my face as I tumble forward. She grasps my temples, squeezing, intent on either smothering me or twisting my head right off my shoulders. The tendons in my neck crackle.

Shoving my left hand in her face, I force her back, giving myself room to breathe. She pushes back, her hand on my forehead, forcing my face backward, bending my neck, exposing the veins. My arm trembles against the dead weight of her bulk and I dig my feet in, throwing my whole body into resistance. My shoes slide against the gravel and my elbow buckles. The woman's snarl jolts forward, a forearms width away from tearing a hole in my jugular.

My only option is to let go of the Glock. Christina stumbles back with the sudden release of tension. My free right-hand grasps for the handle of the knife strapped to my thigh. Straining my neck away from the teeth, the muscle creaking under the stress, I slide the blade out and cock my arm to my shoulder to bring it crashing down into the chunky zombie girl's upturned eye. The midnight purple explodes in a gelatinous sludge. The skewered beast hovers for a second and then teeters back, toppling face-up, spread-eagle over the white-suited leader at our feet.

I dive for the knife stuck in her face, grasp it with both hands, and heave. It sucks free, the blade prone, as I pivot to face the girl I don't think I can shoot in the head—not until I know for sure, not until there's no other choice. From behind me, the abrupt crack of a gun freezes my heart. For a split second, I wait, my breath caught in my lungs, anticipating the shock of a bullet in my back.

Impossible! They're dead! A zombie isn't going to figure out how to pull a trigger. My head whips back to face Christina, or what was Christina, her motion frozen, the gun limp at her side, a quarter of her face a slimy purple mess. Nicolas stands right behind her, his gun still touching the back of her head.

The air breezes out of my mouth as her legs buckle and she crumples to the ground like a pile of clothes with no person left inside.

The doctor looks a little stunned. Opposing emotions rip at my heart: relief that I'm not dead and cutting sadness that this orphaned child couldn't be saved. I don't blame Nicolas. I know it had to be done, but I held her hand a couple of days ago, warm, pulsing, sweet, and innocent. The purple blood washes over the half of the face that I recognize, obliterating it.

Running my fingers through my hair, stiffening my shoulders, I refocus on Nicolas and the rest of the compound, sigh and then lean over, my bloodied hands on my thighs. I breathe until I can think again because, during the fight, the beast takes over. Everything is reflex. I'm not in control.

My first rational thought warns me that all that noise is bound to have attracted some attention. In the back of my mind, I'm hoping some of the attention was from Greyson—if he's still here.

Shuffling over to my rifle I sling it up by the strap. "What the hell was that?"

Nicolas isn't sure what I'm talking about and looks like he might be working on an apology for blowing the face off the zombie girl.

"They came after me, Nicolas; not you. They were hunting! Hiding in the shrubbery like my cat, stalking us! I thought you said they died."

"Well, that's the hypothesis. We didn't know for sure. That's why we're here. The evidence suggests that the virus is controlling the brain functions of the body once the victim dies. Anything that would be a normal animal instinct is available to the virus as long as it controls the command center—the mind. I'm not completely sure why they ignored me and targeted you." He looks over the scene, trying to read the info from the bodies.

"I think I know." Shuffling over, I kneel at Christina's body. "It's the smell. You probably don't pick it up, but I do. Sam's scent always triggered the virus into firing up my fight or flight instincts. Like he was a predator." I have to pry the Glock out of the little girl's stiff fingers.

"If that's the case, then their instincts probably mark you as competition."

"I haven't got any proof, but in the thick of the attack, it felt a lot like I was a lone lioness hunting on hyena territory."

Shoving the Glock back in my pocket, I wipe the purple gunk on my jeans before sheathing the knife. Nasty stuff. Normally, I'd be disgusted, maybe even a little nauseous, but the virus is rioting in my bloodstream, and the beast inside thrives on gore. "Let's go. If Sam's still here," I motion to the new breed cluttering the gravel, "which I think he is, he's going to be in the Hall of the Judges."

The point of the rifle leading the way, I turn my steps to the passage between the corners of the men's dorm and the church.

Nicolas tugs at my sleeve. "But, if what you say is true, you're not immune. I mean they're going to come after you, not just me."

"Yeah." I keep walking forward, sniffing the air for immediate threats, peering into the bushes and trees. "Sucks to be popular." I glance at my watch. Our little stroll through the yard cost us about 20 minutes.

Chapter 31

Three sets of double doors beneath a columned portico mark the entrance to the Hall of the Judges, only twenty feet behind the church. The center pair is much taller, in line with the carved white pediment above. About six shallow marble steps lead the way up. A mosaic of bloodstained footprints, coming and going, reflects as much purple as red. The fatalities depicted in the blood smears are mutants as well as the uninfected. What just happened out by the Jeep isn't an isolated fluke.

Greyson's blood is as purple as mine. For a second, my forced sangfroid falters, my knees feel a little weak. All our differences aside, the connection between Grey and me runs deeper than our purple blood. I'm not sure I can walk in here and find what I'm going to find. Judging by what we've seen so far on the grounds, the devil got into Ms. Ashley's holy plans and turned the flock against the shepherds.

Halting at the top of the steps, I lean against a column out of view of the open parkway between the Church and this building, resetting my head, and blocking out my emotions. Essence of predator zombie overlays the whole compound; it's hard to pick out individuals. Even though that's why we're here, I'm not actually hoping to catch a whiff of Sam. It's Greyson I'm hoping to find…or Cameron.

The way the two virus strains seem to be staging a turf war, ignoring a tasty morsel like Nicolas, I wonder if there's an outside chance a ten-year-old boy could fall through the cracks, maybe hide in the corners. The tough part will be prying him out of his cover…unless he's the hunter now, not the hunted.

The grassy courtyard displays evidence to support my theories. Half the bodies are shot neatly in the head, their clothes smeared in the red blood of the uninfected they must have devoured before they turned on the ZVs; the other half are mangled at the neck, their own blood crusting in a royal purple mantle over their shoulders.

Nicolas takes up a position next to me, his back to the column, his eyes darting, his chest heaving. His normally rich complexion looks a little pale. "Maybe we shouldn't do this?" He steadies himself on the column. "I didn't realize you'd be in danger."

"Your brother is in here, Nicolas. It's the only place he can be."

His head falls and he clenches the fist that's not holding his gun. When he raises his eyes to meet mine, they're brimming with resignation. "He might not be my brother anymore."

"He'll always be your brother, no matter what she's done to him. You can't walk away without knowing."

There's gratitude and uncertainty in the nod he gives me.

Honestly, there's nothing I'd like better than to cut loose and head back to Amber on the nice, safe French aircraft carrier in the gulf. But I can't leave without giving my aunt everything I have to save her boy. She gave me everything she had. And I can't leave without at least warning Greyson about the purge. He probably already suspects, but he can't know he's only got a couple of hours to get out before all hell breaks loose—or maybe that's already happened.

I take the whole conversation to an altruistic, scientific level that Nicolas won't be able to refute—that I can't refute. "Whatever Sam is, we need what's running in his veins. We all need what's running in his veins." With the point of my rifle, I indicate the purple-stained steps exiting the building. "Because the demon he spawned is out there now. And there's only you and me to go in there and get the samples."

The doctor's jaw sets. Nicolas isn't really meant for fieldwork, he's more of a lab guy, but the boy has heart. I dash to the set of doors on the right in front of us. I'd rather not make a grand entrance, front and center.

The entrance dumps us into a foyer. Opposite the entrance, another two sets of white, ornately carved double doors beckon us to a chapel. Two hallways extend east and west off of the foyer. From our end we can make out the writing on the small plaques that decorate each of the chapel doors:

Please maintain a quiet and reverent attitude before the holy altar of the Resurrection

Exchanging glances with Nicolas, I push the door on the right open about an inch. My hand shakes imperceptibly on the handle, whether from the suspense or the adrenaline rush of the virus, I couldn't say. The role of prey triggers a unique chemical cocktail, totally different from the flavor of dodging Snatchers. This feels so much more vulnerable.

The door pushes in quietly, casting a dull bar of light on the mostly somber chapel. Some sort of yellowish haze washes vaguely from the center front toward the two-inch crack I've opened. Nothing growls.

Widening the gap, I push through. Nicolas follows, his shoulder sliding in after mine. Stillness hangs heavy in the chapel. About twenty rows of wooden pews sitting on marble tile separate the doors at the back from a raised dais that showcases an altar under a domed section of the roof at the front. White carpet, stained and blotched, covers the aisles between the pews. Towering above our heads, enormous, colorful paintings of Lazarus, the widow of Nain's son, Jairus's daughter, the angel at the open tomb, the travelers on the road to Emmaus, and a couple more I can't make out, testify to the reality of the resurrection.

A single yellow light rains down on the purple velvet altar enshrined in gold plate. In the recesses of an alcove behind the altar, loom the shadows of three large wooden chairs, carved thrones really. The center seat stands taller than the two on the sides, the one on its right slightly more prominent than the seat to its left.

Approaching the altar, I step more cautiously, one toe at a time, a syncopated beat in between, scanning the dark emptiness between the benches. A tortured giggle cracks the silence, my stomach hops, and my heart double times. My rifle whips around to target the trinity of thrones under the dome. As my night vision adjusts to the sickly light, I realize the owner of the voice is sitting in the throne on the right hand of the center.

"You're too late for the wedding feast." She sweeps her long dark hair over the white robe on her shoulder. "We began at dawn, as the sun rose in the east." Her hand waves majestically to the eastern wall of the dome where a strategically placed, oval window would catch the morning sun. Bereft of their purpose, her fingers fall lightly to her neck, stroking the skin across the curve where her throat meets her clavicle.

Apparently, Ms. Knight's bubble has finally popped, but she's still trapped in the puddle of the deflated delusion.

"Where's Sam? I want to see my brother. Now!" Nicolas stalks up the aisle and pushes ahead of me.

Ashley Knight is obviously suffering from acute psychosis, which would normally invoke his charming bedside manner, but he's justifiably pissed about being cut off from his brother. Of course, that's why we're here. It's not our job to clean up the mess Ashley made. Someone else will take care of that—I glance at my watch—in a couple of hours.

"Ashley, this place is going to be a fire pit by noon." I try to appeal to any part of her brain that's still with us in this reality. "You need to get out of here. They're evacuating. You can find some soldiers and get on a transport. But tell us where Sam is so we can take him with us."

"Yes!" She nods, smiling serenely. "The earth will be burned and the wicked will be consumed in the flames of wrath. But the righteous," she holds up to heaven a single finger of exception, "those who have been changed, they will be lifted up." She stands, staring into the light streaming through the window as if I've just brought hope into her world of gloom. "I must tell my father."

I sidestep forward, my eyes shifting about the chapel, my nose poised, searching for pockets of stench that would betray a stalking predator. If we're going to get any coherent information out of Ashley, we're probably going to have to walk her through this. She was teetering on the edge of insanity before, but whatever has happened here has pushed her into the ravine and she's cracked and broken on the rocks below. "Your father died, Ashley. Remember?"

Her head snaps away from the window, glaring at me from the shadows, pointing accusingly at my skeptic heart. "Liar! Your eyes are closed and you will not see. You have ears, but you will not hear. He is not dead, but liveth!" She puffs up, but then her shoulders sag and her finger sinks as her alternate reality vies for playtime in her mind. "For I have seen him with my own eyes. He lives at the right hand of Death."

"Evelyn!" Nicolas hisses to catch my attention. "Didn't she call my brother 'the messenger of Death'?"

I turn away and whisper so Ashley can't hear. Reason tends to upset her. "Yeah. Sam was riding the pale horse. If Ashley takes us to her father, he may be with Sam."

Cautiously, checking each row of pews for hidden zombies, I make my way up the white carpet of the western aisle.

Ashley shifts into reverie. "I thought my father was murdered for my sins because I fed human flesh to Gavin." His face, illuminated in sickly light, laments her wrongdoing and then stiffens in resolve. "But it made him stronger. How could it be a sin to heal the one you love so deeply, with all your heart? How could it be a sin when Providence, itself, provided the sacrifices lost in the woods, just as it provided the ram in the thicket?"

She glares down at me as if I were the one contradicting her rationalization instead of her own conscience. "I judged my own father and the truth was hidden from my unbelieving eyes. And when our dearest Gavin changed him, in front of my very eyes, I doubted. I could not see the truth and thought him dead in his sins." She shouts, shaking her fists, angry at her lack of faith.

"But he was not dead," a triumphant smile spreads serenely over her shadowed cheeks, "only seeming so, that the coming of the Great and Last Judgment might be manifest in his rebirth." She holds her hands to the heavens in gratitude for her epiphany.

Gavin. So that's where it all started, just like Ryan imagined. Sam and Gavin had the same reaction to the virus, producing these full-blown, walking dead—or should I say running dead—zombies. Gavin mutated and then murdered her father. He was, indeed, the first fruits of this demented resurrection.

My heart sort of cringes for the crazy girl. The whole gruesome story is starting to make sense now. Ashley was in love with her cousin Gavin. I don't even want to think of how it happened, but he must have taken a bite out of someone, found that it improved his strength and convinced her to bring him more. The thought turns my stomach. And then I realize that's probably why she got Miguel working for her. Ms. Ashley isn't the type to get her white gloves dirty.

"Did he die, Ashley?" I probably ought to gather as much information as I can from the source.

"I told you! My father lives!"

"No, not your father. Gavin. Did he die when you started feeding him your followers?"

Indignation and horror streak her countenance. "I did not feed him my disciples—only the goats, caught in the thicket, sent by Providence. Only the sacrifice of their soiled hearts could bring the holy strength that filled his soul. Gavin did not die. He lives! Immortal. Bringing about the Judgment beyond the walls of this holy garden."

So, there we have it. Once the virus had made him stronger, Gavin took a bite out of her father, turned him into one of these ravenous monsters, and then left her flat. It must have been hell. No wonder she doesn't want to look reality in the eye.

She's not much different from the rest of us. We all make our own reality, something that we can live with. Hers is just a little more extreme than the rest of ours. She's been trying to dress the demons in white, paint silver clouds over the smoke, and build paradise over the inferno.

I can't help but feel sorry for her in some little corner of my soul—sorry for everything she's lost, sorry that her love spurred her to such atrocities. But mostly I loathe her. I loathe her in the same part of my soul where I cherish Amber. How could someone kidnap children and intentionally feed them to these deranged monsters? Even worse, what kind of monster manipulates people's faith and altruism—and fear—to serve her delusions?

It feels devious, but I figure the best way to manipulate the manipulator is to buy into her delusions. "Ashley, can we see him, your father…so that we can believe also?" I grimace at Nicolas, who, for once, is totally on board with the deception.

Apparently, I've just dislodged one of the pillars of her precariously perched world. Her head shaking ambivalently, her face contracts into a frown of fear all mixed up in reverence. "He…he…sits at the right hand of…of…Death." She looks to the western wall of the building. They must be in one of the rooms on the other side of that wall. If I haven't lost my bearings, the basement room with the bars on the windows that the late Brother Jacob strategically pointed out to me should be on that side of the building.

That Sam is hanging out with zombies isn't exactly good news for Nicolas. My eyes check him at my side. His jaw is taut, the corners of his eyes pinched, dealing with the implications.

With a flicker of the light from above, and a ripple in the air from an unseen vent, the significance of the chairs on the dais piques my curiosity. Now that I've gotten used to the predator fumes, I can smell the shadow of Greyson hanging on the air. "Ashley," I glide closer, peering at the hue of her skin underneath the yellow wash, "on whose right hand do you sit?"

She doesn't comprehend my question. I've jumped from the nightmarish reality of what her father has become to the foamy, world of bubbles floating in her imagination. She looks back at the chairs, trying to find an anchor in the concrete world, her fingers fumbling with the delicate silver cross at her throat, and then straightens up, squaring her shoulders regally. "I sit on the right hand of War, on the right hand of the Sword."

The Sword. Greyson.

The sliver, the one that pierced my heart when he drove away, twists; the tender muscle spasms around it. This is what he came back to—this throne, this cracked girl, this world of smoke and clouds. He left me for this. Okay, so, left me is too strong; I'm the one that got out of the car. But I'm close enough to see her clearly now. And I'm close enough to make out the evidence of his infidelity: the puncture wounds, a passionate purple ring at the base of her neck, the grey tint of her skin, the purple rimming her eyes.

The image of his teeth piercing her naked flesh slithers up and haunts me. My eyes burn and I bite my lip to stifle the tears. I knew it would happen, one day, but I didn't want to actually see it. In the end, I've been as delusional as she is, creating my own reality, a reality where Greyson is what I want him to be, not what he is.

"'For he must reign until he has put all his enemies under his feet'..." She rambles on, oblivious to the damage she's done, not just to me, but to the world; she's unleashed the beast. "We should have ruled them." Her head shakes incredulously. "But they would not be ruled. They...they...they hunt!" She stares back at Greyson's chair, her face a mask of mystification and horror, baffled and terrified by the joke that's been played on her.

Nicolas has had about all he can take. He stomps up the stairs and grabs her arm. "Look, you crazy bitch..." The bad news is, when it comes to people, Nicolas is color blind; he hasn't taken note of the purple tint to her skin. Or maybe he's just blinded with anger. I've never actually seen Nicolas fly off the handle. Not that I don't sympathize. If she had Amber locked up, I'd have clawed the girl's eyes out ten minutes ago.

Ashley scowls, her eyes wide at the audacity of his rudeness, and she rips her arm out of his grasp. The moment his Sunday Brunch flavor hits her nose, her eyes narrow and she growls low, catching Nicolas off guard. Clearly, she hasn't been vegetarian long enough to establish the neural pathways that help resist the cravings.

I don't have time for anything but sprinting up the stairs and tearing across the stage to tackle them before she makes the conscious, virus-driven choice to lunge for a juicy morsel of Prime Nicolas, right out of his neatly carved six-pack. My chest collides with his back, dominoing all of us to the floor. Slapping and clawing, I gag Ashley's mouth as she writhes and snarls beneath us. "Get out of here, Nicolas!" I shove him from between us.

Nicolas scrambles out from the mess of writhing mutants and heads for the stairs. My chest heaving and panting with the sudden exertion, I slam Ashley's head against the floor. She may be stronger now, but she was always a lily. My knee in her stomach, my hands pinning her bare shoulders to the carpet, I growl, "You are not immortal. You are no angel. You have become the Beast, with eyes and claws and teeth, and if you don't control it, it will devour you from the inside until you're a brain-dead nightmare just like those monsters you've used Sam to create. The only difference is, you'll know you're a monster—it'll be a choice."

Our eyes locked, I wait until the lucidity creeps in, and then the tears. She's not going to stay in my reality for long, but I want to plant an image of it in her foggy brain.

Pushing off her chest, I toss a little free advice her way. "You're trapped here now. They won't let you out of the quarantine zone. If you've got a bomb shelter or someplace like that on the compound, now would be a good time to hang out in it."

Her eyes glaze over again and she refuses to look at me. "No. I'll wait here. He said he would come back for me."

I don't bother to ask "Who?" I already know.

Chapter 32

Darkness swallows the west hall of the foyer. With the sharp blade of jealousy, I lop off the part of my heart that was infected by Greyson. "Come on, Nicolas. It's this way." Touching his sleeve, I lead us into the shadows with the nose of my rifle. At the end of the hallway, there's an illuminated sign indicating stairs. Directly underneath it hangs a painting of the Judgment separating the lambs on the right from the goats on the left. We're heading the right direction.

Very few doors line this hallway that leads along the chapel. Indicating the stairway at the end of the building, I put my finger on my lips and pause. A couple of yards before the threshold, an alcove, vaguely lit from above with a drinking fountain sign, casts an eerie green shadow on a narrow door opposite, slightly ajar. Just beyond the open door, at the end of the hall, there's an emergency exit. Judging by the barely two or three feet of hallway extending past the open door up to the back wall of the building, the room can only be some kind of utility closet or office.

Veering away from the stairway side of the hall, I slow down, advancing one step at a time, my finger hugging the trigger, the barrel pointed at the crack in the doorway. Behind me, I can hear Nicolas huffing, trying to hold his breath and stay quiet, and then exhaling in panic.

The stairway to my left is blind, a perfect spot for an ambush. These new zombies are stalkers, so I'm not venturing down the stairs until I know no strays are lurking in this small room waiting to attack me from behind. My eyes fixed on the weakly green-washed gap, I peer, sniffing, into what turns out to be an office.

A pocket of zombie stench saturates the air, assaulting my nose. I brace, my trigger finger itching. The scent breezes by again, on the move, but not from out of the closet. It's behind me!

A low, rumbling growl jerks my head around to the drinking fountain. A snarling camouflaged soldier leaps from the alcove. My first instinct is to cover Nicolas. Whirling, I clip him with my elbow as the nose of the gun drops. Losing his balance, Nicolas tips backward, his head thumping against the wall.

But soldier zombie isn't interested in the doctor—at least not yet. Claws grasping, teeth gnashing, he dives for my neck. My finger triggers a shot before he can get to me. The bullet plows through his gut, jerking him back. I scramble to re-anchor the gun against my shoulder so I can get a shot off through his brain to put him out of his misery—and ours.

Seizing a fistful of the barrel as he falls back, the zombie drags me forward, jerking the rifle. Firing wildly, not even trying to aim, I blow his cheek off as we fall. The muzzle of the gun dive-bombs the floor, vaulting me over on my side. The zombie's head smacks the wall, smearing purple ooze as he slides down. Hardly noticing his new face job, he throws himself at my foot, hooking my ankle and sliding me forward, growling and snapping. I scream as his jaw clamps down on my leg, ripping away a mouthful of jeans and wool socks, exposing the skin under the frays. Shit! For all I know, I could be as susceptible to this new strain as any uninfected victim.

Somehow, through all the months of infection, dodging Snatchers, and hanging out with Greyson, I came to consider myself immortal, not immune to pain and suffering, but exempt from death. The thought of dying and coming back a ravenous, stalking demon—no hope for a cure, no drive to save my sister, my body hijacked—infuses into my blood some kind of human survival instinct the virus was never able to trigger.

The beast spits out the denim and dives for the exposed bite of flesh. My muscles practically spasm, as I whip the gun around. The barrel whacks the zombie in the head, detouring his jaws from my exposed calf. Another shot explodes, but not from my rifle. Nicolas is standing over us, his pistol pointed at the head of the now silent camouflage zombie. RIP.

Exhaling loudly, I grab the hand he offers me. "On second thought, Nicolas, I'm glad you didn't wait in the car. I think that makes twice you've saved my ass."

He manages a nervous smile. "Who's counting?"

Actually, I am, and with good reason. All the shooting we've been doing worries me. Every organ sucker in the place knows we're here. We should have done this quietly with knives, but how? They hide and wait, come at us so fast, we barely have a chance to get a shot off.

Considering all the maneuvering difficulties I'm having with the rifle in the building, I think I'd be better off with the handgun. Lifting the strap over my head, I leave the semi-automatic on the floor near the top of the stairs to retrieve on our way out—hopefully. It's better for picking off zombies coming at us from farther away.

Nicolas raises his eyebrows at the gun abandoned on the floor.

"It's slowing my reaction time down. They're pretty fast." Knowing he'll want a lab before he gives me a definite answer, I ask anyway, "Why are they so fast? They're dead already."

"I'd have to do some testing first…" my back is to him as I eye the stairs so he doesn't see me smile, "…but an educated guess? In vegetarian hosts, the virus adapted in the brain, enhancing all the essential predator functions. Now that it's adapted to kill the host and then reanimate the brain functions necessary to ensure its survival and propagation, it's only natural that those hunting instincts are part of the reanimation."

"So, pretty much, there's a virus driving the instinctive, reflexive parts of the human engine."

Nicolas doesn't go in for oversimplification. His head vacillates between me getting the general idea and the wrong idea, and then he goes for 'good enough' with a qualified nod.

With the muzzle of my gun, I motion at the painting hanging over our heads. "Just so you know, if Sam is down here, and the odds on that are pretty high, the place is going to be crawling with his minions."

Nicolas responds by awkwardly swinging the gun dangling at his side out in front, and then supporting it with both hands like a cop in a crime show.

"Thank God for the movies." Grinning, and then checking my watch, I crouch down and peek around the corner to get a handle on what's waiting for us in the stairway. It's clean—for the moment—but halfway down there's a landing and then the stairway doubles back to the basement. I'm starting to hate basements. Nothing good ever comes out of the basement— then again, I came out of a basement. Motioning to Nicolas to follow, I creep down the first half of the flight.

My nose is the best defense we have at this point. But, other than the disconcerting film of predator that always hung about Sam and permeates this place, I'm not picking up anything but Nicolas, which means if something's waiting for us down there, it can track us with its eyes shut.

Poor Nic! I glance back. He's totally out of his element, a baby rabbit hunting hawks. Beads of sweat on his forehead glisten in the green emergency light, and I can hear him sucking in air. Hell! I can practically hear his heart thumping. Or maybe that's mine. I'm not exactly an experienced hunter. I'm more of an escape artist, a survivor. At least I'm equipped with the same biological weapons as the enemy.

No scent of Greyson. Disappointing. Why he left his Queen Bee alone in the chapel remains a mystery. In my deranged reality, the only reason he'd do that would be to remove the threat from the woman that drives him. It's pretty safe to assume, maybe hope, that when everything went wrong in Ashley's resurrection scheme, Greyson jumped in and handled the mess. He would have come down here and dealt with Sam to stop the carnage.

Pausing on the bottom step before the landing, I put my hand out to stop Nicolas. Maybe Greyson did come down here. Maybe the mess handled him.

My heart skips a couple of beats as my imagination conjures up the scene. Sam was pretty strong when he had that episode—stronger than I was—even Greyson was a little surprised. These new virals I've been running into, they're not a bunch of walking targets, and they're protecting their turf from the competition—Greyson and me.

Closing my eyes, I bite my lip, and lean my head against the wall, trying to reassemble the pieces of my courage. The virus snarls against the fear, injecting toxic fight chemicals into my veins.

My nose following the barrel of my Glock, I slide down the last step onto the landing, crouch behind the beam that separates the up and down sides of the stairwell, and peek around the corner. We're at the west end of the building. The bottom stair spills onto a hallway that mirrors the one we just left. To the west, the building will end about two or three feet from the stairs, just the length of the switchback I'm standing on above. The hallway doubling back to the east is where we'll find what we're looking for—and maybe what we're not.

Wedging my back to the east wall of the stairway, I sidestep down the stairs. I figure there's more chance of unwelcome company emerging from the east side of the building and the wall at my back will make sure I see them before they see me. Of course, if there's a new-breed zombie out there, he smelled me coming the minute I turned on the landing.

Nicolas follows one step behind me. The closer I get to the bottom, the louder my heart thumps. By the last step, I realize I'm holding my breath and force myself to exhale slowly before inhaling and peering around the corner. Wouldn't it be nice if a bunch of brain-dead specimens were conveniently milling mindlessly about the corridor so we could pick them off like apples bobbing in a barrel? No such luck. Oh, there are zombies in the corridor, but none of them are standing. An occasional heap of military camouflage and purple sludge mingles among shadowed, bloodied, white suits, glinting green in the random lights of the signage. This is where the carnage began.

But if Ashley has already held her Final Judgment Zombie Fest, where are all the living dead? She had several hundred willing sheep and who knows how many unwilling goats. A shiver syncopates my breath. The footsteps by the gate ran across the road into the trees. Other than the bodies in the courtyard, there's not a living—or nonliving—soul around. If the hundreds living at the compound aren't here, casualties of the religious civil war, then they're roaming free on the outside, heading through the trees to the city.

Once Holland gets a look at one of these predator zombies in the flesh, he's not going to wait a couple of hours before calling in the fire.

All he wanted from us was proof. But the proof is on its way to him and the reality is a whole lot worse than the theories. And what about Gavin? Ashley said he left before Sam got here. He could be anywhere. Who says he's not already outside the quarantine zone?

My watch ticks loudly enough to remind me we're losing time with every step the escaped cultists take toward the city. We have to find Sam and get back to the research building before the last helicopter has flown.

Sam and Cameron…and Greyson.

My eyes flick to the piles in the corridor. Is he stacked up in there, one of the bodies with its throat ripped out?

No. No! Greyson does NOT die here in this hellhole. Not after…not after everything. In my reality, that doesn't happen—that never happens.

In the underground darkness splotched with fluorescent green, my eyes target the couple of alcoves on the wall opposite me. No movement. The signs indicate one is a restroom and the other a drinking fountain.

I think Nicolas is sweating again. A little burst of his flavor puffs by. "When we get out in the hallway," I whisper, glancing back up the stairs, "walk backward behind me. Cover these stairs, in case something follows us down."

Ashley didn't seem lucid enough to track us, but she has some new skills that make her a threat I can't ignore. Nic nods and I break into the hallway, my back brushing the wall.

Down here, instead of three sets of doors, there are only two: one, a few yards in front of us, and the other, several yards farther down. From the amount of space between them, I guess that the basement has two rooms. We're on the west end. This is the side with the window that Brother Travis was trying to get me to notice. This is where we'll find Sam.

Tiptoeing gingerly between bodies, I glide along the wall. The dead that could still move have long since extracted themselves—I hope. But by the looks of it, this is a take no prisoners, leave no survivors kind of war. Maybe we won't find

Sam. Maybe he's wandering free, outside the compound, hunting at the head of a herd of his own creation.

The double doors loom just two bodies away. Nicolas's breathing rises and fades, underscored by the beating of his heart as his head wavers back and forth between the threat ahead and the threat behind. The adrenaline rush adds a salty tang to his aroma.

Right now, I'm glad I'm a ZV. If Nicolas gets off a nervous shot, hits me in friendly fire, the damage won't be quite so serious—well, unless it's a lucky—or unlucky, depending on how you look at it—shot to the head.

Which makes me wonder…I always thought we mutant ZVs could only be killed with a bullet, or a bat, through the brain. Maybe that's just the fastest approach. These corpses have clearly died from bleeding to death through their jugular. The blood of a mutant ZV is the vehicle for the virus, so it's possible my brand of the virus can't stop the flow of blood fast enough when the jugular is severed. In that case, lack of blood to the brain would kill the victim. Or maybe the attack snaps the spinal cord and the virus can't communicate with the body anymore. Or…maybe the new strain is contagious—even to ZVs—and these were infected with the new virus which killed them, but wasn't able to resuscitate the body because of the injury to the spinal cord or jugular.

"Nicolas," I pause to glance at the rip in my jeans, checking to make sure the bite didn't break the skin, "do you think the new strain is…you know…contagious?"

He looks at me like I've lost my mind. Everyone is dead. Of course, it's contagious.

"No. I mean for ZVs. If they don't kill me, if I get bit, do you think…?" I'm just asking because I should know in advance what I'm looking at. If one sinks its teeth into me, I'd rather die than come back.

He shakes his head, his hands flying up at the total impossibility of responding to that question. We don't have any samples, no data. When it comes to medical studies, Nicolas doesn't do tactful. He either has the research or he doesn't.

"Then listen, Nic. You don't take any chances." It's a command, not a statement. I stare him down, glancing at the gun that just never seems comfortable in his fist until I'm sure he knows what I mean.

His brows crease with the mental struggle going on behind them. Nicolas hangs on. He doesn't let go. Hope defines him.

"Amber is everything!"

Finally, he nods, slowly, like an oath.

Reassured I focus my attention on the doors. They swing in. No locks. But there's a chain wrapped around the handles. The key sticks out of the lock. Whatever is in there isn't hiding. Someone locked it in. Greyson? Is this the reason why he left Ashley upstairs, wallowing in the failure of her ascension? I can't help myself. I scan the faces of the bodies strewn over the carpet before dragging my eyes back to the lock.

Shit! My hand shakes as I reach for the key. The fear ripples anger through the virus. Twist, click, slide. A couple of rattling rotations and the chain clatters to the floor.

Nothing happens. No sound. Only the overwhelming smell of Sam, much stronger than it ever was. From behind the cover of the wall, I slide my hand to the center of the door and push it open a couple of inches. Inside, a small window shrouds the room in a vague morning residue. No movement.

Straddling a body, one of the disgorged, I place my weight against the door and lean cautiously back. The door swings wider and I lead through the gap with the Glock. Crouching low, I prop the door open on the foot of one of the corpses.

Nicolas navigates slowly into the room behind me, watching our backs.

Inhaling, I pivot and stand, peering into the shadows inside the room. Nicolas takes cover behind the open door. It'll take a while longer for his eyes to adjust to the sickly rays spilling from the window on my left.

The scooped-out carcasses of mottled red and white-clad young adults litter the floor, nothing left but a smeared crimson hollow of bone between the pelvis and the rib cage. Ashley segregated out the few adults in her congregation, goats to offer up in sacrifice to the Beast. Or maybe this is the fate of the adults Miguel rounded up—food for the gods of the resurrection. I stop to swallow two clashing urges.

The monster runs wild in my blood willing me to feed, but the gore on the floor has my brain convulsing. My mind is still mine and it overrides the instincts of the virus, willing my whole being to vomit up this image. I'm glad Nicolas can't see what I'm seeing.

"It's like watermelon." The chuckle comes from the raised dais at the back of the room.

My head snaps up, my eyes adjust to the darkness lurking beyond the range of the window's glow. There's only one chair there. The shadow in it can only be one person. Sam. Nicolas jumps at the sound of his voice, springing around the door and into the room, gun abandoned to his side in relief.

Chapter 33

"Thank God! Sam, are you all right?" Nicolas trips over one of the mutilated corpses as he emerges from behind the door.

Sam doesn't move, instead, he tilts his head wistfully. "The sweetest parts are at the heart. Why bother with the tasteless garbage around the rind?"

Nic stumbles over a leg, landing on all fours, his palm planted in the vacuous center of a half-eaten carcass. The light from the window dimly illuminates for him the mess of bodies scattered and mutilated on the floor between him and his brother.

If it weren't so pathetic, the cackling laugh that chokes Sam as he watches the relief on his brother's face turn to disgust would be terrifying. "Blind to the end, Nic?" He sounds almost sad, a little indulgent…almost. And then he leans forward, as if his brother can't hear, and snaps, just loud enough to be on the wrong side of the line between sane and hysterical, "Look around you, bro'! Does it look like I'm all right?" He leans back in his chair, decompressing, and then sings out, "No, no! I'm good. I feel great!"

Nicolas's mouth hangs open as he stands. On the east side of the room, Sam's left, the side I couldn't see from the door, bodies, dressed in white, mostly adults, and shot through the head, slouch over each other, a thin topping of purple icing drizzled generously through the piles. On the west, Sam's right, Nicolas is wading in the grisly carcasses of his brother's leftovers.

"It's the diet," Sam explains, nodding appreciatively. "All the weakness, the nausea, the pain. Gone. A strict diet of human giblets and suddenly I'm 110%. Strong, fast, increased sensory acuity! Of course, I owe all that to Reverend Knight. Don't feel bad, Nic. Your premise was just off. You were looking to conquer the virus when the solution was to embrace the transformation, cuddle up with destiny."

He leans forward, almost whispering. "I am the mouth of God, now. I judge. The goats consigned to be demons of hell on my left..." His hand sweeps over the shot corpses. "...the lambs for the slaughter on my right." He gestures toward Nicolas, his head tilted, an oblivious smile, vaguely visible in the morning light, pasted to his lips.

Frozen, unable to speak, Nicolas stares, shocked, his incredulous gaze bouncing between his brother's silhouette and the massacre on the floor. We knew this was possible, but the reality is so much more gruesome than the anticipation could ever be. Nicolas is a doctor; he's seen stuff, lots of stuff, but nothing like this. He leans over, retches, and finally spews his churned and minced breakfast into the cavern of the body at his feet.

"Tsk. Nicky, you're contaminating the research." His brother stands up to explain, a professor at his podium. "You see, Her Reverence sent me the adults, and the occasional odd teen caught cheating on the diet. The Reverend knew I was sent to judge them. It's so obvious; everything is so clear now that I've stopped kicking against the pricks. My calling has enlightened me." He raises his arms to the ceiling, which is only the floor below the chapel above.

Sam hasn't just been nibbling on organs; he's been sipping the Ashley Kool-Aid. My instincts tell me to grab Nicolas and get the hell out of hell, but we can't leave without the samples. As bad as the slaughter on the floor is, I know there were hundreds more here in this compound. If Greyson didn't infect them, then Sam did. And now they're gone, out of the cage, headed toward the rest of humanity, hunting.

Sam rambles on while my mind cranks through all the possible action plans. The bug driving my head screams at me to shoot him down. This is the queen bee, the mother of the hive. But, there's no way I'm going to murder Nicolas's little brother in front of his eyes. So, I watch him, intently, and wait.

"Of course, I knew you'd want your data, Nicky." He shifts his posture, changing characters for a new scene, pushing his hand grandly out in front. His voice deepens sarcastically. "Our parents' research must go forward."

Nicolas has nothing to say—or maybe the words just won't come out.

He and his brother had a few issues we only glimpsed on our long road trip, and the virus has supersized them all in Sam's brain. "Given the origins of the virus and its connection to ancient mummification procedures, I wanted to examine the Egyptian practice of removing the heart, lungs, liver, stomach, and intestines. May I just add on a side note, nothing academic, just a personal anecdote, mind you, that these morsels are quite the craving quenchers, exactly what the virus is looking for. You'll be quite happy to know that the subjects bitten but then deprived of their internal organs do not transform."

His complete lack of emotion as he indicates his pile of "test subjects" chills my whole body. "But this is a most interesting finding." He indicates those on the other side of the room. "Even the ZVs which the messenger of war—that's Greyson—created to lead my children into battle, they transform when I bite them again!"

For the first time, Sam shifts his focus to me. "The mutant ZVs are NOT immune to my strain of the virus!" His eyes narrow.

The air seems a little thinner. My chest pumps harder, sucking in more of it. Nicolas glances my way. We have the data for the question I asked him earlier. The killer strain carried by Sam and Gavin infects ZVs. That explains why Christina, a teenager, was one of the zombies that attacked me in the yard when Sam was supposedly only 'judging' the adults, turning the goats into the living dead monsters of hell.

"…And a little child shall lead them." I remember that from Sunday School. Apparently, Ashley was counting on the 'obedience' factor encoded in Greyson's bite victims to be present in the new strain infected by Sam. She must have been hoping her lucid ZVs would be able to lead his zombie minions into battle against the infidels.

I can't help but wonder why, when the master plan went south, Greyson didn't kill Sam right here, on the spot. The only reason I can think of is that I've lost him. He's stepped over the line. He's a convert and he's not going to raise a gun against a fellow god…or…he's lying out there in the courtyard with his throat ripped out…or…he was bitten and now there's nothing but a deep purple haze staring from his golden eyes.

"Of course, we're still in the early stages of the research." Sam is clearly mocking his brother. "The tests I had hoped to conduct on the mutant ZVs were postponed. We had difficulty…collecting the necessary samples—such an appalling lack of specimens here. The disciples weren't faithful vegetarians for long enough."

At least now I know Greyson's body isn't one of the dark heaps on this floor in here. I'm sure Sam would have thoroughly enjoyed passing along that piece of data.

Sam turns glibly back to Nicolas. "I must admit I was quite surprised by my findings and repeated the experiment multiple times to verify the data. As theorized, they all died within 5 or 6 minutes and then resuscitated, transformed. 'Resurrected' as Ms. Knight would prefer to term the metamorphosis. But that would be an unsubstantiated term requiring further investigation. I must apologize for the lack of precision in my research. I was not appropriately equipped to conduct it in a more professional manner."

Nicolas drags his fingers through his hair and finally finds words. "Sam, stop…" but that's all he can manage before his voice breaks.

"Oh, but I'm not finished, Dr. Vadlamani. My findings are even more spectacular. You see the secondary infected subjects, my children, the children of the angel of death as Ashley classified them, they are as lethal and contagious…"

"Stop it!" Nicolas commands.

Sam bristles.

Nicolas, his palm still tangled in his hair, pleads with his brother. "We have to get you out of here. I can undo what she's done." He waves the gun limply at Sam's 'experiments' on the floor. "This is just the virus infecting your brain. I'm sure of it. We can cure you. All I need…"

Impossible to tell if Sam is angrier at the big brother telling him what to do, or at the implication that he's sick and needs to be fixed.

"You still don't get it, do you?" He shakes his head. For a moment I get the impression he's lucid. "The tide is rushing in, Nicolas, and I'm the heavenly body pulling it." Maybe not so lucid.

I'm sure in his little make-believe world, he makes perfect sense. Very slowly, I slide the aim of my gun up, targeting his forehead, wishing I'd had more practice at this. The room, not quite as deep as the chapel above, is still pretty long. I'm not that good a shot from a distance. But then, Nicolas is only a few yards away from me and, realistically, the only reason I'll be shooting is if Sam comes after him. That's a long shot. Sam climbed over his brother to take a bite out of Amber. If he's got that kind of sub-conscious control, the risk is so much lower. But then again…his whole worldview has changed.

"I'm not the one who needs fixing." The faint lilac that should have been the whites of his Sam's eyes narrows. My arm tenses, my finger twitching. "You're the one wallowing around in your fragile helplessness—weak and vulnerable. All these months—years!—you've fed me your cures, taken your samples, worked so hard to remove my symptoms, to make me like you. Have you ever thought that maybe I'm the one who has the cure for what's ailing you, frail human?"

"Sam…" Nicolas struggles for a response.

"Join me, brother!"

Sam literally launches himself off the podium. He's not wearing white like all the others. The black robes of the Grim Reaper fly behind him as he tramples over the pillaged cadavers between him and his brother.

My gun blasts through the stillness of this ghoulish graveyard.

"No!" Nicolas shouts, but I don't know if he's talking to his brother or me. He retreats, tripping over a tangle of white-clad legs beneath him.

Of course, I missed. It's not like I'm a trained agent with hours of moving target practice on my resume. Sam growls at me, twisting, his purple eyes flashing, his cloak flying to the side as he changes direction. In the light of the window, I see his canines have actually grown and my neck is now their target.

He's angry. He's angry that I shot at him. He's angry that I've kept him from 'converting' his brother. Who knows, maybe he's angry that I'm standing here reminding him that some of us are choosing to embrace our humanity. My finger squeezes as my feet retreat from the snarling charge.

The crack of the gun jerks Sam away howling and grabbing his shoulder, but the bullet only slows him down. In a final, crazed leap, he rams me, his arms binding my waist. Oh God! He's strong.

We tumble over onto the carpet of corpses. My head dents the soft belly of a dead zombie, her white skirt billowing up on impact, her body reverberating.

I get off another shot that shatters the window before my hand slams against the floor and the gun thuds away out of reach. Even if it were close enough to grab, I wouldn't have time. Sam has judged me.

I'm not a sheep for the slaughter and I'm not a goat to be damned and transformed into a demon with a single bite. I am simply the enemy. He's going to rip out my throat, sever all communications from the virus to the body, and remove me from the battle—permanently.

The virus in my veins erupts, flooding my limbs with its brand of survival juice. Crossing my elbows over my face, shielding my neck, I jab my knees into his gut. "Nicolas, for God's sake…!"

The wind rushes through Sam's bloody teeth in a grunt as he doubles up long enough for me to throw him off my chest and scramble to my feet. I'm guessing Sam wasn't much of a physical guy before he went zombie god and I might be able to make up in Karate tactics what I lack in strength.

Struggling to find solid footing in the sea of flopping bodies, I manage one kick to the side of Sam's face as he vaults up. I'm hoping to knock him to his stomach and straddle him, pinned, so that Nicolas can get his samples. But let's be real. I don't see that happening.

My back to him, and not a nano-second to check on him, I have no idea whether or not Nicolas is still in the game—and worse, if he is, I don't know if he's still on my team.

Extracting the knife sheathed at my thigh, I pivot for one more kick to Sam's back to flatten him out on his stomach. He swings around and intercepts my foot. The momentum crashes me back onto my butt, but Sam loses his balance, tripping over the bodies of his dead followers.

Clambering to our feet, viral battle cries hissing from between our teeth, we charge, my knife poised to strike. If nothing else, I'm going to make sure the zombie maker doesn't leave his dungeon.

We clash and grapple, our eyes locked, he's not even sweating. Holding his head at bay with one desperate fist jammed in his throat, I ram the knife down toward his skull. My fist stops short, caught in mid-thrust, snagged in Nicolas's hand.

Shock and dismay drop my jaw; Sam sneers and thrusts his head forward against the force of my arm. My elbow snaps back and the cold mist of his breath hits my neck.

A gunshot shatters through the snarling in my ear.

Chapter 34

Pure astonishment smeared across his face, Sam crumples to the floor, a pile of flesh and black robes.

Staring at the body of his brother, Nicolas opens his fist and drops my wrist.

"Nicolas…" I pant, catching my breath from the exertion of the fight, but I don't even know what to say. My brain transposes Sam's lifeless form with Amber's, places the gun in my hand. My heart wrenches for Nicolas, doubles over with the kick of his loss. My fingers grasp his arm, but he doesn't acknowledge the touch.

There's no cure for this wound. He looks diminished, standing there in the narrow column of light, mourning the part of himself that he severed with the pull of a trigger.

The infection, the apocalypse, the demented glory, they've disappeared. It's just the face of his little brother. It's just the smoking gun in the hand that was supposed to protect the boy lying at his feet.

"Nicolas…"

His eyes fixed on Sam's, he stuffs the gun in his jeans and then pulls the syringes out of his pockets. Tearing back the sterile plastic wrap, he bends down to the body and gently slides his brother's sleeve up to his shoulder, exposing the vein inside his elbow.

Nicolas's hand lingers on the edge of the boy's chest. His eyes squeeze shut. Mine don't. A drop of hot sorrow wells up, breaks free, and dribbles down my cheek as I stare at what he's done, what he had to do, giving up everything he's worked for, blowing away in the violent wind of a tiny squeeze of a trigger finger, the soul that shapes his life.

My teeth work at the flesh of my lip as he wraps, mechanically, the constricting band around his brother's bicep.

The needle poised against the purple vein, Nicolas hesitates. His head falls, and from his chest, a death knoll rings out. His shoulders convulse, the damn breaks, the grief gushes out in a flood of tears.

Bending down, I throw my arm around his shoulders and reach for the syringes. He shrugs me off, violently shaking his head and swiping at the tears. He bends to the task with sharp, experienced professionalism. The tubes are full in seconds.

Nicolas wraps them carefully, not just because they hold the delicate weapon of salvation from the virus, but because they hold the last remnants of his family, the legacy of his brother. Gently, he inserts them into a padded case that he tucks into his sweatshirt pocket. He stands and walks to the door, navigating blindly the bodies under his feet.

"Nicolas…"

He turns back, eyes vacant.

I don't dare thank him for the choice he made. I might as well slap his face. "What about the body? Do you want…?"

"We burn our dead." He pulls the gun from his jeans and leans through the crack in the door propped open by the legs he jostled when he tripped.

Hopping over torsos, I catch him before he can step into the hallway.

We know the zombie disciples have already been sent out in swarms, but we can't be sure there aren't a few stragglers left behind to tend the hive. I'm more worried about Nicolas now than I was when we first came in. He's lost something. His reason for living was to protect his brother. His love, that's been ripped from his being, fueled the zeal that propelled him to the cure. I'm not sure how long it takes for that jagged hole to repair itself.

My hand on his chest, I nudge him aside to take the lead. He shuffles in his pocket and produces the case.

"You'd better take these. Your chances of survival are better than mine."

I take the case, but I don't agree. "No, Nicolas, our chances of survival are exactly equal. If they get to you, it will only be because I'm already dead."

"You can't die..." He chokes on the words and I know what he's trying to say. If I die, then why the hell did he just shoot his little brother?

"Let's go." Poking my head into the hall, I peer into the darkness. Our goal is the top of the stairs and the emergency exit. But there's another door the other direction down the hall. I glance at my watch. We have less than an hour, although I'm pretty sure our time ran out the moment the first swarm of full-fledged zombies left the compound and headed toward the city.

I tap my heel, biting my lip. I can't just leave without looking for Cameron. Too many people have lost the ones they love, putting themselves in jeopardy to save my grey skin. I can't walk out of here without trying to find him.

"Nicolas," I wave him ahead, "go up the stairs. Get the rifle and wait for me. I have to check out that room." I nudge my gun toward the doors at the opposite end of the hall.

He shakes his head and glances at his watch. "If we miss the helicopter..."

Even down in this basement, a distant boom gently rocks the walls, a low roaring growl from the east, toward Houston.

We both know what it means, but I'm the one who says it. "The helicopters are already gone. We're on our own."

"You can't know that for sure. Dr. Pêsqué..."

"...didn't have much choice once the zombies showed up. If the military is bombing already, it's because the rabid hordes invaded the place like the plague. Can you imagine? There were several hundred people in this compound, Nicolas. There aren't nearly that many bodies. Now we have gangs of mutant ZVs raiding and damned predator zombies hunting. I'm sure Holland evacuated everyone..." the thought occurs to me before I have time to censor it "...unless they swarmed so fast, he couldn't get everyone out."

Nicolas already looked blanched. Now he's hyperventilating.

The only question I can't answer for myself is did Ryan evacuate Amber right when he left me? He told her they were going on a helicopter ride. He had to mean right then, didn't he?

"We'll just have to play it by ear, drive to Galveston, and take our chances at being able to catch a ride. Ryan told me the aircraft carrier was just offshore in the Gulf. We'll swim if we have to." My neck swivels reluctantly toward the other door down the hall. Another shock rumbles through the corridor, like the leftovers of a distant earthquake.

Nicolas steadies himself and moves toward the stairway.

"We're done here, but I have to look inside that door." I lean my head toward the other room. "Cameron might be in there. They might have been holding people there before the judgment."

Nicolas nods. He's not going to argue. He knew before we came here what he might find when he found Sam. But he had to see for himself. He had to do everything he could. I don't expect to find anything better than Nicolas found. But I can't walk away without knowing.

Another bomb thunders and reverberates through the building. It's louder, probably closer. It makes sense that this compound would be a prime target. If the zombies are showing up in town, they know where they're coming from.

"Go! Grab the rifle at the top of the steps and wait for me. I'll be up in two minutes." I don't offer a plan B, mostly because we don't even have a plan A.

Picking my way through the bodies, I close in on the door. My toe snags on a dark sleeve and I stumble. Behind me, Nicolas whirls round to cover me. I'm not reassured. From this distance, I'm in as much danger from his gun as anything that jumps out at me.

Catching my balance, I raise my hand and nod, calling him off. At the bottom step, he lingers, his eyes flashing between the stairwell and me. Another bomb shakes the walls. This time, plaster falls off, leaving a glow of green dust shimmering across the ray of light from the exit signs. They're getting closer—probably in the woods.

The sign above the door bathes in green the grey of my fingers as they press against the wood. There's no chain on this one. Whoever locked up Sam—hopefully, Greyson—didn't think it was worth the trouble. But for all I know, the jailor could be dead under my feet.

My head spurs me forward. "Do it! Do it! Just do it!" A tribal war dance stomps through my arteries, drums thumping in the chambers of my heart. The door slides inward. It can't go the other direction, which is why the press of the zombies inside hasn't opened it yet. A potpourri of ZV blood swooshes out the gap laced with the thick fresh meat aroma of uninfected blood. There are both kinds in this room.

Three inches in, the door sticks. I lean in to see what's blocking it, although I think I already know. My attention is focused on the floor, assuming I'll find in here what I've found everywhere else, so the hand that shoots through the opening, aiming for my neck, catches me by surprise.

The low, rumbling growl behind it, makes me think these zombies haven't been exposed to the war yet. This one clearly just doesn't like the way I smell. Jerking back, I pull hard on the handle. The bloody, grey wrist catches, the fingers writhe, and then the whole room rumbles with a snarling, exhale of zombies aroused from their stupor.

"Cameron! If you're in there, you have to let me know!" Reason tells me that if he was in the dark void, they would have sniffed him out by now, even if he was hiding. I just have to be sure.

No response but the growling of the brain-dead beast on the other side of the door; he is not happy. His buddies are crowding toward the smell of me, pressing forward, forcing the door shut on his wrist. No wonder whoever locked Sam in didn't think this crowd needed chains. They'd have to figure out how to pull the door open and all they can do is press forward relentlessly, shutting it. "If you don't say anything, I'm going to leave and look somewhere else. I'll never know you're in there. You have to let me know you're there so I can help you."

Only the mouth connected to the hand responds, not in pain, just angry snarling. The hand thrashes to get free as the press from the growling crowd strangles the wrist in the closing gap.

Another bomb rattles the walls. Closer. "C'mon!" Nicolas beckons me from the bottom of the stairs, one foot testing the ledge.

There's nothing I can do here. Unless they evolve in the next 5 minutes, the crowd of zombies behind this door will keep it shut.

Picking my way through the corpses, I catch up with Nicolas and then take the lead. "Watch our backs." I peer cautiously around the wall of the landing up the next flight.

The party is over in this building. We doused the last of the festivities on our way down the stairs. Motioning to Nicolas, I creep up. At the top, I reach for the rifle. I'll need it again once we get out and can see them coming. It's not there.

"Did you pick it up, Nicolas?"

He shakes his head. "Don't worry about it." He holds up his gun. The way it droops in his hand, it never seems to make me feel any safer that he has it. At this point, the only suspect capable of picking up my rifle is a mutant ZV, probably desperate to defend itself from the carnivores.

Nicolas trailing behind me, I dash for the front doors of the Judgment Hall. A veil of smoke in the parkway, between the back of the church in front of us and the insane asylum behind, washes out the putrid, smolder of zombie we've been wading through inside.

Dashing for one of the pillars, I survey the damage outside. It looks like most of the bombs are hitting the woods to the east of the compound. A white cloud billows up over the horizon above the church. Flaming auras shimmer the tops of the visible trees. The bombs are meant to destroy the nests, but if Holland and company already know about the new breed, it's because some of them have reached the city. From what I saw here, these ravenous predators will run through Houston like the plague. What's worse, whatever death and gore they leave behind will rise up to join them.

Nicolas nudges my shoulder, nodding toward the eastern sky. A plane, looming on the horizon, bears down on us.

Cameron could still be here. The boys' dorm would make sense as a hiding place and it's on the way back to the car. I could just take a look. What I want to do is run through the halls yelling his name so he knows I'm here. But we have no idea how many little pods of zombies are hiding in the bushes waiting to ambush unsuspecting prey. A fruit salad of blood smells saturates this place. It will be hard for them to smell me coming, but we need to at least attempt stealth.

But I also really need to get Nicolas on a helicopter to that French aircraft carrier—Nicolas and the blood samples in my pocket. Deep down, I know the chances of Cameron, alive, hiding somewhere in this compound, are slim and fading. But I can't let him be dead in my head. The boys' dorm is a mirror image of the girls' across the courtyard still twinkling with red, green, and gold bells wreathed in evergreen garland. I'm sure there's a door at the church end, just like the one I came out the night I ran into Miguel slinking around.

"C'mon! I just want to check that building for Cameron before I leave." Nicolas's eyes contract. Cameron dead is a little more possible for him to picture, especially since he just left his brother, still and extinguished, bleeding on the carpet. But he doesn't object. A heavy film of pity slides over his face, pulling down the corners of his mouth, and he only nods and falls in line behind me, covering our backs as we go.

The plane is coming in fast. I'll barely have time to get inside the door and who knows what kind of ghoulish mess I'll find in there.

Motioning to Nicolas to wait on the little porch, I slide inside the door as he takes up a guard spot, his back to the wall of the building. At least on this side of the courtyard, which doesn't back the huge clearing that leads to the barn, there aren't trees and bushes surrounding the door. He'll be able to see any of the new breed coming at him with plenty of time to shoot.

One shot from outside, and I'll have to leave, with or without Cameron. Nicolas is what matters most now—Nicolas and the blood samples in my pocket. But if it were Amber that might be up there, I'm not sure I'd be seeing that decision so clearly. I have to think like my Aunt Esther, have more skin in the game.

The stairwell at the back is empty. A small window looks through the door into the hallway. I noticed the sound carries pretty well in the dorms. I'd be safe calling from here. The zombies don't seem to be able to handle doors.

Yes, I am a little concerned about the arm I left jamming the door in the Judgment Hall. His Z buddies were pressing up against it so hard, forcing it closed, there was nothing I could do. But if they back off once there's no more bait outside, the monster will have a foot—no, an arm—in the door that he could use as leverage to push through. And once the door is open…

The lights are out. I think all the power is gone. Only the neon green signs that must have their own power source seem to be alive and kicking. The putrid smell of zombies here is fainter; even the *eau de mutant* is almost imperceptible. A couple of brain-dead teens wander the hallway aimlessly. A little tide of hope ripples through me. A kid could have survived in here, locked up in his room.

The hinges creak a little as I open the door. The zombies jerk around to the sound, snarling and sniffing the air. My smell must bristle them the way theirs bristles me. This won't be too hard. They're not in any shape to attack anyone. These two were meat before they became zombies. Their white suits are a kindergarten finger-painting nightmare in red. The important parts weren't eaten though. There's still enough left for the virus to function.

My arm slides through the door as they charge—sort of, mostly they hobble. I can afford to wait until I have a sure shot. They didn't catch me off guard like the healthy one under the Jeep. Steadying my aim on the edge of the door, I squeeze the trigger and land a small purple hole in the middle of the first teen's forehead. It's hard to feel bad because I'm not the one that killed him. I've just stopped the pain—still…he was a little boy once.

The second one, smaller and younger, but in worse shape, stumbles over the body and thrashes around for a while. He's not getting up any time soon, so I don't waste a bullet. "Cameron! Cameron! It's Evy! You have to come out. I have a gun. The hallway is clear. We have to get you out of here. I don't have time to check all the rooms."

Nothing happens. Frustration reacts with the adrenaline in my system. "C'mon, Cameron! Get out here! I'm going upstairs and then I'll stop here once more and you better get out here!"

He's used to Craig yelling at him like that. If he's in here, my tone will give him more confidence to come out.

Slamming the door, I sprint up the stairs, grateful my ZV powers let me see in the dark. Looking through the window in the door, I'm even more encouraged. This hallway is empty. I wonder if the brain-dead hunters have trouble with stairs. That would be a good thing if Cameron is hiding here.

This door doesn't squeak, but no breeze of zombie rushes out when I open it. "Cameron! It's Evelyn. I can get you out of here. But you have to hurry." The hallway echoes my call. The place is a graveyard—figuratively. The chances of my cousin being alive and hiding are highest in this hallway.

"Cameron!" I let the door shut behind me as I penetrate a few paces down the empty corridor.

"Camer—!"

The muffled shot from outside sends me spinning on my toes back to the door. Nicolas is only good for putting down a single zombie at close range. He's going to need back up before the second shot. Taking the stairs two at a time, I hit the entry and tear the door open.

Chapter 35

A hive of ZV hunting zombies swarming the porch would have disturbed me less than what I see in the sunlight drenched doorway. It's only a silhouette in the glare streaming into the dark passage, but I don't need any more than an outline to know that face, that body, that voice. It haunts my days, haunts my mind, haunts my soul. Damn him! Damn him for being there like he said he would be. Damn him for making me love him, over and over and over again. Damn him for coming back after I kicked him. It's like opening the door and finding the heart you thought you'd ripped out and thrown to the dogs pumping frantically on the step.

"Go! Go!" Greyson waves his hand in the direction of the girls' dorm. He fires backward around the corner at the entrance to the Hall of Judges. To my left, Nicolas is already ten yards into the courtyard. But he's not alone. Trailing behind, his hand hooked into the doctor's, a little ginger hoofs it to match Nicolas's long, runner's strides with his shorter ten-year-old leaps. Cameron!

"Greyson! Thank God you're safe! Where did you find him?" I race to help cover. What I really want to do is throw my arms around the boy who is the glue to all the broken pieces of my life. But I know I can't, not just because we're running from a herd of zombies, but because he's one of the pieces that has broken off. The missing part makes me feel like I'm shambling and hobbling with only half a body.

"He was here when I got back. I hid him in the men's room when they brought him in for the ceremony." He doesn't look at me as he fires off a few shots toward the smoky steps of the Hall of Judges, drawing my attention to the target.

"Oh, my God!" The doors, which open outward, are vomiting zombies, healthy—well, except for the fact that they're dead—intentionally bitten zombies. I was wrong. They have no trouble with stairs. Greyson has downed a couple of them in front, which is bottlenecking the flow of traffic as they stumble over the bodies. They're kind of tunnel-visioned to their prey and don't really watch where they're going.

"If you were going to set them free, it was nice of you to leave me a gun. Mine ran out of bullets in the first wave." He peers through the scope, pulls the trigger, takes a step back, and squeezes out a couple more shots. Two more zombies drop in their tracks.

But those last two are a mistake. Now there's just a purple carpet of zombies for the others to trample over.

"Shit!" Greyson grabs my hand because they're fast, and now that they have momentum, we're about to be overrun by a wave of snarling carnivores defending their territory. There's no way the two of us can mow them all down before they get to us—and the threat of bullets doesn't deter them. "Run!"

"Where?" I take off after Nicolas, Greyson on my heels. "The car is back there by the gate. We have to get to Galveston. There's a French aircraft carrier in the bay. They've got Amber and they'll get us out of here." I'm not sure he hears everything because he's twisting back as we run, firing off shots at the pack leaders.

They're gaining. They're faster than we are. They're not human anymore.

Brain signals to run faster crowd all my neural centers so I don't remember what the faint buzz in the back of my head is.

A young adult, a couple strides ahead of the others leaps for us. Greyson stumbles; the rifle belts out a short volley of shots into the oncoming mob.

A whistling whirr draws my head to the plane that's just dropped its package. The missile dives for the center of the dorm. "Look out!" I seize Greyson's arm and run for cover as the boys' dorm explodes into splinters, smoke, and shards of glass.

The shock tumbles over us from behind. A sharp blow to my head joggles my brain, knocking my nose into the grass. Wet ooze globs down the side of my face. A flying brick of shrapnel slams into my calf. The crack resonates up my leg, colliding with the throbbing rippling out of my head. "Greyson!" I yell, but it's only a moan when the word actually makes it through the muddle in my brain.

I'm still reeling, but he's there beside me, a trail of purple blood leaking from his forehead. Scrambling up, he wraps his arms around my waist and hauls me to my feet. I can't get my balance; the world is spinning, still rocking from the blast.

"Go! They're only dazed for a second." He's practically carrying me across the courtyard. "What's going on here? They're bombing the compound?"

Running takes all my focus because my left leg doesn't seem to be responding and most of the forward propulsion is coming from Greyson. I have to sort through the mess of images, dust, and information floating in the debris of my bombed-out brain to find an answer to his question, and then getting the words out takes an extra effort.

"Eli…it's like Eli…burn it! They're going to…they're bombing the hell out of it."

"The compound?"

"Houston…all of it…" I break into a splutter of coughing, "…they invaded the city…the new zombies escaped."

He stops short in front of Nicolas, who has doubled back to help me. I can feel the blood trickling down my cheek. "Where…?" Cough, cough, hack, wheeze. "Where's Cameron?"

"Dr. Pêsqué sent the helicopter to pick us up here!" Nicolas gestures in the direction of the gap between the western end of the church and the girls' dorm. The place is a fog of smoke and debris, but I can make out the grey silhouette of my ginger cousin, scrambling toward the structures. "I saw it land in the field behind that building before the bomb hit. We have to go. Now!" He reaches his unarmed hand for my shoulder, to pull me toward the trees.

"No! Don't wait for me, Nicolas. We have no idea what's hiding in those bushes. Go after Cameron." My cousin is only here in this nightmare because I brought it to his doorstep. It's my job to make sure he gets escorted out. Amber is safe; Cameron is the new priority. Greyson is the only support I need to stall the oncoming tide before it washes over us and drowns my cousin.

Reaching into my pocket I wrap my fist around the case holding the tubes of Sam's blood. Holding onto Nicolas's wrist, to support myself and keep him from taking responsibility for my stability, I wrap his fingers around them. "Get Cameron and these samples to the helicopter!"

The doctor hesitates.

"Go! Now!" I break away from Greyson, hobbling forward a step or two. It hurts like hell, but I have to show him I'm right behind him. He leans toward Cameron but can't quite get his feet to run away from me. Planting my right leg firmly for balance, I give him a shove that sends him sprinting after my cousin, tucking the samples away as he runs, his gun leading the way.

I reach a hand toward Greyson to rebalance myself. But he's not looking at me and I teeter, grasping at the air that separates us. He's searching the sky above the clearing smoke and peering at the twitching lumps of zombie littered in front of the building. The virus has had some of its communication lines severed and it's having trouble getting the bodies back online. But they're far from immobilized. There's a lot of rolling, jerking, and growling going on. "They're coming back for another drop." Greyson points at a minuscule plane on the horizon above the smoke.

"C'mon!" Gritting my teeth, I power through the pain in a half run, half shamble. I ran the 4x4. I'm no stranger to the burn. You do what you have to do to win. "Once they have the blood samples on the helicopter, they're not going to risk hanging around. It's our last chance to make it to the carrier."

My face bleeding, my leg broken, hobbling after Nicolas and my cousin, I finally fit the zombie part I've been cast in. It's times like these that I actually appreciate being infected with a virus that doesn't give a damn about broken parts. It just shuts down the blood flow and strangles the nerve impulses. I won't heal—the tub of cream Nicolas offered me this morning rolls in my pocket—at least not right away, but I won't die or feel the full impact of the pain either.

A little irritated because it's taking so much effort to get my butt across the courtyard, I turn to see why Greyson isn't a couple steps in front of me, dragging me along. I know why he hasn't scooped me up to carry me, but are we really so awkward now that I can't lean on his arm? Between the black and the white swallowing up our reality, the grey can't survive alone. Sooner or later you need someone to cover your back, shore up your weak side.

Greyson is obviously torn between the church and me. Catching up with me in a couple long strides, he demands, "Where's Ashley?"

My heart snags on the words and rips. This is so not the moment, it's so self-centered, so petty. But I can't stop the sudden rolling thunder of betrayal that makes me stumble on my weak leg. It's not because he's angry with me that he doesn't have my back, it's because he's done with me. He's done with me. He's done with me. If I say it to myself enough, maybe the rage will kill the pain.

But I knew this would come, didn't I? I knew what he was before I remolded him in my head to suit what I wanted him to be. The reality was bound to bust through my flimsy cast of wishful thinking.

As quickly as the rent slices through my chest, I seal it up. "She's in the Hall of Judges." I look away, focusing on the gap between the buildings, focusing on my cousin, focusing on Nicolas with syringes in his pockets, willing my legs not to buckle beneath me. "She's waiting for someone to come back for her."

"I have to go after her."

"Of course, you do." I squint at the target ahead of me, refusing to look back at the boy that doesn't come after me anymore. I walk—limp—away from him, leaving him to his new religion. I've reached the sidewalk that runs around the grassy square in front of the buildings. Nicolas and Cameron have disappeared through the trees and bushes encircling the girls' dorm.

From behind me, Greyson grabs both my shoulders and swivels me around to face him. His eyes are a little more purple than they used to be. I just hope mine aren't pink and moist.

He's about a head taller than I am, so I can feel the intensity of his gaze, looking down into my face until I'm compelled to lift my eyes to meet his. "You still don't see me, do you, Ev?

What the hell is he doing? I want to slap him…no, I want to ball up my fists and punch him! But no! No, I don't. I want to throw my arms around him. I want to hold him until we're remolded into two people that fit together because every tiny molecule inside me screams that I want to be with him. All the hormones and memories, and maybe even the virus, they all demand that I embrace this boy that it's impossible for me not to love. But I can't love him.

So, I don't move. I just shift my eyes away from the hypnotic draw of his. And there, behind us, a white-suited zombie, dyed grey in the dust and smattered with his own purple blood, has risen from the rubble and is charging, before he can even stand. Close behind, a raven-haired girl with only half a dress and her left arm smashed and hanging limply to her side wobbles furiously toward us. On the horizon above their heads, a small plane grows larger.

Pushing Greyson back, I raise my Glock and fire. The bullet finds the zombie's chest. He jerks backward, but keeps coming. Greyson swings around, ramming the rifle up against his shoulder and pulling the trigger in almost a single motion. A little purple hole opens up in the zombie's head. He takes one more step and then falls forward.

Greyson pushes me toward the trees, "Go! Go! I'll meet you there." More of them are rising up behind the girl. The tiny speck of silver in the sky is now a kid-size model plane. It's coming faster than we think it is and we have no idea how many of the zombies I released are still inside the smoke and debris from the boys' dorm.

"You can't make it! You don't have enough bullets. That bomb will drop before you get out!" We veer in opposite directions, Greyson to Ashley in the Hall of Judges, and me through the trees to the helicopter, to Nicolas, to my cousin, to Amber, to Ryan and the French research team.

Grinding to a standstill, I whirl around and fire on the first zombie in the line rushing toward us. My shot misses her head, but pierces her thigh. She stumbles, her face planting in the bark of a flowerbed giggling with winter pansies. The virus in me celebrates the vanquishing of a predator; the girl in me feels cruel and desperate. "Greyson!" The shot already caught his attention. "Please! Come with me. It's the only way you'll make it out of this war hole alive."

Greyson pauses long enough to take out the oversized-choir boy tripping over the top of the zombie rug I just made. "I always make it!" He grins and disappears around the corner of the church...around the corner of my heart...and around the corner of my life.

Chapter 36

Breaking through the trees, I run toward the deafening whir of the helicopter parked in the field—*he's gone, he's gone, HE'S GONE!* Don't cry; just run. But the treacherous, burning sting has already welled up a drop that blubbers down my cheek. I swipe it away—I'm about 50 yards behind Nicolas and Cameron.

The helicopter blades churn up the tall grass and hog all the sound waves. Squinting, I can just make out the pilot. It's definitely Ryan. He's looking straight on at Nicolas and Cameron, yelling and pointing off to their left.

My legs keep churning. The virus has done its job strangling off the pain from my run-in with flying building parts. There's hardly a pitch to my stride, but that can't be good for the bone. The pain is meant to keep me from damaging the leg any more than it already is. I'm gaining on Nicolas who has caught up to Cameron, but Ryan is still yelling and pointing emphatically at the little playground I noticed the night I snuck out.

Without breaking my stride, because I know what's already hot on my heels, I crane my neck to my left to see what's got Ryan all worked up.

Yellow. That's the first thing I spot. Another couple of steps and the rest of the images file across my neurons. Jeans, burned and tattered, only part of his t-shirt clinging to one blackened shoulder, Miguel sprints across the lawn, trailing one leg awkwardly, targeting Cameron and Nicolas. He obviously just barely made it out of the fire at my aunt and uncle's. Once he shot my aunt and she crumpled limp and lifeless into his arms, I shoved the two of them into the flaming gorge left by the collapsing hallway and then fled out the window.

Miguel's not here for lunch; he's here for revenge. That's how he operates.

Our paths make a V, converging at the helicopter, but he's closer to the target than I am. We need to collide before we get to Nicolas and Cameron so I shift my trajectory by a couple of degrees to intercept Miguel sooner. Cameron has reached the chopper and Ryan is busy hauling him up, yelling at Nicolas. Nicolas turns and spots Miguel, raises his gun and shoots, but totally misses—twice.

Getting off a shot while you're running full speed with a handful of sprinting zombies behind you isn't exactly a skill you pick up on the fly. At least the crack of my gun draws Miguel's attention from Nicolas to me. He looks demonically happy to see me.

The doctor's third shot rings out just as my head butts into Miguel's chest. The two of us roll, grappling, a few yards outside the radius of the helicopter blades. "Shoot...shoot..." Ryan's French-tinged accent rings from the helicopter, but I know Nicolas won't. I'm not sure he has any bullets left, but he and I both know he's not a good enough shot to fire into the tangled mass of Miguel and me.

The shots coming out of the helicopter are flying over our heads into the small mob of zombies drawn to the kill scene. Ryan's preoccupied.

I'm on my own.

What I need here is a clean, close-range shot. The gun's still in my hand and I wrench my arm free to bring it around to his flaming purple, mottled face, aiming right through the tattered yellow bandana probably melted to his temple.

"Bitch!" He grabs my wrist. He's still incredibly strong, but I can smell on his breath that he's been dipping into the human flesh cookie barrel. The weakness has a scent.

Hard as I try, I can't get my wrist out of his fist. He rattles my hand, trying to shake the gun free. Wrapping my left arm around his neck, I squeeze, pulling him away. His other arm breaks free and swings around, his fist catching my jaw. For a fraction of a second, the world shudders. I lose my grip, the gun flies loose, and my back slams against the lawn.

Miguel's knee lands on my chest, pinning me as he dives for the Glock. Nicolas turns back, running crouched under the spinning blades and skids forward to kick it out of his reach, but Miguel grabs his ankle and sends him crashing onto his back.

The dozens of zombies rushing the helicopter completely absorb Ryan. On the off chance that Greyson manages to slip out of the Judgment Hall before the plane drops its load, Ryan will take him out with the rest of the grey enemy swarming down on us. I have to shove Nicolas into that chopper and call off Ryan before that happens.

Grasping Miguel's leg, I roll, flipping him and dislodging his grip on Nicolas who scampers to his feet.

"Go! Go!" Nicolas can't hang about the danger zone to help me. Miguel lurches up, swinging, but I block with my forearm.

"Get in the 'copter!" Ryan fires off orders with his machine gun rounds as if Nicolas isn't moving fast enough. He mows down the front-runners in the snarling mess of frenzied dead streaming from the trees and then swears. "*Merde!* They're coming from the other side as well."

Miguel isn't as formidable a foe as he used to be. His cannibal lifestyle has taken its toll on him. I catch him off guard and my fist connects with his jaw. As he stumbles back, I see the gun in his fist and dive for it.

Ryan shifts the direction of the gunfire to the opposite end of the girls' dorm on the other side of the playground. "I can't wait here much longer. There are too many of them!" He doesn't dare to fire into the locked, wrestling body of Miguel and me.

Nicolas's voice isn't quite as forceful and the racket of bullets and helicopter blades drowns out half of his words as he sprints for the helicopter, "… bomb…less than a minute..."

Miguel twists violently, yanking his gun wrist out of my grasp. Dropping my head, I ram him hard in the gut, tackling him to the ground beneath the blades roaring above.

"We have to get up in the air or we'll get caught in the blast radius," Ryan hollers as Nicolas reaches the cabin. I'm not sure Ryan realizes Miguel has my gun now. I can't just wave good-bye and hop in the chopper. I scramble to my knees to make another grab at the Glock poised in his grotesquely burned hand as Ryan peppers the perimeter.

I don't know if the bomb is targeting the church or the girls' dorm…and what if the bomb drops before Greyson makes it out here?

He's gone, he's gone, he's gone.

In the split second that I crane my neck, rolling slightly toward the gap between the buildings to flash a glance there, reflexively searching for the boy that's always been there, hoping to see him at the edge of the orchard, Miguel swings his arm around, pulling the trigger. A hot ripping penetrates the left side of my chest; the kick of the bullet exiting my back thrusts me forward into Miguel as I scream. He falls backward beneath me, my chest riding his.

The earth vibrates in a low rumble beneath his back and my knees. Another bomb must have hit the woods. The impact rumbles through our bodies sprawled beneath the tenacious whirring of the helicopter blades.

The crack of the bullet and my scream bring Nicolas careening back into the fray under the constant stream of bullets pouring from Ryan's gun. Miguel is already dragging himself out from underneath me and twists around to seize Nic's leg.

The wound in my chest has the virus on full survival alert. The smell of predator hits my nose hard. With Ryan's focus split, some of the new strain are penetrating his defense. Beyond the deafening whir, the low buzz of an overhead plane grows, bearing down on us.

My left arm feels frozen, a heavy lump of pins and needles, but the other hand slides down to the knife that hugs my right leg. Nicolas crashes the butt of his gun down on Miguel's head, which means he has no bullets. Miguel reels, face planting back into the grass, but doesn't fire back at Nicolas. Oh, God! There's only one reason why he wouldn't just shoot the doctor on the spot…

As Nicolas rushes to help me, Miguel lassos him from the ground, roping his legs together and toppling him. Nicolas's face lands near my shoulder, his legs sprawled to the side of Miguel's head.

"Oh, God, no!" Dragging the knife out of the sheath strapped to my thigh, I realize I only have one lunge in me. The left half of my body still quivers, numb from the shot. My head flops and bubbles inside. I can't get enough air like I'm sucking it through a straw with a hole in it.

Miguel's neck is a good two feet above my head. Snarling and snapping, he lunges for the exposed skin around Nicolas's ankle. Propelling my right shoulder and hip forward, I slam the blade down, ramming it just below the knot in his charred yellow band.

My blade slices into the dent beneath Miguel's skull, tearing through the tendons and muscles, severing nerve pathways, right into his spinal cord. His blood squirts out the hole around the handle, damp and cool on my fist.

Some sort of satisfaction should overwhelm my senses because I just put an end to the bullying and unbridled violence of a monster, but still, I just want to wretch. He was alive, and now his legs are limp beneath mine. His head flops to the side. He doesn't even scream.

But Nicolas does.

The doctor, the man on whom our hopes for humanity rest, screams as he rips the flesh of his ankle out of Miguel's bloody jaws—his infected, putrid jaws.

My mouth drops open and the whole scene rips because this was never supposed to happen. Nicolas CANNOT be infected. Nicolas does NOT get infected; it just can't happen.

But the reality is there, two feet in front of my nose, a nasty serrated oval on his ankle.

Raising my body sends the blood rushing out of my head so that the whole scene wavers thin, a figment of my demented imagination. Grimacing, Nicolas extracts himself, lumbering up and bending over me.

"Get her in here. Now!" Ryan fires savagely in both directions, his voice splintering under the bulky sound waves of interminable spinning. He's so caught up in flattening the zombie hordes rushing the helicopter that he probably doesn't even know what just happened. Nicolas is stronger than I gave him credit for. He hefts me up pretty easily and lugs me over to the cabin door. Pain rips and shreds my lungs. Letting his gun drop for a few precious seconds, Ryan drags my semi-useless mass across the floor.

"…Greyson…" I gurgle.

"Where is he?" Ryan demands.

"In..." I can't get enough air to respond. Ryan shakes his head and runs back to grab Nicolas by the scruff, hauls him in, and then hefts his rifle to shower the perimeter with another spray of bullets. His absence has let the tide flow closer.

Thrusting the semi-automatic into Nicolas's arms, he heads for the pilot's seat. "Keep them off us! We have to get the hell out of here."

"…Greyson…" Someone has to go back for him. He's the one that always goes back for the man down. Someone has to go back for him. Someone has to!

Nicolas can't hear me because I can't god damn push enough air across my vocal cords to project the words. Poor Cameron is a crumpled mess cowering in the back corner of the helicopter.

The gun rattles, shaking Nicolas's shoulder. Ryan adjusts his headphones and pulls on the stick.

Greyson! Someone has to go back for Greyson!

The doctor isn't as good at house cleaning as French boy. As the copter lifts off, a couple zombies dive for the doorframe, hauling themselves in, growling, teeth snapping.

At close range, Nicolas isn't hard-pressed to make a clean shot to the brain of the closest intruder, but while he's blowing off one head, the other rabid stow-away grabs his chewed ankle and pulls. Nicolas slides forward, hollering, falling on his butt. The gun hurtles out the open door. We're already a couple feet off the ground and the zombie dangles from Nicolas's ankle as Nicolas clings to the base of one of the back seats.

He grapples against the weight of gravity tugging on the zombie clutching at his ankle. Frantically, he shakes his foot. His fingers, pale from gripping, slip from the metal bar. I have to do something but I can barely move.

Clawing at the floor I haul myself over. The virus isn't shutting off the pain the way I thought it would. Maybe there's more damage than it knows what to do with. My chest spasms and hot sparks shatter through my lungs as I drag myself forward. I'm going to have to lean out the door, and unwrap the mostly dead ghoul's fingers from around Nicolas and let the laws of physics do the rest. Nicolas winces and strains against the drag. I'm almost to his head. "Hang on, Nicolas!" I groan at his ear.

By the time I reach the open door, we're about ten feet off the ground. Even leaning out of the cabin, my fingers don't quite touch the zombie's. They're too far, too far, too far. Inch closer. God! The pain is excruciating, radiating from the hot center at the side of my chest.

Nicolas hollers as one of his hands slips and his whole body jerks downward, collapsing toward the weight of the zombie that dangles oblivious in mid-air, its driving purpose to snap a chunk of flesh from Nicolas's bloody rare leg.

I can't reach.

"Get off him, you freak!" Stretching forward, I rip the hole in my side wider. The scream tears out of my lungs, airless. And then I feel the little hands on my feet. Cameron has ventured out of his corner, anchored himself, and grabbed my ankles. Nicolas groans with the strain of hanging on. I have to try once more. Reaching, stretching, tearing, I extend my hand toward the snapping teeth, the tips of my fingers still inches away from the grey grasping hand...

And then, from the ground, from the corner between the Hall of the Judges and the girls' dorm, from the barrel of the gun I abandoned at the top of the stairs, a resounding crack breaks through the rhythmic chopping of the blades. The bullet pierces a hole in the back of the predator zombie's head and explodes out the front, peppering my face with purple gunk; the growling mouth hangs vapidly open. The grey fingers relax, Nicolas's foot jerks, and the living dead corpse plummets.

On the ground below, I see him, the boy who always has my back, dressed all in bloody grey-smeared white, the scope of the automatic rifle still at his eye. He lowers the site as the zombie free-falls, then he turns and grabs the hand of the brunette behind him, firing into the onslaught of predators hot in pursuit.

Before my heart can break, before his name can grace my lips one more time, another explosion on the compound rocks the cabin. Nicolas and Cameron grab my feet as the helicopter lurches in the blast. The whole field below disappears into smoke as Ryan swears and grapples with the controls trying to keep the copter stable.

And *he's gone, he's gone, he's gone!*

Chapter 37

The world rolls slightly. My chest throbs. Air comes reluctantly. My eyes fight to open because I'm in blackness; my head is emptiness. I need input. My lids flutter; the light hurts. Metal. The ceiling is grey metal. And *he's gone, he's gone, he's gone.*

"Elle se réveille. Allez chercher Lt. Samson et le docteur."

I know what those words mean. She's waking up. Go get Lt. Samson. Lt. Samson…Ryan. The lights go on in my ransacked brain. The world isn't rolling, my chest isn't throbbing because *he's gone, he's gone, he's gone*, it's because I'm on the French Aircraft Carrier and I was shot and *he's gone, he's gone, he's gone*, lost in the blast and the smoke.

The scene plays back in my head: the gunshot, his eyes meeting mine from so far away, his hand reaching for hers, the bang and jolt. My eyes release the tension of deep loss surging up from the molten cracks in my heart. A tear wanders aimlessly down the right side of my face and pools in my ear.

The metal hatch door swings open. Nicolas steps in. "Merci." He nods and the male nurse in French military issue steps out.

Limping slightly as he strides over to my bed, the doctor rubs his hand across my damp forehead.

"…Grey…" the word rasps across my throat, airless.

His hand pulls away and he looks down into my eyes. Something is missing from Nicolas's face. The bold determination and fearless optimism have faded away. In their place, something greyer plays around the corner of his eyes. "You shouldn't try to speak too much." He lets his fingers slip encouragingly down to mine. They lie neatly outside the blankets of the medical cot I'm tucked into. "The bullet chipped a rib and grazed a corner of your left lung. The virus preserves the organs and that's why it didn't just shut down all the pain centers. You're actually quite lucky. This is one of the few spots on your body that will heal. The wound on the surface wouldn't, but I'm treating it with some of the cream from your pocket."

He's all doctor now. Other than his fingers in mine, I could be a patient in an emergency clinic consigned to the capable hands of well-meaning strangers. But his fingers are there in mine—and they're grey, oh, my god, they're grey, like mine—and we are connected now much more deeply than my hand in his.

He's trying to protect me, but I can't let him. "…Grey…" I wheeze and then break into a cough that wrenches and twists my chest.

"Don't…" He can read the pleading question in my eyes without me having to sound the words. His head bowed, he breathes in heavily, the words refusing to come until his eyes meet mine, and then the pitiful begging compels him.

"The second bomb, you probably don't remember, was a firebomb. The Judgment Hall burst into a flaming inferno. There was no turning back…the chances…" He shakes his head mournfully. Seconds, minutes, hours, maybe eternities tick by before he moves on and his words register and confirm the lamentation in my head: *he's gone, he's gone, he's gone.*

The tears flow freely, springing up from buried memories and hidden corners of myself that I molded with the bonds between Greyson and me. Now those corners are just gaping holes because *he's gone, he's gone, he's gone.* My chest shudders with more than one shock of pain.

Nicolas squeezes my hand, looking away, staring into the stark grey metal that encapsulates us. The labored breathing of my sobs pinches and cramps my lungs and I have to stem it off, restricting the mourning to my eyes—*he's gone, he's gone, he's gone…*

"He saved us, over and over again. He came back for us, and we…" Nicolas tries to soften the blow of a brick with a thin, white tissue. He's standing here, infected, without his brother, and I'm so buried in my own pit of despair I haven't even reached out to give him a hand in his darkness.

My left moves more reluctantly than my right, but I don't want to let Nicolas's hand go, so I struggle to swipe the streams off my cheeks. Concentrating, gathering up and storing the air, I shake my head. "We all...saved...each other."

Nicolas is still mourning Sam—he had to put a gun to his own little brother's head and pull the trigger—my loss pales in comparison. Lifting our hands, twisting them to compare the shades of grey, I offer him the only words I can manage, "So sorry..."

"Don't be." He shrugs.

"...should have...saved you."

"You couldn't." Looking down, he shuffles his feet, takes another deep breath, and lets his head fall back, so that the flickering fluorescent lights play on his face as he exhales. When he looks back at me, his head tilted to one side, he confesses, "I was already infected."

My mouth hangs open but nothing comes out while I try to figure out what he's talking about. How? How is that possible? He was never bitten...unless Sam...

"My temperature was dropping by the time we arrived at your aunt's."

The questions are written all over my face.

"Traveling together, the constant exposure...it was bound to happen. The injections..." I remember the syringe I surprised him with in the barn "...they were keeping the symptoms at bay...but now...well, at least I'm vegetarian."

"But...hormones...couple," Nicolas is the one who told me the virus needed a very specific soup of hormones to incubate from exposure. That's why only couples contracted ZV in the beginning. You had to be experiencing all the chemical reactions of being in love...oh.

His hand slips away from mine. Oh, my God. "I'm..." the coughing chokes me, rifling through my chest, "...sorry."

"I'll go get Amber. She's been asking for you."

He walks out the door without looking back. The fingers of my right-hand strain through the thick strands of my hair as if they could sort out all the conflicting emotions tangled in my head—*he's gone, he's gone, he's gone.*

Everything that I'd made my life to be is now just a haze of smoke. I don't even have any right to rail against the gods because he left me. He left me. I let myself need him and he left me. I imagined him into something he wasn't and he shattered the mask that I molded. And that's the way this world is now. The people you need leave you. And Nicolas is infected. This is not how it was supposed to turn out.

Before I can push the whirlwind of thoughts out of my head, the door swings in, crashing against its hinges, and Amber dances into the room, Ryan hot on her heels, the smile on his face a contradiction to the doom and desperation on mine.

"Evelyn! We're going to France!" She skips up to the bed and scrambles up the side to sit beyond the guardrail at my thigh. Ryan swoops in beside her, shielding my bandaged chest from her exuberant hugs without quelling them.

Not daring to do say anything for fear of giving away how sick I am, I muster up a grin and hug her little face to my tummy until she pops up. Her blond hair flips from side to side as she swings her head every direction, searching the tin box of a room. "Where's Greyson? I thought you were going back for Greyson." Dangling over the side like a monkey, she checks under the bed, sure he must be hiding somewhere.

He's gone, he's gone, he's gone!

Thank God for Ryan. He scoops her up in his arms before I have to say anything—or start bawling again. "Did you tell Evelyn who came to stay on the big boat and go to France with you?"

A huge grin cracks her face, and she tosses her arms in the air, her fists in victorious balls like she just won the lottery. "Cameron!" She's so excited, she plants a big, smacking kiss right on Ryan's cheek before explaining how bright her future looks. "He doesn't have to go to Montana with Craig, and Paula, and Prudence. He gets to come with me!" She pushes Ryan's face away a little and leans over to confide a secret. "We're sharing the same room. I get the top bunk."

"Of course, you do," Ryan agrees, even though he wasn't supposed to hear. "You're the princess."

A hint of grey clouds the color in her face. "What about Evy? Where will she sleep? Won't she be scared to be all alone in here?"

"I'm fine, sweety." I nearly break a sweat trying to say that in a single breath.

"Evelyn isn't feeling so well, Amber. We're going to let her stay here with the nice doctors and then I'll take good care of her."

Her eyes brighten up. "Maybe Ryan can stay with you!" And then she leans over so far to whisper in my ear that he nearly drops her. "Promise him you'll be good and you won't cry and he'll bring you the yummy chocolate from France." She nods conspiratorially.

He's gone, he's gone, he's gone.

"Promise!" she insists.

"I promise I won't cry, Ryan." The lack of air fires off a choking fit that I try to strangle.

Finally satisfied, the little imp reaches for a hug. I can't refuse, no matter how much pain I'm in. Being there when her little arms reach out for someone she loves to hold her is the goal that keeps me grounded in a shifting reality. It's all that matters…*he's gone, he's gone, he's gone*…it's all that ever really mattered.

Amber brushes her left cheek against mine and makes a little smacking sound with her lips that I return and then she flips coyly to the other cheek, her eyes fluttering in mock sophistication and repeats the little ritual.

At the end of the ceremony, Ryan hauls her back up and stands there misinterpreting the pain in my eyes.

"Now, you!" Her index finger commands me imperiously. "It's how the Frenchies say good-bye."

Ryan dutifully tilts forward, but he can't quite reach with Amber in his arms and the guard rail between us, so I'm forced to lean forward until his warm lips touch, ever so lightly my cold, grey cheek. They glide past my lips until our cheeks brush on the other side. A sharp pain rips through my chest and I'm not sure if it's my heart or my lungs.

He's gone, he's gone, he's gone…

ACKNOWLEDGEMENTS

Many thanks to my daughter Natalie, who supplied the raw material and encouragement to write this story. Thanks also to Elizabeth, Connor, Rebecca, and Esther who read for me, to Elena, Chris, and Jared, my accomplices in writing, and to Janie who shares my obsession. Deepest thanks to Curt who loves me despite the whole writing thing.

Amazon Reviews for the Walking Grey Series

—couldn't stop reading…hope there's a second one coming.

—turns the zombie genre upside down.

—a twist on the typical love story.

—perfect mixture of intense action and softly suspenseful moments.

—dying for the next one. And please for the love let there be a next one.

"Narrated with spunk and humor by a zombie who still has sex appeal, Grey Matters is a fresh take on the undead meme where the enemy comes from within, literally. One of the most original and shocking takes on zombie literature I've ever seen. Grey Matters is humorous, acutely terrifying, and thoroughly gripping from the first page to the last." —Katherine Boyle, Veritas Literary

The WALKING GREY Series

Raw suspense and edgy romance. Zombies for the insatiably romantic. The Walking Grey series chronicles the desperate story of Evelyn Cross and Greyson Childs in a dystopian world infected with the Zoser Virus. Infected, the virus has made them look like ZVs and crave human flesh like ZVs, but instead of slowly consuming their organs and brain, it has transformed them into super predators, fighting both sides of a looming conflict to protect Evelyn's uninfected little sister Amber.

GREY MATTERS
Book 1

They bash our heads and chain us up because we're different. Well, maybe knowing we would happily throw on a bib, rip out their guts, and devour them like hotdogs on a stick, without the stick——or the bib for that matter—probably has something to do with it. No one really wants to hang out with a girl whose idea of a Slurpee is grey matter and blood splashed in the snow, hold the straw.

Evelyn Cross has everything: shampoo commercial hair, a letterman jacket, a tiara, a 3.98 GPA, and now the Z-Virus that is infecting teenage couples in the small town of Eli. The virus has made her look like a ZV and crave human flesh like a ZV, but instead of slowly consuming her organs and brain, it has transformed her into a super-predator, fighting both sides of a looming conflict. And she's not the only one of her kind—here's also Greyson Childs, the vicious pack-hunting player that dumped her best friend when they all got infected.

GREY KNIGHTS
Book 2

Angels or Demons? The grey is fading. The Z-Virus has mutated and the infection looms large on the Texas horizon. As the rushing tide of the apocalypse smears the lines between heaven and hell, Evelyn and Greyson escape the fire of one quarantine zone, only to find themselves fugitives in the inferno of another.

GREY DAZE
Book 3

The chilling finale of Rachel DeFriez's Walking Grey series. Book 3: Grey Daze.

The Zoser Virus has gone global. It's not the first time mindless monsters have invaded France, set up defense positions, and devoured the inhabitants.

Evelyn Cross washes up alone on the Marseille coast. What she finds there is not exactly a dream vacation on the French Riviera. To make her way back to her little sister, she'll have to join the dystopian New Order that the greys of Marseille have raised up from the ashes of the apocalypse. And if she plays her part well, maybe, just maybe, somewhere in the rubble, she'll find love again.

OTHER BOOKS BY THIS AUTHOR

I AM KRONOS

It's not every day you get a friend request from a dead girl.

I Am Kronos is a thrilling blend of gaming, sci-fi, and supernatural romance.

Keven Meyers, gamer and classic underachiever on the fringe of cool, gets a friend request from Sierra Sands, recently deceased and haunting his video games. Sierra is stuck in the Nexus, the center where all the universes and realities collide. She desperately needs Keven's help to stop Silas, another lost soul using his diabolical understanding of the world between the worlds to prey on gamers.

When Silas attacks Keven in his video game, Sierra drags Keven's soul through the game and into the safety of the Nexus where he becomes painfully aware that he is inextricably connected, across universes and realities, to this dead girl. But with the infinite possibilities of multiple realities come options—options like his best friend Lexy Granger.

Only the strength of the ties that bind Keven, Sierra, and Lexy, on multiple levels, in and out of existences, are strong enough to overthrow Silas.

Rachel DeFriez brings us a spine-tingling supernatural thriller that delves into the metaphysical world of the multiverse.

ABOUT THE AUTHOR

Rachel DeFriez is the author of the chilling zombie romance series WALKING GREY: GREY MATTERS, GREY KNIGHTS, and GREY DAZE. She is also the author of the paranormal sci-fi thriller I AM KRONOS.

Coming Soon:
RAVENS AND LAVENDER in Romance
7 SECONDS in YA

Her books have won multiple prizes in the 2018 and 2019 League of Utah Writing Contests.

Due to her husband's nomadic nature, Rachel has taught French and Creative Writing in a variety of states including: Texas, Massachusetts, and Utah. She is particularly surprised to find herself writing YA horror since she's afraid of the dark. Visit her at www.racheldefriez.com